WISH
DEAD
LIST

ROBERT TAYLOR

EU Conformity Declaration

This product complies with the following safety regulations and standards to ensure consumer safety and product quality: Regulation (EU) 2023/988 of the European Parliament and of the Council on General Product Safety (GPSR): The Consumer Product Safety Improvement Act (CPSIA), Section 101. The Californian Safe drinking water and toxic enforcement act. (Proposition 65) EN71-Part 1: Mechanical and Physical Properties EN71-Part 2: Flammability EN71-Part 3 Migration of certain elements.

Produced by Chelmerton Books
Published by Softwood Books
EU Responsible person: Maddy Glenn
Office 2, Wharfside House, Prentice Road, Stowmarket, Suffolk, IP14 1RD
www.softwoodbooks.com
hello@softwoodbooks.com

EU Rep:
Authorised Rep Compliance Ltd., Ground Floor, 71 Lower Baggot Street, Dublin, D02 P593, Ireland
www.arccompliance.com
info@arccompliance.com

www.roberttaylorauthor.co.uk
Facebook and Instagram: @roberttaylorauthor

Paperback ISBN: 978-1-0369-0949-9

Reviews

'Love, love, loved it. Brilliant. I was gripped to the end'

'From the first page I found myself hooked on this fast paced action packed story'

'Have finished your very entertaining book. The plotlines are quite believable and drawn together in a very exciting climax'

'You have a bestseller on your hands. I really enjoyed the story'

'I enjoyed reading this book and felt the interest level and pace were maintained throughout'

PROLOGUE

Libya

The town was two-hundred-and-fifty kilometres south of the Libyan capital of Tripoli. It was decayed, dry and dusty. The roads serving the area, though, were the match of any in the modern world. A man, known only as Dragon to his Russian counterpart, sat in a tent just outside the God forsaken place. Yes, his country's Belt and Road initiative had given this backward country the best roads in the world, well, in places anyway. The BRI was buying influence in all of these backward countries where the Chinese leaders were convinced that the minerals that drove the modern world were laid down in megatonnes just below the surface. He had to concede that the initiative had been a hugely successful policy, thousands of kilometres of asphalt had stretched their way across the Eurasian-African continents reaching out like tendrils from the centre of the world, Beijing. Not since the great Silk Road of antiquity, developed during the Han dynasty to link the important civilisations of the Mediterranean world to the East, had such a scale of communication been conceived by his rulers. They had had reservations at the People's Republic of China's Ministry of State Security but these were set aside when it was learned that the roads would be constructed like no others and would be capable of supporting rapid troop and artillery movements to put down any resistance to Beijing strategy. The roads would easily support the heaviest Norinco Main Battle Tanks.

The area was still full of heathen tribesman queuing up to kill each other in this blighted landscape. It was hot, or bloody hot as the English would say. He continually swatted flies from around his eyes, nose, and mouth. He kept loosening his shirt from the sweaty skin underneath. He was pissed off. He looked at his watch, a gold Rolex purchased from a street-vendor in Hong Kong, and it didn't seem to have moved since the last glance. The Bear was late.

He was just wondering if he had been lured into a trap when he heard the engine. The tent-flap opened, and a man dressed in tribal robes announced that the Russian was coming.

"Thank you," the Chinese said. Now get out of my space, he thought, you stink like a dung-heap. "Show him in, please."

The huge Russian ducked inside the flap. He was like a Slavic monolith hewn from granite. "Ah! Comrade Bear," Dragon welcomed his Russian counterpart, using the agent's operational name for this meeting. It was a pointless pretence, each man knew everything there was to know about friend and foe both.

Dragon rose and held out his hand. The Russian took it before letting go and pulling the small Chinese into a suffocating embrace, a bearhug. Dragon cringed, hoping it wouldn't show, and then it got worse as the big Soviet lump moved in and kissed both cheeks. Dragon hated being touched by men let alone kissed and hugged. He feared he might turn homosexual so resisted any such advances from men. He tolerated it on this one occasion but did not return the felicitation.

"Please sit," Dragon instructed the newcomer. He hoped it sounded like an invitation rather than a command. He needed to remain diplomatic to entice the Russians to do China's bidding.

"You have the money?" growled Bear in his deep guttural voice.

Dragon mused that the Russian's codename could not have been better selected. The man was built like, sounded like and behaved like a big brown bear. He, like Dragon, though, had harnessed the ability to breathe fire when required. "I do."

Dragon removed a small black plastic box from his briefcase and laid it on the table. The Russian bent in for a better look as the lid was removed. It revealed two English twenty-pound bills. The elderly monarch of the British Empire stared up at him. Bear, when attached to the Russian Embassy in London, where he had first met the Dragon, had read about British history, and knew it was unfair to label all Britons as imperialist empire builders and knew that, really, it was the English. They had, at first, subjugated the Scots, Irish and Welsh. He did concede that it could be considered a Wessex Empire as they were the ones who had, at first, conquered the other ancient kingdoms of England before turning their ire on the whole of Britain.

"They look the same, except for the number," observed the Russian agent. The two serial numbers were sequential - indicating both notes had come from the same batch.

"They are. Now take them out and look at them and tell me which is the original and which is the adapted one."

Bear felt the two bills. He folded them, unfolded them and tried to tear them. He studied the patterns, the swirls and the layouts. No difference was discernible. The appearance of the English money had changed so much since his attachment to the embassy in London's Kensington Palace Gardens. They used to use paper money, but this was like strips of plastic that would be as much at home being employed as temporary barriers for crime scenes if they were joined end-to-end. He shook his head. "I can't tell them apart," he said. "Which is the forgery?"

"Good," said Dragon as he pulled out a small telescope like instrument from his case. It was less than a hundred millimetres long. "Now look through this," he said, flicking a switch as he passed it across to his Russian counterpart.

The instrument looked tiny in the paw of the man opposite. "He raised the small tube to his eye. One of the notes appeared to be plain under what he assumed to be some sort of enhanced light, maybe ultra-violet, whilst the other one glittered like it had been sprinkled with shiny shards of metal or hard plastic. "I can see the difference but still don't know which is the genuine one?"

"None of them is a forgery. Both are very real and can be spent in any shop in the UK. My government acquired five hundred thousand of them straight from the factory. The glittery one has been engineered to carry the lethal load."

"Please tell."

Dragon explained how their research unit in Wuhan had heard that the English had used a biproduct of beef production called tallow which is like a gelatine that is mixed with the polymers to make the ink. The Chinese would never have known about this but the West's obsession with transparency meant that all of the ingredients were declared. Then vegans kicked up, saying that they would never use the new money as it contained animal products. He observed that neither the Russians nor the

Chinese would be so stupid as to let the general population know what was used in anything, let alone banknotes! "Our lab was developing biological weapons, and one clever scientist realised that the gelatine like product could be used as a key, to glue a virus to the note. A little accident meant that the virus escaped before it had been fully developed. Whilst the Americans and the Europeans tried to beat each other to an antidote, we continued to develop our knowledge. The coronavirus that escaped in 2019 is nothing compared with the fully developed weapon."

Bear growled a sort of understanding, but it was already getting too deep for him.

"They were then able to impregnate the gelatine with the virus that is held in microscopic polymers themselves. That is the sparkling effect you get through the optical enhancer you just used. Eventually, through much use, say fifteen to twenty rubs, the polymer will disintegrate and let the virus out into the air."

"Fascinating," he said holding the glittery note up. "Does this bill hold the viral load?"

"No. That is perfectly safe. Now rub the bill on your pants or shirt, say twenty-five times or so, and then look through the enhancer again."

Bear did as instructed. He was wary of his opposite number from the Chinese agency. As soon as Dragon moved to leave the tent he would stop rubbing and kill the creep. Dragon stayed, imperturbable, in his chair. Bear picked up the enhancer, activated the light and peered at the surface of the money again.

The sharp appearance of the sparkles had been replaced by what looked, to him, like starbursts. "So, if this had held the virus it would be now thrown into the atmosphere?"

"Yes. And, about two-hundred times more than a man sneezing and, for that matter, about fifty times stronger than that let out in late twenty-nineteen."

"It will take a long time to infect a good part of the population. how will we stop it spreading to our own countries?""

"Once the virus is exposed it will spread like any plague throughout history. Yes, it is true we might need to be patient and wait for the notes to be circulated for the disease to take hold but once it does the growth will be exponential. There will be collateral damage within our countries as some people get back in from trips abroad but if you do what we do that can be limited."

"What will you do?"

"We will keep our people under lock and key, lockdown as the west call it, until the objective has been achieved."

It could work, thought the giant Bear slowly nodding his acknowledgement.

A smile spread across the Chinese's face.

Bear grimaced as the smile widened, appearing to make the supercilious eyes even more slitted than normal. It was like the oriental face was lit by a bright shining bulb. The face, he conceded, was one he could easily pummel into a red pulp. "Okay," he said. "But won't their vaccines counter the effect of the virus."

"We don't see how. We spent five years developing an antidote and they claim to have developed one in less than six months or so. They will do anything to make their people think they are safe. It is impossible. Their propagandists will come out with all sorts of rubbish to spread a false sense of security. They always do."

"Even lie about the effectiveness of a vaccine?"

"Yes. Even we, who have the original recipe, are not sure we have the antidote correct yet. What chance do they have? They have some clever people but none of them is a match for our researchers."

Russia

Ten days later a train pulled into a station close to the Sino-Russian border, just on the Russian side. It was a miserable day. The rain had been falling in sheets from glowering grey metal clouds since before dawn. There was no sign that there would be any let up in the deluge. This was good as it kept the spying eyes of the American satellites at bay with the clouds offering a security blanket better than any electronic cloaking. Chinese agents exited a carriage toward the rear of the train and formed a protective cordon. One held a red umbrella high and awaited the VIP about to alight.

President Mikhail Drozdov of the Russian Federation watched through the bullet-proof window of the waiting room as his guest emerged from the train. Useless, he thought, even he, at his advanced age, could take out over a half-dozen of the inadequate idiots if he wanted to. He had ordered a meeting table brought from the Kremlin to be placed in the station's waiting room which, normally, would have been full of passengers pondering whether their trains would be on time. Today, for the commuters, was one of those unpredictable days when the station was closed for no reason. For most it meant no wages for the shifts ahead. Then, the age-old question, heat their home or eat?

Drozdov took his place at the opposite end of the table to the entrance, donned one of the infernal medical masks his guest's nation had forced the world to wear over the last year and a bit. He hated everything about the Chinese. He hated their strutting ways as they strode on the world stage, he hated them for developing their own weapons, becoming less reliable on Soviet exports and, most of all, he hated their claim to be the equal of any world power, up there with the Americans and ahead of the Russians.

President Ding Jang Li of the People's Republic of China strode into the room between his bodyguards who, to Drozdov, looked about as lightweight as a box of cobwebs. Kremlin cronies guided him to a position at the other end of the five-metre-long table. He was wearing a mask cut from the same cloth as his tie and kerchief. I hate this asshole, thought Drozdov.

The Chinese uttered something in his sing-song voice which Drozdov could not decipher. An interpreter voiced the greeting, "Good to see you, Mr President. I hope you are keeping well?"

Drozdov knew that Ding didn't mean a single word of it. They may not even have been the actual words spoken but the interpreter hadn't flinched or grimaced so, maybe, they were. The interpreters on both sides sometimes took licence with the true meaning when translating insults. They had, on many occasions, saved the world from major incidents by informing their leaders of a more diplomatic translation. Nothing would please Ding more than to see the Russian topple over on the spot.

"Can't say that I agree with you, you piece of panda-shit," said Drozdov.

The interpreter said. "Good to see you too, Comrade."

They both wore wan, forced smiles under their masks and bowed to one another. There were no chairs so everyone in the room had to stand.

Pleasantries over, Drozdov started the meeting going. "We can do business regarding the money you showed us in Libya."

"Good. I thought you would like that."

"What do you want in exchange for sharing it with us?"

The Chinese had said they would provide the impregnated banknotes for no charge and Drozdov didn't believe them. The Chinese never did anything for nothing, at least not as far as the Russians were concerned.

"I understand you will be invading Ukraine next year?"

Why was Drozdov not surprised? He had only shared this plan with five of his trusted inner circle. It always seemed to get out, though. "If we are?"

"First, you will not do this until our Winter Olympics are over and, secondly, you tell us two days before so that we can fly sorties into the Republic of China."

13

"We can do that. You will have Taiwan back by the end of next year." Drozdov continued smiling under his mask, hoping it didn't look obviously false. He also noted that the bamboo-chewing slime had referred to their western-most state as Ukraine so he would call the island state Taiwan. He saw it had hit home as Ding went slightly darker with annoyance. "Does that include the event for the invalids as well?"

"No. They are not important. We don't care for watching dwarfs or legless people try to do men's things or blind men wandering around like drunkards in a race. It is like Barnum's circus from a couple of centuries ago. It makes me want to throw up!"

We are agreed on that at least, Drozdov thought, and the smile flickered into a genuine recognition of the other's candour. "Okay. Agreed."

"We also want Australia."

That did not surprise Drozdov either. "You can have it. You have just as much right to it as the English."

"We won't even need boots on the ground. We have some of their politicians under our full control and they will do whatever we want."

"Well, comrade," Drozdov allowed. "We will not be stopping at our south-westerly state. We will regain the entire empire as it was in 1989."

"As you wish, comrade."

"You have the currency on your train?"

"Yes. We have five million pounds worth. How will you get them into the west?"

"We have ways. The EU hates the British and the British hate them just as much. It is amazing how easy it is to persuade the French to look the other way on occasions. The British Prime Minister," he stopped and thought for a second as he pondered the work of the Scottish National Party in destabilising the so-called United Kingdom before correcting himself. "The English Prime Minister is weak. He will be caught up in more scandal. His former adviser cannot stand him and will do anything to bring him down. We would have had the treacherous bastard taken to Lubyanka, broken, before casting him away to some out of the way place in Siberia."

Ding chuckled. "Good. Yes, he is weak and seems to worry about what his people think. Truly amusing! Can you imagine such a thing?!"

Drozdov watched as Ding boarded his train. "I do not trust the bastards. They will side with the west as soon as it suits them better," he said to no-one in particular.

President Ding sat in his armchair on the train and looked back through the bullet-proof glass of his bomb-proof carriage at the now maskless smiling face of his Russian counterpart before commenting to no-one in particular, "I do not trust the bastards. They will side with the west as soon as it suits them better."

CHAPTER ONE

Monday 13th September 2021

Norfolk

Today has been my best day for nearly eighteen months. I had an appointment with the top cancer specialist at the hospital this afternoon and he informed me that, in his opinion, I had less than six months to live. I have heard many people say that those words stop you in your tracks like you have been hit by a Challenger tank. To me, though, they were the very words I had dreamed of hearing. They ushered in the release of all my pent-up emotions. They brought to the fore plans I had been holding in my head for the last two months; in fact, two months ago yesterday. I am a very angry man, and some people are going to pay. I am sharpening my knives and cleaning my guns.

The doctor's name is Mr bin Laden or something like that; I never could get my tongue around his real name. To be honest, it is nothing like bin Laden but he has, probably, overseen more deaths than the infamous terrorist. I am not actually sure that he is the top specialist either, but he does seem pretty important, if not in the global eye of the NHS, certainly in his own mind as he assures me his career is on an upward trajectory to the top. I can't complain, though, he has performed admirably and done exactly what I asked although he had no real choice in the matter. He does bear an uncanny resemblance to the now deceased Al Qaeda leader except he was dressed in a suit rather than tribal robes.

My wife, Kate, passed on 12th July. This - so called - genius of a cancer expert missed my wife's breast cancer returning. It probably wasn't entirely his fault as things have changed, worldwide, in the last eighteen months. It was March of last year when we were informed by our jerk of a Prime Minister that thanks to the coronavirus pandemic, now known as Covid, we were going to be locked down as a country for the following three weeks. They, I mean the government, would assess this as they went along but they seemed convinced that we would beat this thing and be back to normal by the summer. I hold the Prime Minister more culpable than bin Laden. He did have his advisers who prophesised doom and gloom by the bucket-load. They are, in my opinion, witless and imbalanced, the Chief Medical Adviser and Chief Scientific Adviser to the United Kingdom government respectively. It is these three who are, in my mind, jointly responsible for the death of my wife. They should now pay. They have blood on their hands.

Kate very quickly went downhill in the last couple of weeks of her life and the only joy she took from it, as a massively keen tennis player and fan, was to watch a previously unknown girl show potential at Wimbledon. On Saturday evening last, I wept with both happiness and sadness. Happiness in that the impressively young Emma Raducanu won the US Open tennis championship without losing a set in the entire competition including the qualifiers. Sadness in the thought of Kate missing out on this quite brilliant moment for British tennis, indeed, British sport. I had held her hand as she watched and listened to the progress the now new US Open champion had made at Wimbledon. It was mainly listening as she usually laid with her eyes closed seeming to let the audio brush over her. It was as if she were waiting for the final's weekend to complete before letting go. She passed on Monday, 12th July, the day after the men's tennis final and the football Euros final. I sat and watched whilst she lay, eyelids resting as normal, with me - not sure how much she could hear of what was going on, but I am convinced a smile lit her sunken face when England scored the opening goal in the football final.

Her last day is misted in melancholy memory, but the final moments are as vivid as if they only happened earlier today. It was so peaceful as she took her last breath or, at least, what I took to be her last breath, for a few moments later, the final exhalation came, and the pulse fluttered away. The nurse we had employed to care for Kate in the last few days left me for a few moments alone with my now deceased wife. I leant over and kissed her on the lips whispering "I won't be long, love. Just got a few things to sort and I'll be following on behind you. Keep a place at the table for me." A most strange thing to say, but it really was a magical moment. I had shared many special times with this wonderful woman since we were both at school, and this was no different as she slipped across into the next chapter.

I glanced at my watch, and it was a quarter-to-eleven in the morning. The nurse agreed to do all the formal bits like organising doctor and undertaker. I took myself into the countryside and found our favourite spot overlooking the village that had become home. Summer was a magnificent time, but the trees were full of leaf which meant the village was mostly hidden behind the green barrier. I could see the church tower sticking up above the treeline but not much else. Cows were grazing on the heath, a couple of horses were being ridden along the lane in the distance, and birds filled the hedgerows with song that seemed to lament the parting of our ways. I crumpled onto the rickety old bench that had been placed there many years ago. I turned to look at the top rail and noted there was no tribute. I would speak to someone at the parish council, I assumed, and order a new bench. It would say "In memory of Catherine Jane Wells who loved this spot" with the second line reading "1960 – 2021" and the final line, simply saying, "Rest in Eternal Peace."

Early in the first lockdown, Kate had an appointment with Mr bin Laden which was changed from face-to-face to that bloody Zoom thing.

"What is that?" asked my wife, understandably so, for apart from a few nerds, very few of the general population had ever heard of Zoom. Within a few weeks it had become synonymous with Covid.

"Oh," his secretary replied. "We can't do face-to-face anymore as we could be putting you and us at risk from being infected by the virus. So, all first appointments are now over the computer." She spoke the last bit as if she were speaking to some old fossil born over a hundred years ago and the very tone pissed me off!

I think the appointment was for the next week or very soon thereafter. In the meantime, we tried to find out what Zoom was. Of course, we couldn't go and see anybody so that they might show us what it was and how to use it. It's ever so easy had been all the secretary could tell us. I suppose it was - if you were a child of about five who had been born with a silicon chip implanted in their brain. We were born before it had been the government policy to plant such chips! What idiots these anti-vaxxers are! If only they knew it was the injection of the vaccine that activated the government's tracking device! The chip was already there! Idiots! In more recent times, this small group of conspiracy theorists has been trying to persuade us all that the vaccine is a way of injecting some sort of locating element into us. So what, if they are, surely you only have something to worry about if you have done something wrong! There is no question that I will test this theory out, over the coming months, as I seek my revenge for Kate's premature demise. For some reason I am fully vaccinated in that I have had two injections. There is now talk of a booster jab, though, which I suspect I shall never have. What's the point? I will be off to join Kate as soon as I can.

Anyway, we worked out the Zoom thing and my wife sat down in front of the screen and waited for bin Laden to come online. Sure enough, after a while, there he was. The lighting couldn't have been much good in his office as his brown skin had developed a yellow hue. The long beard adorning the front of his shirt, like a second tie, glistened in the strange light.

After a few pleasantries and discussions about the lump's development over recent times, he asked her to remove her top for a visual examination. He asked her to highlight the lump and got her to show how she had examined the area when she first discovered it.

Then, that was it. Kate pulled her top back on and sat back in the chair for the summing-up. He complimented her on her physical appearance, which in my mind was stepping over the line. Well, for her age anyway.

She had only recently turned sixty. In fact, we both had, for our birthdays were the same day, 21ˢᵗ April 1960, so I had no reason to forget her birthday. To make things really easy, we got married on the same day nineteen years later. A great package. Although I found Mr bin Laden's compliment cringeworthy in the extreme, I had to agree with him, she was in great nick. Of course, it wasn't only her physical appearance that I liked, it was the whole person, and I worshipped the ground she walked on; still do. I loved her beyond anyone or anything else in the world. I miss her but, as I now know, we will meet up again very soon.

I am not really religious, whereas she was a regular church goer, but I do share a spiritual interest that will see us through to the other side. Can't put my finger on it or explain it to others. We have a young vicar in the village, Jordan, who was an absolute blessing toward the end, often standing in when I needed a break. I feel bad now, but he kept coming round after she died to check on my wellbeing. I shunned him every time. Maybe I was frightened that he might convert me to the forgiveness thing? I certainly didn't want that. What did the Lord's Prayer say? 'And forgive us our trespasses; As we forgive those who trespass against us.' At the time of Kate's death, there was not a forgiving bone in my body. There was only one goal left to me and that was retribution and revenge. I was not in the mood for turning the other cheek.

As was always the case, she remained polite at all times and thanked him for the clumsy courtesy.

He decided that it would be worth getting her into the clinic for a more thorough examination. "Ordinarily, I believe it is just a fatty lump but given your history I think it would be prudent."

No shit, Sherlock, was my thought but it stayed in my head.

The Zoom connection was terminated and my wife swivelled around to face me in my office chair. I had been sitting on the floor out of camera shot quietly observing developments, biting my lip at the man's outrageous behaviour. I wondered if he knew I was in the room with her. I also wondered what some of these perverted bastards got away with, in the privacy of their own consulting rooms.

I stood and held my arms toward her. She fell into my clutches, and I held her tight, never wanting to let her go. She did not cry but I did. She had always resolved that, after the first time, she would never let it dominate her life ever again, should it return. She coped better than me; always did.

"Come on," she said. "Let's go for a walk."

We wandered aimlessly around the paths and by-ways, across fields and paddocks, up and down dale until we arrived at our favourite bench overlooking the church. We held each other tightly again.

We slowly made our way back into the village and called at the Store. Technically, they were only meant to sell essential goods. We both agreed that, on this occasion, a couple of bottles of wine were most essential.

We had polished off one bottle in pretty quick time, at which point, I went through to the kitchen and rustled up a pasta dinner. Afterwards we finished the second bottle a bit more slowly than the first before retiring to bed. It was like we were living in some sort of parallel world to the one where she had just had a consultation with a doctor, who had almost confirmed she was suffering from cancer again. Again, we held each other tight. I kissed the top of her head.

We didn't know it at the time but that would be the last time we ever made love. A treasured memory. It was almost like we knew it was the last time, so it was extraordinary. Isn't it peculiar how young people's ardour for sex develops into lovemaking as one gets older. Indeed, we hadn't had sex for the best part of forty years; we always made love.

We started going out with one another in the last year of primary school. She went on to university, reading architecture, whilst I joined the army. I won a place at Sandhurst before joining up with the Royal Marines.

We always wrote and spoke on the telephone when we could. The phones at both ends were hung on walls in very public areas. It was the Easter break of 1979 that I drove to her university and collected her in my battered old Ford Escort. After a cup of tea in the university refectory, I asked her to marry me.

"Yes," she responded without delay. "When?"

"I don't know," I said. "Well, how about this week? Let's go to Gretna Green?"

"Why not," she smiled.

So, we did. She tossed some things in a bag, and we set off straightaway. I can't exactly remember times of day, but it was getting dark when we spotted the sign for Carlisle. We found a pretty-low grade hotel on the outskirts. It was before Trip Adviser and, to be frank, I am not sure it would have registered a rating of zero today. Those were, of course, different times, we weren't exactly rolling in cash and all we needed was a bed for the night. The bed was as narrow a double as you could call double, although we didn't mind, as we would be in skin-to-skin contact all night! Little did we know! Kate went to shower. Within only a minute or so, she tapped on the door and asked if I would come and stay in the bathroom with her while she bathed; there was no shower! The bathroom was shared with every other room on our floor, maybe another ten rooms or so, can't really remember. The water glugged and gurgled in the quaking pipes before a gelid trickle appeared from the hot tap. We later learned that the boiler was on the blink. I leant against the door, it had no working lock, whilst she took a cold bath. I had never seen her bathe before, and it was a wondrous experience. I didn't, at first, notice the tap on the door.

The second one was a thumping of the door with a rattling of the doorknob that I held onto to stop it being forced open. "Come on, for fuck's sake, my mate needs a shit, and you've had the room for too long," commanded an aggressive voice from the other side.

Kate stepped from the bath, rubbed herself nearly dry on the threadbare towel, which if memory serves me correctly, was shared with all the other bathroom users, and pulled her clothes on. I was going to hop in after her. As we had gone in search of the hotel, I had pictured a lingering relaxing hot bubble-bath with us sharing for the first time. That notion was quickly kicked into touch when we saw the facilities on offer.

The doorknob rattled again, the door shuddered under the

thumping of two or three fists. Kate ran her fingers through her wet hair, and I pulled the door toward me to find a group of four men waiting there. We found out the following morning that they were lodged there whilst working on some nearby road construction project.

"Umm!" the man on point said. "Nice bit of stuff. Up for sharing her? Is she good? Looks a bit more expensive than the one we had last week!"

I didn't say a word. I could sense Kate getting behind me. I locked eyes with the talker, the one I assumed was the leader or foreman or whatever they called officers in civilian life.

"Well?" demanded a lieutenant.

I carried on staring into the eyes of the leader but said "No. She's not for sharing and no, she's not for sale. She's all mine and we are going north to get married."

"How sweet," the lieutenant said. For a moment I thought he meant it. The smile, however, quickly changed to a sneer. "Come on, love. How about it with some real men rather than a boy? We'll give you some valuable lessons to stand you in good stead on your honeymoon night and we won't even charge you a penny for our services."

"No," I repeated. "That isn't gonna happen."

"What you gonna do about it, little boy," he responded, trying to taunt me.

"Whatever I have to," I assured him. God, I was arrogant back then. I knew I had two advantages. The first was that only one at a time could get through the narrow door and the second was that they had all had a tad too much to drink whereas I was stone-cold sober.

"Oh yeah," a third contributed. "I don't see an army at your back."

"Don't need one. I am the army!" I'm not sure, looking back, whether arrogance was a virtue I was proud of, but I had it in spades.

The leader stepped forward, cracking his knuckle joints but leaning into the doorway slightly at the same time. It was like the bridge of his nose was coming into my heading zone like a perfect cross from the wing. I flexed my neck muscles, and with hardly any back move, I pounced forward and, although the connection wasn't perfect, I felt the nose give under the assault from my forehead. As I retreated into the safety of the bathroom, I was surprised by the amount of blood pouring from the wound. I was rewarded, though, by his look of wide-eyed shock. His legs wobbled, his body crumpled, and his face dropped from my field of vision. The three remaining blokes looked as shocked as the victim. The lieutenant made toward me but a colleague, who maybe hadn't drunk so much, held him back by laying a hand on his arm.

"Okay, mate," he said. "We'll call it quits there."

"No, we won't," I snarled. "We'll call it, I won." There was that arrogance again.

"Whatever you want. We just don't want any more trouble."

Two of them helped the groggy leader to his feet and guided him, carried him back along the corridor whilst the fourth took over the bathroom for his shit. Kate and I returned to the room. I could feel my head begin to ache. I guess that was as a result of the less than perfect connection. And, I wanted to piss.

"I need to use the toilet."

"Well, I'm coming with you," she demanded.

I must have looked quite aghast by the suggestion.

"I mean, if you only want a wee and not a number two."

How polite we were to one another back then!

We gave the man occupying the bathroom a reasonable time to perform his ablutions before heading again in that direction. She stood inside the stinking room with me whilst I stood at the pan and poured into it. Afterwards I rinsed my hands under the cold water and looked into the misted, cracked mirror, noting the slight bruising coming out above my left eye. I reckon that'll hurt in the morning, I thought.

We squeezed into the bed and fell asleep. We didn't get any visits in the night, and neither were the protagonists there in the morning when we went down for the pathetic breakfast on offer. The tea was tepid and weak, the bacon burned beyond a crisp and the egg like a piece of shoe leather.

Different times! I am pretty sure we have never stayed in anywhere quite so squalid since. I remember when we went on our fortieth wedding anniversary cruise to Australia and New Zealand we stayed for a few nights in a luxury hotel in Bali. I remember commenting to some wealthy Americans who were on our trip that I had stayed in worse places. That single night in Carlisle was the first thing that came into my mind as I made the quip.

We continued on to Scotland and three days later we were married. Needless to say, both sets of parents were appalled by our actions and, of course, their friends, never short on advice, told them, and us, that it wouldn't last. I suppose, in a way, they were right as Kate was taken from me far too early.

The lockdown went on-and-on and before we realised it three months had passed. Kate had not heard a thing from the hospital. "Oh. I won't bother them," she had said. "I'm sure they are run off their feet with the virus."

"Maybe so," I agreed. "But I don't give a monkey's about that. It is you I care for, over everything else. I really think you should at least call the doctor."

The lump was now, probably, twice the size it had been, and I was sure it was not a fatty growth. I'm no expert but I felt it was something far more sinister. We agreed to give it another month. She simply didn't want to come across as too pushy with so many people suffering in the world. That was Kate. Our old school motto had been "God First, Others Second, and Self Last." I definitely didn't go for the first bit despite our spiritual reflections, and I didn't always agree with the second bit. Kate always went for the "self-last" notion. There was always someone in the world more in need than her.

It was in late July of last year that she picked up the phone to our doctor. The lump had, I think, got a little bigger although she thought it roughly the same.

The gatekeeper at the surgery explained that bloody covid had caused many hold-ups and she was sure someone would be in contact soon.

"Okay," said my wife. "That's fine. But perhaps you would be good enough to let the doctor know of my concern."

I jumped over to her side. "No. It's not bloody fine!" I roared and hooked the handset from her grasp. "You listen to me, you fat bitch. It is not fucking fine. Do you understand?"

My curtain of self-control learned in the army was beginning to fall open. It seemed like the other end had gone quiet and no-one was there. "Hello," I said. "Hello. Hello." I stared at the phone as if my look would will someone on to the other end. I tossed it on the table and ran my fingers through my grey hair.

She put her hand on my shoulder, and we hugged. "It's fine," she whispered. "I'm sure it'll be alright, love."

I felt desperate. It all seemed so unfair. We had always dreamed of a long retirement. The situation was getting out of control. "I'll be buggered if it's fine," I said. "I'm going round there. I'll sort that bitch out once and for all."

"No love. It'll be alright. I'm sure they will get back to us."

I burst into tears. The salty cascade flooded down my face and caught on the corner of my mouth on one side before dropping onto her shoulder. I held her tight. She held me tight. I didn't want to let her go.

"I know," I said. "But…. But…. Look, I couldn't face life without you and it's getting to me. Nothing seems to be happening and that, what with this damned lockdown, well…. well, it's getting me down."

She stroked my hair and nibbled my ear. I wasn't in the mood, though, and pulled away. She plucked a tissue from the box by the side of the phone and dabbed away my hurt. How on earth was she keeping so calm about this? Resignation? I really was at a low ebb and could only envisage one outcome, an abyss which I did not want to fall into.

Neither was I in the mood for letting this one go. I went round to the surgery. Of course, the surgery was not open. I held my finger on the button by the intercom. I didn't let go. I could hear the bell ringing inside. Eventually a voice asked how I could be helped. Not the same fat bitch who had spoken at us on the phone earlier. I was fuming again by now.

"You can help by getting my wife better for starters," I shouted at the intercom.

To my utter surprise, Dr Helen Chambers herself came to the other side of the glass door. She pushed the release to the side, allowed the door to swing open toward her before stepping through into the sunlight.

"Hello, John," she greeted me in a calm and controlled manner. She indicated a wooden bench seat across from the entrance. "Shall we?"

I followed her to the bench and sat down beside her. I didn't look at her. I sat with legs slightly apart, elbows resting on knees and stared at the ground between my feet. The silence enveloped us for long seconds. Traffic whirred past in the distance, birds flittered from shrub to tree and summer scents filled the air. Helen eventually cut the ice.

"You've upset Simone, you know," Helen started. "She is very distressed by your outburst."

I let her have it from both barrels. "That fat bitch can take a running jump. You know no-one in the village can stand the bitch. She thinks she's in charge here. She speaks to people as if they are shit and I'm not putting up with it any longer. All I want, Helen, is the proper follow-up for Kate. It is over four months now since she had that Zoom appointment with the Asian doctor at the hospital. He said he needed to get her into see him in person, but we've heard nothing. I want…. No, I demand, that something is done. We haven't said as much to each other, but I think Kate is dying. She seems to be getting more tired daily. What will you lot do? It's not too much to ask. After all, it is what you are here for."

She rested her hand on my right forearm. The touch was just enough to set me off again. The tears flooded out. I rubbed them away with my hand. Helen produced a clean handkerchief, and I wiped them away. I sucked in a couple of deep breaths and handed the cloth back to her.

"I haven't checked the notes, John, so can you just fill me in?"

I went over the ground from first noticing the small lump, through the virtual appointment until this morning's outburst.

"I understand," she said in a comforting sort of a voice. "I will check into the matter and promise I will be back to you personally. This afternoon or first thing in the morning."

"Okay," I agreed nodding my head. "Thank you. I put my left hand over hers, still resting on my forearm, and gently squeezed. "I mean that," I continued. Thank you."

"This is totally off the record, but it really does look like, on the face of it, that we have let Kate down. I will do everything that I can to push this along."

"And, what are you going to do about that gatekeeper of yours? You surely know that I am not the only one to have voiced my concerns?" I looked up from the ground and looked into concerned eyes.

"I know," she said gently. "She needs to be dealt with, but Doctor Williamson thinks she is the best thing since sliced bread. Let's get Kate sorted out first."

Within ten days or so she had had a face-to-face with bin Laden and had a small procedure known as a biopsy. We waited a few days before the results were back. This was followed up with scans and other examinations. The news was devastating. She had an invasive angiosarcoma, rare in itself but not totally uncommon for women that had already had treatment. In layman's terms, it was stage four breast cancer. The options were limited, and it was terminal.

We discussed it for days. She was so brave; oh, so brave. In the end, she decided that she would live out what life she had left without medical intervention. She had chosen good quality life for as long as possible rather than medically assisted life for an extended period. All she asked was that she would have the pain managed as best as possible. Her worst nightmare was breaking down in front of friends as a result of the pain for she did not want them thinking she was frightened of what might await her after death. As much as I was terrified of losing her, she tried to buoy me along by listing all the things I could do, and that I was not to worry, as death was as much a part of life as being born. Unbelievably brave!

Within the limits of lockdown, we did do some nice things. We took the opportunity of visiting places in the UK, rather than going abroad so we became part of the staycation (hate the word) trend. We walked on beaches in the sun, we sauntered through woods in autumn as the leaves fell about us, we celebrated Christmas together for what we suspected was the last time and we marked our birthdays and forty-second wedding anniversary with a home-cooked meal. She wanted to celebrate as wildly as we dare so we had far too much to drink. "Drinking too much might take years off my life," she had joked.

It was just after we had marked our birthdays and our anniversary that I noticed it first. On getting up from the toilet pan one morning, I glanced down at the contents and noted a red tinge within the brown. I looked a little closer and it was most definitely blood. I monitored it over the next few weeks, but it didn't really seem to be getting any worse although I couldn't be sure. Neither was it getting any better. I didn't say a word to Kate and didn't seek medical advice while she was alive. Whilst she was fighting her own battles, it felt churlish to burden her with my own concerns.

Within a year of diagnosis, she was dead.

CHAPTER TWO

Monday 20th September 2021

Suffolk

Duncan Cobbold, head of an elite under-the-radar government squad, the Home Security Team, which consisted of several partnerships each with a former special forces' veteran and a leading ex-police officer, strolled through the open bar door of the Fox and Hounds pub in the Suffolk village of Oakshott. It was a warm evening for the time of year and, whilst many groups sat outside lapping up what could easily be the last balmy sunshine of the year, he expected his contacts to be indoors.

The bar was immediately in front of him with a couple of men standing supping their beers. The space was empty over to the left at the darts board and toilets end. Sitting at a table in the front corner to the right were two couples. The first, with their backs to the wall giving them an uninterrupted view of the room, old habits and that sort of thing, was one of his crack teams. A bulky, muscular not fat, shaven-headed black man. Sitting next to him, closest to the window, was a white woman with a lithe muscular frame, fair hair, tied in a ponytail, and piercing blue eyes that caught the light as she glanced over. The brilliant eyes locked on his, like lasers seeking a target. The other couple were one of the country's leading investigative journalists and his wife.

"Well," Cobbold announced as he stepped over to the table. "…if only the devil would choose to cast his net now. What a catch!"

The woman with the blue eyes spoke first after giving the newcomer the up-and-down. He was wearing an old tee shirt from a Rolling Stones concert, football shorts and flip-flops. No neutral observer would place him as the head of one of the country's leading security organisations. "If you are the horned fisherman, the devil is most definitely not wearing Prada! What do you look like?"

"Thanks for the compliment, Sue-Beth," Cobbold smiled. "May I get a round in?"

The two men downed the remainders of their glasses in one and passed them to the buyer without saying a word.

"Two Ghost Ships?"

The men nodded their acceptance.

"Ladies?"

"The New Zealand Sauvignon Blanc for me, please," Walters answered.

"By the way," said Cobbold. "A belated happy birthday for the sixteenth, Sue-Beth."

"Thank you. God! Forty-three. Where does it keep going?"

"And a white wine spritzer for me, please," said the journalist's wife.

Cobbold took the two beer glasses to the bar leaving the women with their unfinished drinks. He ordered the drinks, delivering them to the table one-at-a-time as they were poured. The last trip from the bar to the table saw him with a glass of orange juice. He hadn't drunk alcohol since a night, many years ago, when he had got so obliterated on booze, that it had taken the best part of a week to feel back to his proper self. That was the day a young black man called Dwight Carter had been imprisoned for his part in post office robberies in the West Midlands. The sentence had been a shock to Cobbold, but it was merely a ruse to show that all culprits had been punished according to law. Whilst Cobbold was touring the drinking holes of Birmingham the mysterious wheels of motion set running by the sham imprisonment started to rumble. Dwight Carter, a small-time villain turned police informer, had supposedly been killed in prison, a charade only helped by the false claim of the robbery gang leader that he had ordered the execution of Carter for his betrayal, and Curtly Richardson was born. Richardson, given a second chance, changed his life around. A crammed education allowing him to pass GCSEs and "A" Levels before progressing to university and, eventually, the police force. Later, when Cobbold had been tasked with putting the Home Security Team together, one of the first on his list of recruits was the more than capable officer from Hampshire Police.

He dragged a chair across from another table and placed it at the end, the head, of the occupied table. "Cheers," he allowed, holding his orange juice high.

"Cheers," the others reacted in unison with a clinking of glasses to follow.

"You took your time," Richardson said.

"Got held up with the Home Secretary this afternoon. He sends his regards by the way."

"I don't even know him!"

"No, but he thinks he knows you. And that's what counts. He has your career files on record, and you are all his family as he sees it. A good man."

"Ha! What've you got for us, then? I assume that's what your meeting with the Home Sec was about. I also assume it is the reason you wanted to find out if we were all available this evening? I suspect this isn't a social visit? So, it must be important?"

"Do you know, you really should have been a police officer! You have a nose for investigation. It is important but, as usual, I had to give him time to unload on me about the top man."

"What about him? Some juicy gossip?" Walters enquired.

"Juicy gossip? No. Usual shit. He is too heavily influenced by wine, women and song. The latter two are as a result of too much of the first. After a few glasses, he thinks he can sing like Pavarotti but sounds more like a piglet being castrated. He then thinks he is God's gift to women. He nearly caused a diplomatic incident when his hand lingered on the Spanish ambassador's wife's bottom for too long last week."

"Sleazy bastard! Why don't they just get rid of him?"

"There are some who would like to, I am sure, but, apparently, he is too popular with the people."

"Really? Me and Curt could do a job on him easily enough," she joked.

"I'm sure you could. All these things will get ironed out in the fullness of time. They always do!"

"I suppose you would like me to go and find something else to do right now?" the journalist's wife, Amelia Bryant, put in.

"No hurry. I can get to that a little later. Have you all eaten? My shout. I'm famished."

"If that's the case," replied Sean Bryant. "I'm pretty hungry too."

"More than likely the Home Sec's shout," joked Richardson. "I'm starvin'."

"Is there a menu?"

"Don't be stupid," smiled Bryant. "You and your big city ways! It's fish and chip night. So, you can have fish and chips or fish and chips! It's up to you."

"Welcome back to Oakshott," joked Richardson. "By the way, you could have just chips or just fish!"

"One day there will be an improvement. I guess it'll be five fish and chips, then?"

They all agreed and Cobbold headed back to the bar to place the order. On returning, he carried five sets of cutlery and a box of condiments.

"Go on then," demanded Richardson.

"It's actually one for all three of you," Cobbold said as he retook his chair.

"Not me, though?" Amelia put in.

"I daresay there is no good reason to ask you to leave anyway Amelia. I am sure Sean will fill you in in any case. It doesn't really impinge on national security this time. It does fall under the remit of the Home Sec, though, and it's something he just can't get sorted out. Hence, he has asked us to take a look."

"How come it's for me?" Bryant asked between sips of his beer.

Ordinarily, like in the case of the missing girl in Corfu which was eventually linked to a Russian betting syndicate who used their influence to control results in European football club matches or the so-called vegan vigilante, Bryant had played second fiddle to Richardson and Sue-Beth Walters. Since he had helped crack the case of the neo-Nazi terrorist organisation headed up by the former Army general, also known as the Lionheart, he had been used for his investigation skills in exchange for the rights to the book and, in the case of the Lionheart, the subsequent movie. The three books thus far and the film had proven lucrative, and he had gone freelance after the publication of the Lionheart story. His former newspaper, the London Echo and Post, had allowed him to leave without delay as long as they were granted first refusal on the future books' serialisations. They even threw in a nice advance for his maiden venture into freelance investigation.

Cobbold leaned back in his chair before steepling his fingers and sighing aloud, "The Home Sec, as you know, is fully aware of your role in helping to solve the three previous cases. Indeed, you could not have banked your small fortune without his approval." Although referred to as "he" the current Home Secretary was, in fact, the fifth since the Lionheart case; the position had been held by two women as well as the three men. "Indeed, this is his idea. He thinks it will make a good cover for what we need to find out. And, for what it's worth, I agree with him. I think it's a good idea. No pressure, though, you don't have to accept it. It will have dangers but not that bad."

"And, if I don't take it on? You never know, I might be doing something else at the moment!" Bryant was, in fact, doing something else. He was ghost-writing the autobiography of a former leading football manager, and it was hard work. The man might have had a brilliant football mind, but his grasp of simple spelling and grammar were almost non-existent. The subject of the book had given him notes made during his career that needed an ever-present interpreter. You know what, he thought, I could do with a break from the supposed stresses of the football world where mediocrity appeared to be rewarded with enormous pay-outs. The bombastic son-of-a-bitch would have to go on the backburner for a while. "I'm in," he agreed.

"You don't know what it is yet," Cobbold countered with a glint of victory in his eyes.

"It can't be as tedious as what I'm doing at the moment."

"We don't know what it is either," said Walters. "We might have something else on as well."

"You, I am afraid, don't get any choice. You are both in the employ of HM Government and will do what you are told." It was all banter and the sparkle in Cobbold's voice showed that he knew it too.

The Chief turned his attention back to Bryant but was, really, addressing all three of them. "You will all be aware of the issue surrounding the migrants crossing the Channel, almost on a daily basis. Most of the organisers pose no threat whatsoever, others pose a horrendous threat and will be monitored by the necessary authorities. Our chaps, and they are always men, are somewhere in the middle. What they do, though, is depraved and they make small fortunes out of it. Bear in mind that they have already made more than you get in a year from trafficking one boatload of unfortunates from France to England. One would've thought, that would be enough but, no, they want more. Greedy bastards."

"How come the Home Sec is involved?" asked Richardson. "I didn't think he was involved in operations during the investigation stage?"

"He isn't. He suggests our participation but that's it. He is never kept up to date with operations on a daily or ongoing basis. He will give me a brief at the outset, and I will give him a report at the end. That's it. I might ask him to bring pressure to bear in certain circumstances, but he will never know why in most cases. Sometimes he might take a keener interest, especially if there is pressure coming from elsewhere. He will never direct an operation, though. The Government are struggling to keep a lid on illegal immigration, so he is asking us to help him out. We're not subject to the normal rules of engagement."

The fish and chip suppers arrived. They ate the meals and decided to retire to Richardson's house for coffee and further discussion.

The sky was now darkening in the east while a sublime red with flashes of glorious pinks, purples and golds lit up the western horizon as the sun sunk below the far treeline. The band turned away from the sunset, passing the school to their left. Amelia spotted Richardson's surreptitious glance through the fence at the headteacher's office in the front. He always looked in that direction. It was a habit he could not break. It was only recently that there had not been a tear rolling down his face. She never talked to him about it but knew he would confide in her if he needed to. He now had Sue-Beth for that sort of thing anyway. After the school they turned left into Church Lane before reaching the Richardson residence on the right, a two-storey cottage style house with a pale-yellow render finish. Richardson punched in the security code to the keypad in front of the first pair of steel gates.

Walters pulled out a key and unlocked the front door before letting them all process inside single file. Passing the three-flight staircase on the left, they entered the dining room which doubled perfectly as a small conference room. Cobbold took a chair along the length of the polished oak table on the far side where Bryant joined him. She and Richardson took two chairs opposite them.

Amelia chirped, "Shall I get the coffees?"

"Please. You know where they are," said Richardson, before continuing in a jocular manner. "And, black for me. It's not bloody difficult you know. I am the only black in here and I am the only one who has his coffee black. Colour association should do it if nothing else!"

Amelia saluted and stamped her feet together in a mock attention, "Sir!" She did know where everything was. Sean and her had owned the house before selling it to their friend and his then new wife, Gillian. She couldn't help but wonder how different life could have been. Gillian had been the headteacher at the village school before being hounded to suicide by a racist thug who had encouraged his eight-year-old son to bombard Gillian with offensive slurs about her spawning the devil's own child with a jungle bunny. One day the lout had picked up a claw-hammer belonging to a workman and crashed it into Gillian's pregnant abdomen. The injuries were colossal, and the baby died despite the hospital's best endeavours. Gillian never recovered mentally from the ordeal and one morning, when Richardson had been away on a job, the school-caretaker found her hanging from a beam in the assembly hall.

After more than six months, Richardson had moved Walters, her son, Toby, and her mother-in-law in with him. Both had always stuck to the tale that it was platonic and, indeed, they slept in separate rooms. It was typical of Richardson's kindness. Walters and her tribe had been served with notice to vacate the rental they had in the village near the shop. Richardson had offered up his spare rooms to them nearly five years ago and they had been there ever since. "It's what a house like this should be," mourned Richardson. "A family home."

She set the coffee machine working and as the spitting and gurgling started, she felt a wet nose nuzzle against her bare leg. She bent down and took Richardson's German Shepherd's head in her hands. "Hello, Odin, you handsome thing. Just been for a walk?"

The dog, wagging his enormous tail, was followed into the room by Lady Isobel Walters and young Toby Walters. Just behind them was her own eldest daughter, Poppy.

"Hello, Mum," she greeted her mother. "Thought you were in for a night at the pub?"

"Hello, Amelia," the older woman greeted her. "Are you keeping well, dear?"

Hi, Amelia," Toby put in before Amelia could answer his grandmother or her daughter.

"Hi, Toby. I am, Isobel. Thank you. And you?"

"Well, you know. The bones aren't getting any younger and dear old Odin here knows how to put me through my paces. No doubt, as usual, I shall be as stiff as a board in the morning. Ah! I see you have coffee on the go?"

"Yes. I think there'll be enough if I use the smaller cups."

Amelia turned to her daughter. "Afraid not. Uncle Duncan has appeared with a job for the team. You and Toby got that assignment finished yet?"

Poppy's blush gave her the answer before any words were uttered. "Still in the preparation phase, Mum."

"Oh! I see." She did see. It was incredulous how these two young people who had hated each other so vehemently in primary school had grown to be infatuated by each other through high school and now into sixth form. There interests were similar except that Toby loved cricket, a pursuit only encouraged by living under the same roof as Richardson, whilst her eldest born couldn't stand it; in fact, sport did not really feature in her interests at all apart from the occasional foray onto the tennis court with her mother. It was a shame as she was naturally athletic and was probably a better player than Amelia but chose to shun the game in favour of other interests. The chief of which was now standing by her side, the tall and exquisitely handsome Toby Walters. The physique was most definitely taken from his late father but there was no doubt as to where the looks and the eyes had come from. The eyes in particular; they had the same electric blue laser attributes of his mother and had many-a-girl swooning. Poppy was the school year above Toby and was assisting him with his task. It always seemed to be in the planning stage! They were now at sixth form with Poppy in the upper sixth. There was only about thirteen months between them.

"Me and Toby won't need any coffee, Mum. We're off to the pub," said Poppy to her mother before turning to Toby. "Just go home and shower, hun. I'll try and persuade Daisy to join us. Won't be any more than half-an-hour. Okay"

"Okay. I'll go take a shower too and see you there."

"Huh!" Amelia harrumphed. "Half-an-hour? I think you're safe for at least an hour, Toby. If not longer!"

"Don't take any notice of her," said Poppy. "I'll be there."

Amelia dug out a tray from behind the kettle and took the coffees through to the meeting, leaving two on the side for her and Lady Isobel. Her husband spotted her through the door window and got up to let her in. Richardson dealt out some coasters as Bryant placed the coffees on them. Odin snuck in and laid down at Richardson's feet.

As the door closed Cobbold continued with his, the Home Secretary's, plan. After going through the details for a second time, he asked if there were any queries.

All either shook their heads or confirmed that there weren't.

"One last thing," Cobbold turned to the journalist. Taking out an envelope from his case he handed it to the man.

Bryant opened the small package. It contained a small blue booklet with an emblem on the front, a driver's licence and a few other professional documents. He recognised the insignia on the front of the passport. It had a shield with a kangaroo to one side and an emu to the other. He riffled through until he discovered the identity page. He raised his eyebrows.

"Glen Ponting? Australian? Why?""

"Yeah. We think they will be more inclined to go with that as a cover story. What's your Aussie accent like?"

"Fair dinkum, cobber!"

The other three laughed.

"Umm! Maybe needs a little work," said Cobbold. "Sounds a little more 'Old South Wales' than New South Wales! Might be a good idea to drop the cliches as well. Given that you will be dealing with the French, Albanians and Middle-Easterns, though, I don't suppose it needs to be that fantastic."

"What's the name about?"

"I'll let Mr Richardson here answer that. I am sure he can see the reasoning behind it."

"Certainly can," agreed the former policeman taking the booklet from his friend. "Just like I used the first name of a great West Indian bowler, so you have used the name of a great Australian bowler. Glen McGrath, if I am not mistaken?"

Cobbold nodded.

"My surname is for the great Richie Richardson whereas yours is for Ricky Ponting. I have a middle name, though, taken from the master blaster himself."

"Spot on," agreed Cobbold. "No middle name. Didn't think it necessary."

He went on to explain the other documents which included: a journalist's ID confirming he was engaged by the Sydney Morning Herald and business cards with a number for the London office which would be answered in a room in HST headquarters. He also explained that they had received amazing co-operation from the Australian security authorities who had sanctioned all the documents to be genuine. They would all check out if the French authorities so wished. There was, however, no chance of the passport being accepted at the Australian border. "It was made perfectly clear to us that if you ever try to enter Australia with these documents you will be arrested, thrown in a cell and the key chucked away. Got it?"

"Yeah. Loud and clear. It does look a little new, though?"

"Stick it in your back pocket for the next week or so before you go, drop it down the side of the chair and put your coffee cup on it. Should do the trick. Any more questions?"

"When do we go?" asked Walters.

"In the next week or so. You two will drive Sean to Dover. An open return ticket is included in your package. As a foot passenger, you will be able to board just about any ferry."

Sean and Amelia Bryant took their leave and headed for

home. Past the pub and shop, they continued into Ampsley Road. The evening had cooled since they had left the former, so they walked arm-in-arm in a bid to try and keep warm. Amelia keyed in the number at the gate and let it swing open enough to pass through. She waited on the other side for her husband who, as usual, had stopped to wipe the keys with his shirt. "Don't know why you keep doing that?"

"Can't be too careful." He had a theory that someone could toss some dust at the keys which would stick to the four most used keys. Then they would be able to work at the code even if it took them a few attempts. "You never know who's out there!"

"Like who? In any case, if they go down the side, all they need to do is hop over a four-foot high fence!"

"It's my little game!"

They strolled along the drive, past the old cannon sitting on the lawn and approached the front door. Amelia inserted the key.

"We're home," she shouted as they passed through the door. "Anyone home?"

"In the lounge." came the reply. It was Daisy, the younger of the Bryant girls. She was sitting on one of the sofas with the dog's head resting on her lap, stroking its neck. When she looked up to her parents, it was clear she had been crying.

"What's up, love?" asked Amelia, kneeling down beside her and taking her hands in hers.

"Nothing!"

"It doesn't look like nothing?"

After a little back and forth, Daisy reluctantly let on that she and Poppy had had another row. She assured them that she was alright now, though.

Bryant shook his head. He had heard it all before so went through to the kitchen to grab a glass of water. Bella, the golden labrador, thought he might be getting something more interesting than water so trotted after him.

"What was it about this time?" he asked as they laid in bed later that night.

Amelia sighed, "Well, it's just the usual. Poppy going on about Daisy and why she hasn't got or had a boyfriend yet."

"Christ! There's no hurry. She loves her horse-riding more than anything else in the world right now. Her and Maddie are never happier than when they are galloping across the heath. In fact, I would say, Daisy's life is fuller than Poppy's. All Poppy does is drool over Toby all day long."

"Poppy also teased her about being so frigid and if she doesn't do anything about it, she'll miss out."

"Oh?"

"What's that meant to mean?"

"Well…. I assume, you know, Poppy is still a…. well, you know. Oh God! Hardly talking about things from experience!" Bryant was out of his depth discussing his daughters' love-lives.

"Sean!" exclaimed Amelia. "You're not serious?"

"Huh! What do you mean?"

"What on earth do you think it was about when I went with Poppy to the doctor in the spring?" Amelia propped herself up on one elbow and peered down at her husband.

"I never really gave it any thought. Lady problems, I assumed."

"Bloody hell, Sean. She is nearly eighteen and in a very steady relationship. I'll spell it out, shall I? She's on the pill!"

Bryant opened his eyes and stared into his wife's amused eyes. "You mean…. Oh shit! You mean…. Her and Toby are…."

"Hurray! There are no flies on you!"

"With Toby?"

"Of course, with Toby. Who else?"

"I ought to take him to one side and have a man-to-man talk with him and explain his responsibilities. And, if he gets her pregnant, he'll have me to answer too."

Amelia guffawed. "That should make him quake in his boots! What do you reckon? About six-feet-three and fourteen-and-a-half stone, and full of muscle. You and whose army? They are grown up and maybe, just maybe, you should let them live like grown-ups.""

"Right. Okay," Bryant eventually allowed and rolled onto his side facing away from Amelia.

Amelia laid down, wrestled some duvet back and laid in silence for a short while before asking "What's this job about then?"

Bryant righted himself again and faced up to the ceiling before going on to explain the task ahead.

Amelia laid in stunned quiet for a moment trying to take it all in. Sean had never been actively involved in the field before. Not like this anyway. I suppose, she thought, it is only uncovering a story in the same way he used to for the Echo and Post. When working with Cobbold and his crew, though, he had always been a backseat driver, finding out all the information needed online or over the phone. She propped herself up again, leaned over and kissed him on the cheek. "Be careful! Love you!"

"Love you too," he responded. "Now I need some sleep."

51

CHAPTER THREE

Norfolk

Over the last week and a bit, I had started to make preparations for my end. The primary planning was for the revenge I was going to wreak on those that had crossed Kate and me. My mind went back to the final goodbye, at least as far as the parish was concerned. The funeral was restricted to only a few people in the church, thanks to that cursed Covid, but I was staggered by the turnout that lined the short journey from our house to St Michael's gate. It seemed as if the whole of our adopted village had come out to show respect with heads bowed. As I alighted from the car, I heard a lone bugler playing The Last Post. I swear, looking back, that my eyes never dried out that morning.

I had half-a-dozen or so back to the house in mid-August. We sat in the garden and drank, bizarrely in my opinion, champagne. Kate wouldn't have wanted anything less. Toward the end, she had kept telling me that life was for living and death was for celebrating the former living, not mourning.

When our good friends, now my good friends, Rachel and another John were leaving, the man started as if to say something else rather than the usual consoling words.

"Maybe not now, darling," Rachel had said.

She leaned in and kissed me on my cheek. John took my hand, held his free hand over mine and said, "I will pop and see you in the morning, mate."

What was that about, I wondered.

The next day I strolled over to our allotment, Kate's pride and joy, where she had spent many hours in quiet contemplation in her last few months. It was, I suppose, the perfect antidote to lockdown and the inevitable. But, of course, there was no antidote to the latter. I would busy myself under her instruction, deadheading, pricking-out and pruning, weeding, digging and picking fruit. The strawberries were fat and juicy and complimented her favourite tipple, gin and tonic, very well. John found me there and we sat on the deck of our shed. I poured some coffee from a flask into two chipped mugs. One had "John" printed on it and the other "Kate." I let him have the one with "John" on it. I caressed Kate's mug and let my mind drift to happier times. I am pretty sure John didn't notice my eyes watering. If he had, I was prepared to blame hey-fever. Good excuse in summertime

"Sorry. No milk or sugar," I said as I handed him the drink. "Do you know, mate, we came up here a lot over the few months before she died, and this was one of our favourite pastimes, drinking coffee,"

"That's why I assumed you would be up here. I daresay I'll survive without the milk," he said taking the coffee from me and placing it on the deck to the right of his chair. "You might think yourself sweet enough, but I most certainly am not!" And, to my astonishment he took a small plastic box from his trouser pocket and plopped a small sweetener pip into the black nectar.

In all the years I had known John, maybe fifteen now, I had never seen him do that before. "Talk about prepared," I said.

"Always. You never know when tea or coffee might be proffered."

He then produced a sheet of paper from his pocket. He held it in both hands momentarily before saying, "John.... Mate. I have been thinking about this for a while now and how to do this. All my rehearsals of speeches and what have you, have now escaped me. I think the best thing is to simply hand you the paper, you look at it and then we talk. I think it speaks for itself."

"Okay," I said wondering what could be so important.

He handed the folded A4 sheet to me. I opened it out and instantly raised my hand to my mouth and felt sick to the core at what I saw. It was a picture of Kate, topless, cupping her breasts in her hands.

"How? Where did you get this?"

"Well, I hope you won't think bad of me and Rachel for what I am about to tell you."

"No. Why should I? I have seen and heard shocking things throughout my life."

Well... It's like this. Well.... It's that Rachel and me sometimes use porn sites to enhance our sex lives. We never use hard porn or kiddie stuff or animals. You do understand?"

I nodded. "Of course not, John. But where did you get this?"

Well, we stumbled across this one which was headed something like Sick Women."

I raised my eyebrows. "Is that really what it was called?"

He looked away. This must have been really difficult for him.

54

He gazed, not seeing, I am sure, into runner beans. "Um. No. It was actually called Bitches about to Die!"

From the outside I tried to remain calm but, on the inside, I wanted to rip someone's head off. And, I knew exactly who that someone was. "Thanks for this, John. Much appreciated. It took a lot for you to come to me with this."

"Can I give you any more info? Like where to find it or something?"

"I don't really need anything further. I know exactly where it came from. And I guarantee you that that someone will be getting an unannounced visit from me. I might even kill the scumbag."

I am pretty sure that John thought my threat were the cheap words that people often say when they are wronged, but I was serious. I meant it. I did, though, to save time ask him to show me how to get the site up. He drew out his phone and after a few taps and finger movements he passed the device to me. On it was a gallery of several women, differing in age from fairly young to older than Kate. I looked at him inquisitively. Internet stuff was not really my strength. Indeed, Kate had always done everything for us that involved computers beyond the very basic.

"You just tap on the image you want to see more of."

I tapped Kate's image and there she was taking up the whole screen. It was a video recording with music in the background. Moaning noises emanated from her lips along with all sorts of suggestive words and heavy breathing as if she were about to orgasm. I was appalled. The words and noises had been dubbed in by some pathetic actress. How could I be sure? I was in the room when the video was filmed. There was no doubt in my mind, the purveyor of this filth was going to die.

Doctor Helen Chambers had been brilliant with me and had ensured that the attention I received from the NHS was as good as Kate's had been bad. I phoned her the day after Kate's death, and she saw me that afternoon. I was in with bin Laden the following day. Impressive and really quick. He showed me the utmost courtesy and speed. Between Kate's passing and her funeral my concerns were confirmed. I had bowel cancer. Bin Laden assured me that it was early enough that I could make a full recovery. We agreed we would meet up after the funeral again to go through options. I knew I did not want a full recovery so I would reject all treatments on offer.

After John had passed me the still of Kate's performance, I had gone to the hospital and followed bin Laden to his home. He never spotted me, why would he have been looking. I was good at surveillance after many years practice. It is really easy when the target has no reason to suspect they are being trailed. It is not quite as easy when they have a guilty conscience, they are often on the lookout. There was no doubt that this bastard should have had a guilty conscience, but he didn't spot me. Maybe he was so arrogant he thought no-one knew?

I parked in a street of a small village about ten miles from the hospital and, after a short while, strolled up the gravel driveway to bin Laden's front door. The house was detached but modest, constructed of brick with Norfolk flint panels breaking the monotony of the, otherwise, plain facade. To the right of the home, there was a triple garage outside of which he had parked his modest saloon car. What on earth is the reason someone would need a triple garage? Of course, it could have been the previous owners and not bin Laden. For some reason I had been expecting something a little more palatial.

I pushed the bell. He answered the door himself. He didn't recognise me at first. Why should he? My face was one of many he would see over time. Recognition dawned eventually. "Mr Wells, isn't it?"

"Yes"

"This is somewhat irregular but what can I do for you?"

I removed the folded A4 sheet from my chinos' back pocket and handed it to him. He unfolded it, much like I had and his hand, much like mine had, flew up to his mouth. The difference was he soon started to perspire. He stepped through the door and drew it shut behind him before ushering me away to the middle of the well-tended front lawn. I assume there were family inside, maybe children. He certainly did not want them to know about his sordid little side-shuffle. Fear was etched all over his face.

"I can explain," he stuttered.

"No need," I countered as calmly as I could manage. Inside I still wanted to rip his head off.

He brightened a little.

I continued. "You simply have to do something for me. That's all." I went on to explain what I wanted him to do and supported how serious I was, by giving him a brief bio of my life, telling him of the killings I had made as a professional soldier, mercenary and security consultant.

I watched the colour drain from his bearded face. His dark eyes began to water as he came to the obvious conclusion. "Please don't kill me. I've made a mistake. I shouldn't 'ave done it but they threatened my family. If you kill me…. Well, my kids and wife…. Well, you know…."

"You do everything I've asked of you, and I promise I won't touch a hair on your head. And, what is more, you give me the names and whereabouts of the nice folk that threatened you and I will hunt them down."

God! I thought, Me and whose army! Then it came into my head: Major Alan Cooper, ex Royal Marines.

Based on my qualified guarantee, he agreed to every one of my demands. The first of these demands was that he invites me in for a consultation about the bowel cancer diagnosis. During the weeks since my visit to his home, I had received cameras up the arse after some sort of horrific tasting clear-out drink the day before. I went through further examinations and scans before, early last week, I sat in with bin Laden for the planned appointment. He handed me an envelope as promised which contained the name and address of the man behind the threat to him and his family. I was always told that you should never judge a book by its cover. I expected the name to be Asian in origin but was surprised to discover it was British. I felt a little shame, but it shouldn't have shocked me, there are just as many arseholes with English names as there are with Asian, probably more. Names, though, had changed to name, singular!

"I thought there was more than one? You said they?" I asked.

"The others are of no importance. He is the head man."

I shrugged.

It is now the autumn equinox, and, without doubt, the evenings are getting darker. It is nearly seven in the evening, and I've got the lights on and the curtains drawn. Bit too warm for a fire but I suppose it won't be long. I am sitting at the dining-room table with a spiral notebook and Kate's old fountain pen, a glass of her favourite gin and tonic by my side. I didn't bother using the measure, I guessed! It is taking effect, and I can, strangely, feel a clarity of thought coming over me. It is like a battle calm. Bin Laden has stated that I, in his professional opinion, have less than six months to live. That is what I wanted from him.

When I dug out our life insurance policies after Kate had passed, I realised we had missed a trick, we could have claimed a pay-out when it was estimated she had less than six months to live. Mine was caught early so I, maybe, had a few years ahead of me yet. Officially, though, thanks to bin Laden's professional opinion I was now able to claim my quarter-of-a-million quid. It is meant for me and my loved ones to enjoy the little time left to me. Even if we had realised this with Kate's policy, what the hell would we have spent it on? Lockdown after lockdown along with restriction after restriction would have put paid to that. Bastard government! I hate them. I would now have the cash to purchase anything I wished to assist me with completing my wish dead list.

Not sure I get this lockdown business. It, as I understand it, was meant to protect the NHS and its workers; bugger everyone else. Throughout I haven't known a single person who has died from the virus, but I have known three lads in the village who have lost their businesses - thanks to protecting these privileged divas and divos called doctors and nurses. I hate them from the coldest of hearts as I plan to revenge my wife's unnecessary death. Some of the bastards believe that they do not even need to have the vaccines on offer, having fallen prey to the idiot conspiracy theorists, not giving a toss about all of those who have lined up for their jabs even though some wondered at the efficacy of what they were doing. They were doing it, primarily I guess, to protect themselves, but mainly to protect the sainted NHS. God! How I hate these prima donnas. My wife had paid the ultimate sacrifice in protecting the NHS but where are they in turn? They really couldn't give a jot about the people who turned out every Thursday evening to "Clap for the Carers" last spring into summer. Now they had proved their true colours, they can receive my wrath from both barrels. One of the lads who lost his business was later found dangling on a rope in nearby woods. He left a young wife and child. This will be for them as well.

These bouts of reflective desolation often overcome me. I look across at the sideboard where our wedding picture takes pride of place. It is nothing special. No wedding dress, no church archway surrounded in flowers, just us with a stack of horseshoes at Gretna Green. To either side of this are the pictures of Kate dressed in her mortar board and gown clutching a pretend scroll at the presentation of her degree in architecture. To the other side was me being awarded my green lid after passing the physical acuity tests at Lympstone.

My eyes misted and my mind went back. Apart from my marriage to the most wonderful person to walk this planet, this had been the proudest day of my life. Weeks of training had culminated in days of exacting tests finishing with the gruelling thirty-miler. We had to complete the distance in under eight hours, with a twenty-one-pound pack, across all sorts of terrain: through bogs, through rivers, over hills and down hills. Overcoming the physical pain was the toughest thing I have ever done. Our motto was 'Per Mare, Per Terram' or 'By Sea, By Land.' I always used to think 'By Air' should have been added to the eighteenth-century slogan. It would make it clear to the enemies of our realm that they were not safe anywhere. They would have to watch the waves, they would have to watch the hills, and they would have to watch the skies. We always got the job done. Watch out, we're coming to get you.

I take another sip of the spirit and run through the list again. It contains nine unstruck-out names, and I need a tenth. The list, to start with, probably had around thirty names on it but, gradually, I had deleted and added until I had fixed on the nine names left. Some of the originals had already died or, despite all my limited skills on the internet, I hadn't been able to find if they were still alive or not. Substitutions had been made but, annoyingly, I was still one short.

I need ten because I wanted to get to fifty and raise my bat and, hopefully remain not out - although I could be stumped anywhere between forty, my current score, and the milestone. During my life, I had killed nine men in the army, three in the Falklands and six in the first Gulf War; I never saw service during the second Gulf War; I had then seen off twenty-two as a mercenary in the pay of the British government in some nasty places around the world including Columbia, Yemen, East and

West Africa; and, finally, as a so-called private security consultant, a euphemism for private mercenary, I had taken out eight nasty individuals, drug dealers and people traffickers among them.

The only ones I felt any type of regret over were the ones I despatched as a professional soldier. They, you see, were amateurs, conscripts. Some, possibly, had only held a gun for the first time when they went out to face us that morning. They didn't stand a chance. The Sunday League Dog and Duck stood more chance against Liverpool or Man City than they stood against us. We were well-trained professionals compared with the bakers, butchers and candlestick makers of the enemy.

There was also one individual I had killed by accident. About twenty-five years ago, Kate was about four years into running her own architectural practice when she hit the buffers. She had taken on the dream job of designing a multi-story office and residential block in London somewhere. The project was worth tens of thousands to the business. Can't remember exactly how much. Then her world fell in. The developer got himself in too deep and pulled the plug on the project leaving many builders and designers out of pocket by what I recall as millions. The annoying thing was, though, he had set some sort of limited liability company up to run this development and, to my simple mind, had run it into the ground. He owned other companies and properties and assured all the creditors he hadn't broken any law. Kate couldn't survive it and one Friday evening, after she had had to let all her staff go, one of the younger ones decided to come and pay her a visit. Luckily for Kate, I was on leave. Unluckily for the tanked-up idiot, I was on leave. He banged on the door with his fists and kicked at it before I pulled the door open. The situation wasn't a whole lot different to that night in Carlisle. A drunken protagonist who thought he could take me out and wanted to get at Kate. He was probably more drunk than the roadbuilders in Carlisle and stepped into the narrow gap that was our front door. This time my head connected perfectly with his nose. As the drunken architect collapsed to the floor, he caught his head on the slightly raised kerb or low wall we had to the side. He died in hospital three days later. We went through a police investigation but in the end, it was decided I had no case to answer as I had used reasonable force to defend my wife and property. It had come to light that as he drank that night, he grew more and more malevolent toward Kate and was, apparently, going to teach the rich bitch a lesson. Others in the party couldn't convince him that she was as much a victim as the members of staff.

In short, I knew how to kill and although I hadn't seen meaningful action in just over ten years, I was still sure I could out-fox any prey. This, I suppose, is going to be my last career move: I am going to become a serial killer.

CHAPTER FOUR

Suffolk

The dark Mercedes GLS SUV pulled up outside the gates at Crouch Hall Farm, the Bryant residence, just outside the village of Oakshott. It was still dark and the driver had to use his phone-torch to illuminate the keypad. He punched the numbers in, let the gates open and drove through passing the antique cannon and swung round in front of the main door. The door to the house opened and Sean Bryant stepped out into the cool morning. He got in the back behind the passenger.

"Morning, mate," Curtly Richardson greeted him.

"Morning, Curt. Sue-Beth."

"Ready for some real work, then?"

"Ha! It's a while since I have left the house in the dark at this end of the day."

Richardson and Walters had, the day before, kitted Bryant out with government issue clothing. This included a mid-season jacket to protect against the cold mornings. Every item of clothing, including the socks and under-pants, had a micro-tracking device sewn into them. The trainers had the appearance of being worn in. No-one would know unless they looked inside. The consensus was that the smugglers would not check in so much detail, if they checked at all.

They had made good progress as they approached the last junction on the M25 before the Dartford Crossing. Dawn was now breaking and the glare of brake-lights coming on alerted them to an incident ahead.

"Surely they're not queuing for the bridge already?" said Bryant.

"Probably," answered the driver.

"Shit!" said Walters. "I don't reckon. The line is only about ten cars long. I tell you what I reckon it is. It's one of those bloody Insulate Britain demonstrations."

"Great!" exclaimed Richardson.

"We could be here all day," said Bryant.

"No, we won't," said Richardson. He found Duncan Cobbold's name on the car's computer screen and tapped the line. The speakers erupted into life with static to start with, as the phone searched out towers to relay the signal, before the amplified ringing tone came in.

Cobbold picked up within two rings. "Got you on the screen. I guess you're caught up with the protestors?"

"You got it. Can you activate Solar Flare?"

Cobbold confirmed that he would. Solar Flare is a jamming device that blocks the working of all electronic devices. No-one within a one-to-two square kilometre area will be able to make or receive texts, calls or emails and send or receive any message on any platform such as WhatsApp. It also rendered the absolute use of electronic devices useless including the taking of photographs, recording of audio or video. It was seldom used. It was only employed when security authorities identified a requirement to protect their own agents in the field. Emergency services communications were not affected by this technology.

"Stay here, Sean," Richardson ordered after he had been assured Solar Flare was active. "Try calling someone on your phone. If it still works, press the horn and we'll rethink our strategy."

Bryant tried to call his wife but there was no response from his device whatsoever. He couldn't open a single app. Christ! He thought. I bet I'm not allowed to write about this when we're done! There were some aspects of HST field work that he was not allowed to report on at any-time. Solar Flare was, without any doubt in his mind, restricted territory in the interest of national security. As much as it was a great story, he would never divulge its existence as his agreement with the HST was too lucrative to break that trust. He would only ever expose activity which compromised levels of his interpretation of law. That had never raised its head thus far. He did, sometimes, feel a little squeamish at the deaths that resulted from HST operations but, to date, coroners had always deemed the killings to be lawful, so his allegiance had never been compromised. Cobbold's lawyers demanded sight of all transcripts prior to publication.

Walters and Richardson walked side-by-side between two lines of traffic. A small crowd of men had accumulated toward the front, and they were berating the protestors. The police had formed a protective line between the idling vehicles and the protestors. It looked like they were going to be offering protection to the demonstrators rather than move them on and get the road freed up.

"Watch out boys," said a man with a bald head. "Here comes bloody Black Lives Matter now." He laughed at his own attempt at humour.

The other men all joined in the laughter.

The pair continued past the group of men. Walters locked her lasers on bald head. The man visibly recoiled as the eyes bored into him. "Best you're not in my way when I come back," she said. "I hate racist bastards."

The man laughed again although his friends did not join in this time. "I'd wait anywhere for you, my little lovely," he allowed. "You're gorgeous!"

Oh dear, thought Richardson. This isn't going to end well.

"Sexual harassment as well," Walters added calmly. "Best you run for the hills."

Richardson took out his identity badge and flashed it at a woman constable. "Who's in charge?"

A sergeant pulled away from a conversation with one of the demonstrators. "I am. Who are you?"

"Home Security Team," answered Richardson brandishing his badge. "I am Curtly Richardson and this is my partner, Sue-Beth Walters. We are on government work, and I need a path through this lot."

"Never heard of you."

"I suggest you go and check us out, sergeant. Don't take too long, though. Lives are at stake."

The man reddened but took the badge to the patrol car. After a couple of minutes, he returned. Richardson took his badge back. Well?"

"This is an awkward one. These people won't go anywhere in a hurry," the sergeant offered up without conviction.

"Either you make them, sergeant, or I will. If someone gets injured in us carrying out our duty, there will be no moment in court for the family of the slighted. The government will not let me or her anywhere near a courtroom. Now get it sorted."

The policeman pulled away from Richardson and again engaged with the same protestor. He turned with the woman and headed toward Richardson. "This is Panther. She is the leader of this protest."

"I understand you are threatening us, whoever you are. We won't be moving for anyone. Our protest is in a bid to save the world by making sure that Tory scum make sure all the housing stock in this country is insulated and heated to acceptable standards. We couldn't care whether you had your dying wife in that car, you're not coming through. You'll be proud you made the sacrifice in years to come."

Richardson's fists balled. He felt a calming hand on his arm from his partner. Walters removed her pistol, a Glock 19, from the holster in the small of her back. "A bad analogy, Panther. This man lost his wife, thanks to a brutal attack from a racist thug. The mission we are on, if it goes to plan, will save hundreds, if not thousands, of lives. Now, before you glue yourself to the road or whatever you are intending to do, let all the cars through as far as that blue SUV and I won't put a bullet in your brain. If you don't let us through, I will shoot you and then put the same

68

request to your second-in-charge. After we're through, you can protest to your little heart's content for the rest of the day for all I care. The rest of the year if you want."

"You wouldn't dare shoot me."

"Just try me. I kill for a living. I'll count to ten before I put a parabellum between your eyes. And, trust me, I won't even give it a second thought. One."

On six Walters raised the weapon to the woman's head. It was as steady as a brick wall.

The woman looked behind her. "Is anyone filming this?" The voice lacked the confidence of earlier.

Someone replied that they could not get their mobile phones to work and that there was some weird shit going on.

"Your choice, Panther. Seven."

Panther took a couple of steps back and was visibly shaking now.

"Eight."

"Okay," she screamed. "We'll let you through."

"Good girl. You know it makes sense."

Panther turned and herded her colleagues toward the hard shoulder. The duty police joined them. Richardson and Walters turned for their vehicle.

The group of four men which were blocking the way between the two lines of cars parted, two each way, as the pair approached. This put bald head to Walters' left. As she got closer, she flexed her shoulders and extended her arms as if she were stretching prior to exercise.

"Thanks, love," bald head said. "Not bad for a woman. How do you get that thing to work with the phones? We all tried to film it."

"You still here?" said Walters before her left elbow smashed into the man's face just below his right eye. Not hard enough to cause permanent damage but good enough to need a paracetamol or two. His legs weakened and he sat down on the road before he fell there. "Keep control of your tongue in future, you racist misogynistic bastard," she growled. "I think it is now safe enough to get Solar Flare deactivated." She whispered the last sentence to her partner.

The man was helped to his feet by the other men. The protestors looked on in disbelief. The police stood motionless as the lines of traffic passed through. Then the police formed a protective rank between the vehicles and the protestors again.

The rest of the journey went without incident and Bryant was now standing on the deck of the ferry waiting to disembark at Calais. He made his way through border control without challenge and found the rendezvous point. A man saw him and got out of a small red hatchback.

"What is the longest river in Australia?" he asked.

"The Hawkesbury," responded Bryant in his best Australian voice. He was not sure of the veracity of that claim, but the challenge and reply had been concocted by Duncan Cobbold and who was he to argue.

The man nodded and opened the passenger door. Bryant climbed in and they were away.

Two hours later he was sitting on the terrace of a clifftop café overlooking the beach at Wimereux, about thirty-five kilometres south of Calais. He had learned that there was a long bit of coast extending to the south and west where traffickers would pitch up with their cargo and cram them into boats. The Rigid Inflatable Boats, RIBs, would often be seen working inshore waters but crossing the open English Channel struck Bryant as a little precarious. The beach was so long that it was nearly impossible for the French police to patrol it effectively, he had gleaned earlier.

About thirty minutes before, he had encountered a gendarmerie patrol near the café and asked them, in clumsy French, what they knew about the people smugglers.

It was a close-run thing. His passport, his Australian passport, had been closely scrutinised by the officers. He couldn't believe his bad luck as one of the officers must have been the only Australian born policeman in the French force. He had no idea whether that was true or not but there could not have been many. His mouth had dried up and his heart beat like a big bass drum.

"Glen Ponting, mate?" the policeman had queried with a perfect Australian accent in English. "Any relation to Ricky?"

Jesus! He thought, feeling sweat form under his armpits. And he likes bloody cricket as well. "No. Not that I know of," he replied in his practiced accent, now the subject of far more examination than he had expected. "You like cricket?"

"No, monsieur, I don't like cricket," the gendarme said. "I love it!"

Oh shit, Bryant thought.

"Whereabouts in Sydney are you from?" the gendarme continued.

Bryant recalled the map he had looked at the previous evening. What happened if this damn bloke came from Sydney as well? Bryant had never been to Australia, let alone Sydney. This cop, on the other hand, might know the city better than the back of his own hand. It was now make or break. His brief from Cobbold had stated that he was born in a place called Hornsby and now lived with his wife and two daughters in a suburb named Turramurra. All he knew was that they were both to the north of the city centre. "Turramurra. Do you know it?"

"No, mate. I come from the other side. Perth. My parents moved out there in the mid-eighties but moved back to France just after I finished high school. If it's any consolation, I still follow cricket like it is a religion and will be rooting for the Aussies in the Ashes."

Bryant hoped that the palpable relief that was coursing through his body did not show. "Good for you. I hope you two can help me?"

Before answering the Australian born gendarme translated the exchange for his colleague. He turned back to Bryant. "How?"

"Well. My paper is very interested in doing a piece on the migrants wanting to get into the UK. I won't identify them in my article if they don't want but I would like to get inside the minds of one of the traffickers. Do you think that's possible?"

The policeman, once again, translated for the benefit of his partner. The partner said something in return, but Bryant couldn't get it. He had a schoolboy grasp of the language but when it was spoken by natives it was usually too fast for him to translate. He soon worked out the meaning when the other gendarme held out his right hand, palm up, and rubbed his thumb and forefinger together."

"Oui, Okay," Bryant said to the French partner before addressing the Australian. "How much?"

"Two hundred each."

Bryant took out eight fifty-euro notes and handed them over, four to each of them. He was told to sit at the café and wait for about thirty minutes. The pair were pretty sure they knew someone who could help.

He waited for another five minutes before his coffee and a baguette were served to him. No-one appeared while he was eating. He took his time over the coffee, a little strong for his liking. When his cup was emptied, he looked around. He couldn't see anyone who resembled his image of a people-trafficker so again caught the attention of a passing waitress. "

"Un café encore, s'il vous plait?" he said in his very basic French.

"It is alright, monsieur, I speak English. A little. You have no time. A man wants you at the steps bottom on the beach." She nodded at the CCTV camera overlooking the terrace.

He looked over and nodded. "Ah! Merci, mademoiselle."

"Ha-ha," she smiled before correcting him. "Madame. I have not been a mademoiselle for over thirty years!"

He handed her a twenty euro note and headed for the stairs going down to the beach. He noticed a man standing away from the bottom step on the sand wearing a white tee-shirt, jeans and trainers. He had fair hair and a ruddy complexion. Not what he was expecting. Surely this was not his contact? The man was looking up at him and after a short interlude, he beckoned for him to descend the stairs. Bryant felt his stomach knot.

The man kept two metres away, observing the Covid protocol. "Monsieur Ponting?"

"Yes."

"You can call me Pierre. No other names."

"Okay." Bryant was trying to hide the surprise from his face that he felt on the inside.

"I am not what you expected, monsieur? Non?"

"To tell the truth, no. I was expecting an Asian or an East European. Albanian, maybe?"

"How can I help you? You want information, oui? Walk with me."

Pierre turned to his right allowing Bryant to step in beside him. They strolled, companionably to any onlooker, along the strand. The sun was shining, the sea a glorious blue and Bryant understood why desperate people might be lulled into a false sense of security when confronted with these seemingly benign conditions. Further out he could see a few whitecaps but nothing to suggest a crossing today would be fraught with any danger. Beyond that he could make out the blue-grey line of the English coast. To get this far and to give up on a dream was unjust. Even more galling were the dozens of lives that were lost every week to the unpredictability of the waters of the English Channel. To be robbed of one's life when almost in touching distance of their goal was even more unjust.

"What do you want to know, Monsieur Ponting?"

"Call me Glen. I want to get a feel for how desperate your clients are and how you go about securing passage?"

"As you wish, Glen. Information costs euros."

"How much?"

"One thousand."

"Five hundred," Bryant countered.

"Eight hundred."

Bryant had been given five-thousand-euros. This would now leave three thousand seven hundred-and-eighty. Should be enough to cover him. He had Glen Ponting's credit cards to cover genuine expenses. "Okay," he agreed and peeled the notes from the roll he had in his pocket and handed them over to Pierre. "Should be right."

Pierre counted out the sixteen fifty-euro notes. "It is. Be at the bottom of the steps tomorrow before dawn. Au revoir, monsieur."

"But…"

"Tomorrow. Before dawn."

Bryant watched Pierre walk off along the beach before he disappeared between two high dunes. The beach extended as far as he could see with a mixture of dunes close by and cliffs a little further along. No wonder it was so hard to police this stretch of coast. A boat could be launched out to sea from just about anywhere.

He thought about trailing Pierre but decided against it. He just had to trust him. He trudged back to the café. He wandered into the small town and found a place to stay for the rest of the afternoon and night.

Norfolk

I learnt with shock over the weekend of the death of a popular Member of Parliament. He was shot to death in his constituency by some crazed Muslim. What astounded me about the whole story was that everyone was concerned that the rhetoric that followed was kept polite and kind. In other words, the victim's family and friends would not seek revenge in any sense of the meaning. It went without saying that everyone wanted justice to be seen to be done. I was once a trained killer, am a trained killer, and in their position the only justice was to see the bastard lying in a pool of his own blood gasping his last.

Yes, I am a killer but have always abided by the law. The death of my wife has changed me. Is it the death of my wife or my own diagnosis? Not sure but I will have my revenge on all of those who have crossed my path with actions that have damaged my family in one way or another. Every action deserves a reaction. To stop any force from gaining traction, it needs a stronger force placed in its path. I fall into moments of deep despair. The despair turns to anger and to calm it, I thump the table or a door or the other palm. I keep thinking the killings will satiate the anger. The MP's family have made me question my desire for revenge. Why can't I be so forgiving? Is there something wrong with me? Am I ill?

I dug out the list again and reviewed it for the umpteenth time. I had, eventually, settled on a tenth name. First on the list was the receptionist from the doctors' surgery, Simone Thackeray. I scratched a line through her name. In essence, I was thinking about killing her for doing her job. This now left me with nine names again, one short of my half-century. I played around for a while looking for a tenth. I contemplated the two scientists who often headed government press conferences. The government, based on their advice, had put us in lockdown and introduced the draconian rules that, ultimately, had led to Kate's passing. Thinking about it, though, all they had done was offer up advice to the government. It was the government who had made the final decision of where to go with the nation's reaction to the pandemic. It would serve no purpose killing two others who also were only carrying out their jobs to the best of their ability even if their advice had cost the life of my wife.

I played with the list a while longer. The mug of black coffee had chilled on the kitchen table. I gulped the rest down and tossed my spiral notebook and pen to one side. It was time to go and meet ex-Major Alan Cooper of the Royal Marines.

I drove into the car park leading to Holkham beach. I parked the car to the side of Lady Anne Drive, paid for my ticket, locked the car, checked the ticket was displaying correctly and headed for the beach. I did not feel I needed to take any special measures as no-one would particularly notice a man walking on his own with revenge energising his every step. I mounted the boardwalk leading to the sand. I bent to coax the occasional dog that came over to me and nuzzled my leg. I have never owned a dog but sometimes wish I had. Kate had always wanted a dog, but we had decided against it as we were always too busy and it would have been unfair on the animal. I nearly bought one after Kate's illness had been diagnosed, to keep her company, but having agreed a price for the puppy was staggered to find, upon the birth of the litter, that the breeder had put the price up by a thousand pounds. Maybe that prick should go on my list? This sort of immoral profiteering had been profligate during Covid and stunk like the whole bloody mess. Would a pet dog give me something to live for and make me forget this crazy rampage of revenge?

I tiptoed along the last bit of the timber walk, more akin to a ski-jump ramp, alighted from the boardwalk and turned right heading toward Wells-next-the-Sea. I sauntered along really. Birds wheeled in the sky, trees swayed in the breeze and more dogs played on the golden strand. When I arrived at the first of the beach huts, I turned toward the sea. I strolled right up to the edge and let the water lap over my feet, the white foam retreating after surrounding me. I watched a bird dive into the waves before reappearing with a fish in its beak. He or she was going to eat well this morning.

"Major John Wells," sounded a voice from behind.

I didn't turn but simply replied with "Major Alan Cooper. Thanks for coming."

He took a few paces forward and was at my side, social distancing of course. "Sorry about Kate, John."

"Thanks, Coop."

Alan Cooper had never married. It was not because he didn't want too but he was a little more practical in his thinking than me. He never wanted to leave a widow and always carried a foreboding that he was going to die in action. He was the same age, give or take a few months as me and was still on his feet untouched by enemy action. Physically untouched that is. I am sure like me he often conjured with images of battle that would still wake him out of nowhere some nights. One could go months without flashbacks or nightmares but then, for some reason, they would crop up for days on end. I have no idea why it happens like that. Like Cooper, though, I just learned to live with it. I never woke up in a sweat or anything like that, which I have heard others say, as I knew they were always dreams.

I turned to my right and looked at him. He was an inch taller but slenderer. His face was tanned, indicating an outdoor life that had been denied to me for most of the year as I had cared for Kate. His hair was full but grey. I hadn't seen him since a reunion in the late nineties. I had borrowed the other John's mobile phone and tried to find a picture of him on Facebook but with no luck. John had seen me struggle with the device and took it from me and tried looking for my old brother-in-arms. Like me, though, it looked like he was not anywhere to be found on social media. Good man! That meant it was down to good old-fashioned detective work. Phone a contact so-on-and-so-forth. He turned to me and the eyes of another trained killer stared back. Cold as granite and just as hard.

"I guess you can now deliver on our promise?" he enquired.

"I can," I responded. "You in still?"

"Too right I am," I've been looking forward to this moment for years now."

"I need to see off one or two more as well."

"Oh?"

"I've made a list of people who have crossed me or Kate in one way or another. Some are just social outcasts, depraved arseholes who have gone too far in their acts. So far that, I am sure, no-one would ever miss them, including their own mothers. I'll need equipment. Can you still fly that sort of stuff in?"

We watched as a huge hairy dog plunged into the sea in pursuit of a tennis ball floating in the surf. He never got out of his depth, retrieved the ball and returned it to his mistress who immediately tossed it back into the water. "Simple pleasures," said Cooper.

"If only life were that simple. Oh well!"

"That sounds like more than two or three? I've never really thought of two or three as a list?"

"Well. No. I have a list of ten. In actual fact, it's nine at the moment but I struck someone off earlier and am thinking of re-adding them. The woman's ineptitude led to Kate's early death and, really, she should pay. I call it my Wish Dead List. I daresay I will add some more and scratch through some of the names until I'm totally happy with it."

"Yeah. I can pretty well get whatever you want. I am expecting new supply to come on-line shortly. The Jonathans have left tonnes of stuff in Afghanistan. The Taliban already have too much and will need the money. The first lot should be in Austria by now. If you need any Glocks, I can get them straight out of the backdoor of the factory in Austria."

It always made me smile when he referred to our cousins across the pond as Jonathans. He always used to call them Yanks or, sometimes, Septics, from septic tank, rhyming slang for Yank. Then he had read an old history book and learned that they used to be known as Jonathans and it stuck. "Christ! I would've thought they would've tightened up by now? I'll get you a list."

"When Uncle Sam stumbles in somewhere, he usually stumbles out in a hurry. I think they call the new bloke Sleepy Joe? He is not so sleepy when it comes to running away, though!"

I chuckled and recalled reading and watching the disaster unfold.

Cooper continued, "No electronic lists. Paper only. Will you need body-armour and night vision?"

"Yep. I reckon. Be useful anyway." Truth be told I could not envisage a time when I would need body-armour, but the night vision would be definitely helpful.

"Okay. I'll get what you want. I won't need a list. I'll get you what I would use."

"How much is this going to set me back?"

"Nothing. If we're taking care of that murderer, Pringle, that's all the pay I need. Did you know O'Keefe's out? Is he on your list?"

"Yeah. I did. And, yes, he is. There is no way he'll be scratched off. Thing is that one'll be a race."

"A race?"

"We'll be one of many who want that slimeball dead."

"True. Here," he said. He had a mobile phone in his hand. "It's what the Jonathans call a burner-phone. For all I know, we call it a burner as well. It is already pre-loaded with money and has another burner already programmed into the contacts list. Mine."

"Good idea," I conceded. We had used them in the day, but I had thought they were almost impossible to get hold of now. It seems like you need at least ten different photographic IDs and a hundred proofs of address to buy anything these days. I chuckled again. "You are very resourceful, Mr Cooper." I took the burner.

"Have you still got that bloke who killed them boys in the Falklands in your sights? Nothing to do with me, that one, but I recall you said he murdered them."

I recalled storming the Argentinian foxhole above Port Stanley. Three Argentines were sitting in there and as soon as they saw me and Bill Yates appear over the lip, they had thrown their weapons down and lifted their hands in the air. They were terrified, one was crying. Yates simply pulled the trigger and sprayed them with bullets. It was a cold, grey day but the brightness of the blood was vivid against the dullness. It looked like a butcher's shop when he had finished. I had looked on in disbelief and shock. I told him that if it was the last thing I did,

I would hunt him down and punish him for what was nothing short of cold-blooded murder. He had laughed. Despite my report, he was never given a Court Martial. To this day, he should still be in the glasshouse in Colchester. He should never have seen the light of day again. I was tempted, oh so tempted, to pick up one of the enemy's rifles and put a bullet through his head. I probably could have got away with it; it would have gone down as a brave lad killed in action in taking an Argentinian machine gun emplacement. Of course, it wasn't a machine gun emplacement, it was a hole in the ground filled with terrified boys just out of school who were armed with nothing more than Second World War single shot rifles. Some of the Argentinian troops were armed with state-of-the-art weaponry, the match of ours, but not all. He hadn't earned that sort of honour, but the newspapers would not have cared and neither did they. We were two brave Tommies, who against all odds, had stormed the aforesaid emplacement at great peril to ourselves. True, we were brave. We didn't know what awaited us on the other side of the earthwork. Revenge is a dish best served cold. He drives a tractor now on a farm somewhere up north. "Yes. He's on the list," I said coldly. "So, I will need an easy-to-use sniper rifle."

"Ha! I don't remember you going to sniper school? Do you know where Pringle is these days?"

"Yeah. He runs tourist flights out of an airfield near Skegness somewhere. That's where your skillset will come in."

Oh?"

I went on to let him know of my plans for Colonel Matthew Pringle.

"Plausible," he had said when I finished the plan. "I'll work on it a little. What else does he do?"

"How do you mean?"

"He ain't making a living taking tourists for joy rides. A, there aren't enough tourists and, b, they don't have enough money. And, c, planes take a lot of that to keep in the air. Safely anyway!"

I assumed Cooper was insinuating that he smuggled something in from the continent. "Don't judge everybody by your own standards," I joked. "Takes one to know one!"

He laughed. He went onto say that he would lend me all the logistical support I needed in finding and tracking targets. Covid had left him at a bit of a loose end and as his type of business wasn't exactly official, he was unable to claim anything in the way of formal government bailouts. Trade was returning but things were still a little slow. He made it clear that he was not moaning from a financial point of view as he had enough money to see him through four or five lifetimes. He was, in simple terms, a little bored.

I thanked him and shared the list with him. We talked about who hadn't made the cut but might be added back later.

"Interesting!" he said.

CHAPTER FIVE

Thursday 30th September 2021

France

It was still dark when Sean Bryant walked onto the deserted terrace of the café the following morning. He felt an anxiety deep inside and his stomach was beginning to knot again. He peered down into the blackness from the head of the stairs leading down to the beach. He grabbed the handrail and carefully walked down the twenty or so steps to the bottom. He stepped off onto the sand.

All he could hear was the sound of the sea lapping on the shore. He could feel there was more of a breeze than the day before. The salty aroma of seaweed teased his nostrils, hiding the scent of the complimentary soap he had used in the shower. He had travelled very light which meant no change of clothes. The shower had been powerful, and he had soaped and cleaned himself down twice. There was no deodorant. He checked his clothing, and he felt that it passed the sniff-test. He was pleased with the HST issue jacket as it was cooler than the previous day.

He had been assured that he would be tracked everywhere he went and if there was any scent of danger he would be pulled out. The bodycam hidden in one of the coat buttons was again fully charged and working.

A shadowy figure emerged from the darkness to his left. There was now a glimmer of dawn to his right, the east, just enough to show the fair hair of Pierre. The man, like himself, was dressed warmer than the day before.

"You came," said Bryant to fill the awkward silence rather than for any real constructive reason.

"Of course, Glen. We had a deal. You did not think I would run off with your money?"

"No," he lied. It had been the only thought that had interrupted his sleep.

"Come with me."

The two men walked off. They passed the point between the dunes where Pierre had exited the beach yesterday and kept going for about another fifteen minutes. The light was improving with every step. Bryant noticed or, rather, sensed activity ahead. It seemed like there were many people on the beach, no more than fifty metres ahead. As the pair approached, he could make out whispering voices. They sounded urgent, even excited. He did not recognise the tongue in which they spoke so could not decipher the exact conversations. He could see they were gathered around a craft now. There were men, women and children dragging the boat down to the water.

"Here you are," said Pierre. "Stay here. I will go and find Joe."

Moments passed before he saw Pierre returning with a man of Asian appearance. Maybe Indian, he couldn't be sure.

"This is Mr Ponting, Joe," said Pierre in English to the newcomer.

"Pleased to meet you," Joe said in a London accent.

He didn't look like or sound like any Joe that Bryant knew. "Likewise."

"What do you want to know?"

"Why?"

"These are desperate people. They deserve every assistance in getting to England."

"Where are they from?"

"Today, they are mainly from Afghanistan. They all live in fear of the Taliban. America promised them everything and now they shit on them."

"How much do you charge them?"

"Five-thousand US dollars for this crossing. They have to make their own way here. Most of these people are wealthy and don't want to hang around to see what the reformed Taliban will do. It won't be pretty, 'specially for the women."

Joe went on to explain how they marketed their services through Facebook, Instagram and other social media platforms. Each time their content was removed, they simply started again. Potential clients used hashtags to search for the services. "It is risky for us," Joe continued. "If we get caught, we pay a big price. Some of my friends are already in prison and for what? Helping fellow human beings, victims of tyranny, dream of a better life. Your country doesn't want them, Europe doesn't want them, America doesn't want them, and England doesn't want them."

When Joe had referred to "Your country" Bryant had thought he had meant the United Kingdom for a moment. Then England was mentioned separately and he remembered "Your country" meant Australia. "Why England? The benefits?"

"No," Joe laughed. "The newspapers tell the English people that that is the reason. It is not true, though. Most would want to go to America but that is too far and almost impossible although some get in but it is more money. It is language. English colonialism has also spread English around the world. That is why. Some have the French and stay here. Not many."

"So, are most of these today, professional people or tradesmen?"

"A mix. We have at least two lawyers amongst them for example. There are nurses definitely, but I also think there are a couple of teachers. I've heard them talking. One of the older men is a truck driver and one is a carpenter. Other than that, I am not sure what the others do."

"How many are there?"

"Twenty-six."

"Your English is very good. Where do you come from?"

"Twickenham."

"Really? Asian heritage?"

"Yeah. Pakistan."

"And is your name really Joe?"

"No. It's Zaheer. It means helper or supporter. Don't you think that appropriate? Now come on. Let's go and speak to some of the passengers. I assume you would like that?"

They walked down to the water's edge where the RIB was undergoing final preparation. Bryant paced out the length. He reckoned on it being somewhere about seven or eight metres long. God, he thought, there is nowhere near enough room in there for twenty-six men, women and children. He was glad he was returning on the ferry.

Joe clapped his hands together. Bryant looked around and saw there were six Asians behind Joe all sporting knives and guns. "Now," Joe announced. "It is time to get on board. There is no going back now. Over there your new life of dreams is waiting for you." The passengers turned to where he was pointing, the south coast of England.

A few of the passengers cheered and boarded. Others were a little more reticent and held back. They were prodded forward by the thugs wielding the knives much like a cowherd would prod cattle to get them moving. Children were crying and being comforted by their mothers. One woman looked terrified and clearly had a change of mind. She tried to make a run for it but was quickly apprehended by one of the thugs. She carried on struggling and tried to squirm free of the man's clutches. He cuffed her across the head and dragged her back to the boat. Bryant was appalled by this and saw blood coming from a wound above her right eye. She was crying and fear was drawn all over her face. When they were all on board Joe turned to Bryant and said, "Now you, Mr Ponting."

"What... You misunderstand. I don't need to go back on this boat. I've got a ferry ticket."

Joe pulled a gun. "I can't risk that. Think yourself lucky I am not charging you for the privilege. Just think, you have saved yourself five-thousand dollars." He laughed. "You wanted to speak to some of my valued customers? Now's your chance."

Reluctantly Bryant moved down to the overloaded boat which was barely staying afloat. Suddenly, he recognised the terror in the woman's face. He was petrified. He was convinced that if he boarded the boat, he would be in the drink within half-an-hour. He might be able to swim back to shore from that far out but didn't have much confidence of making it much further. The alternative was a bullet. He, gingerly, took his place on the death-trap of a vessel. There were less than ten lifejackets between them. One of the thugs tossed in a load of hoops which he realised were inner tubes from bicycle tyres.

"Health and safety," the man sneered.

Bryant found himself sitting on the deck of the craft next to the woman who had been forced on board. Blood had spilled down the side of her face. He had an unused handkerchief in his pocket and showed it to the woman. Her eyes showed absolute fear. Fear that he had never seen before. It was raw. He could feel it. She was shaking.

"Do you speak English?"

She nodded.

"Would you like me to take a look at your head?"

The woman nodded again. Tears were mingling with the blood and pink droplets were falling onto the deck.

He wiped the wound tenderly. He was no medic, but he was pretty sure that the cut had nearly stopped bleeding and the beginnings of a scab was starting to form. A man passed a bottle of water.

"No," the woman said. "That will be better for drinking later."

Bryant wiped away the tears as well, but this only served to smear a little of the blood over her face. It would be a pretty face if it weren't for the wound and the fear that was still etched into it. He could have sworn that life was coming back into her dull eyes. He was hopeless at estimating age but guessed she was in her early thirties.

The craft was stronger than he had imagined when he first saw it this morning. The deck was incredibly rigid. He had thought it would be just a layer of plastic like a kid's paddling pool he used to put up in the garden. Images of his family filled his mind. Funny though, they were not recent images but flashbacks of when the girls were small. Whenever he was in the shit, he thought, he always managed to conjure up pictures of his family in brilliantly sunny weather.

He snapped himself out of the delightful reminiscing. He was now aware of an outboard motor spluttering away at the back. He had seen RIBs used on the Suffolk coast where the engines had sounded more like brand new motorbikes rather than an eighty-year-old smoker coughing his lungs up. It didn't sound very healthy. He looked back and saw that the French coast was dropping back from the craft. It already looked a bloody long way to swim. Small wavelets were rolling under the boat and one or two already had their faces hanging over the sides. This was utterly miserable. As beautiful a day as yesterday had been, today was a grizzly prospect. At least it didn't seem too windy and it wasn't raining. Small mercies. Thank goodness he had the jacket. Seawater splashed up from the walls of the craft, landing on his face and when he licked his top lip he could taste salt. He could not recall a time when he had felt so desperate.

He wondered if he still had any signal in his phone. At least it was fully charged, for he had borrowed a charger from the guesthouse reception. He pulled it out and noticed he still had full data signal. He opened up the Safari app and tapped in "RIBs." Google soon provided him with a list of options. In the general text, there was a brief history of the craft's development. It had been conceived at a marine school on the South Wales coast, Atlantic College, under the watchful eye of a retired admiral, Desmond Hoare. The deck was formed from rubberised layers reinforced with boards to provide the stability.

He selected a manufacturer's name at random, tapped it and watched the screen fill with wonderfully evocative images of two or three people perched on the air-walls of a RIB paddling down a river, water splashes catching the sunlight like diamonds hanging in the air. He scrolled through looking for a maximum passenger load. He wasn't one-hundred percent sure of the length of the boat but the largest capacity he could find in these pages was fourteen. There was nearly double that on board this vessel. He did not feel at all sure of his future. He imagined something significantly smaller than a tsunami taking them out.

Kent

Richardson and Walters were sitting in the Mercedes and had been joined by Duncan Cobbold, Head of the HST, who had taken a seat in the back. Richardson had connected his phone through Bluetooth to the in-car computer screen and they were receiving live pictures from the French coast. Yesterday, they had looked on in absolute disbelief as two French cops had each taken two-hundred euros to enable a meeting with the people smugglers. "That will look good on the accounting form at the end!" Cobbold observed. His political masters loved it when French corruption was exposed, particularly if it meant the stealing of British cash.

The trio now looked on with equal disbelief as their friend, Sean Bryant, had been forced to board the dinghy at gunpoint. This was not in the script and although, with hindsight, they all agreed that they should have foreseen such a scenario, they hadn't.

Shock had set the anxiety for their friend aside when images of the dark-haired woman had beamed into the car. At least the signal from the bodycam and the trackers were all holding up. Cobbold had been assured that they used satellite technology and not mobile phone signals to get through. All beyond his paygrade. He needed to know it would be reliable not how it was delivered. Bryant's hand with a handkerchief in it came into view as he wiped clean, as best as possible, the blood and tears from the woman's face.

Cobbold was now on the phone to the Coastguard requesting a chopper be sent up. He gave an approximate location. They were instructed to standby, observe and not intervene. If a rescue was carried out, they would have to start all over again. They needed some of the migrants to get ashore and make contact with their handlers in this country. A team of surveillance officers were on stand-by, waiting to follow them to their lairs. Rescue was a last resort for the time being.

English Channel

The sea was getting a little choppy. The refugees were bailing the vessel with anything they had. Hats, drinks bottles and shoes. As far as Bryant could tell, they were keeping the boat swimming. Maybe, just maybe, they might make it. Dark thoughts would then creep into his mind when he looked toward the Kent coast, it wasn't getting any closer, yet the French coast was now a long, long way back. As he bailed with his trainers, he spoke to the woman.

Her name was Rosina and she was from Afghanistan. She had been an interpreter working alongside US troops in Kabul. She had been promised a flight out as the Taliban were taking the city back. She had camped out at the airport, but calm stoicism had descended into violent chaos as desperate people fought each other for spaces on the plight-flights. A British soldier had said there were three places left on the next plane, the last scheduled evacuation flight under the British Government's Operation Pitting, and she was pulled through the hole in the perimeter fence. They weren't checking documents by that time; they were simply getting people out. A woman screamed behind her. When Rosina turned round the stranger pushed her two children through the fence. A little boy and a little girl. All three of them were crying. The kids were clawing at the mother, seeking the comfort of her maternal protection; she was trying to foist them upon the lucky woman who had been accepted onto a flight. They were truly desperate moments.

"Please, please, please!" the mother had pleaded. "Please take my children. For the sake of Allah, please take my children."

Rosina remembered it seeming like time had stood still as she stared into the mother's stricken eyes. They were full of desperation. The faces of the men and women in the melee

94

behind her were also full of terror and misery. The Taliban had set a deadline for final evacuations. These people knew they were not going to make it and faced an uncertain future left to the new rulers of Afghanistan. Whipping and stoning among the gruesome destinies they had now inherited. She looked over at the massive airplane sitting on the tarmac. The engines could be heard above the crowd, and it was her salvation, her last chance. She could take the children or ignore the mother altogether.

"It is make your mind up time, love," the soldier had encouraged.

Rosina stepped aside and beckoned to the mother to take her place on the plane. The woman and her children got through the fence and the soldier directed them to a civilian who was taking down details. The trooper turned back to Rosina, took a step to her and flung his arms around her. "God be with you," he said. "I've seen many horrific scenes during my tour but the kindness you've just shown another human being will stay with me forever. Good luck! May your God protect you."

She spent days hiding around Kabul, forever on the move. Food was running short and every minute of every day, and every step of every kilometre was making her plight more treacherous. She moved from safe-house to safe-house, but this was becoming increasingly difficult as the thugs of the Taliban closed in. Corpses were lying in the streets rotting where they had been slain. Dogs were just as hungry as their human owners and would be seen tearing the flesh from the bodies in a bid to survive. One safehouse was anything but and there was a price to pay. She was raped.

Bryant let out a breath, utterly captivated by her tale. Sure, he had read about such brutality and seen the reports on the television news, but to be sitting next to a woman who had actually been through such a horrific ordeal, was moving beyond anything he had ever experienced in the past. He realised that he had stopped loading water into his trainers. He returned to the vessel's primary function, helping his shipmates to stay afloat.

She had about twenty-thousand US dollars stashed in her backpack which, somehow, she had been able to keep a hold of most of it. Every time she had been paid by the US authorities, she had taken cash from her bank account and buried it in a safe box in her parents' backyard. She now had to get out of Afghanistan. Easier said than done.

She heard whisper of a man who was going to drive to Karachi and get a flight to Europe. The man was younger than her and dressed conservatively in robes. They found her some traditional garb as well. The story was that they were recently married and had not had time to change names on passports. They were going to stay with his family in Pakistan. The ride was going to cost her two-thousand dollars. Life was cheap but death was fruitless. It took them eight days to make it to the Pakistani city. They were stopped at checkpoints. The man had to use some of his fee to pay for their safe passage. She reimbursed him for his losses. When they found an hotel, one from an international chain in Karachi, they were able to clean up. Hot showers taken they felt human again. Food was welcomed as they had not eaten a proper meal since before leaving Kabul.

After eating was when it went wrong. The man demanded his bonus for getting her out. And delivering her the salvation she craved. She now faced the real prospect of being raped again. He forced her down onto the bed and pulled his trousers down. He was trying to force her trousers off but he was slightly hamstrung by his own pants as they tied his legs together just above the knees. He gave her the opportunity she needed when he tried to remove his lower dress altogether. A vase was just within reach on the bedside stand. Her fingers touched it, so she wriggled across the bed a little and grabbed it in her hand. As he made to mount her again, she brought the pot, flowers and all, crashing down on the back of his head. The result was immediate, he slumped on top of her, trapping her under his dead weight. It was a struggle to escape but escape she did. Blood was oozing out of a wound already matting his black hair. She had expected more blood but, somehow, the vase had only inflicted a light cut. Once she had escaped his unknowing clutches, she checked his pulse and, to her mind, it felt strong. She didn't reckon on him waking up anytime soon for she was sure that his brain had been shaken around inside the skull enough for a deep sleep.

"I took my money back out of the asshole's wallet, changed my blouse and headed for the lobby. I got a taxi to the airport and ten hours later, I was in Dubai."

"That is incredible," said Bryant. "Did he die?"

"I have no idea. If he did there will be tonnes of evidence in there. I haven't had a problem at any of the border controls. I don't think there is a, how you say, a BOLO out for me so I assume he is not dead. He will be too embarrassed to report it. I reckon, that if he woke up, he would have cleaned the room as best he could, tip the vase into a bin, and hightailed it out of there."

Bryant didn't know what a BOLO was but, given she had worked with Americans, he guessed it was a US acronym for something. Maybe a search for a missing person although he couldn't work out what. No phone signal now so the meaning would have to wait.

From Dubai she took a chance and went straight for Europe. She entered through Athens. The money she had retrieved from Yousef's wallet had made the Greek border control ignore the absence of a visa. From Greece, she got to Italy and a few train rides later, she arrived in Paris three days ago. This was the only time she allowed an indulgence and booked into a four-star hotel. After clothes shopping, shower and food she fell into a deep sleep. The following morning, she went in search of the facilitators who could get her into the United Kingdom. It wasn't until the following day that she found someone and she took the train to Calais.

"And, here I am. I was told that I would be going in the back of a lorry and couldn't understand that I was on the beach back there. I am terrified of the open sea. I used to read stories of wrecks and such things and was so obsessed with the Titanic story that it convinced me that the sea would end up killing me. I told them there had been a mistake but they didn't care less. I could go or I could go. If I didn't go, I would be cut to pieces and dropped in a hole where all sorts of creatures would feast on my worthless corpse. It wasn't worthless when I handed over five-thousand dollars for the journey."

"You have been through one hell of a lot," said Bryant sympathetically.

"So has everyone on this boat. Every single one can tell a

story to equal or beat mine. Take the woman over there in the red sweater."

Bryant looked across the width of the small dinghy to where Rosina had nodded her head.

"She buried her brother and husband on the road. They were hacked to death by people pretending to be Taliban when they refused to sell her to them. Her only child died of lack of food and water. She then spent a week in a Christian charity hospital before making it to here. At least her dreams are still alive, and she is doing it as a tribute to her loved ones."

Bryant didn't say anything. Only to be pimped out as a whore in her land of dreams, he thought. How ironic, these women were being transported to life as prostitutes in a boat developed by a Hoare! Emotion coursed through his veins and, somehow, caught in his throat. He had to stop himself from crying at the incredible bravery of this, hitherto, stranger.

A red and white helicopter was now tracking them.

"Oh God!" Rosina uttered on spotting the machine in the sky. "They'll send us back, won't they?"

"No, they won't. They will make sure we get ashore safely but, I am sure, will rescue us if we need it. It's the coastguard not the police. I do believe you are safe now."

Kent

"Receiving you loud and clear," said Richardson who was actually speaking to a caller on his phone rather than an old-style radio. "Go ahead."

He allowed the other end to say something.

"No. Honestly, I can hear you really clearly. I can also hear a tremendous noise from the engine and the thwacking of the rotor blades. Go on."

He paused and listened again.

"Okay. I've got that. Near Folkestone?"

He listened in to the caller again.

He slapped his hand on his thigh in frustration. How many more times did he have to say he could hear the caller loud and clear? "Yes! Affirmative. I've got that." He ended the call before addressing his two colleagues. "That was the Coastguard. Their best estimate for where they are going to come in is just west of Folkestone. They suggest we make our way to the town centre and await an update."

"Good," said Cobbold. "No more than twenty minutes from here. I'll leave you two to it now." With that, he got out of the car and got in his own car parked alongside.

English Channel

The vessel had now been in the water for just over five hours and, incredibly, the outboard motor was still working. It didn't sound any worse than first thing this morning; it hadn't got any better either. The destination coast was much nearer now. Details of buildings, colours of clothing and swooping gulls could be made out in the town. Bryant was pretty sure it wasn't Dover. Maybe it was Folkestone. His phone wasn't connected out here so getting a measure of where they were was impossible. Perhaps, it was now less than an hour to go until the boat ran aground onto what looked like a sandy beach from his perspective. At least the sun was shining for the final run-in to the welcoming coast of England or, as his fellow passengers knew it, the land of dreams.

"Look, Rosina," he whispered to the woman. "I need to talk to you in absolute confidence. Can I?"

"Of course, Glen. You have been very kind to me. I won't say a word to anyone."

Bryant sucked in a breath before continuing. Whilst it hadn't been in the script that he would travel back with the migrant refugees; he now believed it might be the best thing that had happened to the plan. A golden opportunity had landed in his lap and now he must make the most of it. "Well. My name isn't really Glen Ponting. And, I'm not really a journalist. I used to be but now I write books. Neither, for that matter, am I Australian."

"So, who are you, then?"

"That's a good question. My name is Sean Bryant. As to what I am, in this situation anyway, I'm not entirely sure. I work with a government organisation called the Home Security Team. We are not the police, although we do work with the police sometimes."

"Are we all going to be arrested when we get to England?"

"No. No. Far from it. From that point of view, you are probably the luckiest group of migrants to land on these shores. You will be given freedom to go wherever you wish in the UK. We are more concerned for your safety. I daresay you have been promised work when you get here? And, in the next day or so, I wouldn't mind betting that you are to get yourself to a rendezvous point somewhere to meet the people who are going to get you into work?"

"Yes. I am meant to meet a man named Andrew who will get me work. It is at a place called South Mimms. I think it a type of roadside house."

Bryant laughed. "You could say that. It's a motorway service station. It's massive. Many people stop there every day. Tens of thousands, maybe hundreds of thousands. I'm not sure. It's big."

What do I have to do?"

If she was going to be put off, it was going to be now. The alternative, though, was not a great prospect as it would be weeks, even months, in a migrant processing centre. He went on to explain that Andrew, if that was his real name, would, more-than-likely, take them off to various unscrupulous gangers who would use them for their own purposes. In short, they would be sold as a commodity, much like slaves used to be. It was extremely common for women, especially the more attractive ones, to be sold into the sex industry. They would be expected to take part in pornographic films, entertain in lap or pole dancing clubs. They were nothing more than pieces of meat to be sold and hired out for profit. Many were known to have turned to drugs as a form of comfort and somewhere to hide from the horrors of everyday life.

Rosina shuddered. "I have a degree in modern languages and speak four, apart from my own, very fluently, English, French, Spanish and German. I was told my skills would be sought after in England and I could earn more money than my whole family needed in a lifetime in a year. Are you saying that's not true?"

Bryant saw her eyes were filling with tears again. He looked away, looked up at the helicopter, looked around at other boats now they were close to shore and bought himself thinking time. "No. I'm afraid not. It is all part of the sales pitch. They want you women for the sex industry, the men to run drugs and the children will be used for menial tasks until they are old enough to take over from their parents. There is no pot of gold. Well, maybe there is, if you are willing to wait it out in the centres. You can help us put these criminals behind bars. Then, I am sure we will be able to sponsor you, especially with your skills. Interpreters are in high demand."

"Do I have to help?"

"No. We will not force you. I must admit, though, the alternative is full of uncertainty. Let me introduce you to my colleagues. In fact, I would call them friends. We would do anything for each other."

"How do I know you're not the same as the horrible people you have been telling me about."

"True. You don't. My friends and I will have to convince you, I guess."

The RIB's propeller from the motor snagged on the bottom as they got close in. The man at the back killed the engine and lifted the propeller out of the water. The waves turned the vessel so that it was broadside onto the beach. The migrants, in their keenness to land on British soil rushed to the near side, leaving

Rosina and Bryant on the furthest side from the beach. She only just had time to say that she would help them if it made others' lives better, when the deck of the boat tilted violently. They both slid against the opposite airwall before they were tipped into the water. Both landed on top of others, but the depth was only a couple of feet at this point and they were able to right themselves soon enough. They were, however, soaked through.

By a small miracle no one was injured or killed. Belongings were strewn all over. Slowly everything seemed to be retrieved. Some of the people fell to their knees, kissed the sand and offered up prayers to Allah for their deliverance.

To Bryant's surprise there was a group of onlookers gathered on the beach with blankets and flasks of drink. They applauded the newcomers and shouted "Welcome to England." Bryant, ever intrigued by facts, had looked up the history of migration into the UK. Somebody's illegal migrant was another's refugee. Folkestone had been on the frontline for oppressed peoples' entry to Great Britain. Human beings had escaped tyranny throughout history and the plight of these Afghans was no different to the Belgians who had sought refuge at the outbreak of the First World War or the French royalists escaping the vendetta of the revolutionaries or the Huguenots fleeing the Dragonnades.

Set apart from the group, maybe twenty metres or so away, were Richardson and Walters.

"Come on, Rosina. There are my friends."

Rosina clutched her bag close, took in the large group before moving her gaze to the right where a man and a woman, both dressed in what she took to be a black uniform, were standing.

They struggled up the beach, squelching their way slowly to their welcome. Walters strolled down to greet them whilst Richardson stayed back with his phone to his ear.

She threw her arms around Bryant. "Well done, mate." She then turned to the damp and bedraggled Afghan migrant who had endured well beyond what should be expected of anyone in a so-called civilised world. "Hello, Rosina. I am Sue-Beth Walters. My colleague, partner, friend over there is Curtly Richardson. As you know, we work for the Home Security Team."

Rosina took the proffered hand and looked into her host's eyes. She had never seen eyes like them before. True, she had heard of blue-eyed Europeans but had never met one quite like this. The eyes were gorgeous when smiling. They held the allure of a turquoise sea on a bright sunny day. "How do you know my name?"

Norfolk

On the evening after I had met with Major Alan Cooper, I was still contemplating my tenth target when an item about the Prime Minister cropped up on the news. And there it was, right in front of me, emblazoned on the black glossy door in Downing Street, London, probably the most famous door in the world. Two simple numerals, one, basically, a straight vertical line and the other a slightly extended circle. The number ten. This confirmed it. The person who resided at number ten would be my tenth revenge. After that, I guessed, my mission would be complete, and I could prepare to go and join Kate. Neither of us had really ever broken the law but I think she will be proud of me when I get the chance to tell her what I have done. I don't really see it as breaking the law, it is more enforcing the law that our not-fit-for-purpose justice system so often fails to do. All of my targets are deserving of their fate.

I have played with putting the PM's name on the list before taking it off. I have done this over and over. It was only when I saw the big number ten that it dawned on me that he was the obvious candidate for the final position. I do some brief research and am somewhat surprised to discover that there has only been one Prime Minister assassinated whilst in office. If I had ever given the subject thought, I would have reckoned on more than that. I have no idea why I would have thought more than that, other than, that particular office pisses off more people than it pleases.

It sounds like Mr Spencer Percival was a little above his station. When his predecessor died, he already held the post of Chancellor of the Exchequer. In his bid for absolute power, he decided to take on both roles, Chancellor and Prime Minister. No wonder he made himself a target, I already don't like him. As it turns out I don't think it had anything to do, personally, with dear old Spencer. It seems that he had just drawn the ticket out of the hat at the wrong time.

A deluded maniac by the name of John Bellingham, a Liverpool merchant, who traded with Russia had been caught up in some shenanigans and ended up in an Archangel prison. He became twisted and warped whilst serving his time and seems to have blamed the British government for selling him down the river and not getting him out. Then, late on 11th May

106

1812 the unfortunate Percival was walking through the lobby at the House of Commons in Westminster when Bellingham calmly walked over to him, put a pistol against his heart and pulled the trigger.

It appears that in the ensuing bedlam, Bellingham could well have made his escape. Instead, with a controlled coolness, he simply went to sit on a bench, smoking pistol in hand and awaited his inevitable arrest. He was sent up for trial, found guilty of murder and sentenced to death by hanging. Many appealed that his time in a Russian fleapit of a prison cell had turned his mind and he was not responsible for his own actions when he killed one of the most powerful men in the world at the time. He was eventually executed outside Newgate prison in front of a huge crowd only seven days after Percival breathed his last. Today's practitioners of justice could learn a lot from the swiftness of punishment meted out in the early nineteenth century.

It appears that many were not happy with his fate. He was a hero to some radicals who thought that the Tory scum had got his just-desserts. A public appeal was set in motion, a sort of "Go Fund Me" of its time. Incredibly, despite hardship, thanks to the ongoing war with France, this raised about ten times more than he could have expected in compensation for his imprisonment. His widow and children benefitted admirably from the public's generosity and, indeed, Mrs Bellingham, now a rich widow, remarried the following year. After he was cut down, he was taken to Bart's Pathology Lab where he was dissected. His skull was preserved for some sort of depraved posterity. I wonder what my destiny will be after I've taken my revenge upon the Prime Minister. As far as I am aware, I cannot be executed.

Over two-hundred years later and there are some that still hold to that mantra. Am I the new deluded maniac? I don't think so. My grievance is justified but, maybe, Bellingham felt that his was as well.

I added the last target to the list. I still wasn't totally happy with the overall list and I amended it yet again. This was now final.

Whatever happened after my campaign had been successfully completed, was out of my hands but I did not want anyone going down for offences they had not committed. Equally, to preserve my own vanity, I did not want others taking credit for my achievement. I, therefore, decided to make my Wish Dead List a matter of record. Of course, I couldn't post it up anywhere, even if I knew how, for that would alert my targets I was coming for them. I pondered this for a while over a few glasses of gin and tonic.

Then, I had it! I would put a list on my laptop. Shit! I then thought. John and Rachel are in and out of this house almost more than I am. I also had lent others keys for them to sit with Kate over the final weeks. I wouldn't suddenly demand the keys to my house be returned but would encode the list instead.

If I am killed in action, I need the list to be discovered by the authorities so that some gung-ho cop does not put someone else in the frame for any of the revenges. So, I decided that I would, on all missions, carry an instruction on where to find the Wish Dead List and give them a clue as to the key for the code. I would not carry the actual list, nor would I be explicit about the code. Any cop, with an ounce of nous, would be able to locate it

108

and crack the code. Encryption was not a high-level skillset I had in my armoury but I would give it my best shot.

Kate's bible would be the key. I am not sure that she had any particular favourite text but I riffled through the pages. That's it, I thought, the key would be like an email address, NTSM@SM. I am sure that someone would eventually speak to Reverend Cruz in the village. He seems pretty bright to me. I'm sure he will be able to work out the key. After that it will be easy.

I opened up the computer, found the spreadsheet app, or whatever it is called, and started to encrypt the list. I selected the passage I thought easy enough to follow. I employed a combination of Roman and Arabic numbers so that each encoded letter would appear as a series of Arabic, Roman, Arabic. The first code would represent an "S."

At this point, I realised that I would form a grid in the spreadsheet using squares, each containing one letter. I inserted all the names in the first column using the devised series. I then located all the "Ss" before cutting and pasting the code. Eventually, the list was complete.

The burner pinged on the table and I saw there was a message. "Gift now ready for collection."

That was impressive! I wasn't expecting any deliveries for at least a few days. I wouldn't ask but assumed that Cooper had access to a stock in this country.

I picked up the phone and called the number the text had come from. It was answered promptly. "My car park tomorrow same time," I said.

The phone went dead. No need for a protracted conversation. Cooper and I had agreed some basic rules. My car park was the one located along Lady Anne Drive leading down to the beach at Holkham; his car park, if needed, was the one at the Wells-next-the-Sea end of the beach. We would meet up at eight the following morning.

I then thought I would need to add some more information to the Wish Dead List in order that the revenges could be collaborated and double-checked to places and dates. The next main column, sub-divided into letter squares again, would, on completion of each task, indicate the location of the mission. The third main column would be the date. I think that was all that was needed. Of course, columns two and three could not be filled in until my targets had been eliminated.

Kent

"Come on," Walters said. "The car is in a car park over there." She offered to carry Rosina's backpack but the woman said she would keep hold of it. Who could blame her, thought Walters, knowing there was, probably, the best part of fifteen-thousand dollars in there and she was in a strange land.

Richardson came over and introduced himself. "Nice to meet you, Rosina," he said, also offering his hand. "We understand that you are concerned about our identities. Rightfully so. I have been in touch with our boss and he has arranged for us to go and meet the Home Secretary in the heart of London. Pimps and gangsters would not be able to get that sort of audience, I can assure you of that."

Not unless you are a Russian oligarch or some such, thought Bryant, but kept it inside his head.

"First of all," said Walters. "We need to get you two dry, fed and reclothed. We've booked a suite at a local hotel."

The hotel was a modest establishment set back from the seafront. Richardson had booked the room earlier and gotten hold of the keys. Proper keys rather than pieces of plastic. Quite incredible in 2021! He hadn't yet seen the room. The receptionist had eyed him with suspicion when he declared that he didn't need to see the room or have any luggage.

"We take a very dim view of guests who think to use this as a hot-sheets sort of a place and will not hesitate to call the police."

"I am the police," had been his response brandishing his identity badge. He loved saying that to jumped-up public-spirited citizens doing their best for the nation's security. Otherwise known as busybodies! Of course, he wasn't actually the police but the badge seemed to convince the man he was official enough.

Richardson now let the foursome into the room. It was better than he had expected. A large king-size bed dominated the wall to the left and two generous sofas, facing one another with a low-level table between, filled the carpeted floor to the right. A door to the other side of the bed led to the bathroom. Pretty good! Large bathtub, standalone walk-in shower, toilet and, for reasons he never could fathom, two basins. Dressing gowns hung on a couple of hooks on the door. Towels and toiletries were plentiful.

"You go first, Rosina. Have a shower or bath, whichever you prefer. Maybe let Sean have one of the dressing gowns so that he doesn't catch a cold. Curt and I will go and get you both a change of clothing. If you let me have the clothes you have on, I will take them and get them laundered. I assume they're the ones you bought in Paris?"

Rosina nodded. "How do you know so much about me?" The penny then dropped. "Ah! Glen, I mean Sean, was wearing a recording device? Yes?"

"Nearly," said Walters. "A bit better than that, actually. It was a bodycam hidden in Sean's coat. Let me take a look at that wound on your head. Make sure it's clean."

Rosina took a seat on the dressing table's stool whilst Bryant popped into the bathroom and changed out of his soaking clothes. Walters peered at the injury, took out the first-aid kit Richardson had brought from the car, donned a pair of latex gloves and cleaned around the ugly but superficial cut. "See how it is after you've cleaned up. I can put a plaster on it if needs be."

Rosina took a long hot bath. Bryant waited to use the shower.

"What's a BOLO?" Bryant asked of his colleagues.

"It's an American thing. It means 'Be On the Look Out for.'"

Richardson and Walters, armed with clothing and shoe sizes, went shopping.

They exited the lift into the reception lobby and instantly saw that two police officers, a man and a woman, were engaged in a conversation with the receptionist. "There they are," said the man pointing at the two guests as they exited the lift.

The police officers turned and approached the two capable looking individuals as they crossed the lobby toward them.

"How can we help you, officers?" asked Richardson.

"Can we see the ID you showed our friend behind the desk, sir," the man asked.

"Yours first," Richardson countered.

"Sorry, sir. Of course."

Both police officers drew out their warrant cards. Richardson had no doubt that they were genuine officers but assumed that the receptionist had played the race card. He suspected that had it been Walters who had booked them in they wouldn't be confronted with this, well, stop and search now! Then the black man had turned up with another bloke and two women. He was sure to be up to no good so called the police to report a black pimp using his hotel for prostitution. He diligently checked the documents. He matched the numbers on their uniforms with those on the cards.

"Thank you, Constable Bevan," he said to the man. "And, you, Constable Pritchard." He handed their wallets back to them.

"And yours, sir?" the man said holding out his hand. On taking Richardson's badge he said, "Never heard of you. Home Security Team?"

Richardson refrained from rolling his eyes and remained polite. Why should they? "Call into HQ and ask them to check Home Security Team and get them to punch in my details. They should then come up with a picture of me in glorious Technicolor." He emphasised the suffix and was rewarded with a reddening of the man's face. He then knew that it was, with absolute certainty, race driven by the little shit behind the desk. "I assume I can check on my phone?"

"Doubt it. You don't have the requisite security clearance." He let the insult linger. "Sue-Beth and I will make ourselves comfortable over there whilst you check us out. We are in a bit of a hurry, though, we have an appointment with the Home Secretary and I reckon he will be really pissed off if we are late."

The HST pair took two armchairs. It wasn't long before the male officer came over. Handing him back his ID he said, "Thank you, sir. Have a good day."

With that, they left. Richardson and Walters followed them out into, what was now, a sunny warm afternoon. Not bad for the last day of September.

With the two shipwreck victims restored to cleanliness and satiated in the food department, the foursome left the hotel. Walters did the checking out as she fancied a little sport.

"You're not staying the night?" the public-minded servant on the front desk enquired.

"No. We're done. How much?"

He tapped the computer and after a little while the printer whirred into life. He plucked the bill from the device and laid it out on the counter for Walters to review. She scanned the list, one night's accommodation and four room service meals. "Perfect," she agreed.

The lad passed the card machine along the counter, Walters inserted the card, followed the instructions, ignored the chance to give a gratuity to the racist little shit and the transaction was complete. "I would like to give you a tip."

The man brightened. He liked cash tips for he didn't have to share them with anyone else. "Thank you."

"Two words of advice, if I may."

"Oh?" the lad responded looking a little bashful. He had noticed her eyes before and thought them unbelievably attractive but now they looked like they might cut him in half.

"I'm sure you meant well when you called the police earlier, but I think if it had been me, you wouldn't have bothered. Just because someone is black, don't assume they are up to no good."

He blushed.

"Thought so," she said on noting his reaction. "And, another thing. Get together with your favourite housekeeper and with a little tidy up, you've got a room to let for cash. You only need to replace the towels, dressing gowns and some coffee. Might not even need to do that if you have a favourite whore!"

The blush deepened.

Later in the afternoon all four were sitting in a restaurant, the Strangers' Dining Room, at the House of Commons. Rosina was clearly in awe of the surroundings. And, to think, she had nearly bowed out of the trip across the English Channel. What appeared to be an incredible change of fortune had not yet sunk in. If only her parents could see her now. She hoped they were well, she hoped they were still alive. The upbeat feel left briefly when images of her beloved mother and father came into her head with an evil thug whipping them or, even worse, their decapitated bodies lying rotting in a Kabul street gutter. She knew they wouldn't like her sitting with three westerners in a bar drinking wine. They would be ashamed if they knew she drunk alcohol, but she had developed a taste for it when working alongside the Americans. She was not such a fervent follower of the faith as her parents. But, she thought, my God, they would be impressed to see her sitting in one of the most powerful buildings in the world.

She noticed two men enter the room. One was a white man with a high forehead with greying hair. The other was a man of Asian heritage. The second man was holding the harness of a black dog. Rosina had seen this type of dog before. The American soldiers had used them to sniff out hidden explosives. She remembered how some of the soldiers cried when one of these dogs was killed in action but never shed a tear if a colleague was blown apart. She thought they were called Labradors.

"Hello, Rosina," the white man said. "I am Duncan Cobbold, head of the Home Security Team of the United Kingdom and this is Javid Akhtar, the Secretary of State for Home Affairs in HM Britannic Majesty's government. And, given it is late on a Thursday evening, you must consider yourself very important that he has bothered to stay on so long after knocking-off time."

The Home Secretary extended his hand and Rosina noticed that the hand was only vaguely placed in the vicinity of where she was standing. She took the man's hand in hers and shook it. When she looked into his eyes, she realised that he was not looking directly at her. My word, she thought, he is blind, which is why he has the dog, a guide dog. She had never heard of blind men and women achieving such high status in the previous democratically elected Afghani government. She assumed that there would be no chance of a disabled minister in the Taliban form of government. She was, though, not sure whether either of her assumptions were fact. She was aware that his eyes showed a kindly man behind the mask of darkness.

"I've heard all about your harrowing journey," said Akhtar. "I'm sorry but the west has let you down, off the record of course."

"Of course," Rosina allowed.

Cobbold completed introductions of the other three at the table for the benefit of the government minister.

Akhtar allowed Cobbold to settle him into a seat before speaking gently to Rosina. "I understand that you had concerns regarding the veracity of my team here?" he waved his arm in a broad sweep taking in the four others at the table. "Understandable, given what you have been through."

"I don't think I have those concerns any more...." She answered but wasn't sure how to address the panjandrum in front of her. "Your majesty?"

The minister smiled. It was a warm smile, a friendly smile that highlighted the care in the eyes even more. "Majesty? We save that one for Her Majesty, The Queen. We are not too formal around here. You can call me Javid."

This was unreal. She had seen this man on television from five and a half thousand kilometres away and now here she was, Rosina Ali, sitting in the iconic home of the British government. She wasn't sure where Javid ranked in the hierarchy of the British establishment. She assumed Queen first, maybe then some princes, the Prime Minister and then, maybe, the man sitting and chatting to her most amiably. Perhaps there was a finance man or woman in there somewhere? "Yes…. Javid," she said.

"I'm glad you are on board. My secretary has booked four rooms for you all at the Savoy for tonight. Make the most of it. You have some hard graft ahead. Thank you, Rosina."

"I hope I don't let you down. Does your beautiful dog have a name? He is so good."

"He does. I call him Blair."

"Blair?" said Bryant. "After the former Prime Minister?"

"Yes. He is my first guide dog, and I am still frightened he might lead me into somewhere I don't want to go!"

The four English around the table all chuckled at the jest but Rosina remained stone-faced before smiling in a bid to join in.

"Walters noticed the lack of understanding on Rosina's face and leaned over to explain that Tony Blair had led the country into war in Iraq which many members from all sides of the house had advised against.

"Yes. That's right," said the Home Secretary. "But I am afraid, it is a thankless task being the PM. Everyone thinks they can do a better job. Most manage to achieve some sort of enmity along the way. The present incumbent, unfortunately, is no different. Many would like to see the back of him. In more ways than one."

"Would you like to do it?" asked Walters.

"Of course. But, alas, it will never happen. I am not sure that the country is ready for an Asian or blind Prime Minister let alone both. There are still a number of glass ceilings in politics and, I am afraid, they are all set at different levels. There are many very able Asians who, one day, will have a good claim to the position. Blindness is another matter and I suspect that that barrier is set the highest of all. Having said that I believe I am as well qualified as any and, indeed, have a few supporters in the party."

With that Akhtar stood, waited for Blair to rise and left with the guidance of the Labrador.

CHAPTER SIX

Friday 1st October 2021

Norfolk

The following morning, I drove to Holkham again. Turning into the drive, I saw that Cooper's car was standing to the right next to the first pay station. He was pumping the machine with coins as I pulled up beside him. He had a black Labrador bitch with him, sitting patiently, while he fed the coins. He pushed a button and the ticket appeared. I waited between our two vehicles, mine a white three-year-old Ford Transit panel van I had bought for cash the week before. For another thousand quid, I handed over fifty twenty-pound notes, the bloke had met me in a supermarket car park just outside Leeds with the documents and the keys. He never even asked my name. I still hadn't changed the registered ownership of the vehicle. Number plate recognition cameras were, potentially, going to pose a challenge. Given, however, every mission I went on, I would have different plates I thought it a risk worth running. I opened the back doors.

Cooper took the first parcel from the back of his car and slid it into my load bay. No-one would think it odd if we were seen exchanging one package, even two. We would walk the dog, transfer another package or two, go find some coffee before transferring the remainder. That way, we supposed, we would minimise the risk of being spotted by the same witnesses shifting the loads across. It would have been obscenely unlucky for the same dog-walker to have passed by the back of my van at such random intervals.

"Good idea, the dog walk," I said as I locked the doors for the first time after securing my own ticket from the same machine. "What's her name?"

"Well spotted. Most people say boy or girl. Venus."

"Not after the tennis player?"

"No. Loads of people ask me that. I just called her Venus as she was so beautiful. I think I'd have the woke brigade on my back if I had named her for a black celebrity! Don't you? Poor girl didn't quite meet the criteria to be a guide dog. She was the only one who failed to make the grade from her litter. A friend got to hear of her and suggested I might like the company during lockdown. She's a good girl, though."

I shrugged and we started toward the beach. It was quite a bit colder than the previous time we had met down here and I was seriously under-dressed. Goosebumps covered my arms. My body was still in pretty good shape and my chest jutted forward in my black tee shirt as if I were some sort of icebreaker cutting my way through Arctic pack-ice. God! I was damned chilly.

We wandered down through the woods, past the eco-café, and headed toward Wells. It was a good path all the way now. I hadn't been here since coming with Kate when one needed one's wits about them not to trip over tree roots. The Beach Café, at the other end, was open so we stopped for a cooked breakfast. It was a relief when we found out that they allowed well-behaved dogs inside. I did not fancy an outdoor seat in the morning chill! The warmth was palpable. Two full English did the trick, washed down by black tea in my case and white coffee in Cooper's.

We retraced our steps. Thankfully, since we had been eating, the temperature had risen a few degrees. It was now approaching comfortable.

"You know," said Cooper breaking into our companionable silence, "I really am short of something to do thanks to this damned Covid thing. I can help you big time. I know you said you don't want to incriminate anyone else but one of my clients, in fact, my main client, is considering taking out one, whom I believe, is on your list."

"I'll give it some thought. Not promising anything."

He reluctantly nodded his agreement. "My client has an inexhaustible pot of money."

"And, I said I would give it some thought."

He seemed to accept that.

We stopped off at the vehicles again. Venus sat motionless as we transferred another couple of boxes across. We then sauntered up to the Victoria pub on the main road at the end of the drive. We stopped in for morning coffee. Ordinarily, apparently, thanks to Covid they were only meant to be serving residents staying in the rooms. As there was only one other table occupied in the restaurant the barista let us in, took our orders and returned to the bar to make them up. Neither of us really needed a pastry but we wanted it to look genuine. I mean, who pops into a coffeeshop for drinks on their own, without a bite to eat, in the morning.

"Pringle first?" asked Cooper barely above a whisper.

I looked across at the other table. A woman was sitting with two men and they were talking fairly loudly. I couldn't hear them clearly so assumed we could up the volume a little without detection. "No. Second."

"Okay. Do you want assistance with any of the others?"

He wasn't going to give up. "No need. I don't need to bring anyone else down if I get caught. You can, though, if you want, help with O'Keefe."

"It would be a delight. If only to make sure you do it properly! The offer still stands for the logistical side at least."

I nodded. "Okay. We are the Marines, remember. We get the job done."

The barista brought the coffees to the table, white for Cooper and black for me. "I'll be back with the pastries. Nice dog. Would he like some water?"

"She," Cooper corrected her. "Yes. That would be kind. Thank you."

She returned with the water first. She put the steel bowl in front of Venus who got to her feet and lapped away at the water, splashes going everywhere. That only served to remind me that a dog may not have been a good idea for Kate and me for we were house-proud. I am not sure it would have fitted in with our own lifestyle. Dirty feet after muddy walks, smelly coats after wet days out and keeping the garden clean of muck. No, not for us at all!

"Sorry," Cooper said.

"Don't worry. I'll clean it up when she's finished. What's her name?"

"Venus."

"What! After the tennis player? Isn't that a bit racist?"

"No," he replied. "She is named for the Roman Goddess of love because she is so beautiful."

"That's nice."

Small talk over, she went and collected our pastries and brought them back to the table. They weren't bad. Once we had devoured the food and drink, I went to pay for them whilst Cooper walked Venus outside. I paid with a twenty and let her keep the change. "To help you with the clearing up after Venus."

"That's generous and really nice," she said. "Thank you."

I now had over five-hundred-thousand pounds sitting in my bank account and there was no way I was going to get through that much on my own. It was about two weeks earlier that the life insurance had paid out on Kate's passing and about a week later, after some fairly intrusive questioning, that I received my own pay-out following my prognosis. The house was worth an estimated six-hundred thousand. In addition, I had fifty grand in my Premium Bonds. Kate's bonds had now been returned to me and that is what I had changed into cash. When we had moved into the house, there had been a safe under the floor in the garage for some reason, God only knows why, and that was where my horde was stashed. The bank-teller had offered me fifty-pound notes but I said I preferred twenties as they were easier to change up.

We transferred the remaining packages into the back of my van. I shook Cooper's hand. "Thank you, brother," I said.

"I've got a way in which we can communicate with each other. Well, I think I have anyway. I'll create a new email account and let you have the access details. Password and that sort of thing. That's it, actually, I think."

"I'm all ears. You know how useless I am with computers?"

"I think that once I've set up the account, I can write a note to you in the "Drafts" section and when you go into the account, you will find it there. I'm not sure, but I reckon that you will be able to leave messages for me in the same way. Must remember never to send them and delete them when we're finished. You can change the text but make sure you do it in a different colour. Then, plans will slowly develop."

"I'll take your word for it. Cheers."

Half-an-hour later, still morning, I had pulled the van up next to the shed at the allotment. I took a walk around all sides of the building to check that there was no-one in sight. Another two or three hours and the place would have been buzzing like bees in a hedge with people returning from work. There were a couple on their plots at the other end. Too far away. I was safe enough.

I unlocked the door, closed it behind me and bent down to take up the trap door in the chipboard floor, beneath which, I had dug out a chamber, inserted a steel box and lined the outside with insulation boards. I transferred the boxes, one at a time, starting with the biggest first. None were really heavy except for one of the squat boxes which was the last to be transported to the hiding place. As I went, I opened up all of the tightly packed crates and made a mental note of my armoury. I also took some pictures, so I wouldn't always need to come back, to check what I had.

The first box contained two Heckler and Koch 416 assault rifles, lethal in a close-to firefight. I have always been baffled by the term assault when describing these weapons, as it conjures up images of heavily armed marines charging a well defended enemy position but, in all honesty, it can be used in one-to-one combat or in a defensive mode. Each had four magazines, a tad over the top, which, when filled, would house thirty 5.56-millimetre rounds. I transferred them to their safe store. I opened the next long box to discover my sniper rifle. It was an Arctic Warfare Magnum, so called because it takes a point-three-three-eight Lapua Magnum round, it has unerring accuracy from huge distances. I do recall that when I was serving, I had a dalliance with sniper work but when I was assessed at five-hundred metres it wasn't a case of not being able to hit a barn door, I missed the barn. I probably exaggerate as we weren't actually shooting at a barn but paper targets. I missed at only five-hundred metres, so I took my hat off to a British sniper, I forget his name, who took out two Taliban fighters at a range of two-thousand-four-hundred-and-seventy-five metres. Jesus! I thought, that's not far off the distance to our neighbouring village! At the time, about twelve years ago, it was a world record. I have no idea whether it has been beaten or not? A box of the massive cartridges was also included along with a magazine that held five of the missiles that could take out a target behind armoured glass at a close enough range.

Another case contained two Glock Nineteen automatic pistols. I was more familiar with these even though we had normally been issued with Sig Sauers. A couple of fifteen-round magazines were included along with loads of nine-millimetre parabellum bullets.

Now my favourites, the knives, which I expected would be the choice of weapon for most of the kills. It was certainly going to be used for the first one. The advantage of using a knife was that I could be close enough each time to check the result was a success. Before leaving the scene, I could check pulses before retreating from the field. It would look more gruesome for whoever discovered the corpse. People always seem to be more sickened by a gaping throat wound rather than a bullet through the forehead, thus creating a third eye. True, there would be more blood, especially if the slug stayed inside the skull. I didn't expect any kill with the sniper rifle would be that attractive a look. Whichever way, the result would be the same, another point in the scorebook. Cooper had gotten me a couple of Boker knives.

Other packages contained body armour, optical sights, night vision sights, sheaths and carriers. Everything a fully-fledged mercenary would need in the field. Oddly, he had included a couple of body-bags. I hadn't envisaged using them and wondered what his thinking was. I threw them down into my arsenal anyway, before returning home.

I opened up the laptop to revise my wish dead list again. Whilst having the computer open, I constructed a second list in notes, one that I could refer to without actually having to open up my cache of weapons to check. I brought up my photographs to assist me.

London

After a surreal night in one of London's most famous hotels, Rosina was plenty refreshed and, after breakfast with her new friends, she was waiting in the lobby as, once again, Walters checked out. "Nothing to pay, all met by the Home Office," said the smartly dressed female receptionist. "A parcel has been delivered for you."

"Thank you. Can I just take the key for a few minutes. My colleague needs to change into these. I nearly forgot."

"Which room?"

"Any of them. Doesn't matter."

Walters went up to her room with Rosina whilst the two men waited downstairs. When they were back in the room, Walters explained that the clothes she had been wearing for the crossing had been laundered. She also explained that each article of clothing, including shoes and underwear had had miniature tracking wires sewn into the seams. No-one would ever know she was a walking transmitter. She did add that the team were not sanguine that her handlers would allow her to keep her clothing.

"I am frightened. What happens if you can't find me? Can't you put something in my arm or leg or something?"

"That's what I was going to say. Yes, we can. It is a procedure that will take no longer than ten minutes from walking in the door and walking out again. You won't even know you have it. It will be good for us to track you for around three months. If we haven't made a move by then, we will get you out safely. Hopefully, we are talking short weeks rather than months."

"Okay," said Rosina daring to dream of the time this was all over and she was working again. Maybe there would be a position working for the British government as an interpreter? That would be cool.

When she emerged from the clinic, she couldn't believe how easy the procedure had been. She never felt a thing. Even now, apart from the smallest of bruising in her arm, just like getting the Covid vaccination back home, she could not feel a thing.

The rendezvous was in the afternoon at four o'clock and they all agreed that Walters would be the only one to escort her to the meeting point. It would give Richardson a chance to test the tracking devices. If the one in the arm wasn't working, he would text Walters and they would abort.

Walters signed for a car at the rental office and the two women headed out of the city to South Mimms. If asked, she had picked Rosina up just outside Folkestone and the two had agreed to stop for a meal at the motorway service station. Richardson had gone to meet up with Cobbold whilst Bryant, his immediate work over, had hopped on a train at Liverpool Street and returned to Oakshott.

"What do you want?" asked Walters.

Rosina looked around. She spotted the golden arches of the McDonald's burger place. Many of the Americans she had known had extoled its qualities to such an extent that she couldn't wait to try one out. "I'm not really hungry," she said truthfully having eaten a plentiful breakfast no more than four hours earlier. "But, I guess, we need to make this look genuine so a McDonald's would be good. I've never had one before."

"You didn't have them in Kabul?" asked Walters as they made their way to the open entrance. It was more like a huge booth with a central eating area full of hard surfaces and loud noise.

"Yes. And no," Rosina answered. "There was one but, I was told it wasn't a proper one. Somebody had made a burger-bar look like a real one. My American friends said it wasn't real, though. I never went there, didn't even know where it was. My parents would not have approved. They always said that if I ate American food, I would get fat."

Walters laughed. "Shall I order?"

Rosina nodded. "And I shall pay. You've all been so nice to me."

"You have English money?" Walters knew they hadn't let Rosina out of their sight since picking her up on the beach so there was no way she could have obtained English cash. She had only mentioned the American dollars.

"Yes. When we were waiting yesterday morning, before Sean arrived, we were all given one-thousand pounds each. Fifty twenty-pound bills."

"We say notes. Bills is American. Can I see one?"

London

Walters returned the car and headed for Cobbold's office in the centre of London. She carried, rather conspicuously for her liking, a plastic holdall which held Rosina's dollars.

"I am worried someone might steal my money," she had confessed to Walters. "Can I ask you to look after it?"

130

Walters found a shop that sold luggage at the service station and purchased a cheap bag. She told Rosina to keep the English money as she reckoned that somebody would be expecting her to be carrying this and would want it returned to them.

Cobbold greeted her at the door. The office was inconspicuous when measured against other government departments. From the outside it looked like any other door leading to a flat above any other artisan's shop in the city. Once inside, though, the difference was stark. Inside the street door was a thick secure door operated by eye recognition and, after passing through two more equally secure doors and climbing a staircase to the first floor, they entered an open office full of high-tech equipment. The latest surveillance systems were on show for all to view. All was limited to operatives only. There was a team of nineteen staff offering back-up to the squads in the field, of which, she and Richardson were one. Not even the Home Secretary was welcome here. If Cobbold wished to see him he went to the Home Office, Houses of Parliament or Dorneywood. The latter was in Buckinghamshire and is the official country residence of the Chancellor of the Exchequer but, by the grace and favour of the Prime Minister, the Home Secretary kept a couple of rooms there. Although he could stay overnight, Akhtar elected not to unless the guest of the Chancellor. He much preferred to get home to the tiny Kent village where he lived in his constituency. As with many blind people, familiarity was a source of comfort. He could feel his way around his own rooms, he knew how many risers there were to the stairs and he knew exactly where crockery and cutlery was stored.

Cobbold led Walters through to his own office in the corner

looking out over the street below. The glass was tinted and impenetrable to external gaze. It was also bullet proof. Cobbold placed his index-finger to the touchpad mounted to the side of his door. He pushed through and beckoned Walters into one of the two visitor's chairs. She sat, placed the moneybag on her lap and waited for Cobbold to take his chair. He pushed a button on the phone and asked for two white coffees to be brought through.

"Well done, Sue-Beth," said Cobbold.

After she had eaten with Rosina, she left the restaurant area and sat in the rental where she had an unobstructed view of the entrance. In her windscreen mirror, she saw a battered old coach pull up. It was too big to take a space and stayed idling in a lane. People appeared from all over and accumulated around the bus entrance. She watched Rosina emerge from the building and make her way to the coach.

"Don't do that," Walters whispered as Rosina kept fingering the slightly irritated skin on her arm where the internal tracker was buried in her flesh. "Don't give it away."

It was as if Rosina could hear the admonishment. She stopped touching at the tracker. Walters had told her that it probably wouldn't come to anything but if she had kept rubbing her arm, as she had whilst devouring the McDonald's she, just might, raise suspicion. Unlikely, though.

Six white men appeared from separate vehicles and approached the migrants. One-by-one, until last of all, Rosina stepped forward, they boarded the ancient vehicle. Rosina was coyly looking down at the ground. A man took hold of her chin and raised her face to look at his. He smiled and said something.

Rosina tried to back away. Fear was showing on her face. The man fingered the scar above her right eye and shook his head. It was as if he was deciding whether to accept the delivery of damaged goods or not. Bastard! Thought Walters.

She felt for Rosina. By God, she was brave. It wasn't within her gift, but she had to fight down the urge to extract Rosina from this predicament. She had seen men smile like that before. It was a smile full of lust and want. The man only just managed to stop himself from licking his lips and drooling like a hungry dog. Rosina disappeared onto the bus. Walters observed the vehicle leave the car park before starting her engine and heading back to London.

"She's brave and frightened," Walters said to her boss.

"Don't worry. The signals are all coming through loud and clear at the moment and there will always be two top field officers within four hundred metres of her."

"I know," Walters sighed. "There is one thing, though. Two actually."

"Oh?"

Walters pulled the folded twenty-pound note from her jeans pocket. "She had this."

Cobbold had a quizzical look on his face. "It's not against the law to have English money in England, you know?"

"No. But wouldn't you have thought it unusual for each migrant to be given a thousand pounds each by the traffickers?"

"Traffickers with a moral compass?"

"Bollocks!" exclaimed Walters so vehemently that it rocked Cobbold back in his chair. "They've got to be forgeries and someone wants them distributed in England. Or, what I reckon is, all the cash will be collected from them and distributed by others."

Cobbold mused over his reply before pushing the intercom button on his desk-phone. A woman's voice came through.

"Is Adelaide Wiggins in the building, please, Lucy?"

"Yes. You want to see her?"

"Ask her to step in would you, please?" He ended the exchange by releasing the intercom button. "Have you met Ms Wiggins before? She knows the ins and outs of currency forgery like you know the back of your hand."

"No. Not had that pleasure," said Sue-Beth sipping from her coffee.

A knock at the door heralded Adelaide Wiggins. Walters had expected a willowy brunette, tall and elegant with alabaster skin. She had no idea why she had conjured up such an image based on the woman's name alone. The woman popped her head around the door and Cobbold waved his hand to beckon her in. She was as plain as the image had been elegant. Fairly squat with a severely short red haircut. Her only real concession to elegance were the designer spectacles that made her eyes appear enlarged. She was neither fat nor thin, neither tall nor short.

"Yes, Duncan," she said. "How can I help?"

Walters could never get used to the informality along which lines the Home Security Team operated. Her background was army and if a ranker had been summoned to a senior officer's presence they would snap to attention, salute and say, "Yes Sir or Ma'am?" as they did so.

"Adelaide. This is Sue-Beth Walters, one of the field working on the migrant trafficking. Sue-Beth, this is Adelaide Wiggins probably the best banknote expert in the United Kingdom including at the Bank of England."

"Please to meet you, Sue-Beth," said Wiggins sitting down in the other visitor chair without being invited. "Actually, I was the best in the Bank of England before Duncan came calling."

Never judge a book by its cover or, at least, its description. Not only had she been wildly inaccurate as to her physical appearance the voice was not what she had anticipated either. She had thought the words would fall from Adelaide's mouth like melting honey. Instead, though, she was as Eastend as jellied eels although, in Walters' mind, cultured Eastend. Maybe she went to the Opera. "Pleased to meet you."

Cobbold passed the note across the desk. "Sue-Beth has come across a potential twenty-odd thousand pounds worth of these. They were all given to the illegal migrants to bring across with them. Take a look."

Wiggins reached out and took the promissory note in her hand. It felt alright, fairly new but nothing unusual. She examined it. Queen side first before turning it over and studying The Painter of Light, Joseph Mallord William Turner, and Margate Lighthouse. The foil and holograms all looked perfect. She couldn't discern the veracity of the note. Except, maybe, the feel wasn't quite right. She held it in the palm of her hand and stroked it with the fingers of the other hand. Walters noticed her tongue was sticking out from her satin red lips as she concentrated on the task. Wiggins was holding her breath.

Finally, she exhaled. Walters only then realised she had been holding her own breath and, surreptitiously, let it out.

"Well?" asked Cobbold with a wry smile on his face. Walters knew that he had been observing the two women opposite with amusement at the spell a possible forged banknote could hold.

"It looks real enough," observed Wiggins, pausing before continuing. "But there is something about the feel. It is all a little too firm. I'll take it up to my lair. Coming?"

"Can you give us a few seconds," asked Walters.

"Of course. I'll wait outside."

When the door was closed Walters turned back to Cobbold. "There were two things," she had said as she placed the holdall on his desk. "Rosina asked me to care for her American money. Can you keep it safely?"

"Yes," he said taking the bag. "I'll let you have a note itemising what's in it."

"No need. I trust you."

"It's not a matter of trusting me, Sue-Beth. I'm sure you can. It is a matter that if I die, or more likely get killed, my successor might not easily let you have it. Comprendes? It'll be like getting gold out of Fort Knox!"

Yes."

They joined the notaphilic numismatist in the open office

where she was perched on the corner of a male operative's desk exhibiting far too much thigh than was polite in a work environment, thought Walters, who was by no means prim but did adhere to standards. Wiggins led the way, through even more security doors, up to the next floor. Her room took up about a third of the space. A red light was turned off above the door. She used the same index-finger procedure to gain entry as Cobbold had used earlier. Inside, the light was low making the computer screen that Wiggins brought to life appear bright in comparison.

She scanned the same finger that had unlocked the room door across a pad on a fancy-looking filing cabinet before punching in a code. The top drawer slid open. "Double security," said Wiggins. "No-one can simply chop my finger off and gain entry. It works off a thermal image of the print anyway so if my digit were too cold, it wouldn't work in any case."

Walters saw why the need for care. The drawer was rammed full of notes of all denominations and currencies. "Jesus!" she said.

Wiggins then typed in another code on a second pad. To Walters astonishment, a twenty-pound note, to her, exactly the same as the one she had brought into the office, was mechanically raised up above the rest. Wiggins pulled out a fresh pair of latex gloves, put them on and removed the note. She opened a scanner machine lid, thicker than the ones Walters had seen before, and placed it on the glass deck.

Wiggins typed on the keyboard, after removing her gloves. The screen blinked and blinked again before the note appeared

137

on the monitor. Holding down various keys she was able to zoom in and out even allowing a single one-millimetre squared section to appear across the entire view. "That, my friends," announced Wiggins, "is a genuine English twenty-pound note."

She zoomed out to show the whole note again. Dimension lines showed above and to one side of the object. The one across the top read one-hundred-and-thirty-nine millimetres whilst the one down the side showed seventy-three. She tapped some keys again and after two more blinks, the Turner side of the note came into view. A repeat of the other side and the show was complete. The note was returned to its storage, another button pushed and the drawer slid shut. "If this place was nuked," said Wiggins, "This filing cabinet would be the only thing left intact."

Wiggins now placed the note retrieved by Sue-Beth Walters onto the glass deck. This time she didn't use gloves. After the obligatory blinks again, the Queen's side of the note appeared. The dimensions shown were the same as before. The reverse also looked the same as the original. Wiggins moved the arrow across to the image of a finger in the margin and clicked. The computer paused before a page was displayed. It had identified six different fingerprints. Two were unknown, one of which was, presumably, Rosina's. One print was totally unrecognisable to the system and the three gathered around the screen. The other four were all known. Three were Duncan Charles Cobbold, Susan Elizabeth Walters and Adelaide Charlotte Wiggins. The fourth was Oleg Vladimir Kasparov.

"Who the hell is he?" asked Walters.

"No idea," Cobbold replied.

"Just a moment," said Wiggins. "If we run it under ultra-violet, we can sometimes find any flaws. There is also another little security mark built in which only shows under UV. This note is good, though."

Wiggins killed the lights in the room. "That means the red light above my door is now on and despite the jokes that will be now going around outside, I am not open for business. Anyone come in here and they will be shot without warning!" She laughed a soft giggle, again not in keeping with her appearance.

"Jesus!" exclaimed Wiggins. "I have never seen that before."

"What is it?" asked Cobbold.

"No idea."

For want of anything better to say Walters observed that it looked like glitter at Christmas time. Underneath the glitter, a bright red and green twenty could clearly be seen. This was, thought Walters, the hidden security feature.

Hertfordshire

After she had deposited her bag in the luggage hold, Rosina took her seat on the bus. She reckoned there were more than forty men, women and children on board. They weren't all from her boat and, she thought, not everyone from her boat had made it to the rendezvous point. How she now wished she had been amongst them. Two men started to pass through the cabin. Rosina was toward the back, just in front of the wheel, and wasn't aware of what was going on forward of her as her view was compromised by the seat immediately to her front. She occupied the place closest the aisle, no-one sat in the window seat, and peered around the seat in front of her. One man was carrying handcuffs which he passed to the second man who was forcing the migrants' wrists onto the armrests before locking the devices shut. Many were protesting and she could hear crying, above the din of the coach's engine, from women and children. One man got up and tried to resist the detainment but was punched in the face and slumped back into his seat. The second man applied the cuffs in such a brutal manner that the man yelped like a scalded puppy.

"My God," thought Rosina. It was happening.

The two men got to her. She didn't want a punch in the mouth so laid her hands on the armrests. The handcuffer locked her wrists down. "Now! You're a pretty thing. Speak English?"

Rosina nodded. "Yes." It was hardly above a whisper.

"Didn't hear you."

"Yes," she repeated.

"That's good. If you tell anyone of what I am going to do, I will beat you to a pulp. Understand? Mind you, it looks like someone has already had a go!"

Rosina nodded again. "Yes." It was the same man who had greeted her just before boarding.

She cringed as he touched the area above her eye where she had been thumped on the beach back in France. She closed her eyes as the oaf pulled her sweater and tee-shirt up over her head. He pulled her bra up to reveal her nakedness. She kept her eyes tight shut to stop the tears from running.

"Nice," said oaf. "Look at these little, well, not so little actually, treasures, mate." The last comment must have been to the other man going down the aisle carrying the cuffs.

"Not bad. Nice," oaf two said.

She nearly jumped out of her skin when she felt one of them bend in and kiss her exposed flesh.

A fracas broke out behind. "Leave her alone," a man shouted in Afghan before the sound of a fist on jaw shut him up.

She sensed that the two men had moved on to subdue the man. She shook her torso which allowed her jumper and shirt to cover her nakedness but the bra was stuck and really uncomfortable. She kept her eyes closed and wished she had stayed with the Taliban. Nobody had told her that this went on in the civilised west.

The passengers further back had had time to work out what was going on forward and tried to resist the shackles. Resistance was futile, though, as the unmistakeable sound of fists crashing into skulls occasionally resonated from behind her. Rosina heard other women asked if they spoke English. Clearly, the answer was negative or, more than likely, no response at all. When the screams came, she knew the two oafs were exposing more women and were laughing. A child screamed out as the mother was subjected to this indignity in front of him or her. Rosina could not make out if the child was a girl or a boy.

The violence ceased and all that was left was a sorrowful whimpering. She heard, or rather sensed, the oafs coming back down the bus. "Look at this," said oaf one stopping by Rosina.

"Naughty girl," said oaf two.

Oaf two leaned in and held the bottoms of her jumper and tee-shirt in his fist again. "If I want to look at your tits, bitch, I will look at them." He pulled the garments up over her head again. She could feel goosebumps all over waiting for the invasive touch of her tormentors but it never came.

"What the fuck do you think you're doing," said a third man, oaf three.

"Just having a little fun. They need to get used to it. They are probably all Muslim virgins so need to be shown how to behave." Rosina thought this speech had come from oaf two but couldn't be sure as the voices were muffled through her jumper.

"Don't talk such rot," said the saviour. "There are mothers on here. If you touch one of these women again, I will personally, feed you to my pigs. Got it?"

A grumbled acknowledgement was grudgingly given. Then, showing resistance, continued, "Don't know why we bother with mothers? Most customers don't want spoiled flesh."

"No-one gives a fuck what you think."

A hand gently moved the tops back to where they should be. "I'm sorry," oaf three said. "I don't want you thinking bad of us. My name is Andrew."

The man they were meant to meet. Rosina nodded her thanks but could not control her own trembling. How could anyone carry out this degradation to fellow humans? She remembered tales of such obscenities in the outlying villages of her homeland. But here, in the west? No!

"Give me the keys," he ordered of oaf one. He took the keys before turning back to Rosina. "I am going to unlock your cuffs so that you can dress yourself. It is not for me to do. I need your word that you will not try anything. To be honest, it is a waste of time, you can't go anywhere."

Rosina whispered, "Thank you." She stood and reset her bra and tops. "Can I see to the other ladies?"

"Yes," said Andrew. "Same rules, though."

London

Wiggins studied the image on her screen. "I have never seen anything like this before."

"What on earth could it be?" asked Cobbold.

"Absolutely no idea," Wiggins responded whilst moving the arrow and fiddling with the zoom buttons.

Some of the individual bits of glitter were brought into focus. In the main, they were all of a uniform elliptical shape, each looking like it contained something inside, much like an Easter egg. Some of the eggshells appeared to have been slightly damaged.

"And?" asked Cobbold.

"Still no idea," answered Wiggins. "They look like perfectly uniform eggs which contain something inside them. I am only guessing here but it looks like some of the outer casings, or shells if you like, are wearing a bit thin. Do you think they might contain something biological?"

"How the hell would I know?" said Cobbold. "But I know a

woman who might. Put it in a plastic bag or some such and keep it secure. Can you isolate it?"

"Yes."

"Okay. Good. Stay here and I will give you a shout if we need you again." Cobbold looked at his watch. "Don't go home until I say you can. Sue-Beth. With me."

They left Wiggins securing the note and made their way back to Cobbold's office. "I assume Oleg is a vital ingredient in this?" Sue-Beth mentioned as they took their chairs.

"Just double-check that door would you," Cobbold instructed his field officer who obediently got up and pushed against the closed door.

"Definitely closed."

Cobbold hit the speed-dial on his desk phone. When the display requested a number, he punched in a three-digit sequence. He left the phone on speaker and said "MI6."

The phone was picked up before the fourth ring was complete. "Well," a woman's voice answered. "Duncan. What a pleasant surprise. I assume this isn't a social call?"

"Afraid not, Ness," Cobbold said to Vanessa Forbes-Marriott, the Head of the Secret Intelligence Service, SIS, more commonly known as MI6. "I need to pick your brain."

"Oh dear," Forbes-Marriott responded. "It is a little bit frazzled at the moment. You know how it is? Our masters in Whitehall ask a question and need a reply about two days before they asked the question. One day, I am going to pick up the phone to you and you are going to say 'come on Ness. I've had enough, I'm going to whisk you away to an exotic island where we drink pina-colada and make love in the dunes on the cape after midnight.'"

Walters did her best to supress a smile.

"Vanessa. If only! I have you on speakerphone and have Field Officer Walters with me. She has full security clearance so you can speak freely."

"A pleasure to make your acquaintance, Sue-Beth. I have heard a lot about you. All good. You're quite the legend."

"Likewise," said Walters although, in truth, she had barely heard of the Head of the SIS.

"What do you know of an Oleg Vladimir Kasparov?"

"He is a huge bear of a Russian agent who, until the second half of this year, has been laying low. We thought he might have crossed the Czar somehow and ended up in Lubyanka or some such. Or, even better! No such luck, though. Why?"

"His fingerprint has found its way onto a fake twenty quid note."

"Oh shit! God! About three or four months ago, there was traffic coming out of Libya saying that Bear, a codename for dear old Oleg, had met with a Chinese agent miles from anywhere. They spent their time examining twenty-pound notes but no-one could work out why. I'm sure it wasn't good, though. After that, we didn't hear anything apart from a few days later, there was a clandestine meeting of great minds. There was a meeting of Drozdov and Ding on a train near their border. No idea what it was about. Our informant has now disappeared. Anything significant about the money?"

"We have a currency expert...."

"I know. Adelaide Wiggins. You pinched her from under my nose. Your charms know no bounds! Did you know she is actually a numismatist?"

"No. Who knew? Well, she has put it through some ultra-violet light examination and it shows like egg things encased in the plastic coating."

"Jesus! Do you have it secure?"

"Yes. It's..."

"I'm sending a bike round immediately. We need to get it to Porton Down without delay."

Norfolk

It was dark when the battered old coach pulled off the motorway and tracked its way through minor country roads. A sharp turn to the left jarred the occupants awake as it drove along an unmade lane. Rosina shook her head and tried to wipe her eyes before remembering the fetters that held her wrists to the arms of the seat. Her neck ached from her head lolloping to one side as she had tried to grab some sleep. At least she had briefly escaped the torment during the snatched dozes. The snakes, which had filled her stomach on the beach in France, began to writhe in her belly again. She wasn't going to give these thugs the satisfaction of seeing her cry but she could feel a pricking in her eyes. Images of the Kabul backyard, sitting out with her family under a sail erected to provide shade from the hot summer sun, popped into her mind. Fruit cordials were mixed up and stored in the shade ready to quench the dry thirsts that assailed the family. That didn't help.

Oafs one and two started down the aisle. Other passengers were being released from their confinement so Rosina guessed they must be close to their destination. Ahead she could just make out lights. The light blinked in and out of focus as she realised, they were travelling through a forested area. The darkness wrapped around the bus and she felt more desperate than ever. When she was released from the cuffs, she fingered the small lump on her arm before remembering not to do it. She also resisted the urge to rub at the scar above her eye which felt like it needed a damned good itch but that would only serve to open it up again. She turned around and allowed her gaze to follow the oafs proceeding toward the back. They had not noticed. Why would they suspect anything anyway? After having been secured for two or three hours it would be natural to rub and touch various parts of one's body.

She was confused about where she might be in the country. They had left the roadhouse and merged right onto the motorway. A blue sign had indicated a turning for M11 with a few placenames on it, but she had never heard of any of them apart from Stansted Airport. That didn't help her as she had no idea where the place was in comparison with London or South Mimms. Her entire knowledge of English cities was restricted to London, Manchester, Liverpool and Edinburgh. In fact, she wasn't even sure that Edinburgh was even in England. She could now add Folkestone and South Mimms to her geographical knowledge of places. She was fairly sure the bus had been travelling north through the afternoon as the sun had been setting over to her left.

The bus slowed to a crawl as it got closer to the flickering lights, before turning right into a floodlit yard behind two-and-a-half metre high gates. She saw there was a man holding each gate as they passed through. The vehicle ground to a stop and the driver killed the engine. The relief to the ears was palpable. The diesel engine had been a long way beyond its optimum several years before Rosina and her compatriots had boarded the ancient omnibus.

The engine had been hiding the wailing of some womenfolk. What on earth was that about? Then, as she rose and made her way to the front, she noticed that the men and older women were still secured in their seats. The reptiles moved again inside.

"You're wasting your breath," oaf one said to a woman, maybe the same age as Rosina, who was pleading with him not to split her family up. "I cannot understand a fucking word you are saying you Paki bitch."

Rosina retrieved her backpack from stowage and walked toward where the altercation was taking place.

"Hey. Lovely tits," oaf one called out to Rosina. "Tell this Paki slut to calm down, otherwise I will have to give her a slap across the face."

Rosina felt nervous but called on all of her strength and faced the man down. "My name is Rosina. We are not Pakistani; we are Afghani and proud of it."

"Whatever. Just tell this slut to shut-the-fuck up because, if I have to shut her up, it will give her something proper to cry about."

Rosina turned to the woman and held out an arm of friendship. The woman took the arm and embraced Rosina so tightly that she thought she was going to have all the breath squeezed out of her. She hugged the trembling woman back. The woman's son was holding onto her mother, trepidation in his eyes. Rosina reckoned he was about ten years old. "What's your name?" she asked in their own language.

"I am Amina."

Rosina stroked the back of Amina's head. "My name is Rosina. Just try and do as they instruct. I think it will make life easier for us. And, what is the little man's name?"

Amina nodded and wept some more. She pulled back from Rosina and looked into her eyes. "His name is Fazal like his father and grandfather before him."

Rosina saw dark pits floating in red pools of despair. It was heart-wrenching, and she wondered how she came across to others for she had been crying as well. Never in her life, even after stepping aside by the fence at Kabul Airport, had Rosina felt so desperate. She was sure Allah would protect them and see them through, but doubts were beginning to creep in.

"Where are they taking my husband?" asked Amina.

"I don't know. I'll ask for you." She turned to their tormentor as the bus pulled out of the gates. She watched as the two sentries closed the wooden panels and placed a huge locking bar across the entire width to secure the site. "Where have you taken this woman's husband?"

"Don't know and don't give a toss. We only need the women and the younger children here. They are probably going off to pick potatoes or something. At least, if you play your cards right, you will be able to sleep in some comfortable beds. At times, anyway."

The group of fifteen women and children were escorted to the barn-like structure to the rear of the site. Oaf one opened the crude wooden doors. The lights were on inside and they were shown into a dormitory type of room with two rows of bunkbeds, ten sets against the far wall and eight on the near side. A line of tables and chairs acted like a barrier between the two rows of beds. The floor was painted concrete and the walls were made of undecorated blocks with no windows, the roof was of exposed wooden rafters and the illumination glared like factory lights. It was horrible. There were two doors to the right, Rosina assumed that the bathrooms lay beyond. She wandered over to the bunk in the far corner and laid down onto the bottom bed. The mattress was thin and she could feel the metal slats digging into her back. This was not what she would call comfortable.

Again, she closed her eyes. She wasn't only desperate now; she was terrified as well. Amina came over and took the lower of the beds to Rosina's left. Fazal clambered up onto the top bunk.

Rosina needed the bathroom and went across to the left hand of the two internal doors. She heard the entrance doors to the right close and the definite sound of a key being turned in a lock followed by three sharp clicks, maybe bolts being rammed home.

She pressed down on the lever of the bathroom door but it wouldn't budge. She tried the one to the right and that swung inwards to expose one basic basin, one toilet bowl and a single shower, no curtain or screen. There was no tiling to the walls and, indeed, the finishes were the match of the ones in the dormitory. There wasn't even a lock on the door. There were no windows either, so no ventilation and the place stunk of building materials. Up to thirty-six women and children were meant to share this pokey bathroom? It was disgusting. The present smell was sweet compared to the potential.

She dropped her trousers and peed. After wiping, she sat in the encompassing silence wondering if life could be any worse under the Taliban? Had she really made the right decision? It was time to survive and live for the next minute and see what happened after that. She washed her hands under the tepid water and dried them on a paper towel. She went back to her bed and buried her head in the meagre pillow.

When she turned over, the lights had gone out. All she could hear was the whimpering of women, the tears of children and the comforting voices of mothers. She pulled the cover over and tried to sleep fully clothed. She curled herself up and mused at how different it was to the previous night. The darkness just served to make the position even more pitiful.

Norfolk

I had been watching the fat little woman for over a week when I picked the night to eliminate my first target. Cooper had delivered my arsenal this morning, so I saw no reason to delay, I wanted to get on with it. I could feel a hot anticipation of the immense pleasure that would flood through my being when the task was complete. It had been dark for around thirty minutes when I spied the bitch waddling along the wooded path just outside the North Norfolk coastal village of Thornham. Yesterday would have been good, plenty of rainwater to sluice away the blood. Trouble is, I didn't have the weapons although I did consider a kitchen knife. Today has been fairly dry. Oh well, it is what it is. Rain was forecast for later.

A terrier dog, a Jack Russell I think, was pulling at the lead in front of her. It was a clear night with no moon to cast light across the glade beyond the path. It was incredible how much the stars illuminated the forest floor in this cusp between the harvest and hunter moons. No need for night vision tonight. I always thought the dog would be a problem so was prepared to take it out as well. My experience tells me that these little blighters can be among the most yappy of all terriers. Not proper dogs in my mind.

I tracked her move each night when she left the surgery to go home. I observed her as she went in, prepared a meal for one, ate it, washed up and took the dog out for a walk. I couldn't believe my luck when she elected to walk the dog after dark each night. The weekend had been different, she had walked the little thing about two each afternoon. I had watched her for five nights and on each walk, she had not passed another human being as she made her way across the main coastal road and up a lane into a field. Neither she nor the dog had been aware of me tracking them. This was going to be easy. When I had watched her all the way home, I had traversed the landscape until I found the ideal spot to ambush her. I had placed a flint-stone, about the size of a honeydew melon, on top of a fallen tree and followed in her direction to see if I could spot it. I could not. It was concealed in the darkness of the undergrowth. If she used night vision to take pooch out then, maybe, she would see me but she didn't even wear spectacles.

I was now hunkered down behind the same tree watching her approach. One of the boxes collected from Alan Cooper had contained some black nylon overalls along with matching overshoes. I was now fully dressed from head to toe in black nylon including a hood over my hair. She came level with me. The dog had started to tug on the leash as if it had seen a squirrel or a rabbit. He had caught the scent of something.

"Don't eat that," I heard fatso say.

Too late. Earlier in the day, I had called at the supermarket and bought a prime piece of steak. Nothing unusual about that, a widower buying a meal for one in his grief. When I got it home, I dug out some of the pills that had been prescribed for Kate to help her sleep when the pain became too much. I ground one to dust and forced it into the meat. I didn't want to kill the little thing but was damned if I wanted it snarling and yapping as I took out its mistress. The woman tried to drag the animal away, but it now had the food in its teeth and was munching on it as if it were the first meal it had eaten in an age. Lots of dogs seem to be like that, though. She tried to wrestle the meal from its jaws but this only served to encourage the thing to snarl at her. She backed off.

"I've told you before about picking things up in the woods. One day it will make you ill so don't come running to me when you feel sick."

The drugs were nearly instant. First it sat and then, in slow motion, rolled onto its side. The target shrieked. Shit, I should have thought about that.

I stepped onto the path behind her. She was more concerned with the little love of her life as I caught up with her. Christ! The little thing was still conscious and saw me looming over its owner's shoulder. Other than that, though, it couldn't react and lay his head, I could see he was a boy now, on the grass at the side of the path. The receptionist started to look around sensing that the dog had seen something. She was too slow. I jerked her head up by placing my left palm over her mouth and pulling her upright. The dog stared but couldn't react. Good. She tried to struggle but very soon realised the fight was futile. She tried to scream out below the gagging hand but with no success. She was so short I had to duck to whisper in her ear.

"Do you know who I am?"

I sensed she tried to shake her head but my grip was vicelike.

"Then let me tell you. Do you remember Kate Wells?"

This time there was a perceptible but weak nod.

"Your negligence sent her to an early grave."

She tried to say something but I couldn't make out what it was; I think it was "No." She had pissed herself with fear. I could smell that she had voided her bladder. Good. That made up for poor Kate suffering the ignominy of pissing into oversized nappies and using a catheter.

"Now," I continued. "It is a life for a life. You will die because of Covid not with Covid. Do you understand?" My taunt to the woman about dying because of Covid was a reflection that it was beginning to emerge that not all deaths were necessarily of Covid but a large proportion were with Covid. A subtle difference that the lying saintly NHS love to put out there in a bid to justify messing people's lives up. I loathed and hated a huge chunk of that organisation. Some, probably the majority, like Helen Chambers, were good people and did not gloat about being heroes at every opportunity.

She tried to struggle. I reckoned that if I could have seen her eyes, they would have been wide with fright.

"If you struggle, you fat bitch, I will make your death last a long time. If you stay still, I will be merciful…."

She was trembling now but when I used the last word, I think she sensed a way out and I could feel her body relax. I loved how her fear was now controlling her bodily functions. No matter how good the brain, it is the gut that rules the instinct. I was in control and she had none.

"…And make it quick," I finished. The knife, with a newly applied edge came up in my right hand. As I brought the knife up in my right, I pulled her head up with my left, to expose the neck. I knew I had to put a lot of effort into this revenge. I had done it three times before and, the first time, I had been surprised at how hard it was to cut through tendons, muscle and windpipe. It was quick and clean as I sawed the edge across the white skin and into the flesh below. The carotid arteries breached; blood spurted. It is amazing how far the pressure exerted by the heart could cast the lifeblood of a human being. I had pulled her to the left of the path and let her blood squirt over the undergrowth.

Once the fuel supply had been cut to the brain and the pump ceased working, I felt Simone Thackeray twitch before the body relaxed for the second time in as many minutes. She was now a dead weight in my arm so I let her drop to the ground. I bent to clean the knife on her hoodie before returning it to its sheath.

I skirted back to my concealed lookout and opened a box and removed a body-bag. I hadn't envisaged using any of these but thought it was, after a rethink, a useful piece of kit. I returned to the corpse and loaded it inside the bag, did the zipper up and cleaned the site as best I could. I was counting on wild animals and the forecast rain cleaning the area of evidence. Not that it really mattered as they would take ages to catch me and I would have nearly completed the list by then, even if they did trace me. I threw my nylon rucksack onto my back, loaded dumpy woman over my right shoulder, bent down to pick up the now sleeping dog, checked the site over one more time and headed for the van.

I only had to carry the loads a hundred metres or so. The van had been left with the keys in it and the doors unlocked just in case a quick getaway was needed. I laid the dog on the ground at the rear of the van, opened one of the doors and laid the dead woman on the load-bed. I hefted the sleeping, or dead, dog in beside her. I didn't want to kill the animal but did wonder if I had overdone the dose. I could feel a small heartbeat from his chest.

I had taken the precaution of looking out a similar van to mine in Norwich, copied down the registration number and bought false plates from a contact of Alan Cooper's. His resourcefulness never ceased to impress. It was clear he had ground out a good career living on the wrong side of the line. I kept wondering how he got away with it but the thought soon vanished. If my van was spotted in the area of where the victim had gone missing, I hoped that the local plods would finger the unfortunate true owner of the other van. In time, though, the list would exonerate any unfortunate caught up in this mess.

First stop was a lay-by on a secluded lane that had allowed me access to the rear of the target's house during the observation phase. I took out the dog from the back and trekked across the field until I was behind the familiar home. I placed the dog over the back fence. I took great care not to touch the top rail. Fingerprints. I turned to leave when I remembered the lead. Could I leave fingerprints on the roughened fabric of the leash? I decided to remove it just in case and stuck it in my pocket. Then, there was the dog. God, the things you have to think of to be a criminal! Surely, I can't leave my dabs on the dog? Can I? Surely, they would never dust the dog for prints? I took a chance and left the little fellow in the garden.

"Sweet dreams," I whispered and returned to the van.

It wouldn't have been a surprise to anyone to see my van pull into the allotments. I had used it as a parking place since I purchased it. I drove it alongside the shed before ducking into the building to retrieve a screwdriver and its true plates. Plates swapped, I returned inside and collected the shovel.

I wandered over to a corner of the plot where I had, earlier, started the excavation of a grave. A nosy fellow allotmenteer had seen me digging the grave shaped hole and asked who I was burying.

"You," I quipped. "If you ask to many questions."

We both laughed. I wondered if he would ever find out the truth and confess to someone that he ought to have done something about it.

"No," I said. I am going to put a lasting tribute to Kate here in the form of a bench. I want it to be pretty permanent so am going to put in a concrete base." I never did organise a memorial bench for the top of the hill overlooking the village. I still must do that.

"Oh. That's nice," he replied and left me to the digging.

Now I was back from my mission I extended the depth and tipped in the body. I followed this with all of my nylon overalls and other equipment. Finally, I tossed in the lead. I kept the knife and returned it to the cellar beneath the shed. I hadn't gotten the hole as deep as I would have liked but, nonetheless, threw some stones and rocks in over the corpse before filling the grave to the top with the excavated material. I distributed the surplus soil around the site.

I returned the shovel to the shed and took one final look at my handywork before trudging home. Just before I turned into our road, I felt a splattering of raindrops on my head.

I was knackered. The adrenalin had peaked and was now dropping back. I felt an enormous satisfaction. I left my allotment clothes in the boot-room and jumped in the shower in the downstairs bathroom. I let the hot water run down my body and reflected on a job well done. It had gone every bit as well as I had planned. I dried myself off, put on my dressing gown and went to the kitchen and poured a large gin with a little tonic. I held the glass up and said, "That's number one, Kate. Love you."

London

Cobbold and Walters returned to the HST offices after grabbing a late dinner at a Greek restaurant three doors down. No sooner had they settled themselves into the chairs in his office than a knock on the door heralded the approach of a young man. "Yes, Merlin," said Cobbold.

"Just to let you know, Duncan, the tracker is working well and we are getting a good signal."

"Good. Where are they?"

"Norfolk. A place called Bartholomew's Woods. Looks like a farmyard or something. We're getting satellites lined up with the co-ordinates and hope to get some images pretty soon."

"Good work, Merlin."

Walters waited for the door to be closed as the man backed out. "Merlin?" she asked shaking her head in disbelief.

"I know! Not exactly traditional. He's a wizard with a computer, though."

"Oh. You are nearly as predictable as my esteemed partner."

"Ha! We went to the same humour school! Are you two sleeping with each other yet?"

"No. And we never will whilst we are putting our lives at risk for Queen and country. We love and care for each other too much for that." She was referring to their marital status as widow and widower. Both had lost two previous loves to violent ends and were convinced that if they took their love for each other to the next level, fate would, surely, end their happiness. She shrugged. "You never know, though, we might just try when we have finished with this place."

"Oh well."

They carried on making small talk until nearly ten-thirty when Cobbold's desk-phone sprang to life. He looked down at the caller display. "Ness. Got anything yet?"

"Too right we have. You won't believe it."

"Try me."

Well. Because we found dear old Oleg's prints on it, we thought it might be something like Novichok."

"Was it."

No. It's not as bad as that, thankfully. It is another form of Covid."

"Covid? Why?"

"Don't know why but we are guessing that they want to introduce another strain into the west to mask something they are trying. They know we panic, like sheep shadowed by a wolf, when the west suspects anything Covid."

"Surely the vaccinations we have all had will stop it in its tracks?"

"The theory is yes. It looks like it has morphed, mutated, from the Delta variant. For your information the technical classification is B.1.1.529 colon Sars-cov-2."

"Catchy!"

"Yeah. Those little polymer sacks that contain the viral load are interesting in themselves. They are constructed using a biodegradable plastic which gradually erodes with use and time. They, in turn, are then coated with a film which is why they have that slightly over-plastic feel, which also erodes. In time, of course, the load will be released on our poor unsuspecting nation. And, we assume, there is something similar planned for Europe and our other allies across the world."

"Good God! Why?"

"Not one hundred per cent sure but we are getting traffic out of Moscow hinting that the Czar has plans to annex Ukraine. They, of course, deny this absurd suggestion."

"And, they think that by introducing coronavirus again, we will have our thoughts concentrating on more waves of the pandemic?"

"You got it. Classic diversionary tactics. I'm flying to Brussels to brief my counterparts in the EU, NATO and US. They are most interested in developments."

"How soon will the loads be released into the atmosphere to subject us to another Covid attack?"

"Depends how often the notes are used. All banks, major retailers and post offices have been instructed to keep an eye out for them and reminded of their responsibilities under the Official Secrets Act. It'll cause all sorts of trouble but we are launching a campaign to remove as many twenties from circulation as we possibly can. Any of these treated notes will be removed and destroyed. We won't get them all and some people will catch the disease and may even die."

"Good God!" Cobbold said again.

Vanessa Forbes-Marriott went onto explain that it was still the view of many security organisations around the world that the virus is manmade and was leaked from the laboratories in Wuhan. Some now believed that the earlier release was an accident whilst others think that it was released deliberately to test the free world's reaction. They had probably been delighted when the politicians backed their medical experts and locked the world down. The World Health Organisation had encouraged even more draconian reactions to see off this biggest threat to the planet since the asteroid took out the dinosaurs. There were only a few countries that had actually swallowed the WHO's doom ridden prophecies and cut themselves off from the world. "Now," she continued. "We need to see what our friends in Moscow and Beijing are planning underneath the Covid cloak."

"How do we know that the virus in the notes is not as bad as the ones that are already circulating?" Walters asked breaking into the silence that had ensued after Forbes-Marriott's summing up.

"We don't for sure, but the boffs at Porton Down are convinced that every strain will be less effective thanks to the rollout of the vaccines. They are, though, looking for volunteers to test it on."

"Who the hell would do that?"

"You'd be surprised what restaurant and clothing vouchers

will do to some people's sanity."

Walters shook her head and rolled her eyes. She was astounded at what idiots there were even in the employ of government departments.

Norfolk

Richardson was sitting in his car in a remote lay-by around two miles from Bartholomew's Woods. Two HST field officers were in place with a good view of the entrance gates, across the track from them, of the rural residence hidden within the heart of the wood. He had turned off the road onto the unmade lane through the woods, parked up, killed the headlights and put his night vision on. The car had rolled along the track, keeping a distance from the bus, when they saw it pulling off into a farmstead. The operatives had jumped out of the vehicle, retrieved their packs from the rear and scuttled off into the woods as quick as they dare, before Richardson had retreated to the lay-by. All three had been surprised to learn that this place was by no-means unique. There were another four plots carved out of this arboraceous landscape. He could see from his in-car computer display that Field Officers Michael Jones and Rowena Crawford were in position about fifty or so metres from the gates. Maybe another twenty-five metres, to the inside of the gates, a weaker signal was being detected from Rosina Ali. It looked like she was in a building hence the partial cloaking of the signal.

"Curt," Jones whispered into his mouthpiece. "The bus is now leaving. Headed back to the road."

"Thanks, Jonah."

Michael Jones had been Richardson's first ever partner in the Home Security Team but had left to take up a life of luxury with his wealthy partner, now husband, after which he had joined up with Walters. Jones had become bored with a life living in a cossetted comfort following his earlier career in the Army and SAS. Then Covid had hit, and the couple had not been able to fly off around the world as they had got used to. Jones had contacted Richardson to see if Cobbold would consider taking him back. It couldn't have happened at a better time, as a more than capable young police officer, Rowena Crawford, had been recruited into the HST and needed a steady hand to bed her in. Jones had taken and passed the mental and physical acuity tests that were set as minimum standards of entry. "I didn't say so before but it is good to work with you again, Jonah. Welcome back. How's your position?"

"Yeah," the man of few words replied. "It's good. They'll have to trip over us to know we are here. Lots of undergrowth."

"What can you see, Rowena?" Richardson asked of the ex-police officer, keen not to show favouritism. He also knew that Jonah was over-cautious with the use of words, saying that he believed everyone had a lifetime's allocation and once they had been used up the end was nigh, and he would obtain more description from the former policewoman.

"A nice sized house, probably four bedrooms at least. A high fence runs right into the side of the house and then continues out the other side, if you see what I mean, and just to the right of the house as we are looking at it are the gates the coach just pulled out of. Two ways in from this side, through the gates or through the house. No idea about the back. A front garden is bordered by a short post and rail fence to the front and one side and the house to the rear whilst the side closest to the gates is open to let a couple of cars in. There's also a keypad that I assume is for entry into the site to anyone who has the code."

"See anything inside when the gates were open?"

"A glimpse of the object hugging another woman after it looked like she had an altercation of some sort with, shall we say, a guard."

"A positive ID?"

"Affirmative."

"Affirmative," repeated Jones.

"Okay. Wait there and see if the place settles down. It's now just gone eight. Then you can take a nose around the perimeter."

"Cobbold and Sue-Beth have gone for some grub and will be back soon. I can get them in an emergency but I'll try and let them eat in peace if I can."

About two hours later, the floodlights in the backyard turned off. No lights could be seen from the building to the rear and the main residence only showed a lit room downstairs and one upstairs. The upstairs room did not have a curtain or blind drawn. Jones and Crawford observed a man enter the room, undress and get into bed. A few moments later, a naked woman appeared and joined him. The light went out.

"That was one of the blokes from the bus earlier," said Crawford.

"Yeah," agreed Jones. "When the downstairs light goes out,

we'll give it fifteen minutes before we take a look around the perimeter."

After a while the two officers rose, stretched out the stiffness from laying prone and still for so long, slung their automatic rifles over their shoulders and set off toward the road. Both had now donned night vision goggles which depicted the tendrils of early autumn-dead black branches like ghostly fingers daubed on a greenish background. They crossed the road, a light ribbon cutting through the darker surrounds of the forested verges, before edging their way to the right corner of the front. The gates were now, maybe, ten metres to their left.

There was a gap between the bush of the wood and the fence which was easy to navigate. The soil at the foot of each fencepost was roughed up which along with the smell of the recently sawn timber indicated the fence was newly constructed. There was nothing remarkable about the right-hand elevation. It continued on to the rear where it stopped hard up against the other structure they had viewed from their observation position. Jones measured out eighteen generous paces before they got to the corner of the second building. The building was clad, from very near the base, where there was about a foot high concrete plinth, in shiplap weather boarding. It was the gable end of the barnlike building they were now passing. There were no cameras to be seen anywhere along this elevation.

On turning the corner, the rear of the building continued on for about another fifteen, maybe twenty, metres before dropping down to the fence. Crawford, a goalkeeper in her local football team, thought it was about the height of a crossbar. It certainly would not prove an obstacle should it be necessary to storm this place later. Once again, no cameras.

Richardson was looking at the live feed coming into his car. The three signals were converging. Two dots, Jones and Crawford, were now within a metre of a weaker sign. "If there wasn't that wall in the way," said Richardson. "You would be able to touch Rosina on the hand."

The left-hand elevation was the height of a goal along its entire length as the front building was set in about three or four metres from the corner. Once again, no cameras.

"I don't think they intend to keep anyone out," observed Crawford.

"Agreed," said Jones. "Definitely for keeping people in, if anything."

"How can you be so sure?" Richardson interjected from his car.

"No cameras," Crawford answered.

"Pressure plates buried or detection wires atop the fence?"

"Negative to the former," replied Crawford. "Apart from the post-holes, it is virgin soil. Could be wires but I have only seen them when the fence is sturdier. If you knock into it, it shakes too much. Alarms would be going off all the time, in the wind and when wild animals rub up against it. I think that would piss off the occupiers too much."

"Agreed," whispered Jones.

At the end of the left elevation fence, they peered around the corner and saw that there was about three metres to the side of the house, over the post and rail fence, which extended out to the front by about five metres. There was a small window to the ground floor. Suddenly, both sets of night goggles were filled with a bright light as someone turned on a switch inside the room. Both operatives backed up quickly but silently and removed their night vision. Crawford dared a peek and noticed that it was frosted glass and observed a bulky man, with his back to the window, drop his trousers and sit down.

She retreated back to the cover of the fence and waited for the man to finish. The toilet flushed and after a while, she hoped he was cleaning his hands, the light was turned out. The two made their way back across the road and headed back to their observation point.

"Good work guys," said Richardson. "Set the camera up and make your way back to the extraction point."

Jones dug out the camera, disguised as an evergreen shrub, from his Bergen and set it up. "There aren't any other evergreens around here," he whispered into the intercom.

"Shit," said Richardson. "Set it up anyway. No-one will notice until morning. Is there enough cover?"

"Definitely. Someone would have to trip over it to know it's here."

Jones finished the setup, checked the battery charge, ninety-eight per cent, and set it to movement activation only. Crawford and Jones retreated from their OP and made their way back through the forest to where Richardson was parked. They clambered into the warm SUV at just gone twenty-three hundred.

Richardson drove them to a house three miles from where he had been parked but no further from the house in the woods. He pulled onto the gravel drive, the headlamps washed the flint exterior in bright light and the car rolled to a rest in front of the double garage.

"Come on," he ordered his two colleagues before getting out and approaching the front door. He knocked. The door opened inwards almost immediately. When Richardson had been contemplating a place to stay, he had remembered the owner of this place from years ago and had given her a call to see if he and his team could put upon her. The answer was given in the positive without a second thought. Richardson checked in with Cobbold to authorise expenses, and arrangements were made.

"Couldn't wait to see me?" he beamed at the woman who stood at the threshold.

Eden Marcello beamed back at the man who had helped her get off a murder charge a few years earlier. She leaned in and kissed him on the cheek. Richardson turned to the two field officers following him along the gravel.

"Eden. These are Field Officers Michael Jones and Rowena Crawford of the Home Security Team. And, this is Flight Lieutenant Eden Marcello of the RAF Military Police, the Whitecaps."

"Come on in," Marcello invited the entourage. A dog, a German Shepherd about eighteen months old, sat patiently at the end of the hall appearing to guard the entrance to the kitchen. "This is Sheba."

Richardson approached the animal, knelt and took its scruff in his large hands. "Hello there, my little beauty," he said before turning back to their host. "Still training?"

"Afraid not. She didn't quite make the grade. Even though she could already take a fully grown man down and disarm him. Since my promotion, I am not an active dog handler any longer. She melted my heart when I saw the rejection in her eyes, so I adopted her. She is really good company, though, and I am really lucky to have a pre-trained dog."

"Good girl!" Richardson enthused.

"I thought Sue-Beth might be with you? Don't tell me she's seen sense and got herself a man who will give her what she wants?"

Richardson knew that was a jibe at the platonic relationship he and Walters enjoyed. "No. We're both celibate and will remain so until we are finished with this damned 'keeping the country secure' business. Then we might, just might, settle down for a life of rural bliss in our dotage."

"Good for you," Eden agreed. "Me and you both."

Richardson recalled the conversation he had had with Eden over four years ago when she too had confessed to being unattracted to the physical side of a relationship. Hers was for a different reason altogether. Hers was down to body image. On the outside, she seemed to have a figure most women would envy but when she undressed it exposed the scar from a horrific knife attack years earlier. She was ashamed of the scar, not only because she felt deformed but it always served as a reminder of her last canine partner who had died protecting her outside an RAF base in Cyprus. "And you?" he asked.

"Same," she replied, and Richardson could still see the hurt in her eyes. "Come on. There's coffee on the go and the three spare rooms are made up. I only have the one bathroom I'm afraid plus the toilet downstairs. I had my Waitrose delivery earlier so there is plenty food in the house. Help yourselves."

The three cooked up some pizza and French fries before Jones and Crawford took their leave and left Marcello and Richardson to catch up on old times.

CHAPTER SEVEN

Saturday 2ⁿᵈ October 2021

Norfolk

Following a very deep, dreamless night's sleep I returned to the allotment after opening up the laptop and completing the entry for target one. I encrypted Thornham using the same key as before in the location column. I then added St Therese of Lisieux to the date column, also in code. When I strolled through the entrance, I could see that many of the parcels of land were busier than last night. I exchanged nods of recognition with some before arriving at my own plot. I hadn't noticed the night before that I had brought up so much sand with the excavation and thought it a giveaway that something had been buried deep below the topsoil. I did think the sand was widespread enough and didn't really point to the corner where the gruesome find might lay if someone stuck a spade in the ground. On the way out, with some tomatoes bagged up, I observed some of the other areas where the earth had already been turned for the winter onset, I noticed that many had sand strewn across the surface. Funny what one can see when you know something is there. It is equally incredible what one doesn't see when you have no suspicions. I turned on my heel and sauntered, leisurely, back to my plot and took another peek. Maybe the sand was thicker in the corner, but I convinced myself that no-one would really notice the difference between mine and the other allotments. I might just get away with it for long enough.

I had thought the use of saints' days in the date column a

little fun aside that would emphasise the use of a biblical key if the dates were solved first.

And that was a line scratched through revenge number one!

Norfolk

The camera picked up movement at just after six-thirty the next morning. The three HST officers were gathered around a laptop on the kitchen table. Marcello and Sheba had left for the airbase an hour earlier. Although no longer active with the RAF, Sheba still went along with Marcello when carrying out her duties. Sheba was still a popular member of the team.

"How much do Whitecaps earn? Nice place," said Jones.

"I had been thinking that too," said Crawford.

"Eden has wealthy, very wealthy, parents and they bought this for her after she had been attacked in Cyprus. I think they saw it as a bribe to leave the RAF before she got herself killed," Richardson explained.

"Didn't work, then?" suggested Crawford.

They watched as a scarlet Ferrari pulled up to the gate. The driver stopped at the keypad standing a distance back from the tall gates. He punched in four digits and the leaves swung inwards. The locking bar had clearly been removed earlier, probably as part of a morning routine.

"Good view of the keypad," observed Jones. "Can we get a close-up of that?"

"Yeah," said Richardson. "Don't see why not. If we can't, I'm sure London can."

The gates swinging open had given them a look at the building to the rear. It, in the growing daylight of dawn, looked like nothing more than a barn except that the double-doors toward the right end were only big enough to let in people and not farm machinery. It was also in there that Rosina Ali and her compatriots were now fearful of what the new day might bring. All three were pretty sure that the driver of the Ferrari would provide the answers very shortly.

"Take my car," said Richardson and get yourselves back in position. I'm sure we'll get a full facial of the driver on exit, but I want back-up with pictures from other angles. I want to nail this maggot."

Norfolk

Rosina was awake before the lights came on. She thought she had not slept well but felt reasonably fresh. Eventually the crying and whimpering had faded away to be replaced by the uniform breathing of sleep, a rhythm only interrupted by a snort or snore. She laid on the bed staring at the bottom of the unoccupied bunk above.

"Rosina. Are you awake?" Amina whispered, from the next bed, in their own language.

"Yes."

"What's going to happen now?"

I don't do this every day, Rosina thought, I have no idea, but she said, "Maybe some breakfast first followed by an idea of what we will be expected to do."

The doors from the outside opened and the three men from yesterday walked in, two of them carrying trays of food and drink. Two women then entered carrying further trays stacked with more food, Paper plates and cups and wooden knives and forks. They placed the trays down on the tables closest to the entrance doors. It was a short moment before the smell of the food made its way across to Rosina. She was starving so it smelt good. She had not eaten since yesterday's McDonald's. She recalled the times when she was a little girl when she said she been hungry, and her father had countered with "You know when you are hungry, as camel dung sprinkled with salt and pepper will smell good!" She smiled at the memory and tears pricked at her eyes again.

"Grub up," oaf one announced.

No one moved.

"Come on. You need to feed as you have busy days ahead." He walked between the two rows of bunks scanning to either side until he spied Rosina. "Come on you. Tell them what I said."

Rosina swung her fully clothed legs off the bed and made her way toward the food. She translated as she went. One of the women removed covers from the food before handing Rosina a sandwich on a paper plate. She looked between the slices and saw it was bacon and egg. She had no qualms about eating pig but she expected it would be an issue for some of her fellow detainees. The second woman gave her a paper cup and poured some weak looking coffee into it. She retreated to her bed and sat down placing the coffee on the floor. She placed the food in her lap and took a bite. It wasn't too bad. A little cold but not bad. She picked up the coffee, lukewarm at best, and really not good.

"What's this meat?" Amina asked as she came back to her bed.

"It is bacon."

Amina looked horrified.

"It really isn't that bad. If I am hungry, I will eat anything. I would even eat seasoned camel dung, I am sure."

Amina took a bite, screwed up her face and chewed. "Umm! It really is not bad."

Rosina nodded and finished her sandwich.

Amina took a sip from the drink. "Urgh! Coffee tastes like camel piss!" She laughed for the first time.

Some of the women had removed the bacon from the sandwiches and protested at those who had eaten it. Oafs one and two laughed at them. The older children ate.

After half-an-hour had passed, a man, Asian, strolled into the dormitory. He didn't look at the women and children, going straight for the left of the two doors in the far wall. He produced a key, inserted it in the lock and opened the door. Rosina could see there was light beyond the opening. He closed the door behind him.

Oafs one and two walked along the two rows of beds and picked out two of the children, a boy and a girl, aged somewhere between ten and twelve, Rosina guessed. The boy was Fazal.

Amina screamed out and oaf one clubbed her in the side of the head. A short tug o' war ensued until the man's brutality won the battle. Amina followed the small party to the door where the boy and girl were ushered through. Amina banged, fruitlessly, on the door and oaf two laughed.

Amina slunk back to the bed. Rosina saw the eyes had filled with tears again. She patted her own bed, Amina moved across and Rosina comforted the wretch again. When was this nightmare going to end?

After a short while the two children were brought back to the dorm and reunited with their mothers. Fazal came to his mother but ignored her. He climbed onto the top bunk above Amina's and buried his head in the pillow. He lay perfectly still but fear had been etched on his young face. Amina went to comfort him. He shrugged her off and turned his head away from her motherly care.

"What happened?" asked the concerned parent.

The boy did not reply.

Rosina looked across to where another mother was trying to break down the same walls as Amina with her daughter, maybe a little older than Fazal. The girl was sobbing but was not divulging what had happened. Fazal remained quiet, maybe even stoic.

A woman was invited to the door but held back when she was about to cross the threshold. She screamed but was forced in. The parade of women and children continued until it was only Amina and Rosina who remained. They were led to the door together.

"The guv'nor wishes to see two of you together this time," oaf one sneered.

They stepped through the door together and found they were at the top of a stairwell descending into a cellar.

"Go on." The same man ordered. "Down you go."

At the bottom they went through another door and entered a brilliantly lit room decorated in pale colours. The man from this morning sat in a chair with cameras and even brighter lights facing a wall.

"Do either of you speak English?"

"I do," Rosina replied.

"Very good. Come and stand in front of me and remove your clothing."

CHAPTER EIGHT

Monday 4th October 2021

Lincolnshire

I had let Cooper do most of the planning for the next target. He was equally keen, if not more so, to see the end of this murderer masquerading as a war hero. Colonel Matthew Pringle had been an officer in the Royal Marines and was a contemporary of Cooper and me. He had stayed on after we had left and eventually retired as a Colonel.

Years ago, we had been trying to sort through Iraqi prisoners, separating civilians from militants. It was a difficult operation as militants did not wear nice uniforms indicating division and rank. Equally, innocent appearing civilians could be militants. God, we needed to be careful. We knew the world would be watching and wanting to ask questions if we messed up. Human Rights campaigners and lawyers, who had never been near a battleground in their lives, were persistent in telling us how easy it was to do our job. They were waiting for us to make a mistake, imprison or kill the wrong one and they would hold us to account. What they failed to mention in their ethical rants, was that they were only interested in one type of account, their own bank account. They were not concerned about who got killed or wrongly imprisoned, the more the merrier, for they could extort their exorbitant fees from the British taxpayer in the pursuit of justice for the terrorists. Some they would win, some they would lose, but either way they would hold accounts bursting with cash tainted by greed; their own. They did not care a jot for some soldier going through hell, unlimited stress and anxiety, just as long as the money-tree in Whitehall kept fruiting.

We had put three females in a compound, pretty sure that they were civilians. They were a mother and two children maybe six and eight. The mother started to scream as we put a man in another compound, we thought him a militant, ready for extraction into detention and to be dealt with by the authorities.

He protested very loudly so Captain Pringle, as he then was, clobbered him in the side of the skull with the butt of his rifle. It only served to stun him. "You bastard," he spat at Pringle in English.

"What did you call me?" Pringle demanded.

"You bastard," he repeated with loathing in his dark eyes. "I want to be together with my wife and children."

Tensions were high and blood was pumping. It was hot and dusty. Pringle turned to a Sergeant, nodded and ordered the man released. The man was thankful and kept bowing his head whilst uttering his thanks to Pringle and Allah.

"Stop there," ordered Pringle and the Sergeant put his hand across the man's chest to stop him. "Now let the woman and girls out."

The Sergeant nodded to another soldier who unlocked the civilian compound and ushered the females out into the open space. They met with the husband and father in the middle where the family had embraced. Tears of happiness were running down their dirt crusted faces. I was impressed by Pringle's consideration. The default position, wrong or right, was to consider singles, male or female, to be enemy combatants whilst women with children were considered unthreatening and afforded civilian status. This was not always the case but, without real intelligence, it was a fairly effective policy.

Pringle had placed himself between the two compounds, one to his left and the other to his right, with the four family members ahead of him with only desert as far as the eye could see behind them. Pringle moved the fire-selector on his weapon. I saw a venomous look in his eye and knew, with absolute certainty, he had set the selector to automatic fire. I did not have time to intervene and nor could a stunned Lieutenant Cooper. It happened so quickly, yet looking back, seemed to evolve in slow motion with our feet held by concrete. Pringle squeezed the trigger and I watched in horror as the four, maybe innocents, were shredded to pieces by an entire magazine being emptied into them. Shell cases sprayed from the chamber, blood spurted whilst gobbets of flesh and splinters of bone flew in all directions. He was standing so close to his target that I did not think any bullets would be found, they had disappeared out into the desert, having passed right through the human forms without being slowed. I've seen some grotesque sights in my time but that remains as the prime amongst them.

Pringle casually strode over to the butchered bodies and said, "There you are you loathsome raghead. You will be together for all time. Just as you wished."

Pringle did not even face a court martial but was instead taken out of the front line, given counselling for post-traumatic stress and shipped back to Britain. He then kept his nose clean and rose to Colonel. Cooper and me, back in the barracks at the end of the night, vowed we would get him, if it was the last thing we ever did on this earth.

Now, all these years later, Kate has been taken from me and I can deliver on our oaths sworn in a dry and arid land an age ago.

Now, driving down a pot-holed track toward a cluster of buildings including a small hangar at a Lincolnshire airfield, I carry retribution and justice in my heart. After all, the lawyers fucked up on this one! Cooper had got out of the van on the main road. A main road that was still a country lane. The van was, this time, disguised with plates depicting a similar looking vehicle in Buckinghamshire that Cooper had spied earlier in the week. I had arranged for a flight with a man named Rupert and he had promised that it would be Matt Pringle who would take me up. I had offered him the name of my new hero, John Bellingham, as I knew that, had I given my real name, Pringle would, more than likely, have run for the hills; not that there are many around in Lincolnshire! I wasn't so sure he might recognise me but there was every chance he would. I had rehearsed my patter.

I pushed open the door of the small office and noticed a man standing behind a counter. A camera was positioned on a wall above his head offering, no doubt, an unhindered view of my head and shoulders. "Are you Rupert?" I asked first.

"I am," he responded cheerily. "You must be John Bellingham?"

"Yes. You booked me in for a coastal sightseeing trip with, um, a bloke named Matt?"

"Yes," Rupert said as he stepped out from behind the counter and invited the occupant of a small office to come out and join us.

Pringle emerged from the room and now was only a few paces from me. He stopped in his tracks, recognition, maybe shock, showing on his face. I am not sure that he had placed my face immediately, but something had sparked.

"Mr Bellingham," he said as I took his hand. It was like shaking hands with a rancid memory, but I tried to keep up the charade. His eyes were an intriguing mix of curiosity and fear. His brain was still working overtime. He simply could not place me.

"Good to meet you," I lied. I'd rather have greeted a hungry tiger in its own lair than engage with this murdering bastard. Means to an end, remember.

"A few formalities. Disclaimers, that sort of thing. Don't want Mrs Bellingham suing should we fall out of the sky." A wan smile came to his lips but it was forced. He was still trying to place the face in front of him. He showed me into the small office.

The desk was untidy but he managed to find some forms. He asked me some medical questions, transferred the answers to the paper and invited me to sign the medical declaration along with the 'At my own risk form.' I didn't even read the paperwork. It really wasn't going to matter. If things went to plan, the plane would be falling out of the sky but not with me or Cooper on board. Pringle picked up the forms and placed them in a tray to the left side of his desk. The tray was full to overflowing and not just with disclaimer forms. It didn't look like filing was Pringle's favourite occupation. He went to a four-drawer filing cabinet to the rear corner of his office, opened the second drawer down, pulled something out and dropped it in his jacket pocket. I couldn't see what it was as his pocket and hand were obscured as he turned. I figured it must have been the keys.

I followed him out of the back door and the light aircraft was sitting on the small concrete apron in front of the dark grey hangar. He opened the passenger side door but instead of jumping in, I held the door until he opened his own door. We stepped into the cockpit simultaneously.

He conducted a few pre-flight checks before starting the engine. We taxied to the far end of the grass runway. I had guessed from the direction of the wind that we would be taking off toward the buildings. He made contact with someone on the radio, a form of air-control I assumed, gave his call-sign which was repeated back to him and we were free to go. On turning he revved the engine and we accelerated along the grass strip. I hated small airplanes as they did too much bumping for my liking. I tried to appear calm. At a time Pringle had judged to perfection many times, I am sure, he pulled back on the control and the plane was airborne.

"What's this about, Lieutenant Wells?"

So, he had recognised me. "What?"

"Don't be an idiot. It took a second or two but I soon realised who you were when I stepped out of the office. I suppose you think you're going to kill me. How's your wife?"

184

No point in continuing the pretence now. "She's dead. Cancer, earlier this year."

"I'm sorry," he said, and it sounded genuine for a moment. He then goaded me, "She was always too good for you. You were always punching above your weight."

I ignored his jibe and tried to keep it civil. We exchanged some pleasant words for a while, much like old mates meeting up for the first time in a long time. He hadn't married or had a family, I told him about Kate. He liked many women to keep his bed warm, I had only ever been with Kate. He laughed at the last confession. Then, he gave us an open net for he liked to go up on days like these as it was getting dark and watch the sunset from the air. He put the craft on cruise control and turned to face me.

Then he plucked up some courage. "What's this about, Lieutenant?"

"I retired as Major," I corrected him.

"So I recall. God knows how. You were such a righteous bastard that I never thought you would ever get above Lieutenant. You didn't take chances or use your initiative."

That was bullshit. I had enough commendations to decorate the downstairs bathroom. "Like you, you mean? For example, when you bravely murdered, in cold blood, that family of Iraqis?"

He thought for a while and checked the dials. Surely he could remember that heinous crime under the hot sun out in the desert. I was sure from the fear in his eyes when he confirmed

185

that Bellingham was actually Wells, he knew why I was there. But, maybe not.

We drifted away from the desert heat as we exchanged tales of what we had done since that day. He had, by some miracle or, possibly, favours further up the command chain, stayed in the Army although he stepped away from the Marines. I told him of my life as a mercenary, government and private. He was interested in the work I carried out as a government mercenary.

"They actually exist? I mean I have heard of them but whenever I tried to look into it, I was told they did not exist and I was dreaming."

I had always flattered myself that they only selected the best of the best. Maybe I was right. I had been approached after doing some training in the Australian Outback and asked, recruited I suppose, into what was clearly a clandestine organisation. It was made absolutely clear that, if I were ever killed, wounded or captured, the government would deny any knowledge of my existence and activities and I would be on my own. Not even repatriation of my body. The reward for signing away all of my employment rights was pay commensurate to four times a Major's salary in the forces. In addition, it was tax free as we didn't exist in the eyes of the law. I was intending to kill the bastard so there was no reason why I could not divulge all at this juncture. "It exists," I said before adding, "They only pick the best of the best which is probably why you were never asked."

He snorted at that. "I really don't know why they even thought about you. I suppose your little bum-chum went with you as well?"

"Who do you mean?" I asked, knowing full well that he was referring to Major Alan Cooper retired.

Right on cue, Major Cooper reared up from the back and put his right arm around Pringle's throat. At the same time, he fished a pistol out of the Colonel's jacket pocket. Christ, I thought, I hadn't noticed his pocket had any weight in it. It was at that moment I realised that he had recognised exactly who I was back in the office and, if I were a betting man, which I'm not, I reckon he was going to shoot me and drop my body in the North Sea. As Cooper appeared from the back, I took a hold of the control and tried my best to keep the craft level.

"Careless, Mr Wells!" said Cooper referring to the pistol.

"I owe you one," I admitted.

I didn't have full control of the aircraft as we were gaining altitude. I pushed the control too far forward and the plane felt like it started a nosedive toward the water below.

"Just keep the fucking thing level," Cooper shouted. "The speed and direction will take care of themselves."

"I'm trying," I shouted back. I had never realised how sensitive the controls on planes were before but I was learning fast. The plane levelled out and my heartbeat returned to normal speed.

Pringle was trying to struggle but Cooper had him held tight. Pringle's right hand was trying to reach over his left shoulder and gouge out Cooper's eyes, but he just couldn't reach. He tried with his left which was just as ineffective. When he reached over his right shoulder, he exposed his ribs closest to me so, taking hold of the control with my left hand, I popped him in the side with my right just below the armpit. I extended my middle finger's knuckle forward of the fist as I made contact. It is a tender area there and Pringle let out a rewarding yelp.

"Don't move you bastard," Cooper repeated before reminding me of my prime duty. "Keep the damned thing level, will you."

I looked through the front screen and saw there was more water in the view than made Cooper feel comfortable. I levelled the machine up again.

"As I said earlier, did you use your initiative when you murdered that family in Iraq?"

"That wasn't murder," he said, words muffled in the crook of Cooper's elbow. "I suddenly realised that we had released them and they were in the open and could have been armed and might've turned on us."

"Bollocks," I said.

"It was fully investigated and I was totally exonerated."

"Once again," I said. "Bollocks! Were you ever asked for evidence Mr Cooper, my little bum-chum?"

Pringle reddened and Cooper constricted the murderer's breathing further by tightening his arm around Pringle's neck.

"No," Cooper confirmed. "Were you Mr Wells?"

"No. Those little girls were only about six or eight and you shredded them to tiny bits of broken bone, gobbets of flesh and fountaining blood. You turned around and walked away leaving the mess for someone else to clear up. That, Colonel Pringle, was absolute murder."

"I was protecting my team," Pringle's muffled voice continued trying to defend the indefensible.

"Bullshit," I said. "I reckon you just wanted to see what it was like to kill someone. It was all about you. Your team, my arse, there's no I in team." I snarled the last bit.

"But there is in Pringle," said Cooper and laughed as he strengthened his hold even more.

Pringle gasped and could not release himself from the iron hold around his neck. His words were hard to make out now.

"Let him go a little," I ordered Cooper. "He's trying to say something."

Cooper relaxed his hold enough for Pringle to catch some air. "I'll sell my plane and let you have all my money if you let me live."

"Ha!" was my retort. "I don't need money. I have plenty, you grovelling piece of shit. Do you know, I have never seen a colonel die. I wonder what it's like?"

Cooper tightened his grip again. This time he extended his left hand around Pringle's face to the right side of Pringle's head. "Nnoo!" Pringle screamed.

"Yes," said Cooper and he wrenched Pringle's head around against any natural resistance until a massive crack that sounded like a gunshot, even above the moaning of the engine, signalled the end of Colonel Matthew Pringle. He had pawed at Cooper's strong arms but to no avail. It was as futile as trying to turn a tsunami.

"Shit," I said. "I've never done that one. I thought we were going to shoot him."

"Nor have I but it seemed like the right moment to try and, hey presto, it worked. Why waste a good bullet? Good, wasn't it? A damned sight harder than I thought, though! Needed one hell of an effort." He was panting as he loosened the grip around the broken neck.

"Won't some pathologist be able to work out that the death occurred while I was still in the plane?"

"Maybe if he's dragged out of the drink quick enough. But I reckon the body will be pretty bloated and the sea creatures will already have started on him. The plane will be pretty mangled up as well so I don't think a broken neck will be totally unexpected. You don't even have to make up that thing about the sunset, they will already know back at base."

Cooper clambered into the front seat, forced the body between us and, thankfully, took the controls as I squeezed right up against the door. He took us back to the airfield. I got out of the plane and said thank you. Pringle's corpse flopped over into my place but there was no way that this could be seen from the admin office. We both laughed as Pringle farted, soldiers' humour. The plane taxied back to the other end of the runway. I watched as it whirled around, heard the engines power up and watched as it hurtled toward me before leaving the ground and heading off towards the sea again. I made for the office.

Rupert greeted me. "Enjoy that?"

"Amazing," I said. "I've been looking forward to doing that for years. Brilliant."

"Good. I think Matt forgot to take payment."

"Yes. You're quite right. How much? He did seem to be at sixes and sevens."

"One-seven-five, please"

"Cash alright?"

"Yes. I'm afraid we don't have any change, though."

"Not a problem," I allowed as I took out my wallet and fished ten twenties out and laid them on the desk. "Take it as a tip. Oh! And by the way, he said to tell you he was going up to watch the sun go down. Loves that from up there apparently."

"Yeah. He does. I'd better go and turn the light on. Nice to meet you, Mr Bellingham."

"Likewise."

I headed out the door and across to the van. Now for the journey to collect Cooper if he survives his madcap idea. His plan was to take the plane out to sea, get close to the Norfolk coast, turn it and point it north and parachute out. He could set the craft on autopilot until it simply ran out of fuel and fell out of the sky. He had packed the chute in the back as he had crawled in. I thought this bit was weak. Then, he had some sort of self-inflating raft which he would be able to paddle back to the north Norfolk coast. I thought this weaker. Talk about madcap. Still, I thought, if it didn't work and two bodies were recovered from

191

the North Sea it might be assumed that Cooper had murdered Pringle. That was fine by me in the short term. I know he wanted to help out with the next one but I was certainly capable of doing it myself.

I drove back to Norfolk. It was dark by the time I parked up in Hunstanton, bought fish and chips and waited for the burner to ring. I had just finished scoffing down the meal, placed the wrapping in a bin and got back in the warmth of the van when the phone rang. I looked at the screen, God knows why, as there is only one number lodged in it, and answered. "Where are you?"

"No idea. Thought a "well done" might be the order of the day."

"Well done," I said. "Now get me a bearing and I will get to you as soon as possible. I assume you're in Norfolk?"

"Not sure but I think so."

It was another three-quarters of an hour before he called. "I'm in a place called Brancaster. Do you know it?"

"Of course I know it. I'll be no more than fifteen minutes. Wait round the corner from the church."

I got to him outside All Saints in Brancaster at just gone eleven in the evening and we headed back to mine. As usual, I parked the van at the allotment, swapped the plates back, before we strolled back to the house. I used the downstair shower, Cooper the upstairs before we celebrated a job well done with some of Kate's favourite gin and tonic. I let him pick food of his choice from the fridge and freezer.

And that was a line scratched through revenge number two!

CHAPTER NINE

Norfolk

Jones and Crawford had only just taken over from two other field officers in staking out the yard, where Rosina was being held, when a black SUV pulled into the entrance, punched in a code and pulled through the opening gates. The women and children had been held for just about half-a-week now.

After a few minutes, the SUV pulled out with two more figures in it, a man in the front and a woman, they thought, in the back. The rear windows were tinted making identification more difficult but the stature suggested female. The man in the front was definitely one of the men who had arrived on the battered old coach last Friday. The driver was new but they got a good image.

"Jonah!" a voice came through their earpieces. "That's Rosina in the car. She is on the move. Sue-Beth," Richardson continued. "It's headed your way. Be ready. Don't follow. I'll keep guiding you."

"Okay."

Walters, in her Ford Mondeo estate, followed Richardson's instructions and ended up in the car park of an hotel on the outskirts of Cambridge. She parked away from the black SUV and watched as the two men got out. The passenger opened the rear door and indicated to Rosina that she should get out. Good job we went for the arm tracker, Walters mused, noting the change of clothing. Short skirt, top with a plunging neckline, tights or stockings and shoes far too high for comfort. God, thought Walters, she looks terrified of something. Both men were Caucasian. The driver was squat and dark haired whilst the passenger betrayed a belly over a slightly too tight belt with unkempt light brown hair and stubble. She watched as they went in through the lobby door.

After a little while she followed. Inside she had a counter to the right with a scattering of coffee tables, sofas and chairs in a lounge area ahead and to the left. Beyond the lounge was a bar. None of the three were in the immediate vicinity. She strolled through to the bar and found them sitting at a table with another man. The fourth man was wearing a suit and kept looking around furtively. It was like he was thinking he might be caught out at any moment.

Guilty conscience, you bastard, she assumed. No doubt, married with kids.

The driver was conducting some sort of business, the passenger was leaning back in his chair and Rosina was looking down at the table. The man in the suit passed cash to the driver.

Oh shit, thought Walters. She's been pimped out.

Walters made her way to the bar and ordered a coffee. "White, no sugar, please." She did not look around but felt eyes were on her. Whose she could not be sure.

"I'll bring it over, love," the woman server said.

Walters knew she needed to get in as close as possible. She turned and looked at the small party gathered around the low

194

table. As she turned, she noticed that the two women occupying the area directly to the group's rear had vacated their positions. She moved across and took the just deserted table directly behind the party, which left Rosina looking away from her. Rosina's back was to her but the passenger and the punter were facing her. It was the punter who had been looking at her. Her skin felt like it was crawling with ants. The punter rose. The driver nudged Rosina who also got up but reluctantly. She did not make eye contact with the punter who offered her his hand.

Rosina paused and, after a snarl from the driver, she took it. "You could at least smile a little for this nice gentleman."

The passenger escorted them out of the bar. Rosina never looked back so was utterly unaware of a friendly face within feet of her.

Walters moved position and took the chair next to the driver.

"Hi," she said as she sat down. "It's Joe, isn't it?" God, I haven't seen you for ages. How are you? Just wait until Curt hears I've met with you. My God!"

The man looked at her. She could tell he was trawling through his mind trying to spark recognition. Eventually, none came. He eyed her up and down. He liked what he saw, Those eyes, my word, those eyes. But, who on earth is she? "I'm sorry," he said. "I don't think I know you. Where do you know me from?"

"Ballroom dancing," she made up but he still betrayed a vacant look. "Over in Ipswich."

"I'm sorry," the man said again. "I haven't ever been to Ipswich and I most certainly don't do ballroom dancing."

"Oh," she said. "More's the pity. I can just imagine you doing the samba."

"Who do you think I am?"

She had been fortuitous that the man's name was Joe. She made up a surname. "Joe Kerridge?"

"Ah, there you go. I am Joe, but Joe Burns."

"It is my turn to be sorry. Allow me to get a coffee for you," she said as her drink was placed on the table in front of her.

"Okay," he agreed after a brief pause. "White, one sugar, please."

"Yes, love," the server said. "I'll be back in a jiffy."

"Do you really think you would like to do a samba with me? You certainly look like you would move well," he smiled at her.

Yuk, you sleezy creep, she thought but said. "Don't see why not. Purely from a professional point of view, you understand?"

"Oh. You're a dancer, then?" he was beginning to imagine been close up with this tall, lithe beauty. Maybe a little old but certainly fit.

"Yeah, but not a ballroom dancer. Don't get me wrong, I do love it but I'm still learning the ropes. I am an exotic dancer. I only perform for all girl parties."

"Really? You're a lesbian?"

"You catch on quick."

"What about, um, Curt?"

"Oh, he's gay as well." She sat back, not because she was

196

assessing the man to her side but she knew Richardson would be listening in and was picturing him, steam coming out of his ear, smashing his fist into a steering wheel or down onto a desk. She forced herself not to giggle at the thought.

Joe's coffee arrived and they paused the conversation while he poured the milk and sugar in and stirred it. She spotted the expensive watch around his wrist.

"What do you do?" she asked, knowing full well what the proper answer should be.

"I run an employment agency."

Yeah, sort of, she thought. "Specialising in anything in particular?"

"This and that. For example, you give me your CV and I will match you up with the best employer possible. Interested in my services? You might have to shift your exclusivity and consider male or mixed audiences, though."

She sipped her coffee and made her best effort to make her eyes look like they wanted to seduce him, but all she really wanted to do was reach through his ribs and rip his heart out. She wasn't very good at the seductive look. Joe nearly recoiled from her gaze. She was pretty sure she hadn't given him her malevolent stare but, just maybe, she might have done. So bloody what!

The words dried up for a few minutes as they drank their coffees in silence before Joe asked, "What's your name?"

"Elizabeth Bryant," she answered providing a hybrid of her second name combined with Sean Bryant's surname.

"He took out a wallet, plucked a business card from inside and passed it to her.

"Ah, here are your friends," she said looking up. Rosina had been crying again and looked like a pitiful wreck. Her eyes had been emptied of life. Recognition of Walters ignited a hope within and they shone momentarily. "Why is the girl crying?"

Joe looked into Rosina's eyes as well but quickly switched his gaze across to the passenger trying to beseech him to turn back. He was enjoying his time with Elizabeth. The passenger, who Joe considered pretty dim, did not read the situation and continued to the table. The punter had gone. Walters made eye contact with Rosina and, imperceptibly, nodded. Rosina inclined her head in acknowledgement.

"If I didn't know any better, Joe, I would think you a pimp?"

"That's a hell of an accusation, Elizabeth. As I say, I match up good candidates with the best possible employers.

Walters seriously doubted whether the punter she had seen was the best possible potential. If he had enough money, she suspected, that would be good enough. "Nice looking girl," she said to Joe. "Just a shame about the deformity above the right eye."

"Huh! That'll mend. Interested?"

"Might be. How much? Does she speak English?"

"I do," said Rosina. "I'm not a piece of meat you buy from a marketplace."

"Of course not," he said. "To you, Elizabeth, she is yours as long as you allow me to fix you up with gainful employment."

She nodded. "Okay. Why not."

"Good. Now then, Dale, be a good fellow show these two to the room, you've still got the key, haven't you?"

Dale grunted an affirmative.

Rosina tried to pull away feigning disgust. "Please, Allah. Please don't let this happen to me."

Joe and Dale laughed. Dale, the disgusting frogspawn started to lick his lips. He then ushered the two women out in front of him back to the same room that Rosina had just occupied with the previous punter. As they entered the corridor, Dale jumped in front of them with the key. He unlocked the door and physically pushed Rosina into the bedroom. As far as Walters was concerned, he let his hand linger a little too long on Rosina's backside. God, this man was nothing but a creep.

Walters plucked the key from his hand as she passed him. "Don't want you thinking you might be able to sneak a peek, do we?"

Dale tried to wrestle the key back from her but she took a hold on his middle finger on his right hand. "Shit! You bitch, you're hurting me. I need the key. Joe will do me if I don't keep hold of it."

"Joe doesn't need to know, does he?" She forced the finger back a bit further. "Does he?"

Dale stayed silent but let a scream out when Walters forced his finger back further and a crack sounded, echoing down the hallway like a spitting log in an open grate. Dale plunged his right hand under the armpit of his left arm, winced as the pain shot through his body and danced involuntarily on the spot.

"Whoops! I sometimes don't know my own strength! You don't catch on very quickly, do you?" Walters mocked. "You touch her again and I promise you, you will probably need hospital food. Have you seen what it's like when people can't eat solids. Oh, and those shakes taste like shit."

"You bitch, you will pay for this."

"Ha-ha!"

With that she closed the door and entered the room. Rosina was standing by the window. She looked up as Walters came around the bed and nearly flew into her guardian angel's open arms. Walters held her tight in response to Rosina's bear-like hug. Rosina was trembling and Walters tried soothing her. She stroked the back of her head.

"God, he is a gruesome oaf," Walters observed. "He is a block of rancid lard that smells even worse."

Rosina pulled away and smiled. Cuffing at her tears she said "That's how I think of him. Oaf one, I mean. There is also oaf two who is just as bad. There used to be an oaf three too, but he has a name, Andrew. He is, I think you say, sleazy?"

"Good name for a sleaze-ball!" she commented thinking of the English prince who shared that name. "Look, um, Rosina. This might hurt but any information you can give me will help."

Rosina went on to explain that they would be taken down into the basement where they would be forced to do disgusting and degrading things with each other or on their own. They would be forced to use horrible gadgets that she had never seen before. It was really, really awful. The HST had suspected a basement but nothing showed up on the Local Authority records for Planning and Building Regulations applications. All that had been received by the Council was a request that the owner could build a small barn. The thermal imaging satellite had picked up fainter signatures from the building which suggested a subterranean room. It also gave off an unbelievably bright indicator that Rosina confirmed must be the lights that picked out all their lewd actions for the camera. There had been a man who would turn up once a day to watch. He would take a chair to the side of the cameras and watch. They also did horrible things to the children. Rosina did not know what as the children had seemed to lose the power of speech. They were terrified. It felt like they were in permanent shock.

"Is the man the one who arrives in the Ferrari?"

"I don't know. I have never seen the car, only him. We are only let out for one hour a day but not when he is there. He is Asian and he keeps telling us that it is Allah's will and we should be pleased that we are pleasing him. He keeps reminding me that when I am naked in front of him that God is nature and nature is God. He asked me if I am a virgin. I didn't tell him of the rape as many men think that rape is the fault of the woman and quite often the woman will receive lashes for tempting the man to have wanton thoughts. It is hardly ever the man's fault. He says that I will be welcome in paradise as I will be able to give pleasure to so many warriors of Islam. He terrifies me. That is not my understanding of the Koran."

Walters could feel a loathing rising inside like a pot about to boil over. They were now sitting on the edge of the bed, her holding Rosina's hand, comforting her. She was struggling to find words of sympathy. She was not designed to be an emotional support to anyone for that is what life had taught her. She knew that this brave, oh so brave woman, was reaching out for a shoulder to cry on. She was doing her best, but it was a struggle. Her place in life was to take out the rotten apples from the barrel and cast them away. Don't be concerned with the good apples that were left for that was someone else's job. She feared that Rosina wanted to give up. "I'll get the bastard," she whispered.

"Sorry!"

"Oh nothing. Yes, we have an image of the man who drives the Ferrari but haven't yet identified him. The car is registered to an organisation on an island in the Caribbean. We'll find him, though. Have you a name?"

"The others call him Mr Sajjadi. Don't know if that is his real name."

"Okay." Walters went on to explain what the team were planning to do in two evening's time. Once the place had been locked down for the night they would make their move. She went into more detail and, at least, Rosina could see an end-plan which she could work toward. Rosina agreed to stay on.

"Got all that?" asked Walters of Rosina. "How did the bloke before me treat you? I will hunt him down and teach him a lesson if I have to."

"He was very nice. He did not force himself on me as he said he was a policeman."

"He said what?" Walters tried to hide her surprise.

Rosina went on to explain how they had just sat and chatted

and how he and his team were working toward getting her out. "Was he with you?" she asked at the end.

"No." Walters pondered who on earth could be sticking their oar in on this case. It would not be the first time that two different departments had been working toward the same goal but for diverging reasons. She needed to know more but that would be one for Cobbold.

"Come on. Let's go. Let's ruffle our hair up a bit. Let's try and look like we've had a good time."

Walters pulled the door toward her and standing in the corridor opposite was Dale. His face had drained of colour and he was clearly in pain. "Was that good, bitch?" he asked of Walters.

"Very nice, thank you," she replied as demurely as possible. Not an easy image to portray under the circumstances.

He moved toward her. "You know what, I think I would like to spend time with the pair of you." He tried to get her to go back in the room.

"That's not going to happen. I don't do blokes."

"All the better," he leered as he moved in to smother her back into the room. He embraced her and tried kissing her on the lips.

She recoiled at the stench from his mouth. It was as if he had fed himself from the hotel dustbins. He held her hard. Her normal attack mode against blokes like this was a kick in the balls. Dale's embrace, however, meant that the kick had been negated but the knee was still an option. Whilst holding her smile, trying not to breathe in, and with no back-lift whatsoever, she raised her knee into his genitals. He screamed again and fell to the floor clutching his groin.

"You're playing with the big girls now, you stinking tub of rancid lard. Do try and have a shower before I see you again and, for Christ's sake, brush your teeth; your breath smells worse than an overflowing septic tank. Come on Rosina. I'll get you back to Joe now."

She tossed the key on the floor in front of Dale who was gasping now and trying to get his breath. Brilliant connection, she thought. The two women turned away and went along the corridor. She could hear Dale retching and when she glanced back, she caught a glimpse of the oaf's foot disappearing into the room. Maybe, she thought, with any luck he was seeking out the toilet bowl to be sick.

Joe was still sitting where they had left him with an empty coffee cup in front of him. "Did you enjoy that, Elizabeth?"

"Very good. Can you let me have a tariff of your charges? It really has opened my eyes to what's out there."

"Of course," he replied and dug out another business card from his wallet. "Use this one if you wish to enjoy some of our services. I feel sure that if you let me work for you, I can give you a staff discount."

"Thanks," she said taking the proffered card. "By the way, you'd better go and check on Dale. He's feeling a little queasy right now. And, maybe, you should make sure he doesn't mess with your merchandise." The last words were accompanied by a sideways glance at Rosina.

Walters found her car in the car park. Two evening's time. That was unfair on the women who were living this intolerable life, hidden in a basement only to be brought out to satisfy some bastard's needs. Her thoughts kept running through the takedown and thinking of Rosina. And, the children. Why did pimps like Joe think that this was an acceptable way of earning a crust. No child, or woman for that matter, should ever be the subject of such degradation and depravity. Joe was utterly charming and if she met him under different circumstances, she would never have suspected there was a criminal, perverted, mind just below the affable veneer.

She was totally unaware of someone approaching from behind as she bent to open the car door. "Good morning, Field Officer Walters," a man's voice announced.

Norfolk

Cooper and me were late rising the morning after Pringle had flown off into the North Sea. I turned on the radio and as much as the disappearance of the doctors' receptionist hadn't even warranted a mention on the national news, the disappearance of a well decorated war hero was the leading story. All the usual rubbish was trotted out including the out of character quote, a mechanical fault in the plane, probably a heart attack, that sort of thing. There had been a sighting from a trawler but this had been over two-hundred miles away so had been dismissed as improbable. Pringle's firm never kept so much fuel in the aircraft.

"War hero? My arse!" said Cooper.

"At least there aren't any reports of the plane smashing into a boat."

"It was never going to happen. The chances must have been a zillion-to-one!"

I turned the radio off and we put the finishing touches to our plan for the murderous IRA bastard who had killed one of our brothers in cold blood in a rural bar in Northern Ireland. The man had been lured there by a woman and when he went to the outside toilet, he never returned. He had been found in a pool of his own blood and piss in front of the urinal trough. Eamonn O'Keefe had been released from prison earlier this year and was now living in Birmingham. That was where we were going next.

We decided to have a meal in my local pub that evening. We arrived at just gone five-thirty and the usual crew were in the front bar including the local vicar, Jordan Cruz. We joined the man of the cloth for a beer before we were shown to our table in the restaurant. We both ordered burger and fries along with a bottle of Shiraz.

"The old vicar knows how to put his beer back," Cooper allowed after the waitress had taken our order.

"I know. He's a good man, though. He was brilliant with Kate before she died. They reckon he's the most popular vicar the village has ever had. Kate used to say that women had started going to church just to be near him. Don't be fooled by the drinking. He works out every day and runs at least five miles as well. Unbelievably fit."

"Should've been a marine."

"Christ! He would have breezed through Lympstone! Joking

aside, though, I think he used to be a chaplain. Not sure where or in what, though."

While we were waiting for the wine to be brought to the table, we both became aware of a group of four a table away. They were on their starters by the looks of it. Two women and two blokes. They had already polished off a bottle of wine when one of the blokes clicked his fingers and demanded another be brought to the table.

"Entitled prick," Cooper whispered.

The young waitress was bringing our wine over on a tray when the entitled prick wheeled on her and plucked the bottle from the tray. "Sorry sir," she said. "That's not yours."

I made to rise but Cooper laid a hand on my arm. "Not your fight, my friend."

I nodded and relaxed back into my chair.

"I can't wait any longer for my wine," said entitled prick. "These two old boys won't mind waiting."

The girl looked across at us beseeching our permission.

Cooper smiled and nodded. "That's alright love," he said before adding. "We're not as desperate."

The party of four laughed out loud. Entitled prick topped up the glasses of his friends. One of the women giggled and said "God! I feel a little tipsy already."

"Don't worry about it," the pourer said. "If you feel bad, just call in in the morning and say you have tested positive for Covid. Nobody questions you about it. They never check. I've had it three times now. Just remember, darling, we are the NHS and everybody owes us a massive thanks for us saving their lives, so we are entitled to go and have a little drink now and then, and, by God, we can have a few extra days off when we need it."

"I would feel bad about that," the woman responded. "It is a busy day tomorrow in theatre."

"They'll just have to cancel. We won't get the blame; we're making all the sacrifices. It's the government who will be blamed. We are untouchable right now. We can do what we like. Remember, we are on the frontline where the bullets are flying. Make the most of it."

The four raised their glasses and toasted the man's speech.

I was fuming. It was people like these who had killed my Kate. Our wine and burgers came and we ate in silence. We continued listening in to the tripe that was coming across to us from the table. It transpired that they were all nurses working at the same hospital as bin Laden. Other punters were arriving and it soon became abundantly clear that others were beginning to be pissed off by the sainted NHS, who were about as tone-deaf as a wolf in a choir of sheep.

"You're brooding?" Cooper said to me.

"Bloody right I am."

"Not your fight," he repeated.

I nodded. "Not my fight!"

A fourth empty bottle was now returned as a further full one replaced it.

"I need to piss," I said. The way to the toilets took me past the obnoxious group and to the back of the entitled prick whose name was George. I bent to whisper in George's ear as I passed. "You murdering bastard."

The diarrhoea that had been spewing from his mouth stopped in an instant. "You what?" he slurred indignantly.

"You heard," I scowled rather louder than intended.

The restaurant had fallen silent. I was among mainly friends although there were faces in there that I didn't recognise, but all of them, without exception, took an interest in seeing George brought up short.

"I have never killed anyone in my life," he protested. "In fact, we are all nurses and we save lives we don't take them." The words continued to be trashed by the wine.

"But you don't mind killing tomorrow by not turning up to work. You are on the frontline, are you not?"

"We are, the NHS would not be able to operate without us," he said puffing out his puny chest.

"Bollocks! I'll tell you what the fucking frontline is, Georgie boy. It is storming enemy positions after marching for forty-eight hours without stopping. Seeing friends' faces ripped off by bullets to each side and somehow, bloody somehow, you are spared. Then you clamber over the top and face down two or three machine gunners. Then you snatch a couple of hours sleep and start all over again. That's what the frontline is, Georgie boy. Not getting pissed, having a day off because you fancy it and staying in bed as long as you please. I have been on the frontline

209

and I damned well know what it is like. If any of us felt like having a day off, we would be simply left behind to be picked up by the enemy. Maybe shot. Understand? You have no idea what the frontline is like."

He turned from me and looked to his colleagues for support but they had all found parts of the table to be of more interest. "Yes," he croaked.

"You and your fucking Covid. Because of a balls-up blamed on Covid, my wife died. Understand?"

I don't think he did but he thought it best to nod. I hadn't realised but I had grabbed the back of his collar and was beginning to restrict his breathing. His face was going the colour of the wine in my glass.

"I also know that there were about three young lads who used to come in here for a drink and the occasional bite to eat. They, Georgie boy, ran their own small businesses. And, Georgie boy, do you know what has happened to them?"

"He tried to shake his head.

"You're strangling him," the self-confessed tipsy woman protested.

"I couldn't give a fuck," I snarled.

She returned her interest to the tabletop.

I returned my attention to the piece of shit whose collar I was holding, although I did slacken the grip slightly. "Well, Georgie boy, they hadn't been trading long enough to get help from the government. They're too busy giving handouts to scum like you, and you think, just because you have a little drinkie too much, you can take a day off on full pay. And, Georgie boy, one of them is laying in the graveyard, about three plots from my wife, now across the road. Do you know why?"

He shook his head again and this time, to back it up, managed to croak a "No."

"Of course you wouldn't. You have no idea how the real world works. One of his mates found him hanging in the woods by a rope that had nearly stretched far enough that he might well have botched the suicide attempt, as his feet were only three inches off the ground. Then, Georgie boy, there was his funeral and only a few of his family could go including his wife. His little girl stayed at home to be cradled by Grandma. We used to clap for the carers but, to be honest, that was a mistake. Scum like you, and most people in privileged public purse jobs, can take the odd day off when they feel a little stress. Lecture over, now piss off."

I smashed him in the face anyway. The room erupted into applause. I returned to the table and sat down. The party of nurses rose and made their way, unsteadily, to the exit without paying.

"I thought you were going for a piss?" laughed Cooper.

"I forgot," I smiled.

I even paid their bills for them. Five bottles of wine and four meals came to three-hundred-and-sixty pounds. With Cooper's and mine thrown in for good measure, I handed over thirty twenties and told the server to keep the change. I plucked the remainder of the unfinished bottle from their table and shared the rest of the nurses' wine with Cooper.

As we stepped off the kerb, on leaving the pub, to cross the road a voice hailed me from the doorway. "John. A moment."

I turned to see Ivan, the bloke from the allotments who had joked that I was digging a grave. I hadn't noticed him inside. Shit, I thought, the last thing I want now is to be held up by him for a half-hour. "Evening, Ivan. Never saw you in there."

He stepped into the road and walked toward me. We met closer to the opposite pavement than the pub side. He held his hand out as he came over. "Can I just say that was absolutely brilliant. They were in last week as well and got on everyone's tits then."

I took his hand and he pumped mine vigorously. "It's okay."

"I see you have filled in the hole for the bench up the road."

I had already rehearsed my answer if I was asked. "Yeah. I know. The bench itself has been delayed. I won't get it for another couple of weeks."

"That's a real shame. You know I am on the parish council?"

I nodded, wondering where this was going. Surely, I didn't need planning permission to place a bench on an allotment? "Yes," I answered with circumspect.

"Tell you what. I will get you one. I think it's a wonderful tribute you have planned for Kate. And, what's more, I'll go and install it for you myself."

I always thought that I was good at keeping a poker-face, but at that moment I really feared that I betrayed I had hold of the worst possible hand ever dealt. My heart missed about three beats and I was aware of my shoulders dropping.

"You alright?" Ivan asked.

I recovered my composure. "Yes. I'm fine. I'm just blown away by your generosity. There's no need, though, I have already paid for the bench and it is exactly what I want." A flash of some of the new benches lining one of the walks at Holkham came into my mind. At least I think it was Holkham! They were made from material reconstituted from waste plastic and were, supposedly, very friendly to the environment. I then made up an answer. "It is a specialist bench and the company gives quite a lot of the profit to plant a tree and, more importantly to me, it donates to cancer charities. I'll wait."

"Okay then," he allowed. "Just let me know if you change your mind."

We watched him return to the pub before Cooper said "So, that's where you buried the first body?"

"Was it that obvious?"

"Might as well have been written on a billboard above your head. Difference between me and Ivan, though, is that I know you have started on your list."

I chuckled, hoping I had got away with it. "Thing is, though, I can just imagine that if they ever dig the bitch up, he will be in here telling all his mates: I knew it. I bloody well knew it!"

Cambridge

Walters froze. That was careless, she thought. She had been

213

contemplating Rosina's plight rather than keeping alert for any potential dangers. She hadn't noticed anyone lurking nor had she seen any furtive characters loitering in cars. God, you fool, bloody careless. She kept her hands in sight and slowly placed them on the car roof. Her heart was thumping against her ribs and she could feel blood pounding around her body. She was aware of her pistol holstered above her backside but didn't think she had the speed to turn, draw and fire before the assailant's bullet smashed her against the car's door.

The man laughed. "It's alright, Sue-Beth, you can turn around. I'm not armed but am told that you could be."

Relief coursed through her veins and her heart started to slow. She turned with caution and came face-to-face with the first of Rosina's customers from the morning.

The man held a wallet open with a warrant card on display for her to examine. This was Detective Inspector Joshua Ebeneezer Edmundson of the National Crime Agency, often referenced as the British FBI.

"Ebeneezer?" Walters allowed.

"A family tradition. I'm named after a Dickens character but you sound like you come from the Blue Ridge Mountains of Virginia?"

She smiled and the eyes took on a glowing appearance which she could see nearly melted the man in front of her. If she could get it right, she knew the power of her eyes. Trouble was, though, she didn't often get it right and, more often or not, they would betray the exact opposite of the look she was intending. "No.

Alas not. My proper name is Susan Elizabeth but I reckon you already know that?

"I do. Let's not hang around as Rosina and her two handlers will be out very soon and I don't think it is a good idea we are spotted together."

"Could be comparing notes," she offered and was rewarded by the policeman blushing.

"You drive," he said as he skirted around the bonnet and took a place in the passenger seat as she got in the driver side door. She took her gun from its holster and placed it in a secure safe between the seats. Edmundson looked down at the position where, in most cars at any rate, there would be cut-outs to hold cups. "Impressive."

"Why aren't you armed?" enquired Walters of the man.

"Never done the course or, rather, never passed it. I've been on the range from time-to-time but have never wanted to carry. Don't like them."

"Squeamish, Inspector? Where are we going?"

"Your partner said to tell you just to punch his name into the satnav and you will find where we are going."

"You know Curt already?"

"Not exactly. My guv'nor spoke to yours and he gave us Curtly Vivian Richardson's and Susan Elizabeth Walters' details. I spoke to Curt and he suggested I wait for you and we all meet up."

Walters found Richardson's name on the car's computer

screen, tapped it and brought up his contact page. She touched the map icon and the map began to fill the monitor seeking a location of her partner. Fully loaded, she saw he was in a supermarket car park fourteen minutes away. She engaged Drive in the car's automatic transmission and headed for the hotel's car park exit.

The drive was slow as lunchtime traffic was beginning to build. This journey didn't take them back toward Norfolk but she kept her eyes alert as she didn't want to, all of a sudden, end up in the next lane to Joe Burns and his carload, as he might think the comparing notes excuse a little thin.

"Yes. I am," said Edmundson.

"Yes. You are what?"

"Squeamish."

"Oh, and you're a copper?"

"Yeah. I know. I'm just not suited to it. I like to use my brains to solve crime."

"Maybe all of you cops are the same. Curt's like that too. Well, not exactly squeamish but has a conscience. Always wondering if he could have done things without shooting someone or other. He's killed his fair share, so you would think he'd be used to it by now."

"I don't imagine ever getting used to it. Have you ever actually used your weapon in anger?"

Walters laughed at that. "Never in anger. Always by precise calculation. I have used it more times than I can remember.

Don't keep a running total like some. Maybe too many to count."

"And it doesn't bother you?"

"It doesn't bother me."

"Have you always been a policewoman?" he asked thinking she was like no female police officer he knew.

"Never have been," she replied truthfully. "I was in the Army before joining the HST." She omitted the time she had worked for a commercial security company as it was a period in her life she liked to block out as much as possible.

"Oh yes. The Home Security Team? Never heard of you before?"

"We mainly operate under the radar. What made you get in touch with Cobbold?"

"Don't know a Cobbold. Oh, is he your governor?"

"Yeah."

"It was the way you came into the bar back there. It was bloody obvious that you were an undercover cop. Except, of course, you're not!"

"Must've lived with one for too long. Speaking of which, there he is," she nodded to a solitary blue SUV standing in a bank of parking spaces at the far side of the carpark.

Edmundson scanned the direction in which she had nodded and could only see a Mercedes SUV. "Christ! You get better cars than we do."

"Jealous, Inspector?"

"Not of the car. Just of Curt." Edmundson looked away.

She smiled as she noted his muscled neck reddening. There was something a little vulnerable about him. She liked him. "Don't be. I prefer women. Remember?"

Richardson had got out of his vehicle and waited as she glided into the space two away from the SUV's passenger side. He waited for her to stop, opened the door behind Walters and slid in. "Inspector Edmundson," he announced. "I am Field Officer Curtly Richardson. You can call me Curt. We don't stand on formality in the HST. I suppose my dance partner here has told you that already? What's this about?"

Richardson was rewarded by a glance in the mirror from Walters. He smiled.

"Dance partner?" asked Edmundson.

"An in joke," Walters allowed. "Don't worry about it."

"I'm Josh. It appears that we are working two different cases and all of a sudden, this morning, they have become intertwined. Not the first time it's happened. Basically, we are looking at serious heavy-duty pornography with a fairly innocent, relatively speaking, face on the ordinary internet. If you know the right signals, you can find a portal that takes you through to the dark web. Have you heard of the dark web, Curt?"

"Heard of it but never needed to look at it."

"It works in a slightly different way. It isn't easily accessible and it isn't really a place to visit. I've heard of officers who have been in to have the merest of glances and have needed counselling for PTSD afterwards. Some of the content is quite disgusting. Actually, beyond disgusting. Really depraved."

"How did that get you to a hotel on the edge of Cambridge?"

"They advertise whores on there who will satisfy whatever the worst of depraved minds can come up with. I posed as a punter who liked that sort of thing. It was explained that I could pick one I liked from a gallery and, over a period of time, could get to know her and slowly bring in more and more disgusting acts of depravity. They don't call it that, though, they just list it as services. Some even show tariffs online including things like sex with a corpse. A customer can even kill their own partner if they wish. It was my job to go under cover and expose these people and, hopefully, end up with arrests and prosecutions."

The two HST field officers listened open-mouthed. They did not reply at first. Walters was thinking of Rosina, her friend Amina and the women and children who were in captivity in Bartholomew's Woods. Richardson knew what Walters was thinking and also knew that arrests and prosecutions couldn't be further from her thoughts, as much as they were at the forefront of Edmundson's thinking. After a while Richardson found a question forming but was terrified of the answer. "And, the children?"

Edmundson found it hard to bring this one to light. He was a father, although he didn't live with his daughter, she was with his former wife and he saw her once a week. She was only seven years-old and he had seen images of children much younger than that. He thought of the times over the last few weeks when little Olivia's mother had collected her at the end of the stay and he had all but collapsed onto the doormat dreading his own daughter ever being a part of such depravity. The times he had just wanted to walk away and take advantage of the PTSD counselling were nearly incalculable. Did Sue-Beth have children? Did Curt have children? He didn't believe for one minute that Sue-Beth was a lesbian. He had no idea why but just didn't believe it. "Yes. And the children."

Walters smashed the steering wheel. "Bastards!" she barked.

Edmundson looked at her, almost in shock, as she had appeared to be so calm that nothing would rattle her. He understood her anger and even shared it. The eyes did not dance with joy any longer as they had done when she had been teasing him. They now looked like they carried the venom of a snake about to strike. They betrayed the soul of a trained killer and he dreaded the thought of been on the wrong end of her muzzle now. He fully understood that she never had a second thought about those that she had killed. Maybe he wasn't quite so jealous of Curt any longer. You would never be able to sleep at night in the safe knowledge that you were going to wake up in the morning, if you shared a bed with Sue-Beth Walters.

Richardson broke into the second ensuing silence. "Josh, we have a temporary HQ set up a few miles from Bartholomew's Woods. Can you spare the rest of today and some of tomorrow to join us so we can all be fully briefed? We are planning a takedown in a couple of days."

"Not yet. You can't do it yet. This is big, Curt. We need more intel. It's coming together but we haven't yet got the head of the beast. Quoting your former profession, Sue-Beth, we want the General not the trench-fighters. What's Bartholomew's Woods?"

"It is where Rosina and some of her compatriots are held under lock and key by people traffickers. Women and children," said Richardson. "That's our interest in Rosina. She has been trafficked from Afghanistan. We want to bring down the beast at the top of the trafficking organisation. Arrests and prosecutions would be nice but not essential."

"Okay. I'll come. I know you probably don't want to postpone your operation, but you might have to. It really would be a great help to us. Once we have the head of the beast we can cut it off and everyone walks free."

"If we have to. Also, I think we might know the head of the beast as you say. That's assuming he drives the smartest car."

"Which is?"

"A red Ferrari. And, we think his name is Mr Sajjadi, although we are not yet sure."

"Didn't know that and have never heard of him. None of our surveillance has taken us back to him."

"You can call me emotional if you wish," said Walters. "But we are talking about women and children who have to go through hell if we don't get them out soon. Who knows what desires and perverted pleasures they are going to have to endure just so we can cut the head of the snake?" I don't think we should let them stay there a minute longer than they have to."

Powerful stuff. Another silence ensued. Richardson knew that they had promised Rosina relief in a couple of day's-time but what was the point of releasing them and leaving this Sajjadi character to inflict the same on another bunch of poor unfortunates? Sajjadi might not be the head of the beast. He kept his thoughts in his head for now, though. "I'll see you back at base," he said instead.

Richardson returned to his own car, gunned the engine and headed back to Norfolk. He looked in his mirror and saw that Walters' car was still stationary. God, he thought, I've never known this before but she is too tied in with the victims here. Defenceless women and children, it wasn't nice, but they certainly weren't the first and, most certainly, they would not be the last. Of course, it was disgusting but there is always a greater sacrifice to protect others and if that's what Rosina had to do ultimately, that is what she had to do. Jesus! No-one said it was going to be a cakewalk. Whatever that means?!

Norfolk

It was less than an hour-and-a-half later when Richardson pulled up on the gravel frontage of Eden Marcello's home. He rolled up to the garage doors, killed the motor and sighed. He had sighed many times on the journey back. Walters had to be ditched if she was going to let her heart rule her mind. A flashback came to him of when they had taken down some terrorists on the Suffolk-Norfolk border. Her lover had been shot and despite the murderous scum surrendering she had, calmly to be fair, picked up a rifle, set the selector to three, strolled up to him and turned his face to a jellied mess of blood, bone and brain. He sighed again. God!

It was nearly an hour later when he heard the sound of another car pulling up onto the stone.

"Took your time?" he said and immediately regretted the tone.

"Josh needed a change of clothes and I needed a coffee," Walters responded brusquely. "Something stronger to be honest."

"And did you?" he answered with equal abruptness.

"Did I what?"

"Have something stronger?"

"No. I know my duty, Field Officer Richardson."

Edmundson stood apart whilst the HST pair carried on with their domestic in front of him. He felt that he could see the argument from Richardson's point of view but had just endured the best part of two-and-a-half hours with Walters, banging on about how the women and children were nothing more than pawns in the overall game. "I am no relationship expert…"

"What's that meant to mean," snapped Walters.

"What I mean is, well, what I mean is, that you two probably need to go for a walk and clear your heads. We can do it your way if it is important to you but we will be here again next month, next year, next whatever."

"That's different," Walters said.

"Why?" asked Edmundson calmly. "Because you don't have an interest in one of the, um, victims?" He had nearly said whores but sucked the word back in just as it was about to spill out of his mouth.

"I'm going to clear my head," Walters said. "I don't need

anyone to help me." She turned out of the kitchen, marched down the hall and left the house.

Richardson shrugged. "I'll give it ten and go and reason with her," he said. "I'll show you around. I am afraid we hot bed here. Eden, whose house this is, insists on cleaning the sheets daily. So, don't be put off by it. We're all pretty clean."

Suffolk

Sean Bryant had just finished turning the illegible rantings, of his football manager client, into understandable English, when his wife called him from the lounge asking if he could spare a few minutes.

"Be there in a minute, hun," he replied.

He closed the lid of his laptop, pushed back his chair and strolled down the passage into the sunlit lounge. Amelia was standing at the French doors, gazing out across the ploughed field beyond the garden fence. Their youngest daughter, Daisy, and her horse-riding friend, Maddie, were sitting warily on one of the sumptuous sofas. His immediate thought was that they had got themselves in trouble somehow. He could not imagine how, though, maybe ridden over some farmer's crop and not realised it? Some of them seemed a little sensitive to normal people using their precious land.

"Daisy and Maddie have something they wish to share with you, darling," Amelia said without taking her gaze from the ploughed field.

"Oh?"

"Sit down, Dad," said Daisy. Her face had concern drawn all over it and she spoke gently.

Bryant took a place on the opposing sofa where Amelia came to join him, taking his hand in hers and squeezing it. Just then his phone rang in his pocket. He, instinctively, made to answer it but with the deft movement of a pickpocket, Amelia got there first and declined the call. "It can wait," she said.

"What is it, then?" asked Bryant, aware of a palpable tension building.

"Dad. Well, this isn't easy. Well, it is just…. Well, it is just that I love Maddie."

Bryant stared. What a stupid thing to say, he thought, they had always loved each other since primary school. This wasn't news. "That's nice," was all he could muster as a response.

His phone pinged an alert, either a voicemail or a text. He went for his pocket but once again, Amelia beat him to it, blocked the opening and stopped him from fishing the device out. "It can wait," she said again.

The three women were staring at Bryant now. Amelia had thought that he would explode at the news. She also knew that he was reliably unreliable when it came to matters of understanding the facts of life, when it concerned his daughters. Sex, relationships and that sort of thing were her domain not his! He had always become tongue-tied when one of the girls asked him what they had to do to have a baby. The response was usually that they should go and speak to their mother! Then, she realised, he had not comprehended!

"God, Sean. You are absolutely not with it sometimes, are you?"

He turned to face his wife, a puzzled look on his face.

"God's sake," Amelia said. "Can't you see?"

"See what?"

"Maddie took Daisy's hand in hers. "Sean," she said. "Your daughter and I are lesbians." She waited for the following silence to be filled but it wasn't. "And, we are very much in love. We are girlfriend and girlfriend."

"Oh, God!" was all he could say. He rose from the sofa and made to leave the room. "I'll get back to you on that one."

"Dad…." Daisy started but was quietened by her mother.

"He'll be fine. Just let him come to terms with it. It's not that it's girl and girl. Remember what it was like when Poppy announced she was seeing Toby? He can't let go. He loves you both so much that he can't stand the thought of you going off into the wicked world and fending for yourselves.""

"I s'pose so."

Bryant returned to his office, took his chair and contemplated the enormity of what he had just heard. He pulled the phone from his pocket, looked at the screen and saw he had two notifications. The first was a missed call from Curt Richardson, whilst the second was a text message from the HST operative asking him to give a call at his earliest convenience. He placed the device on the desk, put his elbows on the surface and rested his head in his palms.

Jesus, he thought, but his daughter was gay. He had often wondered what his reaction would be if either of Poppy or Daisy had laid this before him. He had always convinced himself that he would be tolerant and understanding of their position but, even so, it was still a bolt out of the blue. The galling thing was that, when he and Amelia turned the lights out tonight in the bedroom, she would whisper that she always thought it so, yet he hadn't suspected a thing. He knew Daisy and Maddie had been close but never realised. I think the signs have been there for a while, he imagined her saying. Well, bloody good for you because I didn't, would be his retort.

The phone ringing and vibrating drew him out of his contemplation. He picked it up, glanced at the display and pressed the Accept button. "Afternoon, Curt," he answered flatly.

"You alright, mate," came the concerned response.

"Yeah. Only relationships."

"Ha! You and me both. Tell me about it!"

"What do you mean?"

"Well. Nothing really. It's just that Sue-Beth is getting a little close to that girl from Afghanistan, Rosina."

"What? They're lesbians?" Bryant blurted out following on from his recent enlightenment.

"God! No. Nothing like that. She is a little concerned about putting Rosina's welfare below the mission."

Bryant hadn't missed the way one of his oldest friends had

dismissed such a suggestion. He would have to tell him. All of a sudden, he felt an enormous surge of pride for his daughter. "How can I help you?"

"We need some input from you. Can you get up to Norfolk for a prompt start the morning of the day after tomorrow? Bring the HST laptop. You are going to be looking at some ugly stuff."

"I'll be there. Send me the details."

CHAPTER TEN

Birmingham

The third take down was easy. We arrived at a building just outside Birmingham city centre early in the evening, it was just getting dark and streetlights were coming on. I had been able to find out who his probation officer was. Cooper had sought out the officer. Eventually, you will find everyone has a price. This woman's price had been seven-and-a-half grand. Cooper had counted out the fee in front of her in previously unused twenties. The officer's eyes, apparently, had widened when she had scooped the money into her handbag. "This will give my Mum the best holiday she has ever had," she confessed as she handed over a piece of paper with her care's address.

The target had been given a flat on the tenth, and top, floor of a tower block and would, most definitely, be at home between the hours of eight in the evening and eight in the morning. This enforced curfew was a condition of his release on licence. He had to wear an ankle tag and would not be able to leave without an alarm been set off.

Just after nine-thirty, we were in the apartment. We had retained the Covid masks but had dispensed with the Aston Villa baseball caps that had shielded the top halves of our faces from the external and lobby security cameras. This is another thing about Covid, it makes it so much easier to move around without detection. Combined with the peaks of caps or sunglasses, it makes security cameras as much use as using an ice cube to fight a fire. The man opened the door and, without question, let us in.

We said we were neighbours and had heard that he had killed an English soldier in the past and wondered if he would like to share a bottle of whisky with us?

He looked us up and down with suspicion, but this was a man who had had very little contact with other human beings whilst he was under the gaze of the probation service. The last thing he wanted to do was to step out of line and end up behind bars again. "Why not and why?" he replied, in his distinctive Ulster accent, as he removed the chain from its catch and pulled the door inward.

"We used to be in the Army," Cooper explained. "But, in effect, we are deserters. We both ran away when we were in the desert and made our way back to England via the refugee route before rowing across the English Channel before it was fashionable to do so."

That sounded totally implausible to me. How on earth would two white men make their way from the deserts of Iraq to the French coast without ever being challenged on the way. It didn't matter what I thought, though, as our host swallowed the story in its entirety. He didn't even ask us how we achieved such an impossible sounding escape and manage to avoid detection for all these years. He only had eyes for the whisky. Maybe he was keen on the company, thus far denied to him.

He went through to the kitchen and dug out three beer glasses as that was all he had. He even apologised for not been a good host. I poured him a generous portion and slightly less for the two of us.

"Gentlemen," he said. "Let us raise a toast to the single nation of Ireland."

He took a huge glug from the glass. Cooper and me took a dainty sip apiece.

He continued "I don't know what it was all about now, though. If the North joins with the rest of Ireland, it seems like we will be under the heel of another foreign boot, in the form of the EU. God save Ireland."

"God save Ireland," we both agreed holding our glasses up again.

He finished his glass with a satisfied slurp. "Pity it isn't Irish, but it hits the spot well enough."

I recharged his glass twice more with, maybe, half pints. Cooper and me had still only taken the one sip. I felt in my pocket for the Glock. I pulled it out.

The Irishman was nearly at the end of the third glass and found it difficult to focus on the muzzle of the suppressed weapon. The penny eventually dropped and we watched as the colour drained from his face.

"Remember Lieutenant James Bickerton?" I asked.

He nodded. "Of course. I haven't forgotten him in the last nearly twenty years."

"We're here to take revenge. A life for a life."

He simply shrugged his shoulders and nodded again. "I was expecting someone to try at some stage." He took another glug of whisky from the beer glass. "Freedom isn't exactly what I thought it would be. I've heard from none of my brothers-in-arms. I've been left all alone. It is almost like I have disappeared out of existence. All you boys are gonna do is confirm it. Be a shame to waste the last of the whisky. Might not be Irish but it's not a bad drop!"

He continued drinking, not at the same rate he had at the beginning, neither was he sipping it in a bid to extend his life for a few more priceless minutes. This was a man who was fed up with living, and it didn't bother him if he lived or died. It had also probably dawned on him that resistance was futile, as he realised we had hardly touched our own glasses.

He finished his drink and put the glass on the small table to his side. "You know what? I've thought of little else but taking my own life since they put me in here. It's not exactly prison but it's not exactly freedom either. I'll open my mouth, you put the gun in and pull the trigger. That way," he continued with a drunken coolness but slurred. "You won't miss my brain."

"Okay," I said.

He thrust his head and chest forward. I expected some twist but there was none. He opened his mouth; I inserted the end of the suppressor and pulled the trigger. Even with the suppressor, the shot sounded like a cannon going off in such a confined space. His eyes remained open even after the bullet had taken the back of his head off and left blood and brain on the wall behind. I pulled back from the spurt of blood that gushed from the wound in his mouth.

Cooper tipped the small amounts of liquor left in our glasses over the dead man's face and put one glass in each of his own coat pockets. He then picked up the empty bottle, screwed on the cap and found an inside pocket for that. We hadn't touched anything else in the flat since our arrival so no prints would have been left. He removed a linen handkerchief from his top pocket and opened the door to the hallway. Despite the sound of the gun within the lounge of the Irishman's post-prison jail, there was no sign of life in the corridor. We put our masks and baseball caps on again and made our way back to the van, still sporting the Buckinghamshire index number.

It was three days before the death made the news. By that time, I had filed yet another notch on my gun, so to speak, as the fourth one had actually been a drowning. All I heard, Cooper had left me, to return home, the day after the elimination of target three, was that the former Republican terrorist had died. The police suspected in suspicious circumstances.

"Only suspected!" I laughed into my coffee as I started to plan number five in an hotel room near Ascot. "Obviously haven't got Sherlock Holmes on this one." You find a man with the back of his skull blown off and no weapon and you only suspect it is under suspicious circumstances?! God help us!

The report went onto say that a man from Buckingham was under arrest and being questioned at a secret location. That is normally a euphemism for the secure Paddington Green police station in London where major terrorists are often interrogated after arrest. It is a building that bristles with security, almost daring anyone to chance a breakout at the risk of their own life.

"I'm sorry," I said into my coffee again, but addressed the

poor innocent soul from Buckingham. "Just bear with me and when this is over, my Wish Dead List will get you off the hook."

And that was a line scratched through revenge number three!

CHAPTER ELEVEN

Thursday 7th October 2021

Norfolk

Sean Bryant found a place to park on the now over-crowded shingle drive to the address he had been given by Richardson. The door was opened before he got out of the car and his old friend greeted him with a smile and a handshake. "Thanks for coming. Ready to get down to it? Oh, forgive my rudeness, have you eaten?"

"A couple of Weetabix only. Despite their claiming it'll keep you going long enough to build Rome, or whatever it is, I am pretty hungry."

"Okay. Good. Plenty of bacon and eggs on offer here. Come in."

Bryant stepped through to the kitchen. There was a man with his back to him, sitting at the kitchen table, drinking coffee whilst a tall woman turned from the coffee machine at the counter to face him.

"This is Field Officer Rowena Crawford," Richardson introduced the newly recruited operative.

The man at the kitchen table did not move. Bryant could see that he was scrolling through his phone. Bloody rude, he thought before greeting the woman. "Pleased to meet you. I'm Sean Bryant. I work freelance for the HST."

The woman took his offered hand, a move that took him past the sullen gentleman sitting at the table.

"You weren't with the HST," the sitting man growled, "when I bailed you out of the shit ten years ago."

Bryant spun round and was faced with a beaming Michael Jones. "Jesus Christ!" he exclaimed. "What are you doing here? I thought you were travelling the world as the eye-candy trophy, um, I mean personal assistant, of your poor benighted husband?"

"I was," said Jones as he rose to greet his old friend. "Then the Covid bullshit got in the way and, in the end, I got bored. Curt called me and begged me to come back as the HST was falling apart without me."

Richardson provided a scornful laugh from the doorway.

When the Home Security Team had been a fledgling organisation, a neo-Nazi group, the Knights' Tempest, had kidnapped Bryant from outside his office in London. When an article he was writing threatened to expose the hitherto anonymous money behind the terrorists, he found himself imprisoned in a secure facility on the Norfolk Suffolk border. One of his fellow inmates had previously worked for the public face of the organisation, the Civil Protection Group, and found herself incarcerated along with Bryant. Together, they had concocted a plan to escape, later returning to bring down the terrorists and their now infamous leader, the Lionheart. His fellow prisoner was Sue-Beth Walters.

Bryant joined in the laughter. "Good to see you, Jonah."

The two shook hands.

"And where is the cold-as-ice, Field Officer Walters?"

Crawford put a mug of black coffee in Bryant's hand. "Milk

and sugar on the table," she said indicating them with a nod of her head.

"She is in Cambridge," Richardson put in before going on to explain her role. He had said that they had put a plan in place to release Rosina and her compatriots from their hell-hole experience tomorrow night. The HST investigation had now crossed paths with another authority who, it seemed, were hunting the same perpetrators but for different reasons and from a different angle. Walters, in an out-of-character fit of pique, had stormed out of the headquarters to get some air. Richardson had given it half-an-hour before heading off in pursuit. She was easy to find as she was still wearing her trackers. He made his way to the nearby village playground, found her sitting on a swing, pawing at the ground with her right foot in between pushing herself back and forth on the equipment.

It had been an incongruous look, two adults, two HST officers, swaying in the breeze debating their assignment. Nobody saw them, though. After twenty minutes, they had alighted from the swings and returned to HQ with the revised plan clear in their heads. "And that is why she is in Cambridge. As we predicted, Rosina's promised employment did not meet her expectation. She is being pimped out as a whore, among other equally depraved things."

"Jesus!" responded Bryant remembering his role in recruiting her. Even though he had known that this was a distinct possibility, the reality was so brutal when it hit him. "Poor girl!" he whispered.

"Sue-Beth should be with her by now."

"With her?" asked Bryant not fully understanding. "If she's with her, why don't you simply get her out?"

"Because," answered Richardson holding his thumb and forefinger together in front of his face. "We are that close to breaking open this tin of maggots. She is briefing Rosina on our revised plan."

"How can she get so close to Rosina? I'm pretty sure her pimp won't allow welfare visits from her counsellor!"

"She's posing as a gay client to get close."

"Can't get by without the queers," Jones put in.

A shadow passed across Bryant's face.

Richardson registered anger flash into Bryant's eyes for a flutter of a butterfly's wing. He let it pass but promised himself he would talk to his friend later. "Anyway," he said. "Let's get down to it team, shall we? Where's Josh?"

"In the shower," said Crawford.

Wiltshire

I approached the towpath running alongside the Kennet and Avon canal. I was closer to Bradford-upon-Avon than Bath and had turned right heading toward the former. I had followed a man down here from near his home. Except this was no real man. This was a man who had stolen a family's pet dog, calmly walked it along this stretch of the route until he was hidden by woods. He had then found a rock and tied the pet's leash around it like an anchor, itself the size of an adult Labrador, before heaving them both into the canal. What he hadn't planned on was a couple of girls chancing upon the scene as he was capering up and down in celebration of his sacrifice to the water Gods. In one of the girl's pieces of evidence to the Court, she had said that when her and her friend came upon the crime, there were still bubbles rising up from the stricken and terrified animal. They implored the man, they described him as a loon, to rescue the defenceless creature. All he did was mutter that he had quietened the Gods of water who had been plaguing this stretch of canal for the past two-hundred years. They had even told him that if he pulled the dog out of the water, they would not tell anyone. He still refused claiming it was a calling from a greater power.

The lunatic was a local man, often seen walking on his own and muttering to himself. I remember when it hit the news around eighteen months ago it being discussed in the pub. It was a contradiction of human decency what this nut-job had done. Although it did not affect me directly, I was appalled by this cruel, barbaric taking of a life. When I was preparing my list, I recalled this news and felt for the dog, even as a non-dog lover. This innocent creature had put its trust in this seemingly lovely human who had offered him or her, I don't recall the sex of the pet, a break from the tedium of the small back garden in which it had been playing. The garden was only a small ball-toss from the canal.

Then, after the guilty verdict had been handed down and the Judge had been expected to pass a custodial sentence, nut-job had been allowed to walk free from the courtroom. The nation, through the RSPCA, was shocked by the apparent misreading of the gravity of the crime by the Judge. He, on the other hand, had decided that due to the defendant's low level of understanding and his mental acuity, or lack of it as we all said at the time, including the voices of the Gods in his head, he would impose a suspended sentence. During his addressing of this depraved individual, the Judge had said that he was sure there was a nice, caring human underneath who would learn by this misunderstood happening. The dithering old fools who represent our justice system had surpassed their own appalling standards of judgment on this occasion. I really had to toss it up between finishing off nut-job or the judge. It was a close-run thing. On hindsight, I wonder if I should have done both.

Thanks to the recording of the case by, I assume, an incredulous stenographer, this criminal lunatic's address was on record for perpetuity. I had driven here immediately after seeing Alan Cooper on his way. I did have another set of plates in the van, these ones from Nottingham, that I had swapped over the day before. The guise was the same we had used for the previous takedown except that the baseball cap was for Nottingham Forest. With the pulled down hat and the Covid mask, I did not need to fear surveillance cameras. I had selected the backpack to transport my equipment for this takedown. I was loitering, down the road a little, from the revenge target's home and was rewarded within a short time. All I was really doing was reconnoitring, trying to learn his movements. I was prepared, though, and the pack weighed heavy on my back. I supposed it was well over ten years since I had carried a pack with such mass in it. My legs were feeling the pain and, hopefully, nut-job would lead me to a place of convenience which, if devoid of people, would be an ideal place for this revenge.

I trailed him at a good distance, at least fifty metres to begin with, I guessed. A man and woman, arm-in-arm, passed me coming in the other direction and I overheard part of their conversation.

"I can't believe it either," said the man.

"He got off scot-free. Should've gone to prison," the woman replied.

"Bugger should've been put down," the man countered with real hatred in his voice.

They continued their exchange but the words drifted away from me in the breeze. There is no way that I could be sure they were speaking about the dog-killer but I reckoned they had been. I also believe I could second-guess what they had said as they had passed nut-job before coming into earshot. They had clearly said something, for the target of their derision suddenly turned to stare at their backs with a look of surprised affront on his face.

"Do you know who that was?" I imagined one of them had asked.

"Yeah. The dog-killer. Bastard!"

I continued following. The pack was getting heavier and I was beginning to think I might have to abort as my legs were turning to jelly.

My prey entered a wooded area, still going toward Bradford-upon-Avon and the path was clear of walkers in both directions. The tarmac was carpeted in fallen leaves of gold, red and brown. A breeze played in the undressed branches bringing even more leaves fluttering down for the impending winter. I was sheltered from the slight zephyr at ground level and could hear the leaves touch the ground like the gentlest of raindrops refreshing the earth. I tried to accelerate but my legs were spent. I looked down at the ground, forced my muscle-burning limbs forward and counted to fifty. When I raised my head, I had reeled him in, I estimated he was no more than ten metres in front of me. I made up the ground quickly. I wondered if the ridiculous notion of carrying the weight in my pack was going to thwart me for today. My breathing was heavy, even panting. I had been here before, though, in forced mountainous marches with just as much weight, maybe more, on my back. It again reminded me of the thirty-miler test in training. We always get the job done! I only needed one final push.

I put my hand over his mouth and pulled his head back. I was already armed with a few inches of duck-tape and placed it over his mouth. I removed two electrical cable ties from the same pocket of my coat. I yanked his arms behind his back and tied his wrists together. I then forced him to his knees and did the same to his ankles. He was shaking. Good! He was struggling so I whacked him around the head which knocked him to the ground. Good. I had a loathing for this creature now prostrate in front of me. I kicked him in his undefended ribs. He groaned. Good.

"You killed a defenceless little dog and you did not get what you deserved from the Judge. I am here to put that right. Understand." As I was saying this, I unslung my pack, opened it and removed a body-bag along with weights from my home gym. I placed the steel discs in the bag.

His eyes were expressionless like this was just one big

adventure. He clearly wasn't the full ticket, a couple of parabellums short of a magazine. Physically, he was shaking and showing fear. Emotionally, he was showing an ambivalence, a lack of comprehension. Maybe the Judge had been right, but even so, there was no place in a civilised world for cruel, demented clowns like nut-job. I convinced myself I was going where justice had refused to tread.

I forced the medium sized man into the bag, did up the zip to leave a small gap at the top to allow water to get in and tossed him into the cloudy waters of the canal. As I hefted him toward the edge I could feel the last pangs of struggle. Once the splash had subsided, a torrent of bubbles died at the surface.

My legs were done in, so I rested on a bench a few metres away hoping for a quick recovery. The pack felt like I was lifting a rag now. The bubbles slowed to nothing, I closed my eyes and let the dappled sunlight revive me.

I heard voices approaching from my left. It was the same couple coming back down the track. They weren't close enough for me to hear what they were saying but as they drew closer the man said, "Nice day?"

"Nicer now I have gotten this load of my back." I was prepared to offer up that I was in training for a charity night-time march across the Brecon Beacons but neither of them continued the conversation. Sweat had drenched my face and I could now feel it cooling on my back.

All of a sudden, the water surface broke. My heart leapt like the fish that had risen for a fly before plopping back into the depths. I waited for the couple to get out of sight around the next bend to the right before I hoisted my baggage over my shoulders and headed back to the van.

And that was a line scratched through revenge number four!

Norfolk

Rosina, hair ruffled again, was escorted back into the dormitory by Dale. The man had learned to leave her alone after his first encounter with Elizabeth Bryant. Joe had always warned him off messing with the merchandise. He had usually thought why not? Joe Burns certainly didn't frighten him. If he had been working in a sweetshop, no-one could have blamed him for helping himself to a few lemon bonbons. He saw Elizabeth and Rosina as nothing more than lemon bonbons which he could enjoy as much as he wished, whenever he wished. The blonde woman with the killer eyes had taught him one of life's simple lessons, put your hand in the bonbon bag and your fingers could get broken. The finger that the bitch had broken was still throbbing and his groin felt like someone had lent in and tried pulling his balls out through the sack. This time he had not even made eye contact with the bitch. She carried a bigger threat than the tepid Joe Burns; that was for damned sure!

Rosina had been aware that Dale was treating her with circumspection now and, in a peculiar sort of a way, even felt sorry for him. No man back home would be so cowed by any woman. The shame would be enough to drive him to revenge. Dale even afforded Rosina some respectability, offering her extra portions at mealtimes and treating her with a courtesy never shown until his encounter with the bitch with the eyes. In short, he was terrified of her.

She had enjoyed her bedroom meeting with Sue-Beth Walters, and held it very close to her heart, that her days in this nightmare were nearly over, although it was going to be a little longer than she had hoped. She had listened to the outline plan and said she would play her part. She had wondered over the past few nights if being a Taliban soldier's whore could be any worse than this Jahannan had turned out to be? She had been cast into the deepest part of Hades and was now beginning to dream of the sunlit uplands of Janna. Was it not true that classical philosophers of Islam had told her that good Muslims would not be cast into Hell for eternity, but Allah would find them and pluck them from Perdition and welcome them into Heaven. Well, when was that going to happen? I am a good Muslim, aren't I?

Rosina was sitting at one of the chairs in the middle of the room. All of her compatriots were laying on their bunks, faces etched with despair, and she could not tell a single one of them, even Amina, of their imminent freedom. She heard the muffled sound of a motor. It was the unmistakable choking sound of the battered old bus pulling into the yard. The engine was killed. God no! Please don't tell us we are going to be moved away to another place, she thought. The door to the outside was then flung open and she realised it was another intake of women and children being brought here to begin their lives in the land of dreams.

In her trips out to meet clients, she had learned that her group were the first party to occupy this barn. She had been horrified to learn that there were at least another twenty-five similar establishments across England, Scotland and Wales. She had never heard of Wales before, at least not as a place, but assumed it must be a part of the United Kingdom somehow. At least she had passed this intel, as the Americans used to call it, onto Sue-Beth. She seemed to be genuinely grateful.

She was finding the trips out to be debilitating, in that, she would sometimes have to perform tricks three times a day with odious men. None of them were what she would call attractive or desirable. Thinking of whales had reminded her of one encounter.

She had been forced to have a physical encounter with a mentally retarded man of nearly one-hundred-and-fifty kilograms; his mother had paid for her boy's pleasure. How could a woman, especially a mother, force another woman to have sex against her will. In Rosina's mind, the mother was an accessory to rape. Maybe she lived in a deluded world in which she thought girls like Rosina enjoyed being fucked by a backward overweight and flabby lump of smelly jelly? All because she loved her son and didn't want him to go without. Even Rosina had felt sorry for the boy, he was only sixteen, when he grunted his thanks and offered her a half-melted, half-finished, chocolate bar from his sweaty pocket. She politely declined. She knew Sue-Beth was collecting as much intel as she possibly could but even Rosina could not bring herself to tell of the retarded fat boy.

Her heart had swelled in anticipation earlier, when she had been told the lesbian dancer wanted her again, although she tried to show disgust. It must have been a good act because Dale and Joe laughed. She watched Dale in the car's mirror and saw a shadow cross his face. He turned and faced her. He made her promise that she would tell the bitch with the eyes that she was being treated well by Dale. Rosina just smiled her increasingly convincing false smile which she guessed from Dale's blank look, he could not interpret!

She returned to her corner bed and observed the parade of women, there were no children this time, being ushered into the dorm. To her surprise, they were not Asian but European. Well, this was something different?

The whimpering and wailing had started even before the guards had left the room. There were another ten inhabitants to share the meagre bathroom facilities. The bed opposite hers, on the other side of the dividing barrier, had not been occupied as yet and a tall blonde woman shuffled over to it and sat down on its edge. My God, was Rosina's first thought, they have brought Sue-Beth in. The woman turned to face her and the fears evaporated when she saw it was not Sue-Beth. This woman was the same height with a similar hairstyle, long and drawn into a ponytail, but that was where the similarity ended. She was younger, not so firm and possessed a less confident face. Rosina beckoned her to the tables and they met, like at a border control in no-man's land.

"Do you speak English?" Rosina asked.

"I do."

"My name is Rosina."

"I am Petra."

"Where are you from, Petra? I am from Afghanistan."

"I am from Czech Republic."

"I don't understand," said Rosina. "I mean, can't you just come in and out of England when you want?"

"No. Since UK leave EU we have to apply and they take a long time to process passes. My boyfriend, he English, we met in Prague, pay for me to come here. He live in Winchester. We get married and I can stay after."

After what? thought Rosina. You are not getting married any time soon. Is her supposed boyfriend a part of this or is Petra an innocent victim of the murky world of people trafficking?

"What are you doing?" asked Petra of her new confidant. "This is not a proper centre, is it?"

"No," Rosina answered in a low whispering conspiratorial voice.

Petra felt at her wrists. "Thought not. Why the, how you say, um, arm-rings?"

"Handcuffs," Rosina corrected. She sucked in a big breath and slowly exhaled before describing the expected horrors of the next few days. "It might be that Europeans are treated differently to Afghani," she finished lamely, as shock was now portrayed in the Czech's face. There was a wrestling match going on in her brain. Should she divulge the meetings she had held with Sue-Beth and let Petra rest easy in that her torment would not last too much longer or should she keep quiet. Would Petra shoot her mouth off and the plan would creep back to the oafs? Keep it to herself. The threat of punishment would make her keep her mouth zipped, for she did not want to be manacled to the punishment cradle again in the basement. Forced to smile while tied up like trussed poultry in a market and having electronic cattle prods forced into her had lost its appeal. She had been forced to look at the pictures before being tormented by men with abnormally massive attributes. It was degrading and she knew that if she crossed the line again, she would have to endure. It was the children that made her sick to the core. If one of the children was forced down into the basement again, she would kick off in a big way and, even, volunteer for the torture many times over to save what were, at one time, innocent souls.

Norfolk

Sean Bryant had been given the two business cards that Walters had collected from Joe Burns during her first visit to the hotel. One was for a recruitment firm called PHA and the other was for the provision of personal services, PHS. He was sitting with Josh Edmundson in the HQ control centre, the kitchen table, when he had started to explore the content of the websites advertised on the cards.

The first card was, when compared to the second, decent and bordered on an acceptable way of running a business. It was still sick, though. The website offered services which promised to match up willing men and women as escorts for all sorts of social occasions. Rosina's picture had been discovered in a thumbnail gallery of applicants offering their services. It even highlighted her linguistic skills stating that an evening with this highly intelligent interpreter would be the most stimulating night of a man's, or woman's, life. There were pages where the services of exotic dancers could be bought or models for swimwear suits purchased or sisters who could brighten any outdoor shot. In short, it purported to be a model agency where the ladies were banned, under company policy, from offering extra-curricular services. The hint was there, though, when a follow-up statement suggested that they could not limit the earning capabilities of all their experienced staff.

The second website took Edmundson and Bryant into another place altogether. It was a world where different levels of depravity could only be accessed with the purchase of special codes. The services on offer included the use of children, animals and death. Weapons could be purchased for self-gratification. It was disgusting and both the police officer and the ex-journalist were in shock at what they witnessed on these sites. Bryant had heard of the dark web as a place where all sorts of illicit products and services, weapons, drugs and, even, killers to rid yourself of that pesky business partner, enemy or wife, could be sourced for reasonable fees. New identities could be provided for the perfect getaway including the issue of genuine passports, driving licences and credit cards. These were all gross and all highly illegal in most countries but not all, incredibly. Bryant saved it all to the evidence folder he had created earlier.

Bryant found that the services available on Joe Burns sites were all related to the sex industry. He had turned up a loathsome image of Rosina in such compromising positions that he was not willing to share it with Richardson let alone Walters. He remembered the poor woman on the RIB who thought her ordeal would be finally over and a new life of unparalleled potential was waiting in England. Instead, this. The smile was inviting but look closer and the eyes were as dull as they had been as she sat crying next to him, head bleeding, on the cruise to a new life. He saved it all to the evidence folder.

He saw a section headed "A Pinch of Snuff Does You Good." He clicked on it and was sickened by what he discovered. There was a video featuring a black-haired woman, arms above her head, suspended from the out-of-sight ceiling, in metal shackles on the ends of chains, with two men taking it in turns to whip her. The schlap of the leather on her back and her grunt as the first lash landed, leaving a crimson welt across her bare shoulders, made him dry retch. The second one from the other protagonist made her scream out. Before the third one landed, sobs could be heard and she was screaming something in Arabic. The two men, also naked, were relishing their task and were laughing whilst administering their pleasure to the stricken soul dangling from the ceiling. The pair had been aroused by their perverted activity. Bryant muted the audio; the video was bad enough to bear. A few more strokes and she had slumped in her fetters, her back red raw from the punishment. The victim's long dark hair had become matted in the bloodied wounds higher up her back. Fragments of glistening white protruded through the lacerated mess that had obliterated the skin from her back. The end showed the men giving mutual gratification to one another whilst the woman, maybe unconscious, maybe dead, hung in the shackles. Bryant saved it to the evidence folder.

"You sure you want to go on with this?" asked Edmundson whose colour had drained from his face. "I could use a break myself."

"Let's just check these last two icons on this page, get them saved and then, I could murder a pint or three."

Bryant opened the links under the icons. He could not believe what was shown on the first one and quickly exited it and saved it to the folder. The second one was equally as disgusting which he also exited and saved. He slammed the laptop lid down.

"That's it. I'm going to the pub. I hope the damned place is open. I could use a pint or four."

Edmundson said he needed to make a report back to his office but might join him in an hour or so. Richardson said that if he could give him no more than fifteen minutes, he would be along too.

"I'll be outside. I need the air. Apologies if you step in a pile of sick on the drive!"

He stepped outside and breathed in the autumnal air. Fuck it, he thought, I can't wait fifteen minutes. He opened the door again and bellowed through to Richardson that he needed a drink now not in fifteen minutes. The images he had witnessed were imprinted on his retina and if it meant reaching out for a drunken oblivion, that is what he would do. He made for the pub.

The White Horse was a quaint pub with a white picket fence to the front bordering a small garden with a smattering of tables and chairs for the last of the year's outdoor drinking. Christ, it was only just gone four in the afternoon!

He pushed open the front door which led into a small bar with, maybe, half-a-dozen tables, a dartboard to the left and a small open fire in the grate on the same wall as the bar. Three stools stood in front of the drinks pumps like sentinels guarding a citadel. He scanned the pumps and asked the portly bar-tender to pour him a pint of local ale. The beer was placed on a mat in front of him, he picked it up and downed it in two huge glugs.

"Another one, please," he said.

"Christ! You must be thirsty! You new in the village?"

"No. Visiting Eden Marcello, down the road."

"I know her. Bit of a loner? Keeps herself to herself."

"So would you be if you had her history. Got any darts?" He had been brusque but, in his mind, had justification.

The man took the proffered ten-pound note, gave change and found a set of darts in a pint pot on a shelf behind the spirits. He handed the arrows over and took that as a sign that the tensed-up guy did not wish for further conversation.

Bryant took the wallet, dug the shafts out from the inside and fixed the Union Jack flights to the ends. He stood at the oche, made himself comfortable and threw his first three. All three penetrated the board in the larger of the single twenties just above the triple. He retrieved the darts and repeated the motion over and over. He supped on his beer in between throws and was very soon needing a third pint.

Richardson walked through the door. "Alright, mate?"

"No. I'm not bloody alright. I've just watched a woman whipped to death for the gratification of two arseholes who clearly found enjoyment in it. I have never seen anything so sickening in my life."

Richardson took hold of Bryant's empty glass. Bryant threw three more darts at the board with so much force the tips sunk in right up to the barrel.

"What is it?"

"The local one, furthest to the left," he replied, referring to the positions of the beer pumps.

Richardson ordered two pints of the beer and put them on a table to the side of the board. "Wanna talk?" he asked.

Bryant hurled three more darts at the board. "Yeah." He knew he was being boorish but, by God, he had good reason to be. He sat.

"Edmundson has just given me a brief. If it is any consolation, he understands where you are coming from. He says that this site is among the worst he has ever seen. Many of his investigation team can't hack it and are off sick."

"Not surprising. They are nowhere near as sick as the perverts who are carrying out these abuses, though." Bryant went through what he and Edmundson had witnessed on the "A Pinch of Snuff Does You Good" section.

"Jesus" was all Richardson could say.

"And, then the next bit was an image of a butcher cutting a carcass into chunks. And, then the next…" He trailed off, closed his eyes and tried to banish the images from his mind.

"Take your time, mate," Richardson said softly.

Bryant didn't continue immediately, took a slurp from his glass and steeled himself to continue. "And the next one showed…. Jesus. Showed the two killers, still stark naked with hard-ons eating meat. No guesses where that came from!"

"Jesus!" Richardson repeated.

"That's not all. Did he tell you about Rosina?"

Richardson nodded and took his first pull.

"Then there is the price list. Take that snuff video. The two blokes who used the whips each paid twenty grand for the privilege. Anyone who wants to watch it then pays ten-quid. Anyone who wants to buy it will fork out a hundred. It has been downloaded forty-five thousand times. God, there are some sick people out there!"

Richardson stared at his drink allowing Bryant to continue. He was lost for words.

"Did you know you can buy women on there as well?"

"I guess so. That's what prostitution's about."

"Not that sort of buy. Not for a one-off encounter. I mean you can actually buy these women for keeps. Permanently. Rosina is on there for seventy-five thousand. And she's not the most expensive. Blonde women from eastern Europe can fetch well over one-hundred-and-fifty grand. Arab and black women seem cheaper…. Sorry, bad choice of words."

"It's okay. Another drink?" Richardson was stunned by the detail of the revelation. He also knew that there was a danger he would betray a violence, not displayed since the takeout of Gillian's tormentor, in taking these scum down. He questioned whether it should be he leading the mission. He countered this with the argument that someone had to do it and why let a father like Josh Edmundson take it over? Any mother or father would be wrestling with exactly the same thoughts. He was committed really and knew there was no alternative.

"Yeah. Whisky, please. Make it a double. I'd better have it with ginger otherwise I'm going to be pissed. Jesus! I wished I still smoked. I could use a pouch of Drum right now. I reckon I'd chain-smoke all the way into morning!"

Richardson took his phone from his pocket to pay. "Christ!" he said noticing the time. "Sue-Beth should be in with the Prime Minister right now."

"Prime Minister?"

London

Sue-Beth Walters was in with the Prime Minister. She was sitting in a reception room at number ten Downing Street with the Home Secretary and Duncan Cobbold. Blair, a name not unfamiliar within these walls, was laying at his master's feet. The head of the UK government wanted to thank, personally, the diligent operative, who had uncovered the plot to flood the United Kingdom with contaminated banknotes. Not only had the officer realised that there might be something wrong with the twenty-pound note she had confiscated from a migrant a few days earlier, she had done something about it. The woman's alertness had been the only reason why a potentially devastating biological attack from a foreign aggressor had been thwarted. Following the expeditious actions of all the British security forces the country remained safe. It was true that some of the notes had got through but they were suspected as only being a small percentage.

As Vanessa Forbes-Marriott had suspected, the Russians were trying to cloak something more sinister. No, something seriously sinister! Word had been coming out of Moscow that Russia wanted to provoke the west into a world war in which they would emerge as the dominant global force. They would start with non-NATO countries on their western edge, Ukraine and Finland. The Russian leader believed that NATO was so weak they dare not intervene in protecting those two.

He also knew that thanks to the west's weakness in dealing with illegal migrants, he would be able to smuggle biological weapons in with them. His friends, the Chinese, had developed such a weapon. In their Wuhan laboratories, they had developed a virus that would paralyse the west. They had made a mistake, though, and had allowed a leak to seep out during late 2019. That leak was now known universally as the first wave of coronavirus. The Chinese had now developed a method in which a new strain of the virus could be hidden in micro-polymer sacks which, in turn, could be attached to the tallow used in some modern banknotes. This new version was highly virulent and capable of disabling the paranoid west, giving Moscow an unrestricted window to free Ukraine from their oppressive Nazi government. Ethnic Russians would be freed from the stamp of western authoritarianism. And, the Russian empire would be restored, eventually, to its full glory of the 1980s when it was Soviet.

"And thanks to you, Field Officer Susan Walters," continued the Prime Minister. "We have been able to take action against the new covid threat. And, in addition we will be able to release resources to help our friends in Ukraine resist the lunatic dreams of a madman.

The Prime Minister went on to explain that both the Chinese

and Russians thought the west's vaccines to be of no or little effect. All the evidence suggested, though, reality was somewhat different to the enemy axis view. There was no doubt, according to top American, British and European scientists that even though the new threat was undeniably more virulent and powerful than the original, the vaccines would render it useless at best or mild at worst.

China was not going to be an innocent bystander on the world stage. She was not going to sit back and applaud the actions of her ally in invading Ukraine but under the joint cloaks of a covid-ravaged west and the marching of Russian imperialist troops through Europe, China would be regaining the island of Taiwan before turning its attention on Australia.

"If it were down to me, you would be awarded the highest honour in the land. But alas, so I am told, your group's work must never be recognised publicly so, I am afraid, we cannot bestow our true thanks on you, a true national hero. You are up there with Nelson, Wellington and Churchill and no-one will ever know your name. It will be our scientists and the wonderful NHS who will garner all the credit for allowing our defence forces to continue thriving in these most trying of times. We will announce a new mutation of the virus in due course and the successful rollout of our vaccination programme will be lauded in all the media and not, I am disconsolate to say, our unknown national hero, Susan Elizabeth Walters. There is nothing I would like more than to bestow a damehood on you but, alas, I can't. Just know that, thanks to you, the people of this great nation can sleep peacefully in their beds. I am sure you will think that reward enough."

As the Premier approached the culmination of his oratorial monological masterpiece he stood, raised his voice and projected his words to an imagined audience of thousands, even though there were only the three of them in the lounge, plus the dog who remained totally ambivalent throughout the entire ceremony.

Walters became aware, as the Prime Minister stood, that Akhtar's demeanour had changed. She stole a look into his eyes. It was like she was sitting in someone's back garden on a dark night when the living room light was turned on. For a moment she could see everything clearly, maybe not take it all in during that briefest of glimpses, but it was all there. Akhtar was in the room and did not register her looking in at everything on display. The light, eventually, dimmed before being turned off altogether. The contents were there for all to see. Not furniture, artworks or decorative style. Instead, she saw embarrassment, irritation and, just maybe, fury. She really did feel sorry for this good man. It was clear he did not want to be here anymore than her.

She cringed under the weight of the laudation. "Thank you, Prime Minister," was all she could muster in these august surroundings.

The Home Secretary, Cobbold and Walters all stood. The two HST officers allowed Blair to take the lead, guiding his master through the anterooms to the most famous front-door in the world. Since working with Akhtar, Cobbold knew better than to try and guide the blind man, He had been reprimanded, on many occasions now, for offering assistance when it was not solicited. Blind people would make it clear when they wished to be given assistance. "By all means," Akhtar had said, "Ask me if

I need help but never presume. It is demeaning. If I am unsure, I will ask."

The door was opened and they stepped out into a dusk enveloped Downing Street. The indecipherable chants of the omnipresent protestors beyond the security gates could be heard above the din of rush-hour London traffic. It was not until 1982 that the official home of the British Prime Minister had been permanently cordoned off by a barrier. Although the gates are, under planning law, only considered to be temporary as they are supposed to be demountable, there are no thoughts that the street will be made accessible to all. The gates themselves were not, however, erected until 1989.

"God!" sighed Walters. "What a prick. Does he not realise I have more important things to do."

Cobbold smiled but said nothing.

Akhtar shrugged his shoulders and said, "I understand, Sue Beth, but thank you for doing that. It means a lot to me. I am sure he means well but he can come across as a little crass sometimes."

The Home Secretary held his hand out, vaguely in the direction of Walters' voice.

Cobbold grabbed it first and shook it vigorously. "It really isn't a problem," he allowed.

Walters took hold of the hand next with a firm grasp, shook it and, on impulse, flung her other arm around the man's neck. She whispered, "It is a real pity that not all politicians are like you. I feel sure that you will break through your glass ceiling very soon. Look at me and Curt. We have done it. Who would have seen, ten, twenty years ago, a woman and a black man heading up an organisation like ours? Your time will come. You are a good man, Javed."

"Thank you, Sue-Beth. That means a lot from someone like you," he whispered in response. "You never know what the future holds."

When Akhtar pulled back from the embrace, Cobbold noticed his eyes glistened in the streetlight.

The pair stepped back and allowed Akhtar to be seated in the back of his official car. It drove off, out through the gates and left them standing on the kerb.

Cobbold sighed. "Nothing, my dear, could-have-been, Baroness Walters, is more important than the Prime Minister being able to heap even more praise onto the beleaguered NHS. Praise, in his mind, goes a lot further than the billions of funding they really need! Doesn't taste very nice though, does it?"

"What doesn't?"

"Licking the Prime Minister's arse! And, what was that about? He had tears in his eyes when you let him go."

Walters harumphed. "I simply told him he was a good man."

"One of the best."

CHAPTER TWELVE

Berkshire

Apart from number ten, I presumed the next revenge would be the most challenging to complete. After exacting retribution, on behalf of the British public, in numbers three and four, number five was back to the personal. My target was the developer who had bankrupted his company which, in turn, had plunged Kate's practice into a financial abyss it could not climb out of. Although I have, in the main, worked in the pay of the public purse, I do believe it is much harder to make a go of it in private endeavours. It strikes me that if a public body makes a cock-up, it simply goes to one of the magic money-trees, growing in a garden in Whitehall, and plucks a few extra quid from its boughs. When a private organisation messes up, it is much harder for them to recover. The banks cannot pack their moneybags quick enough before running for the hills. Employees, suppliers and the Inland Revenue have to go without. And that is all they have to do, go without, whilst the owner of the business, like a mother having lost her child on the brink of maturity, has to endure unimaginable distress without any recourse to mental support. They have to pick themselves up, dust themselves down and start all over again, whilst trying to smile at the world. On top of that, the occasional arsehole could only see it as the business owner's fault, like the pissed-up idiot who knocked on our door that evening. What Kate went through at the time was unbelievably stressful, and it was only a matter of months before her first cancer showed itself. I am not sure that the two are necessarily linked but I have never believed in coincidences.

There was only one man responsible for all this. His name is Steve Carter. He is now a fantastically wealthy man as he was back then. Back then, though, in my mind, he was a crook. He engaged Kate's firm to design a block of flats and retail units in London. I shall never forget the evening Kate came home and told me the news. She was over the moon; I went out and bought champagne and we celebrated. She took on additional staff, new office space and purchased new equipment. I swear she was very nearly walking on air. If not air, she was carried along by pure adrenalin.

Then one lunchtime, about nine months later, the child was lost. Carter had appointed someone called a liquidator whose sole responsibility was to wind-up the business. A fax had been received and that was it, it was all over. Kate's hopes and dreams were shattered, broken on the floor like a porcelain doll shaken from a shelf by an earth tremor. There was no putting it back together again. She was an absolute wreck. Time does, sort of, heal but she kept thinking she was a failure. I tried to buoy her along and, I must admit, the Marines were brilliant giving me all the time I needed. About four months later, Kate got a phone call to say she had been the top candidate for a position in an international practice which could mean travelling all over the world. The dream job! Within a week, though, another porcelain doll had fallen on the floor, when she was referred to a specialist with suspected breast cancer. A couple of weeks later, it was confirmed.

Now, as I awoke in a budget hotel near the racing town of Ascot, I was going to obliterate the bastard who had jointly, with the saintly NHS, killed my beloved Kate. Steve Carter was in the cross hairs.

I had checked into the hotel the night before, having driven from Bradford-upon-Avon, using the name of my new hero again, the Prime Minister slayer, John Bellingham. The lad on the desk, he was in his early twenties I reckoned, found it nearly impossible to allow me a room as I only had cash and no form of identification. I explained how I had a job in the area the day before and it had over-run. My boss always gave me a cash float and I hadn't needed a driving licence. Eventually, three twenties tucked in his back pocket, he relented and gave me a key for the room. I signed the register giving the number of a fellow guest's car I had spotted in the carpark. All seemed in order and I was able to have a good night's sleep. If necessary, I would have slept in the van.

In the morning, I took the key back to reception, a young woman had replaced the officious young man, and went in search of breakfast. A drive-through McDonald's did the trick. The muffin was okay and the coffee was good enough. I intended to be at Carter's office at ten o'clock but traffic was light, and I arrived earlier than I had expected. I was armed with a photograph of the man lifted from the website of SC Developments. I slid the van into a kerbside parking spot about fifty or so metres from the firm's carpark entrance. By chance I spotted him, nearly missed him actually, coming toward me in a red sports car. I watched him pull into his business through the driver side wing mirror. I gave it fifteen minutes, picked the burner from the glove box and dialled the office number.

One thing about these serial financial crooks is that they have more front than a large seaside town. I don't believe that they think they have done anything wrong, just because what they do

264

is not illegal. I learnt a long time ago that the moral compass always pointed in a different direction to the legal compass. In fact, I would say, there is no such thing as a legal compass as the proponents of that particular profession seem to follow their nose rather than directions. They only follow the money and fuck anyone else who might get in their way. Steve Carter was one such person who hid behind the legal smoke that concealed their moral duty. Money is king to these people. I engaged first gear and pulled away into the traffic.

"SC Developments. Good morning. How may I help you?" the telephonist greeted me.

"Is Steve Carter there, please?"

"Who shall I say is calling?"

"My name is John Bellingham."

"Will he know what it's in connection with?"

"I doubt it," I said. "I haven't seen him for nearly thirty years."

She asked me to hold the line and her breathy voice was replaced by a turgid repetitive electronic tune.

"It was a while before she came back on the line. I had expected that. I could imagine Carter working his way through his memory and drawing a blank. I had not expected the next words. "Just putting you through, sir," the woman said.

Really, I thought. I imagined having to elaborate a little and, if I'm honest, I did not expect to get through to him.

"Mr Bellingham," he said in the familiar growl of a voice I

remember from all those years ago. "I'm sorry, I can't place you. Please forgive me."

I had thought that if I used my real name, he would refuse to speak to me. "Sorry," I said. "Did you just call me Mr Bellingham? Your girl must have got it wrong. It's John Wells. You remember? Kate Wells' husband.

A moment passed before he lied, "How nice to hear from you. What can I do for you? How's Kate doing? Gosh! I can't have spoken to her since before the pandemic."

He was effusive in his greeting. I had been nervous about using my real name as I had nothing but a scornful contempt for the crook, which I expected he had known. Kate, on the other hand, had always treated him with decent courtesy. He was always trying to persuade her to go and work for him again. In a strange sort of a way, she took his compliments and said that she must have done something right, as he always repeated what a fantastic design she had put together, and how good it would be to work together in the future. She always finished the conversations by saying she would consider his proposals, but never had any intention of picking a pen up for him ever again.

"I'm sorry to say that Kate passed away in July. Breast cancer."

"I'm sorry," he said sounding like there was sincere concern in his voice.

Now I had to encourage him out of the office. "I was in the area, your area, and had hoped to pop round and tell you personally. I'm afraid I overran in my work yesterday and am behind schedule. I'm not sure I have enough time."

"Not that you can't come and have a coffee, though, surely? I'll clear my diary for you."

I suspected he didn't really have the time nor the inclination to drink coffee with me but getting my excuse in first made him seem magnanimous in his invitation.

"That's really generous of you. "I don't know," I sighed. "I suppose, though, as you are being so gracious and cancelling your diary…. Why not! I'm just round the corner from you."

"Office or home?"

"Home," I said, before lying, "Don't know where your office is."

"No worries. I will see you there in less than twenty minutes. Be prepared for bad coffee, though. I live on my own now. Linda and me divorced a couple of years back. Took me for a packet, the bitch. Most of it went on the bloody lawyers, of course."

Good, I thought! I had wanted to check he was in his office first before I sprung my trap. I had been prepared to walk into his office and shoot the crook at his desk if necessary. He was, miraculously, falling into my clutches. I had never, in my wildest dreams, ever expected him to play into my hands. Never look a gift-horse and all that! Since making the call, I had been wending my way to his home, a biggish pile in the countryside down, as I recall, a no-through lane.

A few minutes later, I pulled off the main road and headed along the mile or so to the well-remembered pair of steel gates. To my astonishment and relief, he had no security camera and nor did he have a keypad. As far as I could tell, he would have to get out of the car to open the gates. And, incredibly, he now had no Linda. I did not wish to take anyone else out as part of my list but collateral damage always remained a possibility. so be it. I did not pass a single vehicle coming in the other direction along the remote lane. To my professional eye, he appeared careless. Not my problem, though.

I rolled past the gate on my left, pulled over as close to the hedge as I could and stepped out of the van. I opened up the back door and removed a Glock from my arsenal. A gunshot out in the countryside would not raise any alarms. The sound would be one among many from gas-powered bird-scarers, vermin control and shooting parties. I walked back to the gate, pistol tucked in my belt, hidden by my jacket, and waited for Carter's arrival. This was so easy. In fact, so far, they had all been easy. I think Cooper and me had over-complicated the second revenge. It could have been so much easier but, by God, it had been fun!

I heard the throaty roar of the engine approach before I saw the red sports car. Carter pulled off the lane and parked in front of the gates. I am not good with cars, never really had a great interest in them, but I now recognised the prancing horse badge of a Ferrari.

It was at that moment I realised I had messed up. I had never given any thought to a car's dashcam. Shit! The van wasn't an issue as it had the new plates, this time from Devon, but I did not have the luxury of a covid mask or football club's baseball cap. Idiot! I chastised myself.

He got up out of the driver's seat, extended his hand and we shook. Too late now. I had to abort, accept the offer of coffee and drive away. Or, I could go through with it? I had noticed, however, that he did not suffer too much from an egotistical vanity as the car did not display personal plates, instead showing a standard seventy-one plate indicating that the car was only just over a month old at its oldest. I could smell the newness from where I was standing and reckoned, as it was a new toy, I could ask petrol-head type questions about it. "Nice car," I offered lamely.

"Is, isn't it. It was a bit frivolous, I know, but I treated myself to this when Linda and I went our own ways," he agreed. "Ordered it the year before last you know. It was on quite a long lead-in then, but thanks to covid it only arrived last month. Tell you what, after a cuppa I'll take you for a spin. I'm truly sorry about Kate. Didn't know she was ill. Really sorry. She is... Was... Such a wonderful woman. Leave the van there. No-one ever comes down here, only the occasional tractor, and he'll give me a call if he needs you to move it. I still can't believe it about Kate."

His sympathy came across as entirely genuine. His eyes betrayed a sorrow that I did not believe could be put on. Have I got the wrong end of the stick on this one?

"What sort of horsepower is the car?" I asked wondering if that was a sensible car question to ask or not.

He went on to describe, having captured my interest, almost everything there was to know about the car. He might as well have been speaking in Chinese as far as I was concerned. I didn't know a sparkplug from a cylinder.

"I guess it has all the modern accoutrements like fantastic audio, satnav and dashcam?"

"Of course," he confirmed.

I hoped my shoulders had not visibly dropped. I was like a football with a puncture, in that, I had lost my usefulness but was still being kicked around. "I'd like a drive in it, Nice of you."

"Great, he said not seeming to have noticed my negative reaction to the inclusion of dashcam. "I turn the dashcam off, though. I don't want anyone going through my records and finding out I was doing in excess of one-fifty somewhere."

I feigned laughter. "Of course not," I agreed with relief as he turned to unlock the gates. I took the Glock from my belt whilst he was seeing to the lock.

Carter turned back to me. "Shall… What the fuck?"

"Hands on your head."

He obliged. "Look! We can talk about this. If it's money you want, you only need to ask."

"You didn't say that thirty years ago when you owed Kate that money from that development that you pulled when you went tits-up. Then, thanks to you, Kate got her cancer and now she's dead. As far as I am concerned you, in conjunction with the NHS, killed her. Just to let you know, I now have cancer myself, and before I go, I am taking out my revenge on all of you lot who have crossed me or Kate over the years."

"Why me?" he asked, fear showing in his eyes. "You know the apartments thing in London wasn't my fault. Like the whole supply chain, I felt the pain as much as anyone. Had to re-mortgage this." He took one hand from his head, not too far, and jerked his thumb in the direction of the property beyond the gates.

"It took me ages to get back on my feet," he continued. "It was right in the middle of the recession of the nineties, house prices dropped through the floor, even in London and our partner, it was a joint venture, went, as you say, tits-up, leaving me holding the baby."

I hadn't known any of this. I was almost feeling sorry for him except that I could not understand how he had been able to retain a multi-million pound property. I suppose, though, Kate and I had held on to our house but that was down to me. I also had a salary and our home was a lot more modest than the pile sitting behind the gates. His company's collapse had made the news all those years ago and quotes in the report had inferred he was a typical wideboy who had ripped all the subbies and suppliers off and was still living an apparent life of luxury. No reference was ever made to him re-mortgaging, no reference was ever made to him fighting tooth and claw for personal survival and no reference was ever made to another partner in a joint venture.

"I had even offered to pay Kate her money as I had made it all back and, to be fair, quite a bit more. Apart from Kate and about four, maybe five, others I have paid everyone up. In fact, that was the start of my marriage going down the pan. Linda was very greedy and said I should not be paying them off as she thought we might be able to have a yacht, or even a private island, in the Caribbean. Not my type of thing, though." At the last assertion, he glanced down at the car.

My face must have betrayed disbelief as he continued. "Kate had always refused my offer."

"That's rubbish," I said but without real conviction now.

"No, John. It's not. Honestly, it's the truth. She always felt that if she took my money she would be obliged to come back and work for me. She never wanted that pressure. I wanted her back working for me because she was, quite simply, the best architect I ever worked with. The money would not be a bribe, I really did want to settle all my debts. I can let you have Kate's share if you would like? It was only some years later that I found out the real reason for her not accepting my offer. I had a development we were doing up in East Anglia, so I called her. First, she thought I wanted to talk her into coming to work for me again. We met for coffee a few times in some garden centre, I forget its name, and it was then that she told me about the cancer thing, the first-time round, and she said that she wanted to make the most out of life. Your money, at the time, was plentiful enough to survive on. Over the years, I have had occasion to go to Norfolk on business, and sometimes we have met up for coffee. Not since the outbreak of covid, though."

God! I thought. I felt a sense of confusion descend. Where had the no secrets thing gone. This was a side of Kate I didn't know about. Coffee only, I wondered? I was trapped in a melee of indecision. Part of me thought I should put a bullet through his forehead whilst part of me wondered if he was telling me the truth. I searched my mind to recollect Kate's telling of Carter's calls. Not once had she said that he had offered to pay off all the money he owed. Not once had she said that they had met for coffee. I knew the garden centre and, as far as I knew, she had only been there with a mate. A mate? All I can recall is that she had said Steve Carter had been in touch and wanted her back, but she had declined the approach. I had said that that was good. And that is where we left it. No other detail. I was wavering. Bloody hell! This was a fool's errand.

I think he could feel a procrastination settling in in my brain. "I can prove it. I have a list indoors of forty-odd creditors, all of whom have been paid off in full. You can contact as many of them as you wish. One, two, ten, all of them if you want?"

Would a genuine man offer me that sort of access to information if it weren't true. Also, why would he have such a list if it weren't true, just on the off chance that a mindless idiot like me might just happen on by? I concluded he was telling the truth. The dilemma's horns were really sharp now. I had no doubt that I could pull the trigger, walk away and, probably, never be caught. Atop the other horn, if I didn't fire, he would run off to the police. "Oh, Jesus!" I said.

"Who else?" he asked calmly.

"Who else what?"

"Who else do you have in your sights?"

"Oh! You won't know them. Army people in the main. Two of them killed in cold blood and they deserve to die for their crimes."

"That's it?" he said calmly given that there was still a gun pointing between his eyes.

I didn't think I would reveal all the names and reasons as they were mostly a fancy on my part except one. "Apart from you…" I answered jutting the weapon towards him indicating that I still had the upper hand, "…a nasty piece of work who distributed some pornographic images of Kate that he filmed in secret."

His face twitched a little, no doubt at the shock of being told of something that even crossed his line of decency. And I was beginning to think that is exactly what Steve Carter was, a thoroughly decent human being.

"You're thinking what can I do now?" Carter said calmly, hands still on his head. "Do I still kill him and probably get away with it or, on the other hand, if I don't, he could go off to the police? I won't go to the police, I promise. It will take too long out of my busy schedule. There would be interviews, court appearances, adjournments, all that sort of thing. I would rather get on with life and make money."

I lowered the gun. He sighed in relief and dropped his hands.

"And one more thing," he said. "One of the charities my business supports, and I realise Kate didn't really fall into this category, is an organisation that deals with abused women. With your permission and providing you don't want the money yourself I would like to donate Kate's share to them. What do you say, John?"

I nodded my head slowly. "No. I don't need the money. I have plenty enough to see me out. Send it to the charity with my blessing."

"I will. Now, for that coffee?"

"No," I said. "I'll be on my way."

"Okay. And, John, I hope you get the bloke who made that image of Kate. Any idea who he is?"

"Absolutely. I know exactly who he is."

"Good luck!"

Thank you. And, for what it's worth, I believe you." And I did.

I opened the door to the van but paused in the opening. "One more question." Mate?

"Oh? Fire away."

"Was it just coffee with Kate?" My mind was in a turmoil. I hadn't seen this on the horizon this morning. I felt the question needed to be asked. I was terrified of the answer. "I mean…. Did you and Kate…"

"Did we have an affair?"

I nodded.

"One thing you need to know, John, is that I am a very loyal person. Have always employed the same people, have always used the same subbies and, most of all, have always been faithful to Linda. Not sure it was always reciprocated though. So, no John, we never had an affair. Never."

I nodded again. "Thank you."

I climbed into the driver's seat, started the engine, turned around and drove away. I glanced in the wing mirror and saw him holding his face in both hands. I'm sure it was relief. He had just faced down a crazed gunman who a few minutes earlier had wanted him dead. Had I, though, just fallen for the best deceit ever conceived. I drove on and never looked back again.

I had now killed four people in less than a week. If you drink too much you get drunk, if you eat too much you get bloated and, I have thought, if you kill too much you lose your edge. I wondered if the hunger for revenge was diminishing. Had I already satiated my desire?

And that was a line scratched through revenge number five!

Norfolk

Walters was sitting at the kitchen table with another woman whom Bryant did not recognise through the alcohol infused befuddlement that had overpowered him.

"Morning, Sean," Walters said as he slumped into one of the chairs, placed his elbows on the table and rested his head in his hands. "What would you like for breakfast?"

"God! Nothing," he said feeling like someone had poured a barrel of flour into his mouth whilst he slept. There was a pounding in his head comparable to a blacksmith hammering out steel on his anvil. "Maybe some coffee and water. God, I feel awful. Might need some fresh air."

"Coming right up," said Walters trying to conceal a smirk. "By the way, Sean, this is Eden Marcello, our host. This little beauty down here is Sheba. Eden is a Flight Lieutenant in the RAF Police, the Whitecaps. Get some coffee inside you and I'll come for a walk with you. Eden's not on this morning so maybe she will join us?"

"Of course. Sheba can never get enough of walking," agreed Eden.

"Pleased to meet you," Bryant mumbled.

The coffee, water and a tooth-brushing cleared the mouth and helped to alleviate the clanging in the head a little. He could not recall the last time he had felt so bad. Then the images from yesterday came back to haunt him. The whisky induced sleep had wiped the despicable visions from his mind. He knew he had to do more and quickly. He had a foggy recollection of Curt referencing a takedown as soon as possible. The exposing of the woman in the snuff video had made his mind up that they needed to get the women and children out before any others were subjected to that torment. God only knew how many others had been through that punishment but Bryant, for one, was not going to be finding out anything further. He had scratched the surface, but he would leave it to someone else to itch the sore until it bled.

It was a grey morning with a persistent drizzle hanging in the air. Leaves that still clung to branches were glistening like jewels on necklaces. The trio were all well-shielded from the damp, although Bryant had borrowed Richardson's coat which was a few sizes too big. They took the road past the pub before turning off onto a path that cut through a small stand of managed pine trees. Marcello unleashed the German Shepherd who stayed to heel until she said, "Run free."

"I suppose Curt has told you that he thinks I am getting too involved emotionally in this?" Walters started.

Bryant glanced at Marcello.

"Can't hear a thing," the RAF cop said and covered her ears. "Anyway, I am now involved as I will be acting as liaison between the HST, NCA and RAF. I was hauled in before Group Captain Ashton who gave me the order yesterday. Apparently, I was best placed to do this."

"Yeah," replied Bryant. "He has. He suggested the same thing to me last night. It is bloody difficult not to become emotionally involved when you see what I saw yesterday."

A silence ensued.

"I spent nearly six hours on that boat with Rosina," Bryant continued. "She has been through so much already and now she is a pawn in a huge chess match in which she has no real interest. All she wants is a better life. When I watched that woman being whipped to death, her back torn to shreds, I imagined Rosina hanging there. I imagined Amelia and my girls hanging there. Trouble is, Curt does not have children and cannot empathise with those feelings. I'm sure he thinks me weak. Why can't we simply finish this right now. Just go in and get them out."

"We are close," Walters allowed. "Rosina is safe now. I know she is still in the barn, but we now have microphones in there. Jonah and Rowena got them through the walls last night. We know exactly where Rosina is within the building thanks to the tracker, and we drilled a larger hole and got her two small listening devices that she can conceal down in the basement. That is where they film these videos. Or at least something like this as there are a lot more of these around the country. We have identified many more properties and with the help of the NCA we are going to take most of them out. Then, we should be able to find the rest and close them down. I met with her yesterday morning and I taught her to pick a lock so she can plant a device in the basement. If there is any suspicion that these women and children are going to be subjected to anything like you saw yesterday, we will be in there like a dose-of-salts to get them out. I don't think any of us thought that their treatment was anywhere near as bad as it is until Josh Edmundson joined in. Whilst we haven't witnessed what you did, we have heard about it. One thing is for sure, though, they are careless. Their security is, basically, woeful."

They walked on a few more paces, now progressing along the edge of a field sprouting the green shoots of next year's wheat. "Okay," said Bryant. "I'd better get back and dig out some more stuff, at least that which identifies the weirdos who partake in this stuff."

"We are mainly looking for the head of the organisation. Take him out and it falls apart at the seams."

"Surely, we're not going to ignore the perverts who pay over their money to do these things? The one I saw yesterday had forty-five thousand views and downloads. Every single one of those actions hides a sick bloke with a distorted view of what is decent or acceptable. They should never see the light of day again."

"Our conjoined aim with the NCA is to close the thing down first. Then they will put a separate team onto it to track down the clients and decide, along with the CPS, whether any crimes have been committed and launch prosecutions if necessary. We suspect that many of the forty-five thousand sickos will be from abroad and outside our reach. All files will be sent to prosecutors in those countries as well. Let's hope they're not all in the UK as we haven't got enough prison space!'"

"Try murder to start with!"

"On the face of it, yes. We don't know that the film hasn't been doctored in any way."

"Why can't we just go and take out the head?"

"We don't know who he is yet," she allowed before adding hastily, "Or she."

"Have we got anything yet?"

"A red Ferrari. It's registered in the Caribbean somewhere, though. Curt and Josh are on that today. They have access to all Ferrari records in the country to find out where it might be serviced."

Bryant shrugged his shoulders at that. "It's got to be a bloke. Surely?"

They were back in woods now and Sheba came crashing through dying ferns looking very pleased with herself having retrieved a tennis ball from deep within the darkness hidden by rhododendron bushes. She dropped the ball at Marcello's feet who picked the slimy projectile up and launched it in the opposite direction for the dog to hunt again.

After a few more minutes of silence, Walters interrupted the individual thoughts. "Anything else, Sean?"

"Don't think so. Like what?"

"I had a call from Amelia yesterday evening. To be honest it came in whilst I was speaking to the PM. Or, rather when he was speaking at me. I didn't take it, of course, but called her back when that charade was concluded."

"Daisy?"

"Yeah. She asked me to keep an eye on you. She wonders how you might be coping?"

"I think I'm okay with it now. It wasn't what I was expecting, that's all. The annoying thing is, though, Amelia reckoned that the signs have been there for a while. I didn't see them."

I know we are all meant to be treated equally in the modern world but I am still convinced that a woman possesses intuition that men lack. And, for that matter, probably vice-versa. Even me, as some men call a man-woman, I sensed there was something between Daisy and Maddie."

"A man-woman?" Bryant scoffed. "I think you have the best of both worlds. I've seen you scrub up like the most glamorous in Hollywood when you want to. No. I'm fine with it now. In fact, I am hugely proud of her. These things can normally be put right with whisky and Curt."

"Even if he doesn't understand?"

Bryant laughed. "Even if he doesn't understand! What was the Downing Street thing about."

"Utter bollocks. Total waste of time. Something he wants to take credit for and not me. Just wanted to explain that he and the nation are extremely grateful, for my dedication to duty, but there will be no formal thanks. It was a pat on the head, a tap on the bottom and a 'My word, you are a good little girl!' When it eventually comes out, it will be the NHS and the vaccination rollout that will be given the credit."

M25

I was driving back home. Was I beginning to tire of killing? I was definitely getting drunk and bloated. The pressure was building for me to call it a day. Steve Carter had made me rethink. Not everything was as it seemed on the surface. He had made me take another look and made me reconsider. First, I went through my list starting with the revenges I had carried out thus far. The first one: maybe that one was wrong? On the other hand, though, she, along with bin Laden, represented everything that is wrong with the NHS; on balance, I think, I got that one right. Colonel Matthew Pringle: no doubt about that one, he was a murderer and deserved to die for his crime. Number three: not sure I needed to do that one, I think I could have filled him full of whisky, left him the gun and he would have done it himself; life was not what he had expected after his release from prison; there was no hero's welcome and he was disillusioned with his beloved Ulster stepping out of the UK pan into the EU fire. The dog-killer: on balance, I think I got this one right but was it my fight; anyone who did what he did to a poor defenceless creature does not deserve to be a part of humanity; he was, most definitely, not all there. I am convinced that he would repeat his crime, over and over, for he could not understand what he did wrong in the first place. When Carter is added to the list, I can now say I have drawn a line through half of them.

Was I doing this for Kate? After my meeting with Carter, I could now see why we should all search out the good in everybody. I think I had raised a bloodlust to such a level I thought it would only be quenched when I had revenged all ten on the list. I was just about to contemplate and assess the remaining five when the burner phone suddenly came to life through the van's speaker system. Nearly made me jump!

"Yes," I answered.

"I've found him," said Alan Cooper.

Cooper had taken his leave from me after the revenge on the IRA man. He was finding the tasks gave him something to do. After all, ever since he had left the military, he had lived on the wrong side, and never been caught. Being caught was pretty unlikely as he still worked undercover for the government in some less than desirable places. He had contacts, though, and that's what the mandarins in Whitehall liked, plus he knew where the bodies were buried. He also believed that he would not be allowed to grow old gracefully, as the mutterings of a senile old git, as he had put it, might prove dangerous so, on one dark night he knew he would see the blinding flash of a blade and it would be all over. That was still a while off, though, as he was as physically fit as someone half of his age and while there were others to operate the computers and point him in the right direction, he still proved useful for the heavy lifting.

He had volunteered to track down one of the revenges for me. He had agreed with me, that the man was a worthless piece of shit, who had not only killed in cold blood, but had done it in the name of the Army. We knew Bill Yates was working on a farm, somewhere in Yorkshire, but we weren't sure where. Cooper, as resourceful as ever, had contacts who knew their way around social media, which is how he located him first of all. Then, yesterday, he had taken a trip to God's Own county and followed him from his work right to a pub. "A creature of habit, our Bill, he stops off for two pints of best bitter on his way home every evening. I followed him into the pub and struck up a conversation with him. I said my father used to be a farmer and I was really interested in seeing how a modern farm works."

"Was he?"

"He was actually."

"I never knew that before. Whereabouts?"

"Kent. You'll never guess what? He has only gone and invited me to go out with him tomorrow."

Cooper went onto say how he had been involved in the Falklands War when in the army, something else they had in common, but when he got back, he couldn't wait to get out. "He even mentioned you, not by name of course but it was definitely you. Same story but with his own take on it. He reckons that when you went over the lip of that Argentinian foxhole, he was scared stiff, and made a mistake, and filled the three Argies with lead. You were appalled and said that if it was the last thing you ever did, you would hunt him down and kill him. I thought yeah, that sounds familiar."

"I did."

"To this day you haunt his dreams. He expects to see you around every corner, he thinks you are every tap on the door, even jumps out of his skin if a stranger walks into the pub." He went on to describe how he had never got married or had children as the fear of you walking back into his life, and theirs, was more than a man should have to bear. He had never signed up to social media because he thought the first person to look for him would be you. It was through an Instagram post on his employer's platform that we traced him. "In short, my friend, I think it is safe to say that you have messed with his head and messed with his life. What is left of it in any case."

"How do you mean?"

"He has been diagnosed with early lung cancer. He is undergoing treatment."

"But he still works? What sort of bullshit is that?"

"What else would he do? Sitting at home in between treatments would only give him more time to think about you. Not a great life."

"What did you say?"

"I just said that it was probably an empty threat as it was nearly forty years ago, and most people who make idle threats to kill never carry them out. He thought you were deadly serious, though."

"I was. I'm on the M25 now heading for home. I'll turn off onto the M1 and join you in, what, four hours or so? Does he know you and me are linked?"

"No."

I killed the call. Had I punished him enough already? I never actually realised that anyone took seriously threats to kill them. I never have! I drove in a continued contemplation trying to go through the rest of the list. By the time I had got to the sign indicating that the M1 and Leeds was the next junction, I had made my mind up.

Norfolk

"We've got him," Richardson whooped with delight in the kitchen in Eden Marcello's home. He had just got off the phone with Josh Edmundson, who had needed to return to his office, as his boss would not allow him to bring NCA hardware to a conjoined HQ with the HST, as he had never heard of the fledgling group before.

"Nothing like working together, then," said Walters. "Where is he?"

"Not sure where he is exactly but his car is serviced at a Ferrari dealer in Oxfordshire."

"And, they have an address and phone number?"

"Yep. The address has already been checked and is false. The number is a mobile and we know who it is registered to. A bit careless."

"Who?"

"A Mr Manzoor Sajjadi."

"Bastard!" Walters spat. "So how do we find him?"

"Next time he arrives here, we let the RAF Police know."

"Eden?"

"Yeah. They have all sorts of drones that operate out of Marham and they will put one up, find him in the woods and follow him to wherever he goes next. He won't even know he is being followed. Brilliant, hey?"

"And we will get live feeds so we can track him?"

"You got it."

"So, we can now plan the rescue of the women and children?"

"I am proposing Monday night into Tuesday morning. If things go to plan."

I continued on through the list. After Bill Yates came the woman who was the head of a county's social services department in the south of the country. Over the last decade or so there has been a litany of failures to protect the vulnerable, especially young children. There has been physical, mental and sexual abuse by the bucketload. I lost count of how many there have been since Covid reared its head and gave another group of pampered prima donnas, the opportunity of working from home whilst taking public money for not doing their jobs properly.

'Don't feel like going in today? Oh dear! What a surprise! Look! I have just tested positive for the virus. Better not go in for a week or so and, unlike the private sector who pay my wages, I will still be able to draw full pay. There is a poor three-year-old girl in nasty part of town? Oh well, that's a shame, someone else will add them to their already bulging workload but, hey, I can have a week off in the lovely weather and sunbake in the garden.'

Trouble is, there is no-one left to visit these poor defenceless children. And guess what, they suffered whilst the social services back was turned. And, I thought, Mr Prime Minister, this all lies at your door.

There was the case of the little girl who had been left with the stepfather, a drugged-up piece of shit from the gutter, who had found the child's constant crying too interruptive whilst he filled the child's whore of a mother full of his own seed. They followed this by shooting up. All the time, the child carried on crying. The only reason the child continued to cry was that she had a wet nappy. Eventually the man got up to see to her with the mother in her drug-induced stupor, filming it on her thousand-pound phone. The man picked the child up, a pause in the crying was heard as the child reached out for a rare bit of love. Instead, the bastard took the child by the ankles and swung the head against the wall.

In the end, the child was discovered with nearly every bone in her tiny little body suffering a break. The mother in her drug-induced stupor then tried to claim that the child had fallen down the stairs, forgetting to delete the film from her phone. The sad thing was that the couple had been highlighted as concerning by the local social services department. Of course, they, probably rightfully so, claimed that they were underfunded and understaffed. On the day of little EJ's death, it was later revealed that there were twenty social workers away from work on covid induced holidays. That is why I had put Ursula Sullivan's name on my Wish Dead List. Following my confrontation, with the selfish group of nurses, in the pub last Wednesday, I had given more thought to Ursula's position on the list. How can an officer perform miracles, in the face of the enemy, if they are commanding mutinous forces, who don't want to be on the frontline. Many people will say that my view is distorted, but how come it is the public purse that is so over-run? That is my view anyway.

I remember Ms Sullivan standing on the steps of the courthouse, looking like she had aged fifty years from her pre-case public pictures, trying to defend the indefensible and stating that her department would learn from the findings. One day never, I thought, wondering why this same scene had to keep repeating itself up and down the country on countless occasions.

In a stupor of my own, gin induced, I had added Ms Sullivan to the list. Now, as I was driving around the M25, I had decided to strike her name off. I know a good tradesman should never blame his tools, but I think they can, especially when those tools are the cheapest money can buy and would not normally be the trade's own choice. Come on government, pay your top professionals what they deserve.

The next three on the list were not for moving. Patrick Hunter, supposedly bin Laden's handler, who had, somehow, forced the cancer specialist to start sending him images of naked women being assessed for treatment, so that he could edit them, before distributing them for profit at the expense of someone else's misery. No reprieve. Then there was bin Laden. I know I said I would not touch a hair on his head but he is definitely guilty. I never said I couldn't wrap his beard around his neck and strangle the bastard! no reprieve. Finally number ten at Number Ten. He is the worst culprit of the lot. He has brought us so much misery and now, we are hearing, he was possibly travelling the world on drunken jollies when the rest of the country was making all sorts of sacrifices. Some, including my Kate, made the ultimate sacrifice. If I only carry out one further revenge, it will be the Prime Minister. No single person deserves it more. Like the great John Bellingham, I feel betrayed by the modern-day Spencer Percival.

I am now level with the slip road that will take me onto the M1 and off to exact my revenge on Bill Yates. I had been peering down at a nearly complete thousand-piece-jigsaw sitting on the table with just five pieces to find a home for. Now, as I was nearly finished, a massive gust of wind had blown in from a clear sky and deposited the puzzle onto the floor. I wasn't sure I could be bothered trying to put it altogether again. I push the call button on the burner and it is picked up as I leave the motorway, not on to the M1 but the M11, headed north, not to Yorkshire but for home.

"Yeah," says Alan Cooper.

"Let him go. It sounds like he has suffered enough. I have had him on Death Row for all these years. It has crucified him. Every time a warder came to his cell, he thought it was for the final walk."

"Right decision, my friend."

"You can tell him that you have researched me and found out I am dead. Thanks for all your help, Coop," I said and ended the call.

And that was a line scratched through revenges numbers six and seven!

CHAPTER THIRTEEN

Sunday 10th October 2021

Norfolk

It was just gone breakfast at the conjoined field headquarters of the Home Security Team and the National Crime Agency. Empty and half-filled coffee cups were on the table, used dishes and saucepans were in the sink and a council of war had been convened. Plans were now being thrashed out to rescue the captive migrants from their purgatory.

Curtly Richardson was in the chair. He was flanked by Sue-Beth Walters, to his right, and Michael Jones, to his left, Rowena Crawford and Josh Edmundson were further along the table to the left and right respectively and at the other end was the RAF Liaison Officer, Eden Marcello, the link with the Whitecaps at RAF Marham. Retired RAF Dog Sheba sat to her owner's right hand-side; ears cocked as if she were listening in on every word to learn her role. Neither of the RAF personnel would be expected to join in other than liaise and monitor. Sean Bryant was not present having now taken his leave, task complete and had passed, despite his protestations, the evidence folder to Walters. He had shown concern about how she would react to the content, but Richardson assured him, that in spite of the emotional stuff of the last few days, she was still a professional and would carry out her duty. She now had her game head on.

"Okay," said Richardson. "All the pieces now fit in. The only thing is, as we have observed thus far, that we have never seen

Sajjadi and Burns on site here at the same time. They both seem to come and go with scant regard for the other. Sometimes they miss each other by mere minutes and other times they can be hours apart. We are now sure that it is not a scant regard but by design. They exchange messages with one another using WhatsApp. Can't tell what they are saying because of the encryption used by WhatsApp. We suspect, though, that they carefully plan their arrivals and departures from the site so that they are never here together. It would be good to have them here at the same time. Surprise will be our best weapon in what happens the day after tomorrow. Sue-Beth. Over to you."

"Curt and I are not exactly singing off different hymn sheets at the moment but we are slightly out of tune with one another. Curt wants to storm this place with all of our resources. I want to go with Josh and take down Burns separately. We need him and Sajjadi at the same time, to see if we can squeeze their balls hard enough that they will bleat like castrated rams."

"We need to treat them with the right amount of respect in the eyes of the law," Edmundson put in. "Such as properly executed arrests, rights and that sort of thing."

"Which is why you and Sue-Beth are taking Burns," said Richardson. "Once we get Sajjadi here, we won't be letting him out in a hurry. We want the bastard broken and begging to tell us everything. Contacts here, codes for clients, contacts abroad. In short, we want them all. The traffickers, the pimps, the officers and the soldiers. There must be a network of hundreds involved in this, all taking a profit from misery. I have never seen any people sink so low."

They went through the plans, repeated the plans and knew their roles inside-out.

Richardson had noticed that Crawford's demeanour, was becoming more and more sullen, as the plan was developing. "If there's something on your mind, Rowena, say it. We need to be going in there with the plan clear in everyone's head. Don't be shy. Say your bit."

"Well," she started, aware of all eyes on her. "It seems like there is a lot of emphasis about me, the only woman, going into the dormitory. It seems like it is in a bid to keep me safe. The poor little woman and...." She tailed off as Walters' eyes had taken on that menacing glow.

"For crying out loud," said Walters, keeping her frustration in check. "The reason you are going in is that you are the only woman. You are right. I can tell you it is nothing to do with sexism. It is to do with victim support. All of the victims in there are women and children. They will be scared. Rosina will be informed of our plans later today, but she will not let her compatriots know until five minutes before we go in. Can you imagine these poor women's emotions, when a couple of bruisers like these two, are suddenly in their faces?" She looked to her left at Richardson and Jones. "I would say that ninety-nine per cent of the abusers have been men. None of us around this table, except I can't vouch for Josh or Eden, are bothered about employment rights. We don't abide by the same rules of common employment. It doesn't matter our sex, race or creed, we do what we are damned well told."

Richardson could feel the heat coming off Walters now and,

as he had done before, he laid his right foot atop Walters' left as a warning to keep calm.

"I'll tell you why you're going to the dorm, Rowena. You're right, it is because you are a woman. Put yourself in their shoes. I have reviewed the evidence files as collated by Sean and I can tell you that every single one of those women and children has been raped, buggered and abused in all sorts of ways that you probably can't even imagine. I know I never could have. We also suspect that a woman was shackled by her wrists to a ceiling somewhere, not necessarily here, whipped until she was dead, later butchered and then roasted over an open grill, for the consumption of two fat perverts, who think that, if they have money, they have the right to buy whatever they want. The last thing these poor souls want is a six-feet-something man, bristling with weapons and clad in body armour, charging into their world, their only sanctuary. You cannot even begin to wonder what horrors they think might be coming their way then. You will go in there, smile and offer all the comfort you can. You will be the only woman as I will be away so it will be down to you. Got it?"

Crawford nodded. "I understand. You can rely on me to play my part." Then, reluctantly, "Sorry."

Richardson broke into the following silence with a sigh. "I concur with Sue-Beth. If I live 'til eighty, I will have lived for the best part of thirty-thousand days, and I don't reckon I will ever witness images like I've seen over the past couple of them. Your time will come. Both the police and ourselves will be joined by further personnel. I don't know who Cobbold is sending from our side but it there is a woman and I think her more suitable, I will give her the baby-sitting job."

"Right," Walters put in, equilibrium restored, "I will be headed back to Cambridge to inform Rosina of the final plan. I have booked her, so to speak, for three this afternoon. Good luck everyone. Go get 'em!"

Norfolk

I drove to Patrick Hunter's address for a reconnaissance. It was Sunday morning, so I did not expect much traffic to be on the roads, meaning less chance of being spotted. I had expected a residential street but, instead, found myself in a business area outside King's Lynn. It looked like Hunter occupied the ground floor of the premises. Bin Laden had given me the address and the ground floor had no signs advertising what it did, whereas the top floor business looked like it was a recruitment firm of some sort. Whilst there was a large window sign advertising PHA on the first floor, there was nothing to the ground floor. As I pulled into the car park, I could see there were brass plaques near the entrance but they were too far away to read.

Yesterday, I had received a call out of the blue from Cooper. I thought we had said our farewells to one another. He urged me to reconsider the revenge on Ursula Sullivan.

"Why?" I had asked.

"My social media expert has found out that she has only been in post for a couple of months and, so it seems, is doing a reasonable job at bringing the department up to scratch. I have the name of the bloke who was in charge at the time of the killing of the little child."

"Okay. Message it to me. For what it's worth, Coope, I had

taken her off the list anyway. I felt that it was not right to punish an officer when she had a mutinous crew."

It was Sunday morning and there was a black SUV in the car park. As I glanced up at the first floor, I could have sworn that I glimpsed a figure retreat from the unblinded window. Someone was in this morning. I parked the van on the other side of the car park from the SUV. I sat in the cabin of the van, making out I was checking through paperwork. What I was really working out was whether I could actually turn reconnaissance into action or not. In the end, I decided I would give it a go. I could always abort if others turned up to the office or I discovered cameras on the inside. There was, of course, no guarantee that Hunter was inside, it might be someone else entirely different.

I approached the front door, scanning the surroundings as I went. No cameras, at least as far as I could tell. Cameras were of less importance now. I only had three revenges to complete and so long as I didn't get caught, I should be able to finish my mission within the next week or so. The next two were going to be easy but the final target would prove difficult. I had sought Alan Cooper's assistance in tracking the Prime Minister so that, one day soon, I could step out of the shadows and cut his throat or blow his brains out. Cooper had declined my invitation to assist. He felt it a step too far "And to be frank," he had said. "It will be impossible. He will be surrounded by good people. You would definitely need someone on the inside. And, if you find this person, you need to trust them. You would be better using the sniper rifle, but I'm not confident you are good enough. Just call it a day when you have taken out your bin Laden character. I'm sorry, I'm not in anymore."

I pushed the intercom button for the ground floor office.

Clicks and static were followed by a man's voice. "Yes. Who is it?"

"A delivery for Mr P Hunter," I said. If he looked out of the window, he would see a white Ford Transit van so a package being dropped off would be plausible. It was weak. Who on earth received or delivered parcels on a Sunday?

"Okay," the male voice said. "Wait there. I'll be down in a second."

Down? I thought. Had I pushed the right button? Was this man being a decent neighbour in taking in parcels for the other office? I then glanced at the two engraved signs to the brickwork on one side of the entrance. The top sign matched the upstairs with PHA Recruitment whilst the one below read PHS Specialist Services. The penny dropped: PH must be Patrick Hunter's initials.

I could see through the glass set into the door and, sure enough, the man did come from the first floor. He pushed the door release to the side of the door, stepped back as it swung inward and stood in the lobby.

"Where would you like it?"

He was dressed in a sharp charcoal suit, crisp white shirt, immaculately polished black shoes and a grey tie. "I don't know. How big is it?"

"Not sure," I said. "Maybe so big by so big," I guessed indicating the size holding my hands at the requisite breadth and length.

"Okay, then. I'll have it in here." He moved to push open the door to the ground floor office.

"I'll go and fetch it from the van. Won't be a tick."

The van was stationed with three standard parking spaces and one disabled from the entrance. I pulled open the doors to the cargo bay, messed about with a few cardboard boxes before appearing to find the one I was looking for. I tugged it toward the doors, made out I was checking paperwork and hefted the thing onto my shoulder. I made out I was trying to regain my balance under the weight of the box which was, basically, the square root of nothing. I kicked the doors closed. I held the proof of delivery in my right hand as I balanced the awkward load on my shoulder and staggered toward the front door. "Are you actually Mr Hunter?" I asked. "It says here that I am only to let this parcel be received by Mr Hunter. Unusual, that one, although not unheard of. Must be something really special."

"I am," he said betraying greed in his eyes which confirmed this type of delivery was not out of the ordinary for him. "Indeed it is."

"Do you have any ID, please, sir," I requested respectfully. "A credit card with your name on it will do just fine."

He inserted his right hand into the jacket, withdrew a wallet and presented me with a black credit card. I scanned the card as I got closer. Patrick Hunter Associates it said. The cardholder was embossed onto the card as Mr P J B Hunter. I guessed this was the place from where they processed bin Laden's videos and made them into a product fit for general circulation. I was now at the core of my wife's death and felt good about it.

"Thank you, sir. That's good. Would you be so kind as to open the door again, please." I indicated the door that had now shut on its automatic door closer, a gesture not really needed as we both knew which door I referred too.

He was good enough to play right into my hands by stepping through the opening into the space obscured from the outside world by blackout blinds. I wondered what he might be expecting from a delivery. On the other hand, I guessed, just about everyone except for old fossils like me and Cooper ordered things regularly over the net. Maybe, even some of them, lost count of what they were expecting and every delivery seemed like a Christmas surprise. He might be dressed sharply but he was off guard and fuddled by modern ways. "Whereabouts?" I asked hoping that he would find a space well inside the office which, in turn, would mean he let go of the door again for it to fall back into place.

He did better than that. He jumped ahead of me and cleared a space between two desks, shoving a couple of chairs out of the way and stepping back from the void inviting me to place the package on the carpeted floor. "I must admit," he said. "It's bigger than I was expecting. Put it there."

I obliged, took a pace toward the nearest desk as if to check my paperwork. I removed my outer glove that revealed a latex inner covering for my hand, fingerprints. I had my back to him, delved into my coat, withdrew my vicious killing knife with its wickedly sharp blade and spun on the unsuspecting Hunter.

His eyes had been dancing with excitement but now narrowed with fear like a switch had been flicked inside. In my left hand was the delivery note. Except it was not a delivery note, it was the image of a topless Kate. His attention moved from the picture to the knife and back again. It was like he was following a tennis match from the court's edge beside the net.

"What's this about?" he managed to ask.

"I was given this by a friend. Do you know who that is?" I was snarling and he was, slowly, backing further into the office. Square flat ceiling lights, obviously linked to automatic sensors, triggered by his movement, came on to illuminate the space. It didn't look much like the centre of a great porn empire to me. It just looked like any old run-of-the-mill office. Desks, chairs and dividing screens, filing cabinets, computers and telephones.

He shook his head. "No," he said softly. His hand was shaking.

"That, Mr Hunter, is my wife. The man who took that picture reckons he owes you money and as a repayment he has been forced to take these videos of his patients and give them to you. You, in turn, then give them offensive titles such as Bitches About to Die, post them on the internet and rake in money at their expense. Am I right?"

Hunter closed his eyes. "No."

"What do you mean no?" I growled. "Don't answer," I continued holding up my hand with Kate's picture. "It is the other way round, isn't it? He is in charge? Not you? Yes?"

Hunter's breathing was becoming a little ragged as he tried to gulp in air. "I can't say."

"Can't or won't? Maybe you're frightened? You tell me the

truth which, by the way, I have always believed, and you can walk away from here alive. I might have to tie you up but you'll be alive. I never once believed that he was not the brains behind this disgusting venture."

He loosened up a little and could see a way out. "Okay," he said before telling me everything. Some of it I had already suspected but his account was like a cathartic release for him. It was as if all his burdens dropped from his shoulders and he was free to soar without being held down by others. Perhaps he even thought he might now be the head of the tawdry business he was in? Who knows and who cares. I had the confirmation I had been seeking and suspected. I now knew for sure that the ninth person on my list would die.

"Thank you," I said as I rammed the knife, point first, into his throat. I forced it home, blood gushing all over me, until the weapon would go no further. I wasn't sure whether it snagged on the back of the skull or one of the neck vertebrae. It didn't matter, the light vanished from his surprised eyes as quick as the lifeblood drained from his neck. The body jerked before flopping into eternity as it was only supported by my strength. I let him drop to the floor where the last of his blood gurgled, involuntarily, for one last time, from the death-cut. I assumed that the air was settling inside and found its way out through the wound. I had twisted the knife as I stabbed thinking it would be easier to withdraw the weapon on completion. There isn't a lot of clinging flesh around the gullet and his body simply dropped from the knife.

"I lied," I said to the corpse. "Scum like you don't deserve to live. You took part in the desecration of my wife's honour. Good riddance!"

I was angry but this revenge felt good. The adrenalin flowing through my body was replaced by an elation I hadn't expected. I removed all of my outer clothing and threw it down next to Hunter. Under the cheap everyday clothing, sacrificed as it was covered in blood, I wore another of those nylon inner coverall sets. There were no fingerprints and DNA would take too long to extract. Maybe some hair remnants might be included in the pile of clothing but not much. I had blood on my face but reckoned I could get away with it as long as I could get cleaned up when I got home. I would park the van on my drive this time and not at the allotment.

The incredible thing was that I had not been interrupted in my endeavours. I turned the radio on just in time for the ten o'clock news.

The business park was very quiet, just a smattering of people and vehicles. The egress road was nearly empty and I only passed a blue or, maybe, black incoming van on the way to the main road and home.

It was only just gone ten-thirty in the morning when I pulled onto the drive. I had turned up a secluded lane and swapped the plates for mine on the way back. I locked the van doors, went through the side-gate which I had left unlocked earlier and went in through the boot-room. I stripped out of the nylon under-clothing, popped it in a nylon sack and jumped in the steaming shower.

I let the hot water cascade around me, washing away any of Hunter's blood from my hair and face. Something wasn't right? I couldn't put my finger on it, though.

All cleaned up, I went through to the kitchen and fixed myself a tuna, red onion and mayo sandwich. I turned on the computer to update the spreadsheet. I checked the Drafts in the email account that Cooper had set up for me and noted another message. Weird, I thought. It read "Need the sniper rifle. Got a job and you are the only person I know with one. I'll get it from the allotment shed tonight. Still got the key you let me have."

I didn't type a response but deleted the draft as we had agreed.

And that was a line scratched through revenge number eight!

Norfolk

The cancer specialist, who resembled Osama bin Laden, was just about to carve the roasted shoulder of lamb when his phone vibrated in his trouser pocket. He stood at the head of the dining table with his wife at the other end and his two young boys, blessings from the Gods, along either side. Bowls of vegetables were set along the centre. Two bottles of wine, one red and one white, were also on the centreline of the table but covered over until a prayer of thanks had been offered up. He was pretty sure Allah would not punish him too much for imbibing a little of the infidel's weakness. The plates were in front of Yasmin who would serve the meals once he had performed the man's duty. He paused, placed the cutting tools on the huge dish and removed the interruptive device from his trousers. He looked down at the screen.

"I'm sorry, my beloveds, I have to go. There is an emergency. Please enjoy the meal without me. When you are finished, dearest, you can put a plate in the fridge for me and you can heat it through for me when I get back."

He was on official business for the company so thought it appropriate to show off his position so opened the garage door, admired the status symbol within, the gleaming red Ferrari, got in and reversed it out into the daylight. He had received a text from his courier who had tried dropping files to the office but no-one had been there to receive them. "I tried three times this morning. There is a light on but nobody is answering the door," the nervous courier had confessed when questioned by his boss.

"I will be there in fifteen to twenty minutes," said the man before asking, "Are there any cars in the car park?"

"One. A black SUV."

"He must be there, then. Has he got any merchandise with him? Anything missing from the woods?" The reference to merchandise meant one of the migrant women. He had the choice of whomever he liked, a perk of the job. He had been insulted by his Head of Operations, chief pimp, saying, on more than one occasion, that he didn't like the smelly Paki bitches that he had been pimping out to anyone who preferred the slightly darker flesh. He knew, though, that the new intake from eastern Europe was more to his fancy and Joe Burns would be like a bull let in with prize cows. Burns was a loathsome sort but, he supposed, anyone in this industry did not exactly carry a halo around with them. He was able to turn on the charm when it mattered, let out the women by the hour, by the night or forever if the price was right. In short, he did his job and the quiet, unassuming doctor from Lahore now drove the red beast as a result of Burns', and others like him, work. He recalled the day when he was approached by a people trafficker from Yemen showing him how to make good money from desperate women who would do anything to live in England. He grimaced at the memory of the unsustainable gambling debt he had built up, not having been able to survive on a consultant's earnings, but he had never looked back. Women migrants were cheap and dispensable, as they were untraceable within the borders of the United Kingdom.

He had blanched when asked if he could provide a whore for two despicable creatures to whip to death before barbecuing the victim over an open grill. That, though, had been the biggest single earner so far from the website, netting the best part of five-million pounds from all over the world in less than a week. He had been pleased that this even crossed Joe Burns' decency threshold, so they had decided to fake it. There was no way that they could have disguised the whipping but, thanks to his intervention when he had declared the victim dead, the two perverts had been taken off for some complimentary refreshments. They had then filmed Dale cutting up some pork meat before handing over loin fillets for the two creatures to barbecue. It had worked.

"It tastes like pork," one of them had said.

He had treated the woman himself with salves before dressing the wound. She still lay face-down on her bunk at Bartholomew's House but, apparently, was beginning to show good signs of recovery. It wouldn't be too long before she could start to earn her keep again. She was no good to him lying on her front in a bed. The darker reaches of the sex industry were most rewarding. Long may it continue.

The Ferrari pulled into the forecourt of the office. To the

right was Burns' car parked next to a disabled space and opposite, in the plot, was a blue Renault Traffic. Both vehicles were owned by the company which, in turn, was owned by himself albeit through his overseas investments. Untraceable, he had been told. The courier was leaning against the van's rear cargo doors but pushed himself off when he noticed the sports car pull onto the plot. He pulled over to the right-hand side and slid the car in, at ninety degrees, front on to Burns' car, taking up three parking bays.

He got out as the courier came around the rear of his car. He scanned the buildings; nothing was out of place. A lone white van was parked in a unit on the other side of the road but, certainly, wasn't unusual.

He recognised the courier as one of the gofers from Bartholomew House but didn't recall his name. "Still no show?"

"No."

"Come with me."

The pair approached the entrance. Nothing seemed out of place. He pulled a key from his jacket pocket and inserted it in the door. "If he's entertaining, he will be upstairs. I'll have his guts-for-garters if he is bouncing a whore up there whilst you're trying to make a delivery."

The door to the upstairs suite was not locked so he led them inside. The blinds were open and there was no sign of occupancy. "Check the toilets," he said. "He might have had a heart attack or something." Although unlikely for his age but Viagra played merry hell with men's blood pressure.

The courier didn't move but stood like a dumb bullock about to be led in for slaughter.

"As if reading the courier's mind he said, "A dead body can't hurt you. I've seen plenty and can vouch that they are harmless. They might smell a little but it isn't that bad. I've seen my fair share of dead ones. What's your name?" he asked the question for he could tell the courier was nervous, maybe nervous of being in the top man's company.

"Adam, sir," the courier answered trying to think where he had seen this man before.

"Okay, Adam. We'll go together."

They crossed the landing. Firstly, Adam pulled open the disabled toilet door to allow his boss to look inside. The single stall was empty. The ladies next, two stalls, both empty. Finally, the men's, one stall and a urinal, empty. The man called the lift, heard it whirr into action before the doors opened onto the first-floor landing. Empty. He let the doors close.

"Follow me," the bearded boss ordered and headed for the top of the stairs. As much as Burns was loathsome, he was reliable. This was out of character. His belly was knotting up. A recollection of a hard face came back to him. The face had drifted in and out of his thoughts for a good few weeks now. John Wells. Had the man been serious? If he had been serious, he wondered what lay beyond the ground floor office door. Maybe he shouldn't have dismissed his threats as the idle rantings of a berserk widower. He could feel his pulse quicken, his heart pulverised the inside of his ribcage and the knot in his stomach was getting ever tighter. He descended to the half-landing and sucked in air.

He held onto the polished stainless-steel handrail against the wall. He wondered if he was going to be sick. He wondered if he was going to collapse. Maybe he shouldn't have been so dismissive of Adam's trepidation.

Adam stared at his boss gripping the handrail as if letting go would cast him into the very fires of hell themselves. Then he had it, the man looked like Osama bin Laden. He had been killed, though, hadn't he? Adam had seen the images on television, with the rest of the world, of the terrorist's corpse. That could have been computer trickery, though. If bin Laden was still alive, how old would he be? This was just fanciful thinking. Surely?

Another gulp of air, A jittery glance from Adam and it was down the last flight. Eight treads including the lobby and the door was no more than four paces away. The door was not locked. Bin Laden, which was what Adam would call him from now on, depressed the lever handle, pushed the door inwards and knew, instantly, with absolute certainty, that Burns lay within. Not only did he lay within but, unmistakeably, he was dead. The metallic stench of blood, urine and shit stuck in his throat like someone had inserted a car-cleaning sponge gag into his mouth to block off the air. The darkness of the temporary tomb gave way to light as the automatic sensors sought out the intruders. They revealed a gruesome scene.

Adam managed to, in the nick of time, pick up a plastic waste bin to vomit into. It wasn't the dead body that made the doctor want to retch, with its sightless eyes, its soaking wet and soiled trousers and shirt. It wasn't the flies, where on earth did they always appear from, gorging on Hunter's mutilated throat.

It wasn't the blood-spattered walls, desks, chairs and carpet. It was none of these for he had boasted earlier that he had seen his share of dead bodies. No, it was the dawning realisation that Major John Wells was delivering on his promise. On a slightly brighter side, though, Wells had promised him that he would live if he divulged the name behind the publishing of his wife's video. He had taken the coward's way out and given up another name and not his own. To compound the matter further, he had not advised Burns that he had done this and that he might like to tread with caution from now on. If he had been so willing to betray Burns maybe, just maybe, in a vain bid to stay alive, Burns had betrayed him?

"Right," said the doctor. "You are going back to Bartholomew's and I will stay here, call the police and join you later. Before you go, though, come upstairs. There is something I want you to take with you."

He was panicking now. For the sake of Allah! He had Wells on his back and if the police came in here, he would have them all over him. Shit, he thought. Come on, come on, how did the computers link with Bartholomew's? What had that creepy pervert, Vincent Clarke, said to him in between salivating over the women and children in the films? That was it! Wasn't it? The computer here held no information but had to be linked to the main server in the basement at Bartholomew's. To gain access to the main server, a newly issued password, encrypted of course, would have to be entered manually each time for remote access. He was fairly sure it was secure from this end.

Adam was still waiting on his instruction. He had been going to tell him to take all the computers back to base but was now fairly sure that was not necessary. "Just go. And, whatever you do, tell Andrew he needs to be extra vigilant. I'll be along as soon as I can. Tell Andrew to get my room made up."

When Adam had exited the car park, he went to fetch some paper towels from the downstairs gents. He opened the door with the sleeve of his jacket. He went over all of their moves since they entered the building. He started with the downstairs office. He looked around. Apart from the door, neither of them had touched anything, so no prints in here. As he turned to grab the door handle to leave, his nostrils were assailed, through the all-pervading stench, by the smell of the contents of Adam's stomach. He bent to pick up the bin, took it to the disabled toilet, always careful not to let his fingers touch any new surface, and poured the contents into the toilet bowl. He flushed the toilet. The room doubled as a cleaner's cupboard with a Belfast sink in the corner. He held the bin under the bib-tap and swilled water into the receptacle before tipping that, too, down the toilet. He flushed the pan twice more, stared into it and was satisfied that no trace of anything was left in the clean water at the bottom of the bowl. He placed the waste bin on the coarse entrance mat by the main door and went upstairs. He wiped the outer and inner handles of the office door, was pretty sure that nothing else had been touched and went across the landing to the bathrooms where he cleaned down the handles and outer faces of the doors. Now, the staircase. Slovenly Adam had taken the steps without removing his hands from his pockets, so it was only where he had touched it himself. Bloody hell, he thought, he had used the outer handrails as guides all the way up, even stopping on the way down to prevent himself collapsing from a wave of anxiety that had nearly overcome him. Outside, he gulped in the much cleaner air not tainted by the festering presence of death, dropped the bunch of paper towels in the bin, tossed the bin in his boot and headed for Bartholomew House.

Norfolk

Something wasn't right? I had turned up to the office and discovered Hunter was there on a Sunday. He hadn't been surprised by a courier turning up. He was clearly expecting to be receiving something. I reckon that someone will be going there to make a delivery and that might raise a curiosity. I would bet my house to a pound that, somehow, there was a link back to bin Laden.

I pulled on some clothes, combed my hair and headed back to King's Lynn. I would pull into one of the other business forecourts and watch. I now had no doubt that the bearded consultant was going to be making an appearance at some stage. He would be concerned that one of his trusted lieutenants had gone on the missing list. If I was wrong, I would hang around for a few hours, go home and go to the pub for a few beers. Nothing ventured, nothing gained and nothing lost. As I went through a village, I passed the community's closed store and noticed a couple of commercial waste bins down the side. I stopped, walked back and tossed the nylon bag into the half-full container.

When I pulled onto the road in which Hunter's business premises were, I immediately saw that another van, a blue Renault Traffic, was parked in the carpark to the front. I am pretty sure it was the same van that I had passed on the way out of the estate. Christ! That had been a close-run thing. I continued on past and pulled into another car park across the road and about three units down from the target address. I was, maybe, a hundred metres away. The units on the same side of the road as Hunter's were all office buildings of brick and tile construction whereas the units on the opposite side were warehouse and retail units of low brick, cladding and plastic-coated steel rooves.

The man was killing time. He was nervous. He paced up and down, lit a cigarette and tossed away the match. He was waiting for someone.

A car appeared at the end of the road. It was a familiar vehicle. Surely, the red Ferrari was nothing more than a coincidence? Steve Carter could not be involved in some sort of lewd business so far from his home near Ascot? The thought pricked at my being. I could not see who was driving the tasty sports car as the sun was reflecting off the windscreen. I thought it was going too fast to pull into the office plot but, suddenly, the brakes were slammed on, smoke billowing from the locked tyres, and it joined the blue van in front of the unit. Carter was a very wealthy man. He had said, though, that he went to Norfolk on business. What business? I dismissed the notion as nonsense.

Hunter's SUV was still in the car park and the Ferrari nosed up to the driver's side of the stationary vehicle. The sports car's offside was closest to me, the driver's door opened and there he was. The low fences dividing the office plots from one another afforded me the perfect view of the long straggly beard, the second tie, of bin Laden. He looked around but never saw me. He must have seen the white Transit van but it wasn't out of place in a business park. I didn't even breathe as his eyes scanned in my direction.

The courier kicked himself away from the van's back doors to greet the newcomer. After a brief exchange of words, they headed for the entrance. A few long seconds passed before I saw the pair emerge into the upstairs suite. Hardly any time was spent in the office and they disappeared again. It was a while before they appeared at the front door. The consultant saw the other man out of the building, spoke in a way that looked like he was giving orders, before the man drove away. Bin Laden showed himself through the upstairs' window again, albeit briefly, before disappearing out of sight. It was quite a bit longer than last time before he appeared at the door, placed something, maybe a bucket, on the floor just inside the lobby. He disappeared out of sight for a second time, I assume he might be wiping prints off surfaces as he had a towel in his hand. Eventually, he let himself out, tossed the bucket in his boot and reversed out of the car park. He throttled the engine and the car accelerated toward the public road network. I could hear the gutsy roar from where I was parked.

I started my engine as he appeared at the door. As he pulled out onto the estate road, I was already within fifty metres of him. I slowed to allow him to pull away. As he turned left onto the main road, I sped up and turned in the same direction. I tracked him out of town. Sometimes, I was immediately behind him whilst at others I allowed up to three cars to get between us. The main road out of the town was pretty busy and following him without being detected was easy. After five minutes or so, he turned off and the traffic was lighter until we turned onto an unmade road. Here, there wasn't another vehicle to be seen. I kept back. He took a gentle curve to the left, out of sight again allowing me to speed up a little. The area was thickly wooded. I passed a Forestry Commission sign announcing Bartholomew's Woods. I had never heard of this place before, let alone been here. As I rounded the bend, I saw him travel up a slight incline before he dropped out of sight over the crest of the dusty road. This allowed me to get closer again and as I went over the brow, I saw him pull off the road to the right. He stopped, dropped his window and reached out to punch some numbers into a keypad.

I was wearing my covid disguise with a non-descript black baseball cap which I lowered over my eyes. As I passed him to the rear, the electronic double gates were opening to give him access. I glimpsed a yard beyond the entrance. There was a smart, four or five bedroom, maybe six, house to the front of the property with a barn to the rear. Nice! I glanced in my wing mirror as I continued past and noted a ground floor window, I think with frosted glass, and two first floor windows. All fenestration allowed clear views along the track through the forest. Another bend in the road allowed me to pass out of sight. I slowed the van and pulled off into a small picnic area. I would be seen approaching the house along the lane so took my walking pole out of the back. I stooped my shoulders, crouched into a shambling gait and set off back toward the property.

Every sixty or seventy paces, I would stop to rest on my pole. I hoped I was giving the impression that I was much advanced of my sixty-one years. I allowed myself a look at the windows as I got nearer and no-one could be seen. Rightly or wrongly, I assumed, the target had not spotted me trailing him. I shambled along to the house and tried to give the impression I was blown away by it. I surreptitiously lifted my gaze to take the property in. No-one appeared to take a peek from the front windows. If I wanted to, I could have walked all around the area, I thought, and not be noticed.

The house that faced the track was timber clad, absolutely in keeping with the surroundings and didn't look like it posed any access challenges. I made my mind up, I would come back later this evening, armed to the teeth, knock on the front door and complete revenge number nine.

I headed back toward the picnic area. I kept up the pretence of age, anyone could glance out of a window at any time. If they did, all they would see was a decrepit old man shambling along a country road.

Something pricked at my senses. I had a feeling of being watched. When I stopped to lean on my pole, I tried to get a sight of the woods to my left. I could hear a faint sound paralleling me in the trees. Every time I took a look there was nothing. Maybe it was a deer. Deer were prevalent in this area so what else could it be except for paranoia?

Cambridge

Walters was on her third coffee in the bar at the hotel on the Cambridge outskirts, the used crockery and cutlery from a consumed snack abandoned on the table in front of her, when she decided that Joe Burns was not going to turn up. She returned to the car, took her phone out of the glovebox and noticed a message, voicemail. She didn't play the message but, instead, selected the option to contact the caller. It rang a few times before Curt Richardson answered. "No show."

"We didn't think so. Burns hasn't showed up here to get Rosina. Interesting development, though, the red Ferrari has shown up here, maybe two to three hours ago and is still here. Come back when you can. We might go tonight. Eden has a drone up just in case he leaves again. It might be getting hot soon."

Walters engaged the car to drive and made her way back to the woods. If they were going to go tonight, she would go to the dorm and Rowena Crawford would get her wish not to be a chaperone for a load of sculking women and children. She reckoned that Rosina would be relieved to have her nearby rather than a stranger, even though female, to offer comfort and protection.

It was dark when Walters drove past Marcello's home. There was no space remaining on the gravelled drive. She pulled into the pub's car park, went around to the boot and removed her combat kit. Health and safety gone mad, she thought, as there was no evidence that anyone inside was armed. She locked the car, strolled along the short distance to the temporary field headquarters, pushed open the front door and went through to the kitchen. A sense of anticipation had built and she could feel the atmosphere, the all so familiar feeling of imminent battle. The adrenalin was firing up the combatants even though they all knew how to control it. Adrenalin was good as it instilled a sharpness that could never really be created on the training grounds. Training was just that, training. No-one was going to be tossing real grenades or firing real bullets. Some training had been carried out under live fire but the chances of getting hurt were minimal, but it did serve to keep the practice honest.

She counted nine people either sat around the table, standing

316

against the wall or leaning on the worktops. The aroma of fresh coffee filled the small room. A move to the right showed Sheba sitting at Marcello's feet. Jonah pushed a cup of coffee into her hands. Hell, what difference would another one make? Cobbold stood near the sink and had clearly taken command. Marcello, Crawford, Edmundson and one other sat around the table. Richardson, Jones and two others were either standing by the walls or leaning on worktops. She assumed the stranger at the table was a colleague of Edmundson and the two strangers standing were HST field officers not known to her.

"Ah! Sue-Beth. Come in, come in," said Cobbold. "We are all here now. Sue-Beth, this is," he said indicating the man sitting next to Edmundson at the table, "DC Giles Worthington."

"Please to meet you, ma'am," the young constable said.

Sue-Beth nodded. "Likewise."

"And, these two," Cobbold continued, "are Field Officers Amy Newcomb and Shane Thompson."

The pair, young, fit and trim, smiled at her and both offered an almost imperceptible bow of their heads.

Walters returned the nod. Nothing else was needed.

"Our friend in the Ferrari turned up early this afternoon and unusually, so I am told, is still here. We have thermal imaging cameras up high above."

"Satellites?" asked Walters.

"Drones. Courtesy of our friends in the RAF." Show Sue-Beth the images, Curt."

Richardson stepped forward to the table between the two NCA officers and turned the open laptop toward Walters. "These images are live. As you can see," he said indicating the outline of the rear-most building on the view, "this is the dormitory building. There is now a total occupancy of twenty-three women and children in there, three are out performing their duties for their owners and, the four lighter images, we believe they are in the basement. Maybe making video. We think one is our friend from the car and the other a permanent member of staff along with two migrants. I'm sorry, we can't tell whether they are women or children. It is non-stop from breakfast to lights out. Rosina Ali is in her corner bunk which we get from the tracker. The brighter images along the walls are radiators and the slightly hooded signatures are the overhead lights. There is no blazing signature coming out of the dormitory which suggests that the rads are either fed from the main building, doubtful though as the drone people seem to think it would leave a heat-print as it crosses the yard, no matter how good the insulation or depth, or, more likely, they are electric."

"What about the main house?" she asked.

"First, the bright print is most definitely a boiler." He indicated a bright image to the right side of the house. "Presently, there is one person upstairs, just taken a shower, hence the better glow. Then there are half-a-dozen lounging about downstairs. Altogether, we are pretty sure the split is seven men, including Ferrari, and three women. The women are most definitely partnered with three of the men, well they share beds anyway. There are five bedrooms on the top floor and one on the ground. As mentioned, three of the bedrooms are each occupied by a couple, another upstairs bedroom is a twin and holds two blokes

318

and the downstairs bedroom just has a single person in it. They haven't moved all morning. In fact, they have been there since we put the drones up yesterday. Maybe they are not well. One of the women has been in and out to visit."

"How can you tell the gender?"

"Good question. We are basing this on trips to the toilet. We assume that if they stand to piss, they are men."

"And the fifth upstairs?"

"This has only been made live this afternoon. First, the heating and lighting was turned on and then, shortly after the Ferrari appeared, someone walked into it. That is why we assume he is staying tonight. And, that is why we think it best to move at four in the morning. The place is as dead as a morgue at that time. I know we don't know about the new arrival but we will monitor that and can alter plans as he dictates."

"Any audio traffic?"

"None that is of any use. Too much jabbering going on, too much radio and too much television. We have been able to make out some sounds like toileting, showering and sex." We can only guess that something big is about to go down thanks to Ferrari's presence."

Maybe another whipping, thought Walters but kept it inside her head. Instead, she said," I think it will be me heading for the dorm and the women? That is, of course, if Rowena agrees?"

"Already discussed and agreed," Richardson confirmed. "We think Rosina will trust you. We need to be fluid in executing our plans, though."

"Okay. Do we know if they are armed?"

"Don't think so but it will be full operation dress."

"There is one more thing," Cobbold put in. "An interesting development this afternoon. Probably totally innocent. We can't come up with anything more sinister than a gawking tourist. See what you think?

"What's that?"

"Josh. Would you be so kind?" Cobbold asked of the senior NCA officer.

Edmundson opened another laptop. He hit the return key a couple of times, and a picture filled the screen. It was taken from the camera, across from the entrance, concealed in the woods. He moved the arrow with the mouse controls, clicked the play button and the picture started to move. A red Ferrari, the red Ferrari Walters presumed, came into frame from the right. Usual procedure, drop the window, tap the keypad, gates open, car pulls in, gates close. Whilst that was going on, a blur of white filled the screen and disappeared out of picture to the left. Edmundson moved the arrow and clicked on the fast-forward button.

"And?" asked a bewildered Walters.

"Wait a minute," said Cobbold who had moved around to peer over Edmundson's shoulder.

The policeman clicked the fast-forward button for a second time which slowed the screen to normal speed. A stooped man, maybe in his seventies or eighties by his gait, needing a stick to support himself, wearing a black baseball cap, peak pulled down low, and a covid mask, shambled into view from the left. The time showed nearly twenty-two minutes had elapsed since the white blur had passed. The man stopped and gazed at the house as if he had never seen such a vision before. He scratched his head before shaking it. He seemed to study it before turning around and heading back, stage right.

"And?" Walters repeated.

"We think it's nothing but he is the man who was driving the white van which went past as the Ferrari pulled in," said Cobbold. "We have a still of him. It's definitely him. What is your view, Sue-Beth?"

"Not sure," she answered shrugging her shoulders. "A bit weird wearing a mask out in the middle of nowhere? Maybe he's trying to disguise himself?"

"Not really," said Richardson. "My Mum never goes out of the house without a mask. Terrified of catching the bloody virus."

"Mine too," said Crawford and Jones, almost in unison.

"According to my sister anyway," continued Jones. "My mother hasn't spoken to me since I turned gay!"

Walters was biting her bottom lip now. "Umm. Maybe, he just saw the house on the way past and thought he would take a look? It is unusual tucked out here like this. I wouldn't mind it if I could afford it. There are only a few aren't there but this is, by far, the most impressive. Can't quite work out why he didn't drive back, though?"

"Amy here has a theory," responded Cobbold.

Newcomb's head jerked up like it was on the end of a string. She glanced at Walters and saw for the first time the legendary eyes boring into her. The face was serious, and she had heard other officers say that they could cut a person in half. "Well," she blushed as she spoke. "I think the old boy is too decrepit to turn the van around and by the time he had thought of it he was too far down the road. Maybe?" she finished uncertainly.

"We all agree that is plausible. Man follows Ferrari, sees it pull into an expensive home in the middle of woods and a sort of material inquisitiveness takes over," Cobbold put in again. "There are two field officers keeping an eye on the gate and one of them trailed him back to his van. He stayed hidden in the woods but watched as the old boy struggled back to his vehicle. He had to stop a few times, in thirteen-hundred-and-twenty metres, just under a mile, to rest on his stick. He was taking in huge gulps of air. There was no way he knew he was being observed."

The room was looking at Walters. She scanned from left-to-right, standing-to-sitting before, despite, a creeping doubt, that they were probably right. She finished off her coffee, shrugged her shoulders again and said, "You're probably right. If you'll excuse me? I need a piss. Should've gone at the hotel but thought I'd get back and now I've had another coffee!"

She washed her hands under the running hot water in the basin after the exquisite relief of the toilet. She looked in the mirror and even noticed the lights go out in her own eyes. Her neck was prickling. There was something in her brain that said this was all going to go wrong. Something's not right. She couldn't put her finger on it. Please don't tell me, she thought, there is a third government department digging around this case? I don't care what they all say, nobody, absolutely nobody, goes for a walk in the woods with a mask on, even if covid has made it fashionable. Bloody covid legislation is, basically, a charter for those with criminal intent to hide their features. And the old boy might have given the impression of being a shambling old fool but he still covered the best part of a mile in only twenty-two minutes. She reckoned that she did a mile in about eighteen minutes when out for a stroll and she hadn't bothered correcting Cobbold when he said just over thirteen-hundred metres was just under a mile; it was actually closer to three-quarters of a mile. Even so? Oh shit!

Norfolk

I needed an excuse to be wandering about in the middle of nowhere on a Sunday evening. I was struggling to think of one. Then I had it. I would walk up to the front door, wait for it to be answered and say I was looking for where someone, a made-up name, lived? I had tried a couple of the other houses in the neighbourhood and they had never heard of the person. They were flying off to America tomorrow and I needed to get a package of documents to them for safe conveyance to an address in Washington DC. I reckoned I could make the parcel large enough to conceal my assault rifle. The knife and handgun could be hidden under my clothing. It was cool enough that I needed a coat.

What happened if bin Laden opened the door? Unlikely as it seemed, I would have my hand resting inside my coat pocket ready to draw the pistol. I am pretty sure he would recognise me so I would lift the gun to his face and pull the trigger. No explanation needed. It might be the briefest period of face-to-face but it would be enough to send fear coursing through his entire being. He must know I was behind the killing of Hunter. No, I decided, there was no way he would open the door.

I couldn't use the Transit van again. Someone might have seen it when I was messing about earlier. I would use my own car, a Volvo saloon, and screw on a set of Transit plates. Time I was spotted by any speed camera or CCTV, I would have completed the task. The plates when checked would show a Transit van from wherever and they would not know where to start in a hurry. Plenty of time to carry out the evening's work. I mapped out a route in my head, played it through a few times and concluded that there were no cameras on the way.

I found some brown cardboard in the garage and made a parcel with a hole in one end where I could access the out-of-sight assault weapon. I didn't have any parcel tape so dug out some electrical insulation tape. This was a better solution as it made the package very rigid. I placed the finished article on the back seat of the car.

I strolled across to the allotment, it was still daylight and retrieved the last of the nylon coveralls. Although I had one revenge to go after this, I didn't expect to be on close personal terms with the Prime Minister so the coveralls did not matter. And, by then, I suppose, who cared anyway? I would either hang around to be arrested, smoking gun in hand like John Bellingham, or be dead from suicide-by-cop. At that time the sniper rifle was still in its home. I wondered what Cooper had in mind for it?

I gunned the car into life at just gone eight in the evening. I drove carefully and slowly to the target. I could feel the adrenalin begin to assail my body as I turned off the paved road onto the dirt track. I proceeded along the lane, around the curve, up to the crest of the hill and down toward the property. I pulled off the track into the space in front of the timber gates.

I opened the door, felt the gravel under my feet and collected the delivery package from the back seat, made out I was checking the name and address, and headed to the front door. The ground floor windows were hidden by drawn curtains with light seeping through where the two hangings met. Upstairs showed two of the front rooms bathed in light. I had thought, maybe, that there were only two or three people here? I now suspected there were more, and what did the barn hold. Perhaps this was bin Laden's headquarters. It struck me that I had been seriously careless. As cautious as I had been with the first one, I was equally ill-prepared for this takedown. It was only opportunism following my trailing of the red Ferrari earlier that had brought me to this destiny in the woods with a man who had desecrated the memory of my beautiful wife. Passion had overcome caution and I thought I might be in trouble.

The gravel gave way to paving flags as the path approached the front door across the lawn. The door appeared to be one of those modern composite affairs with a slim frosted window down the centre. The hall beyond was lit and I noticed a shadow cross from right to left. I was now close enough that I could hear the internal door to the left slam into its frame.

I rapped on the door, stepped back from the opening and waited for someone to appear. Another figure appeared from the right, female I guessed from the stature, followed by a wave of music, and came to greet me. An overhead light came on directly above me, casting me in a shower of illumination. The door opened inwards.

I didn't give the woman a chance to speak first. "Excuse me, ma'am," I started. "I am looking for a Mr Spencer Bellingham?" I think he is a businessman who flies to the States a lot from what I understand. His boss, my client, has asked me to deliver this package to him as he is flying out tomorrow morning. He has given me an incomplete address and the satnav puts you together with some other homes in this neck of the woods." I smiled at the pun but the woman did not catch on. "I have already tried two of the other houses in the area but they haven't heard of him. Can you help at all?"

The woman was in her mid to late twenties, Asian extraction and pretty. I wondered if she was a relation of bin Laden. She spoke English very well but with an Asian, Indian or Pakistani, accent. "I've never heard of him. I don't actually live here. I'll ask someone else." With that she disappeared back into the lounge.

The door to the left opened in tandem with the sound of a toilet flushing. An overweight man appeared. "What sort of bullshit is that?" he asked.

"I'm sorry?" I said.

I noticed he was nursing his right hand. Two of the fingers had been taped together. He didn't look like much of a threat despite his assertive opening. He had a paunch sitting on top of his belt, unkempt lank hair and a look that said he wanted to punch my lights out. "It's bullshit. No-one ever calls here. Goodbye and fuck-off."

He went to close the door but I rammed my foot forward and dragged out the rifle, discarded the wrapping on the floor, shoulder charged the door and rammed the butt of the weapon against his damaged hand. He squealed from the assault on his fingers, stepped back but not far enough to avoid the butt being rammed into his face. He now had a broken nose to add to his, apparently, broken finger or fingers. He crumpled onto the wooden flooring. I stepped in, kicked him in the face for good measure, slammed the door and smashed open the door to the lounge.

The woman was just inside the room as I entered. I slung the rifle over my shoulder, pulled out the pistol and wrapped my left arm around her throat with the gun at her temple. She struggled a little. "Still, bitch," I said.

Two other women and two blokes, neither of them bin Laden, had already stood on hearing the thumping I had given their mate in the hallway. I gestured and snarled at them to all sit on the three-seater settee. They obliged.

"Where's the bloke who looks like Osama bin Laden?" I demanded. "Doctor whatever-his-name-is."

One of the men smiled. He knew who I meant and although he possibly thought the same as me, he had probably never dared to say so to the man's face.

"Don't tell him, Adam," my captive pleaded.

"Over in the barn," Adam offered up without me needing to force the pistol harder into the first girl's head. I heard a door slam from further within the house.

Adam glanced through the French doors that went from the lounge into a floodlit palisaded yard between the house and the barn. A man, the same one as I had clobbered in the hallway, staggered across the yard to the barn. Shit, I thought, how did he get up from that? I dragged the panting woman along with me to the windows, flicked back the handle and pushed the right leaf open. Once outside, I pushed the woman back through the open door and kicked the door shut. Both the men rose from the sofa but soon sat down again when I unleashed a nine-millimetre parabellum in through the French doors, shattering the glass of the left leaf. The man had just disappeared into the barn, so I followed. The group in the lounge retreated back to their seats. I ran across to the barn doors.

It was an impenetrable wooden door with, peculiarly, a series of pad-bolts on the outside as if to lock someone or something in. They were all pulled back to the open position. I barrelled into the door as I pushed down on the lever. The lights were blinding, even compared to the artificially illuminated yard. It wasn't a barn. There were bunkbeds along the back and front walls with a row of tables and chairs down the middle. A group of women and children, mainly Asian, like the woman in the house, with a sprinkling of European women, barely adult, huddled in the far corner. The realisation dawned on me. This was a bloody prison. So, Mr bin Laden, it wasn't only pornographic images of dying women you posted up on the internet?

A dark-haired woman, very attractive save for a scar above her right eye had broken from the group and approached me as I burst in. "I am Rosina," she shouted. "I am Rosina," she repeated.

"Where's the bastard with the beard?"

Norfolk

Rosina and Amina had joined two of the eastern European women, including Petra, at the tables that divided the front from the rear bunks. Amina's son sat on his mother's bed whilst she played cards with the other three women. He observed the activity through his big, frightened eyes. The children had all been numbed into silence by their ordeals, Fazal the worst among them.

The card game was simple. None of the women really knew how to play any real games so they re-enacted the degrading way they had been forced to play, down in the basement, for the cameras. The difference was that none of them needed to remove clothing or perform depraved forfeits at the request of an audience, real or imaginary they weren't sure. Instead, they simply kept a tally of who had picked out the highest card each time. The first to ten was the winner. Then, they would start all over again.

Rosina's mind was only half on the game whilst the other half was trying to second-guess what was going on with Sue-Beth. Last time she had met up with the HST field officer, she had been informed that they would have one more meeting in Cambridge where she would be brought up to date with the final plans to get everyone out. Earlier this morning Rosina had been ordered to dress for the usual female customer. She had retired into the dank shower-room, applied make-up and perfume and dressed in a sexy outfit that she had been told was Elizabeth Bryant's preference.

Joe Burns had been due to collect her in the late morning. She had dared to start dreaming of freedom. The time ticked by and no-one came to get her. No-one came to tell her what had happened. There was no action until midway through the afternoon when the man whom she now knew as the Ferrari driver came into the dorm. He was accompanied by the oaf she now knew as Andrew. Ferrari driver had pointed at Rosina.

"Bring me that one," he demanded.

Her blood chilled. Had these brutes found out the plan? Had they tortured poor Sue-Beth into giving up the details? No, she decided, that was fanciful twaddle, none of these idiots was anywhere near a match for her new friend, client.

Ferrari driver clicked his fingers. "No," he said. "Bad idea. I'll take that one." He pointed to a blonde woman who Rosina knew to be from Romania. "Does she speak English? I think he'll value the life of a woman he thinks might be English. Like us he won't place any value on the heads of the Afghan girls."

"Yes," said Andrew.

Rosina, with relief, had retired to her bunk where she had stayed until Petra had suggested a game of cards with the pack she had smuggled out of the filming studio. Rosina had been over the moon that Amina had accepted the invitation to join in. All of the women had been through hell and worse. Amina had sunken back into herself and it was made doubly bad by Fazal's continued trauma. Rosina had decided to confide in Amina about the so-called client she kept going to see. She could trust the woman she had met on the first day now. Amina had brightened at the prospect of freedom and in the knowledge that

330

she was not actually hidden away out of sight of the rest of the world. Of course, Amina had wanted to share the news with Fazal but she had persuaded her friend that this would not be wise. Amina had been upset by this. "He just needs some hope to cling onto," she had said in her own language.

The group of four women were in the middle of a third game when a loud crack, sounding like a gunshot, shattered the evening quiet. Rosina was convinced it was a shot; she had heard thousands on the streets of Kabul. She immediately rose to her feet. Could this be it?

"Everybody," she announced, loudly but calmly, in English. "Get yourselves over in this corner." Others translated her words.

The women and children all made their way to the corner surrounding Rosina's bunk. They fell out of their own Beds; they clambered over and under the tables or they walked around the far end of the barrier. Rosina stood apart from the group.

She dared to hope and stepped toward the entrance. A man burst in. Bloody hell, as she had heard Sue-Beth say, it was oaf one or as she now knew him, Dale. In addition to the strapped fingers, he now had a bloodied nose and a bruise spread across his forehead. She stepped back as he entered but he only had eyes on the door to the basement. Seconds after he had passed through the internal door, the external door crashed open for a second time. Her hopes were lifted again.

This was wrong, though, she had been told that the HST would all be dressed in black commando style uniforms emblazoned with the insignia on just about every part. This man was wearing an over-sized coat and was grey haired. Whilst he looked capable, he was not what she had expected. He was well enough armed with a rifle slung over his shoulder and a pistol in his right hand. He pointed the handgun at her.

"I am Rosina," she shrieked. Nothing but blankness showed on the intruder's face so she repeated, "I am Rosina."

"Where's the bastard with the beard?" was all the man said.

Norfolk

The three HST pairs were in position early in the evening. Sue-Beth Walters and Curtly Richardson were planning to assail the timber fence adjacent to the barn, Michael Jones and Rowena Crawford were planning to stroll across the road, punch in the code on the keypad near the gate and, simply walk into the backyard and the last pair, Amy Newcomb and Shane Thompson, were tucked up beyond the rear fence. It would be a long wait but they were all expert in waiting out time. Boredom was a virtue of the work and they were all good at it. Richardson and Jones had even perfected sleeping whilst standing up.

The considered opinion was that this gang did not enforce their will with weapons, guns at any rate. Cobbold, nonetheless, still ordered the teams to be fully armed and armoured. No chances were to be taken, even a kitchen knife thrust into the wrong place could kill or maim. Walters kept her thought to herself that, having met Dale, there was no threat from these amateurs whatsoever. She didn't mind carrying but she did not like dressing up like a mediaeval knight charging into battle. If Dale was the epitome of their best protection, she actually felt sorry for them. It was going to be a walk in the park.

Cobbold executed a rollcall through the helmet earpieces. "Can you all acknowledge me by saying, one at a time, your names. We'll start with you, Curt."

"Curt: loud and clear."

"Sue-Beth: loud and clear."

The remaining four followed suit.

"Thank you. Solar Flare will be enabled one hour before we go. You are already set up on the secure channel. You won't hear from me now unless we have developments. We switch to silent mode from now on in."

The teams settled back and readied themselves for the assault. Cobbold, along with Josh Edmundson and Giles Worthington monitored the computer feeds. One laptop showed the view from the drone whilst the other showed the front gate. The former could switch to thermal imaging if needed. It was the latter that alerted them to a change in the status-quo.

Worthington had followed the thermal image of a vehicle progressing along the unmade road but this, in itself, was not unusual. Other residents of this arboraceous community went about their everyday business, ignorant of what was about to go down in the big house with the barn. Other vehicles, although not a regular procession, would sometimes use the lane as a cut-through. Edmundson kept his eye on the feed from the camera across the road. He watched as the dark Volvo pulled off the track and parked in front of the gates.

333

"Hello," the NCA's senior man said. "What have we here?"

Before anyone could answer he said into a microphone, an open link back to his office, "Need an index number check."

"Go ahead, Josh," came the response.

Edmundson read out the number.

Cobbold started to pace. He walked a groove between the kitchen door and the sink occasionally scratching, irritably, at the back of his head. Years ago, he would have started uttering profanities at this juncture but more recent times had seen him curtail the everyday use of swear words at the behest of one of the Home Secretaries. "My dear Cobbold," the man had said." "The regular use of swear words suggests you have a very poor vocabulary. You are better than that, I know." He hated surprises, though and he was becoming tense.

"Josh," said the speaker at the NCA office. "It belongs to a white Ford Transit registered in Buckinghamshire."

"Jesus!" exclaimed Cobbold.

"That's not the whole of it. The plate was owned by a man who was recently picked up for the killing of that IRA terrorist, Eamonn O'Keefe. Remember?"

"Jesus!" repeated Cobbold before saying into his own open line to HST headquarters in London, "Activate Solar Flare, Merlin. Now!"

"On it, Duncan," replied the office-bound nerd who had developed this useful piece of software to assist in fighting organised crime and terrorism. Only the HST currently had use of it, as feasibility committees were still reviewing the equipment's potential for use in mainline security. All electronic communication to the immediate area would be rendered useless by a microwave transmitted from an overhead drone. The drone was already up so it would be a matter of seconds before telephones, landline and mobile, broadband, televisions and radio signals were all rendered useless. The HST hardware was all set to operate on secure channels of communication. Other security services had access to these codes but officers did not know of the reason for this.

"Curt to Duncan. What's going down?"

Cobbold summed up the development to his field officers in case they had not been able to hear all of the audio exchanges from the temporary headquarters.

"Bloody hell," said Curt. "That was a gunshot. Go, go, go."

Richardson reached up to the top of the palisade, grabbed hold of the close-boarded fence timbers and pulled himself up. Except, he did not pull himself up as they collapsed from the arris rails on top of him. Shoddy workmanship he noted as he looked at the nails used in the boards. They hardly protruded enough from the boards to secure them to the horizontal rails. Richardson and Walters clawed at the boards to make an opening wide enough for them to squeeze through. Walters ducked down below the middle rail and went through first, leaving Richardson to pull off a couple more boards. The yard had been floodlit by the activation of a movement sensor. She heard the sound of the door to the barn slamming back into its frame as she forced her way through the fence.

Newcomb and Thompson had the same result as they had risen in the expectation of going over the top. Instead, they too went through. Crawford and Jones raced across the road, past the abandoned Volvo saloon, Crawford arriving first at the keypad, banged in the code they had gleaned from the video surveillance. The electric motor whirred but the gates refused to open.

"The bloody locking bar," said Jones. "We'll have to go over."

Crawford reached for the top of the gate, pulled herself up and dropped down into the floodlit yard. Jones, being the heavier and not quite so agile, dropped down beside her after struggling over the gate. They were seconds behind the other two pairs who had been positioned directly outside the fences. They observed Walters and Richardson get to the front corner of the barn closest to the entrance. They saw the blinding flash of a stun grenade from the back of the house before the noise, shocking even from this distance, caught up with the flash a split second later. Crawford spotted a man appear at the upstairs window overlooking the front entrance to the yard. Her brain slowed the image from the window down. With a sublime coolness, she noted the man raise an automatic weapon, settle on his target, her, and hesitate. She did not hesitate. As he raised the weapon, the muzzle of her own weapon was moving to engage at a faster rate than the man in the window could have conceived. Her Heckler and Koch's shot selector had been set to three. She pulled the trigger and the man disappeared in a welter of smashing glass, shards glittering in the light, and splintering wood from the frames. All three missiles had penetrated the man's ribcage in the centre of the chest. He wouldn't have been aware of flying backwards across the room and smashing into a dressing table as he died instantly from his heart exploding.

"One down," announced Jones to the others. "And he was armed. Be warned."

Crawford smiled at her partner.

"Good shooting," said Jones.

Newcomb and Thompson had followed the thunder-flash into the lounge of the house. The three men and three women had hardly moved since the courier had unleashed his shot. Their eyes were watering, their ears were ringing and they were dazed. Seconds before the first intruder had shot the glass out, the television had suddenly stopped working and the screen filled with blackness. Weird! Even if it hadn't turned itself off, they wouldn't be able to hear it now in any case. Newcomb covered Thompson while he checked for concealed weapons. There were none. Why should there be for they had been watching television less than a minute earlier. The explosion from the decoy had been strong enough to blow ornaments and glasses off tables and red wine covered the floor like blood. Thompson had carried a small fire extinguisher into the lounge room after Newcomb had tossed in the thunder-flash. No need for the precaution because no fires had started up after the explosion. More importantly, no one seemed to be badly hurt. Injuries can result if the grenades are not aimed properly. The cases do not rip apart as is usual for an explosive device so bang would be a more accurate description. The flash causes temporary loss of vision for a few seconds but leaves images on the retina for longer. The noise, up to one-hundred-and-seventy decibels, causes temporary deafness and messes with the liquid in the ear canal, affecting the balance.

Walters and Richardson reached the entrance to the barn seconds after the decoy had gone off in the lounge of the house. Walters was through the opening first. Women and children were cowering in the far corner but one woman, Rosina, was stood apart from the rest. She pointed at the door in the end wall. Walters made for the door and stood to one side in case of fire. "Who's down there?" she demanded.

"The Ferrari driver, one Romanian lady called Benita, two of the guards and the man with the gun."

"Get back over there," Walters shouted before listening in to Edmundson's calm voice from the field HQ.

"Five in the basement," he said. "Stairwell is clear. One standing apart from two with a fourth sitting on a seat or chair. The fifth is in a small room off the main area. I think he or she is hiding. The one standing on his own will be, almost directly in front as you go through the door. Targets in the house are all neutralised. Still a person lying in the bed in the downstairs bedroom. Must be in some sort of drug-induced sleep not to be woken by you lot!"

"Rowena," said Richardson. "Well done for watching Jonah's back. He's getting slow. Slight change of plan so go to the barn for your babysitting duty."

Walters took the steps descending into the basement two at a time with Richardson close on her heels. As they turned into the corridor to enter the room she whispered "Shit!"

The door filled the width of the corridor and there was no cover either side of the frame. They paused when they could hear muffled voices from the other side. Walters pointed at herself and to the right of the door before touching Richardson on the arm and indicating the left. "After three," she said. "One.... Two.... Three!" She pushed the lever down, went in and ducked away to the right.

At the same moment she registered the flash of the gun, she was slammed back by a hammer-blow to her right upper torso. She was punched back against the concrete wall to the side of the entrance. Her back slapped the wall like a fish being tossed down onto a filleting board, her head smashed back from the whip against the partition and everything went black.

Norfolk

I considered for a moment that I might take Rosina as a human shield. I decided against that and went through the door she had pointed at, found the top of a staircase and took the treads carefully. At the bottom, I turned into a corridor which led to a door, the full width of the hallway, which, presumably, led to a larger room beyond. I wasn't happy with this as someone from inside could be lined up ready to pull a trigger as soon as the lever handle was depressed. I wouldn't stand a chance.

I heard the muffled sound of a shot, or, rather, the quick zip sound of a series of shots, only three I reckoned, being fired from an automatic weapon. This was quickly followed by the similarly muffled sound, although much louder, of an explosion from, maybe, the house. I was wondering what was happening, were the residents having a falling out? Then I heard the sound of the external door to the barn being slammed back in its frame followed by footsteps, boots, on the concrete floor above me. This might be a bit tricky. I felt inside my coat for the note I wished to be discovered, should I fail at any stage in my pursuit of total revenge.

I shuffled to the door, pushed on the lever and went into the room. There he was, the bastard, standing in front of a bed holding a blonde woman close to him as a shield. Why should I care about one of his whores. If I was close enough, I could fire a couple of slugs and they would pass right through the woman and still kill bin Laden. Another man was sitting on an office type swivel chair behind the pair. A small cellular room, probably a store, was constructed in the corner.

"You promised you wouldn't touch a hair on my head if I offered you up the name of the man who forced me into taking the pictures of your wife," he pleaded.

"I did and I won't. I won't touch a hair on your head. I'll just shoot you. It's your choice as to whether you let the girl die as well. If I shoot, it will go right through her and still take you out. Depending on what it hits on the way through the girl, I might have to walk over and put another one through your worthless head. Up to you."

The girl tried to struggle, bit bin Laden's wrist and stamped on his foot. He slapped the side of her head making her silent.

"I know you met up with Patrick Hunter earlier because I was watching. You lied to me. He worked for you not the other way around. It's truly amazing what someone will tell you when you give them a chance to live."

"You were going to let him live if he told you he worked for me? But you still killed him."

"I didn't kill him for trying to conceal information from me. No, I killed him for helping you distribute images of my wife which were meant for no-one but you. Doctor!" How much money do you people need to earn? A consultant's salary not enough?"

I knew I was mocking him. The girl's bladder let go under the stress and a trail of urine soaked her shoes before puddling on the floor. "Her trousers are soaked. Let her go. Die like a man."

At that moment the door opened and a figure burst in flinging itself to the left with another one immediately on its tail moving off to the right. I instinctively moved the gun away from bin Laden and his whore and took out the first figure. I aimed for centre mass and pulled the trigger. The shot slammed the figure back against the wall. I turned to the second one…

Norfolk

Richardson followed Walters into the basement room. He was aware that his friend had been hit. The killing weapon turned toward him but he already had his Heckler and Koch raised and squeezed the trigger. It was instinct, he didn't really aim but he had practised these scenarios a thousand times. Like all of his colleagues, his shot selector was clicked to three and all of the bullets hit home on the target. Blood erupted from the head wounds and splattered the walls behind along with splinters of bone and brain matter.

"One down in basement. Sue-Beth has been hit. Should be okay. Bullet hasn't penetrated vest. I can see the flattened remnants caught by the fibres. One target neutralised. Others look like they are surrendering. Jonah, get yourself down here."

Jones was impressed at the calmness in his former partner's voice. There wasn't a sign of panic. He was sure adrenalin would be flooding through his veins. Training had taken over. "On my way."

"Targets in house are all neutralised," announced Newcomb. "Live ones secured with cuffs. Edmundson's squad are on their way." The last sentence had been in response to the faint sound of sirens approaching the site.

"Okay, Good work," said Richardson. "One of you stay there and let the plods in. One come down here. Report, Rowena?"

"A bit of panic. Plenty of tears at realising they have been rescued."

"Stay with them. I'm not sure what their status is officially."

"On my way," said Cobbold who had been listening in to the exchange over the communication line. "Shane."

"Yes."

"Go to the front gate. Remove the locking bar and if the gates don't open, stand back and I'll use the code. Then stand guard there for a while until we are sure the place is one hundred per cent secure. Keep an eye out for fugitives. I don't think there are any. According to the technology anyway. Good work everyone. Curt, how's Sue-Beth."

"Jonah's seeing to her right now."

Jones bent down over the crumpled body of Walters. It was

clear that the vest had taken the bullet. They might stop bullets from penetrating but the force is still enough to bruise, break ribs or, even sometimes, kill. Her eyes were closed but she was breathing. When she had been thrown back against the wall, the helmeted head had whip-lashed against the concrete and knocked her out cold. "She'll live. Amy. Jonah here. Go and fetch my bergen from across the road. It has a first aid kit in it."

"Affirmative. Will do."

Jones and Newcomb attended to the stricken Walters. Arrangements were made to transfer her to the RAF medical facility at Marham. Edmundson, Worthington and Cobbold all arrived separately but at the same time. They could not get entry to the yard so parked up behind the dark Volvo blocking the gates.

"Jesus Christ!" exclaimed Edmundson at the sight of the stranger's contorted body lying on the carpet in front of the set that had, until maybe today, been used to film the disgusting videos that were produced by this hitherto unnamed organisation. He had to stop himself from throwing up.

Worthington turned around, nearly barged Cobbold over in his haste to get fresh air, showed no such control. He fled up the stairs, hand over his mouth trying to stem the vomit erupting from his stomach. It was in his mouth and seeping through his fingers. He only just managed to get to the relief of the autumnal evening before he let go. He sunk to his knees and stared at the pile of embarrassment splattered in the dirt.

"First time," asked a concerned female voice from behind.

Worthington looked up and saw it was the still armoured

Rowena Crawford, assault rifle slung over her shoulder, who had followed him out. "Yes. I'm sorry. Not very impressive. Hey?"

Crawford hadn't actually been down in the basement but she had heard the narrative over the intercom link. Dead bodies were an unfortunate requisite of her role in the HST. "It gets easier. I remember my first. I wasn't sick but I cried myself to sleep for a week thinking what a waste of a life. I beat myself up as to whether I could have done anything differently."

"You killed him yourself?" Worthington asked before correcting himself. "Or her?"

"Yeah."

"I didn't even kill the man down there and it has made me like this. I'm sorry," he said again.

"Stop being sorry. Look, there's a bathroom in there. The door next to the staircase. Go and get yourself cleaned up. We'll have a beer when this is done. Yeah?"

Worthington offered a wan smile. "I'd like that."

Jones worked on Walters for a few minutes. She was beginning to show signs of coming round. "Get me a bucket just in case she chunders when she wakes up," he ordered.

The man, identified as Dale, said there was a bucket in the room in the corner. Newcomb escorted him to the room where he retrieved the receptacle. Cobbold watched with concern as the woman took her weapon from her shoulder and aimed it into the room behind Dale. Dale, bucket in hand, was followed by another man, hands firmly planted on his head. "Well," said Newcomb. "Look what we've got here."

She prodded the newly captured man into the middle of the room. Dale placed the plastic bucket to the side of the stricken soldier. Or, at least, that's what Dale thought these people dressed in black were anyway. He looked down at the blackened face. He recoiled when the soldier's eyes opened. "Jesus!"

Walters focused on the group surrounding her. First Jones, then Newcomb, then Cobbold, then Dale. She tried to sit up when she recognised the pimp's minder. She propped herself on her right arm and then, the pain hit her. Shoulder, head and neck. It all combined to send her back into unconsciousness.

Cobbold looked across at Dale. "You know her, don't you?" The tone was mocking and not really befitting of the head of the HST.

He nodded. "Burns thought she was a client who liked girls. He was delighted, in these days of equality, that we broadened our client base to include women. He thought there would be a good market in invalids as well."

"Where is your Mr Burns?" asked Cobbold.

Dale shrugged. "No idea. He was meant to have showed up this morning but no one has heard from him since."

The man with the beard had been listening in. He pointed at the corpse on the ground in front of him. "That brute of a man killed him. He was going to kill me too. He would have killed us all if it hadn't been for you and your brave people. Thank you."

"Can't say we did the world any favours," said Richardson walking over to the leader of this despicable sex ring. "Knowing what we know about you, it might have been better for us all had he succeeded."

"You can't speak to me like that."

"Says who?" Richardson snarled.

"Well…." The man started. He seemed to lose the assertion that he had the right to be treated fairly. "I thought the police were meant to read us rights, let us have solicitors, that sort of thing."

"They are. I'm sure when Detective Edmundson there…" Richardson pointed to the policeman who had fought back his disgust at the sight of the shooter's corpse and was looking for ID, "…gets his turn he will carry out everything in the correct order and manner. I don't have to do that, though. I'm not the police and, if I want to, I can pull out your fingernails one at a time or pluck out your teeth with pliers. It might be just as easy to pick up that fella's Glock and put a fucking bullet through your brain. It would save us all a lot of bother and our friend there can still take the credit." Richardson smiled.

The man blanched at the thoughts going through his mind. "No need for that. I'll tell you everything you want to know." The voice was uncertain but he was pleading for his life, or so he thought.

"I don't need to know anything. I already know it. Who's he?" the question was accompanied by a finger pointing at the dead man.

"I don't know."

"Bollocks," said Richardson as he stepped in toward the bearded people-trafficker. "Someone you don't know just happens to knock on your door at nearly nine o'clock one

Sunday evening and wants to kill you. I reckon there are probably dozens of people who would want you dead, probably starting with the women and children upstairs. I would imagine that this young lady here," he held an open hand out to the blonde woman who was now shaking, trousers and shoes soaked from her own urine, and being comforted by Crawford who had come to the room with Rosina Ali, "would be first amongst them."

The man tried to step back but found he was already up against the wall and had nowhere to go. "He fell to his knees and held his hands in front of his face and pleaded. "Please. I have children. I will tell you everything I know. Just tell me what you want." He was crying now. "I will tell you everything. Everything."

"People-traffickers. Names, routes, everything." Richardson glanced toward the women. The blonde, Crawford and Rosina. A movement had caught his eye. Rosina had a knife. It looked like Crawford's standard issue.

Rosina stood two metres back from the man who had taunted her nakedness on her first night here. "I cut his balls off."

"No, No, No. Please, please…"

"Tell us everything, then. Starting with your friend's name."

"Hold on," said Edmundson. "There's a note here." He handed it to Richardson. "Can one of you guys check his weapons? I don't know if they are safe or not?"

"Rowena," said Richardson.

"As good as done," she responded and stepped over to the crumpled body.

Richardson opened up the folded note and saw a typed message.

"My name is not important right now just in case this note has been discovered by accident. Following the death of my wife at the hands of the NHS during the so called Covid pandemic. For clarity she did not die of the virus. She was ignored by a consultant who missed her cancer returning. This bastard, in short, condemned my wife to death. I now have no purpose in living and, I assume, if you are reading this note I am already dead. I would not be taken alive until I had completed the Wish Dead List I have drawn up. Providing my fingers are intact you will be able to trace me from my prints. Military is all the clue I will give.

My house number and post code are below. Here, you will find my laptop on my kitchen table. It is on standby and there is no password so simply open it up, find the spreadsheet file titled The List and all you need to know will be there. I have encoded the list so that if anyone else should happen to open it up whilst I am still carrying out my revenges, some friends have keys to the house, they won't know what it is. The key is ntsm@sm. Ask the village vicar, Jordan, for help. He seems like a bright fellow.

"Depending where I am through the list, I entered dates and locations on completion of the revenges, you might be able to free some suspects if they have been wrongfully arrested.

"Finally, my last will and testament is on my bedside table. It contains all the names of the beneficiaries as well as the contact details for my solicitors. The solicitor has a copy of the will. The copy of the will in my bedroom also contains a confession to the revenges I have carried out which, you will find, relates back to the wish dead list. It is suitably vague so that unless you have this note it will mean nothing on its own.

"Trust me, every single name on the list deserved to die."

The note was finished off with an address. There was no indication to suggest that he owned the house but Richardson's assumption was that he did.

Richardson looked up at the whimpering man cowering against the wall. "You're a consultant? A cancer specialist, no doubt? Yes?"

The man stopped the whimpering, surprise showing on his face. He still said nothing.

"Who is this man?" demanded Richardson.

The man, whose eyes were concentrated on the point of the knife, remained resolutely quiet.

"I cut his balls off," said Rosina again.

"He is the husband of one of my patients," he blurted out. "I don't remember his name. Honestly! I'm not saying anything further until I get my solicitor."

Rosina raised the knife.

"Honestly. No." He had started sobbing again.

"It doesn't matter. We have enough in this note to find out who he is. You might have been good enough to help speed things along a little. For what it's worth, though, I think you damned well know who this is. We have had this place under surveillance for a while now and not once have you stayed the night. I suspect your friend, Joe Burns, was killed as you say, and that sent a message to you. You thought you were safe here. What you didn't realise, though, was that you had jumped from the frying pan into the fire. Trouble is, or so it seems anyway, the frying pan over-balanced and toppled into the fire with you. You have subjected the women and children upstairs to a reign of debauched terror and now, Doctor, it is your turn. You're shitting yourself. Good! You deserve it. He's all yours, DI Edmundson. We may need him again but if he has any sense, he will tell you everything for you to pass onto us. I couldn't give a shit if Rosina cut his balls off or not."

Edmundson, Worthington and the NCA had, on this night, broken up a dreadful sex ring. Richardson and the HST had rooted out the works of a people-trafficking gang. Names for both investigations would come out and, he suspected, there would be thousands of arrests. But a third thread had been sewn into the tapestry somehow. That was the next matter to resolve. Who was the corpse?

"Rowena. Get his prints. By the way, how did Rosina get hold of an HST standard issue knife?"

Richardson believed he already knew but confirmation came when the officer said, "I have no idea. Must have dropped out of its sheath in all the excitement."

"Of course it must have. Well done, Field Officer Crawford. I think you have a bright future."

The Home Security Team in the forms of Cobbold, Crawford and Jones stayed at the scene all night with Edmundson, a now recovered Worthington and some forensics bods of the National

Crime Agency. Newcomb and Thompson were stood down. Walters was stretchered into an ambulance and transferred to the medical facility at the nearby RAF base for initial assessment.

The delirious woman discovered in the single bedroom was also loaded into an ambulance and transferred to the same centre before being moved to a better facility in Cambridge. She would be scarred for life but, apart from that, she would make a full physical recovery. Making a full mental recovery was a different thing altogether. Could anyone make such a recovery? The woman was, undoubtedly, the same woman who had been whipped to death in the highly disturbing, but extremely lucrative, snuff video. It was a relief to know that the butchery and barbecue scenes had been fabricated.

Richardson returned to the temporary field headquarters and an evening with his old friend, Eden Marcello. Marcello had not been in when Richardson arrived. Instead, he settled down at the kitchen table to start writing his report but not before he had phoned Sean Bryant to inform him of the evening's events, in general, and the discovery in the ground floor bedroom, in particular.

CHAPTER FOURTEEN

Tuesday 12ᵗʰ October 2021

Norfolk

Curtly Richardson and Sue-Beth Walters found the address that had been retrieved from the note discovered in the deceased's cargo pants' pocket. Richardson nudged his Mercedes up behind Duncan Cobbold's saloon from the same manufacturer. Parked beyond the property's entrance gate, at the kerbside on the road in front of a neatly trimmed deciduous hedge, the leaves mostly gone now, were two police cars from the Norfolk force. Crime site tape had already been stretched around the entrance to the property and extended along the paths to either side of the detached house. The road was full of modest family homes, all detached, with private drives. Some had separate garages whilst others were serviced by integral garages, all doubles. Lawns were neatly cut and, in the main, hedges were trimmed in line with the target home. It was an unassuming village residence. The target property did not stand out in any way from the other homes in the street. If anything, it might be slightly better maintained. No weeds in the gravel or between the cracks of the paths, windows recently decorated and lawn cut to as close to a manicured finish as autumn would permit.

"Right," said Richardson. "We have three hours we can look around here before it becomes an NCA crime site. After we've been here, we will book into the local pub for the night, before going off in search of the local vicar. According to HQ the name given by the deceased is not the name of the vicar."

The HST and NCA teams had spent the previous day sifting through evidence collected from the property in Bartholomew's Woods. Sajjadi and his cohorts had been arrested and taken to a police station in Cambridge. They were probably now beyond the reach of the HST as they were, in effect, under police protection and in the system. Richardson had suggested that if they didn't co-operate or needed to be released, he would reacquaint them with the vengeful Rosina. He also added that a fully recovered Walters might be an option as well!

Edmundson had organised it with the police for the corpse's property to be cordoned off by the local force. The Vehicle Identification Number, VIN, had been taken from the Volvo before it had been put on a trailer and taken back to Cambridge. It helped to identify the true index number of the car which, in turn, showed that it was registered to a John Wells at the address given on the note retrieved at the scene. It looked like the man at the scene was Wells but neither Edmundson nor Richardson would be sure until biological checks had been confirmed.

A search of the car and the deceased's clothing had not yielded up any keys to the house referred to on the note.

Walters had arrived at the field headquarters with Eden Marcello and Sheba in the early afternoon. Nothing had been broken but a massive bruise had erupted, centred on her right shoulder, from her chest down into her arm and up into her neck. "It hurts like hell," was all she had said about the injury. Painkillers helped to ease the soreness and hide the headache. A scan had shown no damage to the brain. Walters, although aching, decided not to rest up like many would, walked, slowly, through the village as far as the pub and back again and again, gradually increasing her pace and mobility. She stood in the secluded back garden and practised drawing and raising her gun, complete with full magazine, eight-hundred-and-fifty-five grams in all, the best part of a bag of sugar. By the time darkness fell, she felt as if she was nearly back to her agile best.

When she had awoken this morning and put a tentative leg out of the bed, the pain came back with interest. More pills and she was ready to go again. The stiffness had returned during the short journey from the woods to the corpse's home. As she got out of the car the shoulder, and the ribs, and the neck and the arm hurt like hell.

"I don't get it," said Walters as the pair approached Cobbold who was engaged in a conversation with a local uniformed sergeant.

"Me neither," Richardson replied. "It, sort of, points to suicide by cop. But, why? This place must be worth half-a-million?"

"At least! It looks like he had one hell of a lot to lose, and to be fair, he didn't look that old."

"Grief can do strange things to people."

"Ah, Curt. Sue-Beth," Cobbold greeted his team. "This is Sergeant Haughton from King's Lynn which is about fifteen miles from here."

Richardson and Walters produced their identities and brandished them to the policeman who waved them aside.

"What do we know about the deceased?" Richardson asked. "Working on the theory it is the owner of this house?"

"Not a great deal really," the sergeant offered up. "His name is John Wells and he lived here alone. His wife died in the summer after a battle with cancer. No-one I have spoken to suspects any involvement in anything criminal and, as always seems the case, wouldn't believe it of him anyway. A neighbour, three doors down, reckons that he got on with just about everyone but the best bloke to speak to would be another John. John Sheringham."

"Does everyone living here have to be named after a Norfolk coastal town?" asked Richardson trying to lighten the mood.

"Huh? Don't think so," responded Haughton. "Oh. Hadn't thought of that. I see what you mean! Anyway, Mr Sheringham is out running errands at the moment and should be back within the hour. He has a key which Mrs Sheringham, Rachel, couldn't find."

"Okay. I guess we can wait," said Richardson before turning to his superior. "Warrants, Duncan?"

"Warrant," replied Cobbold. "In the car. One'll do." I'm sure I can be inventive if Mr Wells owns other properties. It was bad enough just getting the one. Even the judges are short-staffed thanks to covid.""

"I'll leave you folk to have a look-around, then," offered Haughton.

"Thank you, sergeant," Cobbold replied before turning to his team. "From what we know, I don't think we need forensic gear on but we had better suit up just in case."

"Could be booby-trapped," suggested Walters.

"I don't think so," said Richardson. "I think he had every intention of coming home Sunday."

"Keep an eye out. That's all I'm saying."

"Okay."

The three donned white forensic suits, nylon overshoes and latex gloves before making their way toward the rear garden through the gate to the right side of the house, between the garage and the right elevation wall of the two-storey building. The close-boarded six-feet high gate, in the same construction as the fence that joined the garage to next door's garage, was locked.

"Shit!" exclaimed Cobbold. "We won't break it down. Mr Sheringham can't be far away. We'll wait."

Richardson reached over the top of the gate and discovered a pad-bolt just hidden below the top rail. He pulled the bolt back to release it. Damn it, he thought, still locked.

"I'll give you a leg-up, Sue-Beth, and you can see if there is another bolt lower down. With a bit of luck, you will be able to reach it."

He locked his fingers together and held them at a level just below the mid-point of the gate. Walters stepped into the cradle as if she were mounting a horse and pulled herself up over the top of the gate. She held her position for a moment, gasped with the pain from her injury and peered down. Yes, there was another bolt and no, it wasn't locked with a padlock. She reached over and released the mechanism. As she was letting herself down, Richardson's phone rang in his pocket.

"Richardson," he answered.

He listened to the caller.

"Good work. Can you get an image across to me? I've only got one of the dead face which is a bit of a mess. It might disturb people if I showed them that. Not that there is much to see."

He carried on listening.

"Okay. Can you add twenty years to it? But send the original anyway."

He listened again.

"Great. Cheers."

Richardson cancelled the call and pocketed the device.

Walters had opened the gate and was now leaning against the gatepost clutching at her right shoulder. Her face was drenched in sweat from the effort.

"His fingerprints have confirmed him as Major John Wells, ex-Royal Marines," said Richardson noting his colleague's discomfort but deciding not to comment; for the time being. "We obviously got a good set of prints. They have an old photo of him which I've asked them to bring up to date. Should be across in the next few minutes."

"Let's go," said Cobbold seemingly oblivious to Walters' predicament. "And, can I remind you, we do not take anything out of here. We leave it for the NCA and local police. We can only photograph what we need and copy things. Our only involvement is to see if he has a link to our people trafficking friends. I have only negotiated you a three-hour window. Got it?"

"You alright?" Richardson enquired of his partner in a low voice. "Don't worry about him. He's only doing his job."

"I'm fine."

The back garden was given over mainly to lawn surrounded by borders. Moving along the rear of the house, past the kitchen window, they emerged onto a fairly large patio with built in gas barbecue and sink. It was more like a second kitchen but outdoors. The patio was formed like a courtyard with two sets of French doors leading back into the kitchen behind them and to a lounge to their left, in front of them was the fence, same style as before, dividing the house from the neighbour and to the right was the garden. Adjacent to the fence, but still on the patio, was a shed measuring about three by two metres. It was locked. All three looked through the doors into the house.

The lounge was a through-and-through to the front window where they could see a uniformed constable was talking to, presumably, a member of the public.

"Could be our man," said Cobbold.

The kitchen was fairly modern with wall and floor units and a generous sized counter. A round table sat in the middle of the room and as promised in the note, there was a lap-top on it, closed.

"Might as well go and have a word," said Richardson.

The team emerged back onto the drive. "Mr Sheringham?" asked Cobbold.

"Yes," The man replied. "What's this about? My wife said there had been an incident involving John."

All three brandished their identities before Cobbold excused himself to go to his car to retrieve the search warrant. Richardson's phone pinged.

"What's going on," asked a nervy Sheringham again. What sort of incident?"

Where to begin," sighed Richardson as he glanced at his phone. "Ah. That's good."

Two pictures stared back at him. The first was an image of Major John Wells toward the end of his military career and the second was a guess at what he might look like now. Although Richardson had only seen a bloodied mess of a face, he thought the images a good resemblance to the body in the woods.

"Shall we go inside?" Richardson suggested to Sheringham. "I am afraid that this might be a little traumatic. You have the key?"

"Yes."

"Booby-traps?" Walters reminded her partner in a whisper.

"There aren't any. As I said, he was definitely intending to return home the other night. He didn't count on me putting three bullets through his skull!" answered Richardson in an equally low sound before he raised his voice to address Sheringham again. "Mr Sheringham, has Major Wells ever asked you not to visit his house?"

"No. Me and Rachel can come and go as we please really. We don't, of course, but if we have anything to drop off, we just let ourselves in whether he's in or not."

"There you go, Sue-Beth."

Walters nodded and immediately flinched at the pain.

John Sheringham inserted the key into the lock of the part-glazed composite front door. A low bleeping sounded instantly. He moved inside and flicked down the cover of an alarm control panel before punching in the four-digit code. Silence. The three moved through the hall to the open door leading to the kitchen at the rear of the dwelling.

"Let's sit down at the table. Shall we?" said Richardson.

The three sat down. Richardson took the chair in front of the computer.

"He's dead, isn't he? Or been in an accident?" asked the Major's friend.

"We are pretty sure. Yes, he's dead," said Richardson. "When I say we are pretty sure, I mean, the fingerprints of the deceased proved to be a match for Major Wells. We will have to wait for formal identification, though."

Richardson opened up the last message on his phone and showed Sheringham the two images of Wells.

"That's John. Yes," the friend confirmed. "Will you need me to perform the official identification of the body? His wife died earlier in the year."

"That won't be necessary. When he was in the Marines, they carried out thorough medical examinations and we have enough to go on including dental."

Sheringham's face displayed a relief.

Walters took up the narrative. She told how they had been tracking a gang of people in, what they believed, was totally unrelated to Wells' presence in the woods, but they needed to be one-hundred-and-ten per cent sure, though. "Our investigation crossed over with a formal police investigation into another case but involving the same suspects. We think that John Wells presence has nothing to do with what we are looking into but need to check a few things out."

"Jesus Christ!" exclaimed Sheringham holding his hands up to his face.

"I delayed for a split-second. I had had a thought earlier in the day that there was a third government body involved in another separate investigation. Although it had been confirmed that there was not, it was long enough for Major Wells to shoot me."

Sheringham's eyes widened. "Shoot you?" he shook his head in disbelief.

"I was wearing armour but it still felt like I had been kicked by a horse. I passed out when I hit my head on the wall behind me."

Richardson took over and told how he followed Walters in and already had his gun ready. When Major Wells had moved the gun toward the new target, Richardson hadn't given him a chance and pulled his trigger. "It wasn't pretty. And that's why it won't be necessary for you to perform the identification."

"Jesus Christ!" Sheringham repeated. "What were the targets? Something to do with soft-porn, I assume?"

"Porn yes. Soft no," Richardson allowed. "He has, obviously, mentioned something to you about this?"

"Not really. I am putting two and two together and probably, no, possibly, coming up with five. I have a horrible feeling I've hit the nail on the head, though, haven't I?"

Richardson nodded. "Go on. You've definitely come up with four."

"Not much really. But if it helps, I can tell you what I think. I used to work in law and know that you guys like hard evidence?"

"True but we're not the police in a traditional sense. Sometimes gut feelings can unlock the right door. It is then up to us to present the evidence to whomever needs to know. Most of what we do never ends up in a court of law. Generally, our actions are pretty final and we are often dealing with desperate people. Prison-time is often the last thing on these perps' minds."

"Okay. I get it. Understand. And you think John was in that group?"

"Don't know for sure. What made you put two and two together in the first place? It doesn't matter what answer you came up with, four or five, doesn't matter."

Sheringham sighed. He sat motionless for a while, staring at the ceiling. He was clearly torn between a feeling he had been carrying around for some while and betraying a good friend. Small seconds passed before he tore his gaze from the lights. He locked eyes with Richardson. Sheringham's eyes betrayed a feeling that his conscience was fighting in favour of doing the right thing.

"Go on," Walters encouraged quietly.

He turned his watery gaze to the woman. Christ, he thought, hadn't noticed that before! The eyes! They were devastating yet captivating. It was almost as if he didn't need to say a word, those eyes were seeing right into the depths of his soul and mind. No hiding place from them. "I am not sure how to say this."

"Just try," she coaxed him on.

"It's the pornography. Please believe me when I say we only looked at it. We don't make it or anything like that."

"Was… Is Major Wells involved in making it?"

Sheringham shook his head. "Good God! No! He's a victim."

Richardson was knocked sideways by the claim. This man was a former Royal Marine. Who on earth could victimise him. He probably had the attributes to rip any perpetrator's head clean off their shoulders. What is more, he wouldn't even blink an eyelid.

"A victim?" Walters was continuing her line of polite engagement. Richardson let her continue. It was normally he who would conduct the police-style enquiries but, just sometimes, she had a knack of extracting crucial information.

Sheringham removed his mobile phone from his trouser pocket. The screen came to life. A finger-pinch here, a tap there and a finger-expansion here and an image appeared. It was a head and shoulders view of an attractive middle-aged woman with medium length blonde-silver hair. He turned the screen toward the pair of investigators, who were positioned at eleven and one, on the clock face to his six. He proffered it more in the direction of Walters who took it. It wasn't a professional image; it might even have been frozen from a video clip. She looked up from the screen.

Sheringham let out a breath. "That is a picture of Kate Wells."

"Major Wells' wife?"

"Yeah. She passed away from cancer. John was pretty shook up. A couple of times he had had one-too-many and would talk about revenge. Evening the score for Kate." He sucked on a dry mouth. "Can I have some water, please?"

Richardson got up and opened a wall unit door.

"At the other end," said Sheringham. "Close to the sink."

Richardson took out a pint glass, moved to the sink, ran the cold tap for a moment before filling the glass. He placed it on the table in front of Sheringham. Sheringham took a gulp and wiped his mouth with the back of his hand.

"Take your time, Mr Sheringham," said Walters. "I can see from the photo that Mrs Wells has bare shoulders and assume that this is from a broader image?"

"Yes. It is. You can open it up if you like. I don't know why but…" He caught his breath before continuing. "Well. I wanted to save her dignity."

"I understand," she responded and placed the device down on the kitchen table. "No need at the minute. Will need a copy of the file, though. How come you have nude pictures of your best friend's wife?"

Sheringham again looked at the ceiling as if there was a cue-card hanging there. He had a habit of holding his breath for short seconds. He returned his eyes to the woman's before letting out his breath. Jesus! This was difficult. "This is where I ask for your understanding. Look.... I often hear of witnesses saying things that are then taken to court and afterwards.... Well, it is like they become a victim. As far as I am aware, it was only John who knew what Rachel and me did. I don't want it getting out to anyone else. We would be looked down on in the village. Laughed at."

"Mr Sheringham," Richardson put in. "A man, probably your friend, is lying dead in the woods and, if we are to believe a note discovered at the scene, there are others so I think we need to dispense with the niceties. Don't you?"

Walters, unusually, put a calming hand on her partner's arm. "Were you and Mrs Wells having an affair?"

"Good God! No," answered Sheringham decisively. "We most certainly were not."

Walters and Richardson remained quiet.

"Well. We, that's Rachel and me, sometimes use soft porn to spice things up a bit. You know, in the bedroom department."

The pair still remained silent. They simply returned his looks with stares of their own. Sympathetic and understanding in her case but aggressive and malevolent in his.

"One day we were searching for something new and we discovered a new category. I clicked on it and scanned some thumbnails. We both saw that image straightaway. My wife said that she thought it looked a little like Kate. I agreed, so we opened it up and it was Kate. We were shocked by what we found. We thought very seriously about going round to see them about it. Kate was still alive at that point, but we thought better of it. Chickened out really, I suppose. After Kate died, and after the funeral, I went to see John having plucked up the courage to show him."

"Can I just pick up on something there," said Richardson. "You went to see him, not came to see him?"

"He wasn't in so I went to their allotment. They loved it there. Not for us, although we would often sit in summer months having a sundowner or two up there, all four of us. It was absolute bliss."

"What was his reaction when you showed him?" asked Walters.

"Nothing really. Nothing that I think most people in his position wouldn't do." Sheringham shifted in his chair, diverted his gaze for a moment before returning it to the two opposite. The faces showed no emotion. They remained silent so Sheringham continued. "Well, he said that he would kill the bastard. But I just dismissed it as the thoughts of most people in his position. Lots of people say it as a figure of speech but never really mean it."

"Was he violent?" asked Walters.

"Not at all. Well, not really anyway. It's just that… well, sometimes if he had a few drinks he would talk about the revenge thing against no-one in particular. I am beginning to wonder, though…

"A little while back, maybe a couple of weeks ago, the receptionist from the surgery disappeared without leaving a note. The police came around the village and asked some questions but never really seemed to get anywhere. Now, I'm sure I am barking up the wrong tree, but I am wondering if he had anything to do with it?"

"Male or female?"

"A woman. I can't really remember her name, I moved to another surgery when I had a falling out with her. Mind you, I was never alone in that regard. Most people felt the sharp edge of her tongue at one time or another." Sheringham let out a small chortle. "Maybe, it's that there are so many with a motive, that the police haven't yet got down to W? Horrible thing to say, though, is that most people actually think good riddance. Oh, her first name's Simone. Can't remember her surname.

"John also mentioned he knew who had made the video of Kate."

"Who?"

"He never told me but I think it was filmed in their study which is upstairs. You can see the bottom corner of the picture behind Kate? I am sure that is the same picture on the wall upstairs."

"Shall we go and have a look?" Richardson suggested.

The two crime-fighters followed Sheringham from the kitchen, through the hall and up the carpeted stairs to the first floor. They crossed the landing into a back bedroom which was utilised as a study. A small desk in the far corner with a swivel chair turned to one side where the last occupant had vacated it. The wall to the left was given over to shelves with a mix of books and family pictures. Family pictures that consisted of Major Wells, his wife and two older couples both depicted in grainy colour images.

"No children?" Walters enquired having noted the absence of any other photographs.

"No. No children. And, both single children themselves. Worth a bloody fortune, I reckon!"

"Parents?"

"All dead."

Richardson closed the door to reveal the wall behind the chair. Hanging there was a print of an olden days' sailing ship, warship judging by the rows of guns along its starboard side. "Can I have another look at the phone, please?" he asked.

Sheringham handed it to him after holding his thumb against the button at the bottom. Realising the picture was shown in the zoomed-in version, he expanded the picture. "Here," he said handing over the phone. This time the image showed Mrs Wells from the desktop upwards including her exposed chest. The picture, though, was the very same.

Richardson handed the device to his partner who glanced at the screen and up at the picture. She nodded before handing the phone back to its owner.

"Okay," said Richardson. "Let's go and take a look at the laptop. Mr Sheringham, is there any chance you could rustle up some coffee? Is there a shop in the village? I'm starvin'."

"Yes, and yes."

"If you would be so good, could we have two large coffees, one white and one black, please?"

"Yeah, of course. Do you want me to stay around?"

"Wouldn't mind. I would like you to bear witness to what we are doing.

"Just wondered. In that case, I will make three coffees,"

Richardson opened up the lid of the laptop and sure enough, and as promised in the note, it whirred into life. Sheringham searched out the coffee and filters and loaded the machine, poured in the water and set it off gasping and glugging. Walters excused herself to go in search of the shop for some vital sustenance.

Richardson retrieved his phone from his pocket and opened it up to the image of the note they had found on the deceased's corpse. The original had been handed back to Josh Edmundson. He located the file on the machine and opened it. No password protection, also as promised. It was an Excel document. There was no heading but it went directly into sub-headings. Listed in Row 1 were NAME, LOCATION, DATE and, in the final column, Y / N. Under the first heading, the spreadsheet was split into twenty-five cells, the second into seventeen, the third twenty and the end column consisted of just a solitary box.

Each cell in the first and second macro-column consisted of a series of numbers, some Arabic and some Roman. The third column seemed to use similar numbers in the first two cells, with each pair followed by further sequence or sequences of numbers. The final column had one letter inserted into most of the rows, Y, except for the fifth, sixth and seventh which had N. Richardson took the Y to mean yes. "So, Major Wells," he said to himself. "you have five hits against your name, three unsuccessful and two not yet carried out or executed." Executed! Now there was the word. He assumed that Manzoor Sajjadi was row nine.

Some of the numbers in the third, the date, column were MMXXI. No problem with that one, Richardson smiled. They were carried out in 2021. What the hell did the others mean? It looked like the date in the month, if that's what they were, were all the same. Why encode this list anyway? Anyone who found this file wouldn't have a clue what it all meant. Richardson had a degree in applied mathematics but still needed a little more to go on to crack the codes. The dates were clearly dates, but only served to confuse. The first two digits, he surmised, were the day in the month on which the revenges had been carried out. Trouble was, they were all the same day going on the encryption. The following cells really made no sense as there was sometimes more than one word, if that's what the codes represented, for each month? What did NTSM@SM mean?

The coffee machine finished its hissing and spluttering and John Sheringham re-appeared from the hall having taken himself out of the way to the lounge. Richardson had heard him talking, he assumed to his wife, to say that he might be out for a little while. "John. Do you have any idea what the letters NTSM@ SM might stand for?"

"No. Can't say I do. Shall I pour the coffees now or do you want to wait for your partner to get back?"

"No. Pour them now. That would be great. She would want hers to cool down first anyway."

Sheringham opened the fridge door and took out a half-full bottle of milk. He smiled. This was like doing one of those infernal puzzles of his wife's. "John never kept sugar in the house so I am afraid there isn't any. If you want a sweetener, though, I can help you there." He pulled out a plastic box and plopped a white pip into his own coffee before holding the container up to Richardson.

"No thanks. Not for either of us," he said. "Are you always that well prepared? I have mine black and Sue-Beth has a small amount of milk."

"Have to be ready when a cup of tea or coffee is proffered. So many people don't sweeten their drinks any longer and, would you believe, don't even have sugar in their houses."

Richardson was always prepared as well and felt behind his back for his concealed Glock 19. The reliable solidity had often given him the strength to go into potentially dangerous situations without a second thought.

The front door opened and in walked Walters laden with a handful of treats. She hated the unnecessary use of plastic bags so would contort her upper body into all sorts of shapes to avoid committing the cardinal sin of using plastic. Two packets of crisps were hanging from her mouth. She started to unload the shopping onto the kitchen table. "Good. I smell coffee. Mr Sheringham, I got you a sandwich, an Aero and some crisps. Is that alright?"

"No thanks," he replied. "Rachel is doing steak and kidney pudding tonight with jam roly-poly for afters."

"Christ. That sounds good," said Richardson. "You were gone a little while, Sue-Beth? I'll have the extra, by the way. I'm bloody starvin'."

"Had a quick look in at the church of St Michael before popping across to the pub and booking us in for tonight. Well, two nights as they only allow a minimum booking of two nights. Then I went to the shop and bought the food. The woman on the till told me where the vicar lives."

"This probably is out of order but would you like to join Rachel and me for dinner tonight. There's always plenty as she always makes up more for the freezer."

"No. It's not out of order. I'm sure dinner will be much appreciated. We don't need to stand on ceremony like the police themselves. In fact, the Home Sec would encourage it. He hates expenses forms and all that sort of thing, so we are asked to be resourceful!"

Richardson rummaged in his pocket and pulled out a thumb-drive. He found a USB slot and inserted it. He got to work and loaded the file onto the drive. He sipped on his coffee, opened a sandwich and the first packet of crisps, and began to eat. Walters had taken a chair at the table and was doing the same.

"Right," said Richardson. "We have a file which, for some reason is written in code. Apart from the years written in Roman numerals, I am at a loss to explain any of it. The reference on the note recovered at the scene has an acronym, NTSM@SM. Any help would be appreciated."

"Sorry," said Walters shaking her head. "You're the brains of the team. Down to you." She winced again as she raised the sandwich to her mouth.

Snacks and coffee finished, Richardson said he would like to have a look around the rest of the house.

Starting upstairs he looked in again at the study, probably the second bedroom if it hadn't been commandeered as an office, but there was nothing more jumped out at him so he moved onto the main bedroom. Usual furnishings really. Big bed, bedside tables, each with books on, one with a manila A4 envelope, and a dressing table with mirrors. A full-height mirror was fixed to the wall at the end of the bed running from the skirting to the coving. Beyond the mirror was a wardrobe built into the wall. A door led through to an en-suite bathroom. Richardson went over to the bedside table with the envelope. It wasn't sealed and he removed the contents. A small stapled A4 document was inside, the last will and testament of John Wells, along with a smaller unsealed DL envelope. Inside the smaller packet was a single A4 printed sheet. It contained, as promised, a confession to the revenges enacted on those detailed in the wish dead list. That was it, no detail. He scanned the will but there was nothing, except all his worldly goods were to be realised and bequeathed to a local cancer charity. He placed the package back on the table. "Nothing in there. Leave it for the NCA to see if they can make anything more of it." He assumed that this was Wells' side of the bed. The book on this side was a tome about Second World War battleships. The book on the other side of the bed was a bible. He shook out both volumes but nothing floated free or dropped out.

The third bedroom, smaller than the main, was similarly kitted out although the bed, still a double, was smaller. The wardrobe must have been behind the mirror of the main bedroom. The back-bedroom had two single beds each with a side table. A family bathroom stood next to the back bedroom. Nothing remarkable. He would leave it to forensics from here on in.

Off the kitchen downstairs was a utility or boot room, beyond this was a shower room with toilet bowl and basin, off the hall there was the front-to-back lounge and dining room with three-piece suite, dining table with half-a-dozen chairs and a smattering of coffee tables in the sitting zone complete with television and DVD player. At the bottom of the stairs was another door that led to, what presumably would be, a study but was, instead, a second lounge area, a snug, complete with second television.

He returned to the kitchen. "I think we're done here for now, John. Forensics will be here in the morning. Do you know the other key-holders?"

"No. Afraid not."

"Shit! We'll have to get the locks changed. Can I have your key, please?"

Sheringham removed the front door key from his ring and handed it over to the copper. "Shall we say six this evening?"

"Do well. Thank you," said Richardson taking the key and

putting it in his pocket. He glanced at his watch. Three-thirty. They let themselves out the door.

Richardson and Walters looked down the road to where Sheringham had pointed out his house before driving off to the pub and a bit of warmth. The heating hadn't yet kicked in in Major Wells' home and it was unusually cool for mid-October.

Before heading for the pub, they called in at the vicar's address. No-one at home so they would call back again this evening.

A roaring fire was on the go in the bar, which doubled up as a reception area. There were two occupied tables with three men to each. All six, if they had been talking, were quiet now as the large black man and the tall blonde woman entered. The eyes followed them to the bar. Walters introduced herself to the barman and gradually, behind them, conversations started up again. The server took a key out from a small cupboard next to the till and handed it to her. Only one key, thought Richardson and smiled.

She noted the look on her colleague's face and knew what he was thinking. "Only one room left. Oh, and it's twin beds," she said.

"Fair enough. If you were planning on anything, I would still turn down your approaches."

"I can hardly move so I don't think I am planning anything except for a glass of beer and a bloody good sleep. Anyway, it is still the wrong time. We're still not ready."

They found their way to the room, threw the bags on their respective beds and sat down. Walters winced again.

"Why?" asked Richardson.

"Why what?"

"I mean, what made a distinguished veteran go on a killing spree?"

"He did?" I've obviously missed something here?"

"Well, I'm not one-hundred-per-cent sure but the list on the computer, I think, is a list of victims, no, revenges. Maybe the codes will tell us something but it has got me at the moment. The note said that every one of them deserved to die."

Walters' face held a puzzled look.

"Sorry. I forget you have been out of it for a couple of days. You are aware of the note we found on the body back in the woods?"

"Yeah. A little. I think I recall you saying it might cast light on why he did it and if there is any link to the people traffickers?"

"We did. Basically, it is a list of names, encoded, which we believe to be the names of victims."

"How many?"

"Ten on the list but I don't think each one has been carried out."

"Why don't we go get a beer and see what the locals have to say?"

"Good idea re the beer. There were six locals in the bar when we came through and, I daresay, they will come up with ten different theories on what's happening including flying saucers and ghosts and all that crap."

They returned to the bar. The silence that had greeted them on the way in was, again, deafening as they approached the counter. Richardson was pleased to note they had his favourite Adnams' Ghost Ship on tap and ordered a pint and a half. He could hear, rather sense, mumbling beginning behind him so turned around whilst his beers were being poured.

"Gentlemen," he announced, immediately putting paid to any resumption of chattering. "Who would like a drink?"

All six finished off their glasses and, one-by-one, approached the bar. Words of thanks, good man and cheers were directed at him as they slowly accepted their libations and retook their chairs.

"And, one for you," Richardson said to the server. He took the change from two twenty-pound notes and joined Walters at a small table to the side of the bar.

"You two looking into the death of John Wells, then?" asked a man with red hair and a pasty face.

"If he's dead?"

"We heard that he had been murdered in Bartholomew's Woods," said a man, with unruly face hair, from the other table.

"A body has been found," answered the black man. "But we haven't had a positive ID yet."

"He was a good man," said pasty face.

"One of the best," agreed scruffy beard.

The cordon around the house hadn't even been in position for a whole day yet and clips of information were already leaking out. In fact, Richardson had expected the place to be packed out by now. He didn't think he would get any more out of this group. Not yet anyway.

Another man, who had his back to them turned around, and with his arm reaching back between his legs, dragged his chair to the newcomers' table, holding his beer out in front of him. Richardson hadn't noticed before but there was a dog collar protruding, only just, at the neck above the blue sweater.

"Chinese whispers," he said. "Oh, I'm sorry. Allow me to introduce myself, I'm Jordan Cruz and I am, for my sins, the vicar of St Michael's across the way. I saw you, umm…?"

"Sue-Beth Walters, Home Security Team," she replied. "And, this is my partner, Curtly Richardson." She indicated her partner with her right hand and winced in pain.

The man had a swarthy Mediterranean sort of a look. "Pleased to meet you," he said extending his right hand. "Oh, forgive me. It's still my natural reaction when introducing myself to new people." He was referring to one of the Covid restrictions that forbade the shaking of hands.

Both of the HST extended their hands automatically too. "We've both been double jabbed! I'm not even sure that rule is still in place," said Walters screwing up her face again.

"Are you okay, Ms Walters?" asked the vicar.

"Ignore her. She's milking it for all it's worth. She only got shot! Anyone would think it something serious. Interesting name for these parts, Reverend?" observed Richardson.

"Oh dear! Ah! Yes, it is, isn't it. My real name uses many

Spanish forenames and ends with Rivero. The heathen English, present company excluded, struggled with it so when I went to theology college, they gave me the name of Jordan, instead of Rivero, that is River Jordan, and Cruz which is Spanish for cross. It has stuck ever since and, to be honest, I don't mind. Quite like it actually."

Ah yes, realised Richardson, that was the real name HQ had come up with for the man-of-the-cloth.

"Your name, Ms Walters," Cruz continued, "is vaguely familiar. Did you used to be in the army?"

A shadow flashed across Walters' face briefly. "Sue-Beth, please. If you insist on titles, it is Mrs. I did, why?"

"I used to be a chaplain in the army and I recall some years ago a female officer, a major I think, leading a team of commandos down a crocodile infested river, in some African country, to rescue two diplomats or something. Was that you?"

"It was. Don't believe everything you hear. Firstly, I was only a Captain at the time and second, there weren't any crocodiles within two hundred miles of where we were. Finally, we weren't commandos either, we just happened to be on hand. And it turned out that the so-called diplomats had just gone along for the ride for a booze and drug filled evening in the jungle with some locals. Never told anyone of their plans. The evening, though, turned out to be several days. The diplomats, apparently, ended up with a collection of STIs!"

"Oh dear! You're a legend."

"Enough of this idol worship!" joked Richardson. "Now she's

been shot the legend will only grow. She'll be the saviour of the whole world before you damn well know it. Now, what can we do for you, Mr Cruz?"

"Well, we know you are hear in relation to John Wells?"

"Uha!"

"I just thought you might like a little background. Kate, his late wife, God rest her soul, used to be fairly regular at church. Well, until the cursed pandemic. Then, in her latter months she couldn't make it at all because the cancer had taken over too much. So, I visited her at home and something she said has always stayed, lurking in a way, at the back of my mind."

"Go on."

"Well, during one of the visits, John went out for a spell. I sat at Kate's bedside while he was gone. She dozed mostly but, all of a sudden, she reached out and put her hand on my arm. 'Jordan,' she said. 'John is an angry man and doesn't suffer fools gladly. He blames everyone for my condition from the receptionist at the surgery through to the Prime Minister.'"

"Understandable."

Pasty face got up from his chair and manoeuvred past them. "Don't believe anything he says to you. He's a proven liar. He keeps telling us that his mate walks on water and turns water into wine."

The four remaining at the two tables laughed raucously and raised their glasses in further salute to Richardson and Walters.

Cruz knew what was coming next.

"Tell you what, though," continued Pasty-face. "He is a dab-hand at turning our cash into his beer." He laughed at his own humour.

Richardson had thought Pasty face serious at first but after a brief hesitation laughed along politely. "And?" he asked turning back to the man-of-the-cloth.

"She went on to say that she feared John would exact revenge on those he blamed. I am afraid, though, other than the two book-casing the list at either end, I don't know who might lay between them or how many there are. She asked me to look after him. I would pop round from time-to-time but he, although remaining polite, sort of shunned my approaches saying he had dealt with death many times before and would have to deal with it again. He didn't lose sleep about someone dying. That's not true, though. I don't know whether you have met him yet but John Sheringham is a very good friend. I feel I have let Kate down and not protected John from himself."

"Yes, we have," said Richardson ignoring the last comment.

"Okay. You might know then that John S has wondered about the disappearance of the receptionist from the surgery?"

"Yes. He did say that."

"Did you also tell you that he confided this information to me and we both discussed it with the police. They said they would get back to us if they wanted further information but they were very busy because of short-staffing and extra requirements policing covid."

"No. He didn't. Did you speak to a detective or one of the uniforms on the ground?"

"The latter. Did I do wrong? Forgive me, but police are police."

"Possibly. We'll check it out. There is one thing you can help us with, though. We retrieved a note from a scene of interest to us."

"Bartholomew's Woods?"

"Can't confirm that. It led us to a laptop and a certain file. Unfortunately, the file was a list and was totally in code. I think the key to the cipher is NTSM@SM. Any ideas?"

Cruz thought for a moment. "Not sure, but it might be that it is New Testament St Matthew at St Michael's. It was Kate's favourite gospel. We have a bible that is always left in the nave showing a different scripture each day. Kate would often drop by to read a little. I also know that she always kept a copy at home as well."

Oh, bollocks, thought Richardson. The bloody book on her side of the bed. One for the morning before forensics get there. "Thank you, Mr Cruz. We know where to find you?"

Cruz removed his wallet from his back pocket, took out a stack of business cards and passed one each across to the pair. Richardson and Walters reciprocated.

CHAPTER FIFTEEN

Wednesday 13th October 2021

Norfolk

During the night Richardson had woken with the case to the forefront of his mind. He looked across at Walters who was asleep. Usually, he would wake her and seek solutions to his doubts, but looking across at her exposed flesh, showing above her nightshirt, in the lurid orange light, from the car park, seeping in around the blinds, the bruising to her shoulder and neck looked blacker than ever. Best let her sleep, he thought. At least while she was sleeping, she wasn't using her arms and wincing every five minutes! That was unfair, for he knew many, even in security, who wouldn't hesitate to take a month or so off after sustaining such injuries. She was as hard as teak.

It seemed like the bedside bible held the key. He would make sure it was collected first thing in the morning before Edmundson locked the place tighter than a nuclear flask. He also needed to get his hands back on the laptop. There might be further clues to be found and, although he had promised Edmundson he would leave it on the table, he wanted to examine it more thoroughly before letting the NCA have it. Cobbold would use his influence to calm any stormy waters that might result.

He fell back into a fitful sleep only coming wide awake when Walters stirred. He opened his eyes and admired the tenacity she showed as she forced herself out of bed to face another day. A wince here and a groan there and she was upright. She worked hard at getting flexibility back into her shoulder and chest. She moved to the blinds, pulled on the cord and let the wolf-light of morning into the room. She did not care that she was only wearing a slightly oversized tee shirt and, potentially, on view to the rest of the world. When serving in the army, suffering from inhibitions was not the best of attributes. Richardson sat up, rearranged the pillows behind his back, stretched his naked torso, and flexed his hard muscles making them ripple. When he did that, it made the small silver tattoo, emblazoned on his left breast, of a Suffolk Punch trapping a football, come to life.

Walters had always been captivated by the image of the horse seeming to dribble the ball across his heart. Above the emblem of his wife's favourite football club was the word, in upper case letters, 'FOREVER' and, below it, was inked 'GILLIAN.' When he had fallen in love with Gill, he had also fallen for the county of Suffolk, and did his best to fit in. Drinking Ghost Ship was no real sacrifice but adopting his wife's family's soccer team was more of a challenge. Since her death, Richardson always looked for the Tractor Boys' results first, closely followed by his native Aston Villa.

He studied her. Maybe the bruising was not as black as it had looked during the dark hours. There were tinges of yellow now mixed with blue and black. "Any better?" he asked.

"I think so. I'll see after I've showered."

Knowing her penchant for cold showers he said, "Make sure you return the bloody temperature back to normal!"

After cleaning up they made their way down for a welcome breakfast washed down with coffee from a bottomless pot. Feeling satiated, they reviewed the investigation so far. "If you're up to it," said Richardson, "would you go back to Wells' house and bring back the bible from the bedside table in the master bedroom? Then get the laptop from the kitchen table."

"Of course I'm up to it," she snapped.

"Good. I'll go back to the room and bring Duncan up to date," he said whilst digging in his pocket. "Here's the key. I don't think there'll be a problem if the local uniforms are on duty. If there is, though, give Duncan a ring and get him to put pressure on where it matters most. He said to forget changing the locks, when I messaged him last night, the NCA could pay for that."

Walters stood. Richardson noted it would have been easier to slide the chair under the table with her left arm but she moved around to use her right. Every little bit helps! "Oh!" he said. "And go round to the surgery and find out the full name of the receptionist who is supposed to have disappeared. Mr and Mrs Sheringham think it was Simone Thatcher or something like that? I couldn't find anything on the news sites about it."

An hour later he was sitting at a different table in an empty restaurant having been back to the room to bring Cobbold up to date with their work thus far. When housekeeping had appeared, he took his leave and returned downstairs. He had chosen a corner table with a clear view of the entrance. There were no windows overlooking his laptop screen and the glass cabinets, containing village nick-nacks, that might reflect the screen were off to his right. The distressed, another word for crap in Richardson's mind, mirror was hanging to his left. There was absolutely zero chance of any busy body getting a glimpse of what he was doing. Not that they would understand it in any case. Nor did he understand it yet.

The bible and computer were sitting to one side. Walters now sat opposite, her back to the room, a position she detested. Old habits and all that! It forced her, out of those old habits, to occasionally look behind her. Each time she peered toward the entrance or the doors to the kitchen, her face creased with the stabbing pain that served as a reminder that she still had a way to go on the road to recovery.

No glass or mirror behind him, he commenced the cracking of the code. He opened the bible to line up with the relevant passages. He was pretty sure that the code was simple and that the numbers referenced individual letters in the text. The first one showed itself as an "S." He made a second copy of the spreadsheet, inserted a second row for each existing row, and displayed them next to each other on his screen. In the second sheet, he found all the codes that might be an "S," and began populating the newly created interim rows. There were seven others in the first macro column, name, one in each of rows one, four, five, six, nine and ten whilst there were two in row seven. He changed three cells in an incomplete Location column and another sixteen in the date column. Every first letter in the date column started with an "S. He therefore assumed that each second letter in that column was a T, making the abbreviation of Saint. It could work, he thought, the dates were not shown as numbers but Saints' days. He now went through and changed every code that had the same cipher as "T" to that letter. "What was the name of the receptionist who disappeared? He asked of his partner.

"Simone Thackeray."

"Bingo. I think we have just solved a disappearance and, for that matter, a murder." Richardson turned the screen toward her. "Look. I've filled in all the "Ss" and the first one in the name column begins with an S and has six letters. I also reckon her surname starts with a T and has nine letters. I reckon it fits?"

"Okay. I see. Why do the second and third columns only have six entries, and the fourth has eight? I assume that the Ys and Ns in the fourth column are yes and no? In which case, why are some Y and some N?"

"I think he has only carried out revenge against numbers one, two, three, four and eight. For some reason he must have aborted five, six and seven. Nine and ten haven't been carried out yet. I'm not quite sure why number five has a location and date but has a no in the final column? It could be that number nine is our man Sajjadi as that is where our paths crossed and Wells hasn't delivered on that one yet. The surname certainly starts with an S."

"I'm actually glad that he didn't get the bastard. It would have been too good for him. Surely, he will, at least, go away for life for trafficking, modern slavery, pimping out and a whole lot more." The memory of the women in the outbuilding in the woods flooded back into Walters' mind. Ah! That's where Major Wells comes in? That little video of his wife pissed him off a bit?"

"Possibly." Richardson asked that she get in touch with the local police and check the date of Simone going missing and, if they were proving obstructive, get Cobbold to lean on them. Then she was to go and rouse Sheringham and get him to take her across to the allotment. "Have a good root around and see what you can find. Probably nothing but you never know."

Richardson carried on his code cracking. He was so convinced he had it right that he started to fill in the cells to Simone's name. It transpired the woman's full name was, indeed, Simone Thackeray. It took a little time but he was making good progress.

"Excuse me, sir," a woman's voice broke into his concentration. He had been so engrossed in the code-cracking that he hadn't heard her approach. "Do you mind if we have the table back? We need to start setting up for lunch."

He pressed Control and S before closing the lid. Tucking the machine under his arm, he left the restaurant and returned to the bedroom. Housekeeping had been in and given it a tidy. First thing he did was to text Walters with his whereabouts. The only place he could really set up was the narrow dressing table.

Richardson completed the grids and listed out the results. Simone Thackeray; Thornham; St Therese of Lisieux 2021; Y. This was followed by Matthew Pringle; North Sea; St Francis of Assisi 2021; Y, Eamonn O'Keefe; Birmingham; St Bruno of Cologne 2021; Y, Tyrone Smith; Bradford-on-Avon; St Justina of Padua 2021; Y, Steve Carter; Ascot; St Simeon Senex 2021 ; N, Bill Yates; no location and no date; N, Ursula Sullivan; no location and no date; N, Patrick Hunter; King's Lynn; St Paulinus of York 2021; Y, Manzoor Sajjadi' no location, no date and no status and, finally, First Lord of the Treasury; no location, no date and no status.

The next task was to find out the dates on which the various saints' days fell. This completed, he saved his work and closed the computer. He had also made a separate list which he now photographed and sent to Duncan Cobbold.

"Duncan," he wrote. "The attached is a list of names, locations and dates. I believe that if you enter these names in the national computer, you will find that they are either missing persons or unexplained deaths. Let me know as soon as possible. Find out about any progress that has been made into the investigations. Get back to me. Should have things tied up here shortly. Can't see that he was linked to the people traffickers. Curt."

Just as he finished sending the message the phone rang in his hand. Sue-Beth Walters was displayed on the screen. "Hi, Sue-Beth."

"Curt. You'd better get over here quickly."

"How far away is it from the pub?"

"Two or three-minutes' walk, I reckon. No more."

He listened to her instructions and set out for the allotments. It turned out to be closer to ten minutes than two or three.

"What've you got?" he asked as he strode onto John Wells' plot. "And, good morning, Mr Sheringham. Lovely meal last night. And thank you for your assistance again."

"It's under the floor of the shed."

Richardson followed Walters across the deck and into the shed. Inside a trap door stood open and exposed a steel container, protected by board insulation, which had also been opened. He looked down on a small arsenal of weapons. There were long guns, handguns and knives. In addition, there was body armour, scopes and night vision equipment. "Christ," he said. "Talk about being well prepared."

He walked away from the shed and stood in the allotment. He called Cobbold. The phone was answered inside three rings.

"Give me a bloody chance. We're onto it," was Cobbold's greeting.

"Great. You need to get the local plods back here, along with forensics."

"Christ!" exclaimed Walters pointing at a bit of ground to the edge of the cultivated plot. "Look at that. It looks different to the rest. Looks like sand or clay or something has been dragged up from deeper down. Size of a grave, I reckon."

Richardson went over for a closer examination. "You could be right. We'll make a copper out of you yet."

"What's up?" asked Cobbold.

"The list I sent you has ten names on it. I am guessing that five of them have been killed, three of them weren't and two are still to be tracked down. I think you'll find that one of them, if not all the dead ones, will be buried on this allotment."

"Really? Okay. Stay put for now. Stay another night if you have to."

Richardson went back to the pub to retrieve his car. He parked it at the entrance to the land to stop any gardeners coming on. Fortunately, the miserable October morning had thwarted any activity on the allotments. Walters saw John Sheringham off the land and joined Richardson in the warmth of the car.

"How's the shoulder?" Richardson asked.

"Still hurts but getting better, I think. I'm trying to use it as much as possible rather than save it. No idea whether that is improving it or making it worse!"

After short minutes a police siren could be heard getting ever closer. Sure enough it pulled in through the gate behind them.

"God! They love it, don't they?" said Richardson looking in his rear-view mirror as the driver killed the blues. "It's the same sergeant as yesterday. What was his name?"

"Sorry. Can't remember."

Richardson got out of the car and greeted the uniformed policeman. "Good morning, or is it afternoon, sergeant."

"Just afternoon, actually, Sir. I'm Sergeant Haughton. From yesterday. Remember me?"

"Yes. Of course, sergeant," Richardson sort of lied. "Sergeant. Can you secure the scene around that shed. Let's say, well, about a twenty-five-metre radius."

"Yes, Sir."

"Good. We'll be at the pub if you want us. You have my card?"

"Yes, Sir."

"Good. And, ah, sergeant, cut the 'sir' bit. Plain old Curt will do. There are no ranks in the HST."

Both Richardson and Walters were relieved to get into the dry and warm of the bar of the pub. Richardson collected two coffees from the bar whilst Walters warmed herself in front of the roaring fire. Apart from the occasional member of staff putting logs on the fire, they were alone. Time passed slowly waiting for updates from either the scene at the allotments or Cobbold. Richardson started to drum his fingers on the table, downed his coffee and went in search of another.

A couple of customers from the previous afternoon appeared and took up the same places as then. Richardson got up and paced. Then a ping alerted him. Cobbold, email. He opened it. "Now, let's see what we have here, then?"

He sat down again with Walters, who had been copied in. They read, in silence, the emails separately but together. Cobbold started by saying he had included a brief synopsis of each victim. If Curt was going to criticise the spelling and grammar, he could stick it where the sun don't shine!

"Ha!" said Walters. "A little waspy. He never has been good with staying up all night. Usually needs a fortnight off to recover!"

"Thackeray was reported missing when she didn't show for work on Saturday 2nd October. She is assumed to have gone out on the evening of the day before but nobody knows where she went. Her car was on the drive, her dog was in the garden and her keys were hanging on a hook in the kitchen, probably a second set. Dog was pretty bedraggled. No trace of her over the last week or so. Looks like she went out and forgot the dog was in the garden or someone took her when the dog was in garden.

Pringle was the bloke whose plane ditched into the North Sea on Monday 4th October. Only retrieved the plane but no body. No reports of it being washed up so far. It's thought that he either crashed of mechanical failure or got taken ill suddenly.

Interesting aside, he was also in the Royal Marines and served with Wells. The investigation didn't feel a need to explore that connection. They might do now, though!

O'Keefe is a less than savoury character. He walked into a pub's outside toilet near Belfast just after the Good Friday Agreement and shot a soldier in the back of the head. Got sentenced to life but as is the way with these things he was released earlier this year. He claims to be most remorseful about the killing which helped him convince the Parole Board. Could be several in line for this one as an act of revenge. Shot through the mouth from close range. Muzzle in mouth so made to look like suicide. Only trouble is that no gun was found at the scene. Exit wound took off most of the back of his skull. When found he was in a hell of a state and whilst they were pretty sure it was him, from the address his body was discovered, identifying him proved challenging. Fortunately, he received dental treatment in prison so was identified through dental records and fingerprints. By the way, this was on Wednesday 6th October. Two men are suspected of carrying out the killing as they have been seen on CCTV. One man arrested and now charged. Hopefully, we'll get him out today.

Smith is an odd one. Basically, he is a druggie, who for kicks at the beginning of the year, thought it would be fun to weigh a poor defenceless dog down with a stone anchor and toss it into a canal. Weird wanker posted it all over social media. Got off on account he was mentally unwell. Received hundreds of death threats. Police are still following them all up. I daresay they are not busting a gut on this one. Was tied up, zipped into a body-bag, weighed down with gym weights and, so it seems, thrown into the same canal. Died from drowning. Ironic really, right in the middle of a popular dog-walking area. This one was the day after O'Keefe.

Carter seems to have had a lucky escape. No idea why so detectives have been sent to find him in the Ascot area. Will get back to you if we learn anything. It might be that he doesn't know anything about it. There are quite a few people in the area with that name so might take a while.

Bill Yates is similar to Carter, lucky escape. There are a number of William, Bill, Yates so might prove difficult to track down. Don't have a location so putting that one on the backburner.

Ursula Sullivan. You will be familiar with her? She is the Head of Social Services down south somewhere. If you don't know her you will remember the case of the little girl who died after continued systematic beatings from her adopted mother and her crazed partner. It was proven that the little girl's midwife and medical staff continually reported the matter to Social Services. There was hardly a bone in her body that wasn't or hadn't been broken. They claimed that due to Covid and a shortage of staff they couldn't really be expected to do anything about it. Not sure why he didn't go through with this one as she seems the ideal candidate. In her defence, though, she had only been in post for a few months. That might have saved her. Lucky escape, I reckon.

Then the one who died Sunday in King's Lynn prior to the takedown in Bartholomew's Woods. Strange one this. A body was discovered early Monday morning by a cleaner. You have listed this as Patrick Hunter. No reference to anyone of that name being killed across the entire country and, for that matter, Europe. The body in KL was our friend Joe Burns. Might be mistaken identity or maybe Hunter was an alias for Burns. Will carry on digging until we are sure. Might call the local force when finished this. The body discovered was stabbed, in the police's opinion, by a professional."

"It looks like our Major Wells was a self-styled vigilante who wanted to take out all of the country's less-than-desired on his own," observed Richardson. "How do you get a knife killing to look like a professional job?"

Walters, who had been scrolling through her own copy looked up and said, "But why? And, what about the final one on the list? Who is he? Get a soldier to do it, by the way.'"

"I have no idea why you jumped in front of that bullet?! If you hadn't done that, I wouldn't have needed to have taken him down and he could have finished the job on Sajjadi. Our friend, Manzoor, would be history now. Instead, I am sure he will get a lengthy jail term but, no doubt, he will be out in next-to-no-time. That is no justice for the poor people who have been trafficked from Afghanistan, Syria, Yemen or wherever. It's quite disgusting."

"The moral to the tale is don't carry out conjoined operations with the police! They have too many rules! He was just unlucky with Manzoor that we were hunting the same prey at the same time. I agree, those poor women who left out thinking they would be living the life of dreams, only to find out they would be forced into pornography and prostitution. No wonder they take to the drugs so easily, it's the only escape. If I'd 'ave known, I would've stood back and watched him take the bastard out... then shot him! Do you think he had an accomplice?"

"He might've done with O'Keefe but the CCTV may have been two innocent people walking out together. I'll ask Cobbold for a still from the video. Really not sure. But I can't work out how he could have done the plane crash into the North Sea without help. Maybe it was illness and simply a coincidence? But how would Wells have known? The thing I'm thinking is, where did he get his weapons?"

"Exactly. I reckon his oppo flew them into some remote airfield. They are so easy to get in Europe. Lots of leftovers from the Cold War. Arsenals full of excess American equipment was bought off for very cheap money and has been circulating ever since. I also reckon that weapons of all types will be beginning to reach Europe after the retreat from Kabul in August. I am sure I read somewhere that the Yanks left seven billions worth of weapons and other military hardware there."

"Dollars or pounds?"

"Not sure. Does it really matter? Let's say it's a bloody lot, whatever it's in."

Richardson's phone rang again. "Really?" he asked as he took the device from the table. "It's Cobbold. Hey, Duncan."

"Inspector Rathbone of Norfolk CID has been in contact. They are pretty sure you are right. There is almost certainly a body beneath the allotment. Did you want to get along there?"

"Will do. Just before I go though, can you dig us out more

information on the disappearance/death of Matthew Pringle? Background could be useful as well as the airfield he flew out of. Where did he serve with Wells and who else was with them. We think he must have had help with that one. We also think that he had help getting hold of weapons. I have a feeling about the profile of his comrade. Possibly worth checking re smuggling of goods including people. This could be the link. Can you also get the best possible still image of the two on the CCTV after the killing of the IRA man?"

"Will do. Umm, that's another thing. The terrorist guys aren't willing to release Kenneth Moseley yet."

"Who's he?"

"The bloke they arrested for O'Keefe's murder."

"Okay. It shouldn't be too long, though. Any news re the death in Lynn?"

"Just come in. It is definitely Joe Burns, ties in with Bartholomew's. We think Wells could have been working on incorrect information. The place he was found was home to firms called PHA and PHS. PH for Patrick Hunter. Credit cards were found in the deceased's wallet with the name P J B Hunter. Maybe the JB stood for Joe Burns. Peculiar!"

They pulled back into the track leading along the side of the allotments. Two floodlights had been erected along with a white tent. Operatives were floating around in white forensic suits and police tape was cordoning off the area. The two ducked under the tape. Sergeant Haughton ushered them over to a figure with their back to the approaching party.

"Inspector Rathbone?" Richardson greeted the police officer from behind.

A woman turned to face them and an expression of surprise, maybe shock, was etched into her face. "We're just about to start digging over there," she answered, pointing at the tent, now covering the same patch of earth that Walters had earlier highlighted as a potential grave. "We had cadaver dogs sniff it out first. Ground radar has now picked out what could be a body under there."

"Nothing else?"

"Nothing showing although that's not a guarantee. Come on over."

The three stepped over to the tent entrance. Rathbone pulled back the flap and they all ducked in. The digging had already begun and a pile of soil and stones was heaped on an adjacent tarpaulin. The odour of freshly turned earth greeted them as they entered the immediate crime vicinity.

"How goes it, Ged?" Rathbone asked of a man, dressed in white, directing operations.

"Already down to the target, ma'am. Not very deep. Looks like it is wrapped in a body-bag."

Another coverall clad operative pulled out a piece of rope, actually a dog lead, and tossed it on the heap. The package was brought out of the hole and laid on a spare piece of tarp. A couple more white-clad technicians, Richardson wasn't sure of their gender, brought in task-lights and examined the outer bag. "Okay," one of them, clearly a woman, said. "We can open it up now."

Rathbone turned to Walters and said, "Ma'am. You might want to step outside, ma'am, as this might not be pretty? I find most women seem to be a little bit squeamish when it comes to dead bodies."

Walters simply locked her eyes onto the Inspector's. After a few moments, the other woman backed down. That usually happened!

"Please yourself," she said. "but don't say you weren't warned."

Richardson had to hold it together as he knew exactly what was going through Walters' mind. "Oh dear!" he whispered for no one to really hear.

The white-clad woman unzipped the body-bag to reveal a decomposing female corpse. Putrefying flesh peeling from the skull, dark hair matted in a black substance and a gash below the mouth which was animated by the wriggling maggots gorging on their prize dinner. Rathbone looked across at the attractive blonde woman who accompanied the tall shaven-headed black man. There weren't any signs of shock or trauma. Rathbone, though, felt a little nauseous.

"She has a stomach for it, Bro," she said to Richardson.

"She also has a tongue in her mouth and a fully operational brain in her skull," Walters interjected. "Rather than talk about me like I'm not here, Inspector, you have my permission to address me directly. I don't bite!"

Much, thought Richardson before saying, "Don't judge a book by its cover, Inspector. "She can bite, though. And, bloody hard!"

"You think it's Simone Thackeray?" Rathbone ignored the chastisement.

"Possibly. No, probably." How quick can you get an ID on her? I also want to know if there are any other wounds and if the slash to the throat was the killer. It is certainly in his modus operandi."

"There are more?"

"A few. At least one with a knife wound."

"By lunchtime tomorrow," Rathbone confirmed the answer to the previous question.

Richardson's phone rang again. It stopped ringing before he could retrieve it from beneath the winter clothing he was wearing. "Cobbold," he said to Walters. "I'll call him back from the car." He pulled a card from his wallet and handed it to the Inspector.

She reciprocated. Richardson looked at the card. "Aretha?"

"You got it man. The Queen of Soul. Mum was a massive fan."

The HST pair returned to the car and headed back to the warmth again.

"I can tell when you dislike someone," smiled Richardson as he put the gear into first and pulled away. "You don't disguise it very well."

"Supercilious bitch. Add to that black racist and female misogynist and that about sums it up."

Richardson laughed softly. "My feelings exactly," he agreed.

"Did you see her face when I, a black man, turned up on her patch. It was the same face that assumed you, a woman, would feel a little squeamish at the sight of a dead body."

They both laughed.

"Call Cobbold," Richardson instructed his phone, now clicked in through blue tooth. The ringtone reverberated around the car.

"Curt. Thanks for getting back to me. I've just emailed you the address of where Pringle flew out of, that fateful day. He ran sightseeing trips from the Lincolnshire coast, just south of Skegness. I will get Colonel Pringle's service history out to you in the morning."

"Colonel?"

"Yeah. Retired as a colonel. And I reckon that you will find Major Wells had some gripes with his commanding officer, if that's what he was back in the day? Maybe he was involved with Wells in bringing women in for Sajjadi? Might've fallen out which is why he ended up in the drink. Yours to find out."

"I'm not convinced there is a connection."

"Check it out anyway. No stone left unturned."

CHAPTER SIXTEEN

Thursday 14th October 2021

Lincolnshire

It was still dark when they arrived at the airstrip near Skegness. There were no cars in the car park and there were no lights on in the buildings, so they sat back to wait. Bleak was not a strong enough word to describe it as the dawn spread from the east over the flat, desolate, featureless landscape. Even the glimmer of sun breaking through, as they unwrapped their breakfast rolls from a service station a few miles back, did not serve to improve the outlook. They had checked out from the pub the night before sacrificing this morning's breakfast in the process. Richardson did not operate well without breakfast. He did not operate well without food.

"That's shit," said Walters as she folded the unfinished meal into the plastic wrapper and dropped it in the passenger well behind her seat.

"I agree but I'm starvin'," Richardson replied before finishing his food, tossing the empty wrapper behind him and retrieving Walters' unfinished breakfast. "Let's see what the coffee's like?"

"Don't hold your breath," she said as she removed the lid. "Oh! Great. It's black."

"Probably just the wrong way round," he said as he removed his lid. "No. Mine's black too. Take it like a man!"

"Bloody awful," said Walters and opened the door to pour the contents into the rutted car park.

"I might've used that!" Richardson complained before taking a sip. He screwed up his face. "Yep. Bloody awful! Like gnat's piss. Must have some caffeine in it, though."

Headlights turned into the track at the end and made their way, bumping over the unmade road, until an old red Ford Mondeo pulled into the car park. It drew up beside them. Richardson turned the ignition to accessory and put the window down.

"Who are you?" a scrawny looking man with a red bobble-hat asked.

"Home Security Team," Richardson responded as he stepped out of the car brandishing both sets of identity. "I'm Curtly Richardson and this is Sue-Beth Walters."

Bobble-hat took the badges. "Looks pretty official. Never heard of you. How do I know you're for real?"

"You don't. We don't want much of your time. It's about a missing person enquiry we took over last night. Matthew Pringle?"

A flash of recognition crossed the man's face. "He used to be a partner in the sight-seeing trips that flew out of here. He either committed suicide or died of a heart-attack or something like that. They got his plane back but haven't yet found him."

"Or he was murdered."

"Really? Shit! How do I know these are for real," he repeated waving the IDs around. "You could be some sort of scammers or something."

"Got a phone that works out here?"

"In the office. No signal out here so need to go inside and use the landline."

"Okay. Call any police station you like and get them to confirm those badges. We'll wait. If you have decent coffee, it would be appreciated."

Bobble-hat agreed and went into the shack that doubled as an office and reception area. He punched the speaker button before pushing a speed-dial key. The phone was answered in less than two rings.

"Hey Rupert," came the greeting from the other end.

"Hello, mate. You'd better get over here. There's a couple of police types here saying that they think Matt was murdered."

"You're kidding. Shit. I can do without that. On my way."

Rupert ended the call before opening up the internet from his phone, now he had a wi-fi signal. He typed Lincolnshire police into the address bar of his browser. He loaded the located number onto the desk-phone before pressing Send. When it started to ring, he picked up the receiver. It rang for ages. Eventually he was answered and, after being put through to three separate departments, in error he assumed, he had it confirmed that the two curiously named officers, or whatever they were, outside, were who they said they were. Before he went out to greet them again, he set a coffee pot going.

He opened the door and called over to the pair. "Please come in."

The huge black man was sipping on a takeaway drink. Rupert recognised the branding on the paper cup. "How's the coffee?"

"Shit!" the woman answered.

"Not surprised," he chuckled. "Old Stan never could make coffee. Or anything for that matter! You didn't get food from there as well, did you?"

Walters and Richardson exchanged glances.

"Oh dear. Hope you are gonna write yer answers down so that there is a record of the conversation should you not make it? Next twenty-four hours will be critical!"

They started heading for the office when their attention was caught by the sound of an engine approaching behind them. Richardson looked over his shoulder and saw a new model pick-up, Toyota he thought, coming along the track. Who's this?"

"Simon Barnes. He was Matt's partner."

"In what sense of the word?" asked Walters.

"What? Oh! Business, of course. There's no way they is poofs."

She smiled and her eyes lit up at the same time.

Jesus, he thought. She can see right inside me. Got to be X-ray vision!

The door swung open and Simon walked in. As scruffy as Rupert was, Simon was the sharp-dressed flyer from the movies. He sported an American style flying jacket with sunglasses on a tanned open face. He removed his glasses to reveal dark blue eyes. "Simon Barnes at your service," he said offering his hand.

The pair both shook the outstretched hand.

"How can I help you folks?"

"Last Monday a colleague of yours, correction, your partner, went missing. We believe he was murdered," said Richardson.

"Don't see how. Police went through everything and it was them, not us, who suggested that it might be a suicide. No way, Matt was too full of life. He always came across as fit but, to be honest, he did eat some crap so it was decided that he must have had a heart attack or some such. It's a bit of a pain as we can't get anything from the life insurance until he has been missing for twelve years. His going missing or death has left us in the lurch a bit. We take it in turn to fly and we had the insurance to cover payments on the plane. The insurance salesman said he thought life insurance with critical illness cover was probably the best way to give us time to get a new pilot and meet the monthlies on the plane. Neither of us considered that the other one might just end up missing. Still, life's a bitch! Hey?"

"What CCTV do you have apart from that one above the counter?"

"None. That's it. The police have reviewed it and seem to think everything is in order and he certainly didn't do anything that was out of character on that last day."

"Have you still got recording from that day?"

"Yep. Have to keep them for six months. Another insurance demand that we have to stick with, so they can avoid paying out if we don't. Those bastards are all take! Load it up, Rupert, there's a good chap. Why do you think he was murdered?" Barnes asked of his inquisitor.

"Tell the truth," said Richardson. "We don't think, we know. Or, at least, are pretty sure."

"Can it be proved?"

"In our opinion, yes, but whether that will satisfy your insurers, I don't know. I can't promise you a pay-day without the body. Never sure, to be honest, whether murder constitutes accidental death anyway. It might not do you any favours even if he was found."

"I'm all ears. I need all the help I can get right now. There'll be no business to pay out if we can't get flying soon. Maybe that's what they want? A pay-out for the smashed-up plane will do for starters."

"His name has appeared on a list. There are four others on the list. Actually, that's not quite correct, there are nine others on the list but five of them are still very much alive. Or at least we think so. Of the others, three are definitely dead and the fifth should be confirmed by lunchtime today."

Rupert brought four mugs of coffee to the desk. "Anyone need milk?"

"Please," said Sue-Beth.

He produced a small bottle from his filthy coat pocket and poured some into her mug. She thought twice about taking in the drink now! She wouldn't feel great with a bad shoulder and food poisoning. But she had survived, so far, Stan's breakfast. Surely, this couldn't be as bad as that?

"Video is all lined up," announced Rupert.

The screen showed a freeze of the view taken from the camera high up behind the counter. It was a still of John Wells, whom they knew, shaking hands with another, Matthew Pringle they assumed. "Can you roll it on?" asked Richardson.

Rupert moved the 'on screen' arrow to the video player button and clicked. The picture moved forward. He clicked another button and the sound came in. Greetings were exchanged by the two although Pringle had a slight look of surprise, even incredulity, on his face. They disappeared from the frame although muffled chat could still be heard as they went away.

"Matt's taking him through to that room there," Rupert indicated the door over his right shoulder. "They get all the formal stuff in there done. Disclaimers, medical run-through, that sort of thing. Enjoy your coffees whilst I tee-up the return."

After less than a minute. "Got it. This is about forty-five minutes later when Mr Bellingham comes back in."

Both officers noted the name but showed no reaction.

The screen showed Major Wells reappear. The voices could be heard clearly as he was standing right under the camera. He said he had had a wonderful time and that Mr Pringle had decided to go out again for one final look as he loved watching the sun go down from the air.

"Was that plausible?" asked Richardson.

"Yeah. He did it all the time. We never saw him again."

"On what you've seen there," said Barnes. "…do you still believe he was murdered? There's nothing in that to suggest anything was awry to me."

"Can you just rewind the video back to where Matt meets Bellingham?"

Rupert found the spot again and started the play button for a second time.

"That's it. Stop," Richardson demanded. "The look on his face, I think anyway, shows a hint of recognition. He looks surprised. Maybe, even, a little shocked."

Sue-Beth bent in for a look. "I see that. Not sure your theory would wash in Court?"

"You reckon Matt knew Mr Bellingham?" asked Barnes.

"Yes, and his name isn't Bellingham, it's Wells. Major Wells. And given that a huge percentage of people murdered in this country are known to their killers, that wouldn't be a surprise."

"Is that man the same man who murdered all the others? And, if he did how do you think he killed Matt?"

"I have a theory but I don't want to divulge that just yet. Is there any chance that a second person could have got into the plane before Matt and Wells?"

Barnes contemplated his answer. "It's possible. I suppose so. We don't ever keep the doors locked during the day."

"No external CCTV?"

"None."

"Okay," said Richardson and pulled a copy of the wish dead list from his pocket. He read the names out one-by-one to Barnes and asked if there was any chance that Pringle knew them or of them? Could they have had any sort of business dealings at all?

Barnes confirmed that he had never heard of any of the names on the list. Pringle only had a business relationship with himself. There was no time for anything else.

"Any chance that Pringle could smuggle anything in from abroad?"

"It's possible but highly improbable. All our flights have to be reported in advance. It doesn't happen very often but Customs can be here to greet us on any random return trip. Just not worth the risk. He wasn't that sort of a bloke. In all my dealings with him, he has always been as straight as a ruler. He is definitely not a risk taker."

Richardson and Walters returned to Norfolk and to the pub to wait for the identity of the buried victim to be confirmed. On the way, they called Cobbold to get him looking into Major John Wells' links with Colonel Matthew Pringle. Could Wells have anything on Pringle and, if yes, was there anyone else who knew? And where had Pringle's military record gone?

Cobbold came back with the answers to the queries just as they pulled up into the pub's car park. Richardson disconnected the phone from the speakers for he knew Cobbold's voice would be amplified so much it could probably be heard from the other end of the village. The phone pinged as he was finishing the exchange with Cobbold. "Yeah. Got it," he said. "Do we have an address for him?"

"Included in the same email."

"Good. Cheers, Dunc."

"See if you can book us in for another night, would you?" Richardson asked of his colleague. "Oh. And see if they have a table for lunch. I'm…"

"Starvin'!" Sue-Beth finished for her partner.

"Ha! Oh. I've got another email. It's from Rathbone." Richardson opened the mail. "Confirmed. It's Simone Angela Thackeray."

Walters went into the pub. They took the same room as before which, because it wasn't booked out again, had not been cleaned so, if it was alright with them, they could have it for the reduced rate commensurate with a three day stay. Lunch was no problem either. The barman indicated a table in the window.

"Thank you," said Walters, "But do you mind if we use that one?" She pointed at the table on which they had worked the day before between breakfast and lunch.

"Of course not."

She ordered a lime and soda and went across to the table. She, too, had been copied in on Cobbold's email. The subject was an individual named Colonel Matthew Pringle. She opened the mail which included an address in Kent. She opened up the military record of the colonel. It was full of plaudits and citations for this and that but, generally, was a record of where he had served and how he had performed his duties. There was one cloud in an otherwise clear blue sky and that was a complaint, brought by two of his subordinates after a shooting during the first Gulf War in the early nineties. According to the allegation

411

Pringle, under tremendous stress and pressure in the midst of an aggressive enemy had killed, in cold blood, an Iraqi woman and her two daughters. The complaint was brought jointly by two lieutenants. One was a Lieutenant Alan Cooper and the other was their man, Lieutenant John Wells. No charges were ever brought.

Interesting, she thought. I assume the address in Kent belongs to Lieutenant Cooper? She placed her phone on the table, extended out her right arm and practiced rolling the shoulder joint. She didn't hear the barman approach.

"A type of yoga or something?" the server asked.

"No. No. Injured my shoulder the other day and just trying to work out how it feels."

"Any better?" he asked as he placed the drink in front of her.

"Just about there, I think."

"We all know why you two are here."

"Yes?" she answered with caution.

"It is just that our pot-wash wonders if he could have a word with you?"

"If he has any information, we will need to talk to him."

"He has information alright. I am just not quite sure how useful it is, though."

"Okay. Let us be the judges of that."

"Thank you. I'll send him over then. His name is Craig. I have to tell you; he isn't the brightest creature on God's Earth."

412

Walters resumed her exercise until she spotted a timid lad approaching from the kitchen. He was young and judging by his face hadn't yet started shaving. "Hello, Craig," she said. "Please sit down. My name is Field Officer Sue-Beth Walters. What have you got for us?"

The lad did not pull the chair out quite enough, snagging his leg as he tried to sit. Then, he more fell into the seat rather than sat in it. He didn't say anything.

Walters said, "What is it? What do you know?"

The lad looked like he was composing himself. In fact, she noticed, he was visibly shaking.

"Take your time," she said but thought, come on, I haven't got all day.

"My Mum and Dad told me I shouldn't bother you with this but I think it is important."

"Let us be the judge of that, shall we. Not your Mum and Dad."

"That's what I said," Craig said, his face brightening at the thought of someone willing to hear him out. "It is just that my uncle and auntie live out in the woods."

"Oh! They're nice houses out there."

"They live in a caravan and they know what goes on all over the woods."

"I see. Go on."

Craig went on to explain how his relatives had seen mysterious lights above the trees and they were sure they were from other

413

planets. A special power had been used to stop phones and things working. It had been really weird.

Walters tried to appear interested in Craig's account. She feared this could be about to turn into a tale of aliens being seen in the area. At the same time, though, she was trying to, surreptitiously, get a message to Richardson. Her fingers fumbled over the keyboard. She tried to keep one eye on the device whilst making the other look like it was concentrating on the witness's story. As Craig finished his tale Walters glimpsed, from the corner of her eye, Richardson come into the restaurant.

Walters held her hand up. "If I can just stop you there, Craig. This is Field Officer Curtly Richardson and he is in charge of this investigation. I think it best you tell him everything you know so he gets it first-hand. I've just got to nip and powder my nose."

The two officers swapped places.

"Pleased to meet you," said Richardson to the witness.

"Not sure she has got that right," said Craig.

"What?"

"My Mum and Dad put the powder up their noses not on their noses."

Yes. No. She means she is…. Oh. Never mind!"

Craig went on to repeat everything he had already told Walters.

When he had finished Richardson said, "Thank you. We will let you know if we need any further information."

"Will the lady have any more questions at all?"

"No. Not to ask at any rate. She might have some to answer, though."

Walters, who had been standing just out of sight around the corner, waited for Craig to return to the kitchen before stepping back into the restaurant. There was no pain on her face any longer. She was grinning from ear to ear.

Richardson rolled his eyes. "Thank you for that. When I got your text saying you had turned up an incredible witness, I thought you were serious and rushed in."

Walters smiled. "Still, at least you might get a drugs bust out of it."

"Funny lady!"

As they were finishing lunch, a Caesar salad for her and a beefburger with all the trimmings for him, Richardson's phone pinged again. It was sitting on the table to the side of his dish. "Umm! Edmundson. I wonder what he wants?"

"Can you get along to suspect's house. Interesting discovery in garage."

The pair ducked under the crime-scene tape, flashed their identities and followed directions to Josh Edmundson. They found him in the garage with what looked like a floor-safe that had been opened. They peered into the hole and shook their heads at what they saw. Bricks of banded twenty-pound notes laid in the hole, along with some loose notes.

"I think everyone should keep back," said Walters calmly. Surely this was not another twist in this tale.

"Why?" asked Edmundson.

"You remember the other day, last week, I had an audience with the PM?"

"Yeah."

"I was there to be thanked on behalf of the British public for my diligence in carrying out my duty. I had, inadvertently to be honest, discovered that a foreign power was attempting to smuggle in twenty-pound notes, millions of them we think, contaminated with another variant of coronavirus. They were giving them out to the migrants who were daring the Channel crossing."

"And you think these could be some of them?"

"Don't know for sure. Can't be too careful. Leave them where they are, I would suggest, and I'll get Cobbold's friend at SIS to send some scientist types along here." Walters bent down to pick one of the loose notes out. "I must admit, though, I don't think these have the same feel."

"And another thing. When we were up at the allotment earlier, a fingertip search was going on, a man appeared and said he was a friend of Major John Wells. He had heard of the Major's death and wondered if he had finished his business before he died? I said that I had no idea and asked him what he meant? I wondered if it had something to do with the allotment but he wouldn't elaborate. We either knew or we didn't."

"What did he look like?"

Edmundson described him. Richardson pulled out his phone, opened a picture and presented the image to the policeman. "Is that the man?"

Edmundson took the smallest of glances at the screen. "Without any doubt whatsoever? I said we, and others, might want to talk to him further. He said fine, no problem, he could be found at the pub later."

Richardson and Walters returned to the pub. "How many rooms do you have here?" he asked of the same barman who had served them their lunch.

"Eight."

"How many of them occupied?"

"Three including yours. Not as many as we would like. Why?"

Richardson presented him with the same photograph of Alan Cooper. "Which room is this man staying in?"

"Never seen him before in my life."

"You sure?"

"Absolutely. Room four has an elderly couple in it and room six has a single woman in it. And, you're in room three."

"I thought you were full when we booked in which is why we had to share?" Walters put in.

"We were but we're not tonight. We might get a couple more rooms out yet. It sometimes happens. Did you want a second room, then?"

"No. Not necessary. I've got used to his snoring over the past couple of nights. Thanks."

They returned to the same table they had used for lunch.

"Do you know? I really should look through the rest of the files, on Wells' computer, before we hand it back to Josh," said Richardson. He lent down, unzipped his backpack and took out the laptop which he had not yet returned to the house.

"Leave it with you," Walters said. "I'm going for a run."

"Is that wise?"

"Probably not. It's my way of getting better. Only one way to find out."

When she returned, about an hour-and-a-half later Richardson was still sitting at the table. He had been joined by another man. It was, without a doubt, Major Alan Cooper. Richardson beckoned her over and made the introductions. Cooper stood and they shook hands.

"I must be going," Cooper announced. "I'm sure your colleague will fill you in. Nice to meet you both."

The HST pair watched Cooper's back as he exited the restaurant. The bar was beginning to fill with a raft of afternoon drinkers. The usual crew were there and Richardson did not want his words to be overheard so they made for room three.

"Good run?" he asked as he held the door for her to enter in front of him.

"As good as can be expected. Don't let anyone ever tell you that Norfolk is flat. This bit certainly isn't. There are some wicked little hills around here!"

She sat on the chair to the dressing table while he stretched himself on his bed, back propped up on cushions like the morning before. He then began his tale.

"Cooper had been to the allotment before going out for a drive. On returning to the village, he called at Wells' house where Edmundson had told him he had just missed us so he had come right over. Of course, he claimed to have no knowledge of Wells' activities. I asked him to come up with a theory about Pringle's death. He said it was purely hypothetical to which I said of course it is! There must have been two men in the plane. Maybe, he said, the plane was put into automatic pilot before one of the two men had broken Pringle's neck. The plane had then returned to the airfield where Wells had got out before the second man, not Cooper of course, took the plane back up, set it on a course directly north and bailed out himself. Wells probably picked him up later somewhere after he had paddled to shore. The plane would simply run out of fuel and come down in the sea. Might have had two-hundred miles or so of fuel left in the tank."

"Sounds like a confession to me," observed Walters.

"Of course it's a confession. I didn't even have to brief him on how Pringle died. Quite the stroke of luck to come up with that, hypothetical or not! He said it was probably justice being served for the killing of the mother and her girls in Iraq. He won't be missed apparently."

"And you simply let him walk out of here?"

"Well, there's the thing, you see. I would say you were still getting changed into your tracksuit when Cobbold called. He informed me that Cooper would be calling into see me and that

I was to take no action. It appears that Major Cooper now has the protection of some very powerful people. Good friends in high places."

"So that gives him the right to go around the country killing people because of a personal vendetta?"

"Nothing we can do about it. For what it's worth, though, it is exactly how I thought it had panned out."

"Okay. Who ordered Cobbold?"

"Wouldn't say. But he is only answerable to one man."

Walters shrugged. "God!" she said before continuing. "So, we're done here?"

"Not quite. Cobbold wants us to hang around for his currency expert to get here and look at that cash. And, by the way, we are to commandeer it if it turns out to be safe. He'll clear that with the NCA."

Walters stripped off her clothing and strode to the shower. Richardson set the laptop up again on the dressing table and started searching through programmes. Walters emerged twenty minutes later wrapped in a white bath sheet, sat on the edge of her bed and dried her hair. Richardson worked through various programmes concentrating first on emails. He started with the inbox but there was absolutely no communication relating to Cooper or any of the revenge killings. Then he scrolled through the sent items. Again, nothing. Drafts, one unsent mail saying, 'Will collect over next day or so.' Finally, he opened the Deleted Items. Walters eventually turned off the hairdryer.

"Bingo!" said Richardson. "Come and look at this."

"Be there in a minute. I'll just get dressed." She tossed the towel onto the bed, riffled through her pack and came out with a set of clothing and some deodorant which she sprayed over her muscled body. She then got dressed: bra, socks, knickers, cotton button-up shirt and jeans. She then peered over Richardson's shoulder at the screen.

There were fifteen untitled files stored in the Deleted Items folder and every single one of them contained instructions, assistance or thanks. None of them had a name inserted in the 'To' row and none of them had a title in the Subject row.

"Okay," she said. "What've you got?"

An inventory of his arsenal. Christ! Was there a sniper rifle in there?"

"No. Most definitely not."

"Okay. Now let's have a look at his recent browsing history."

Walters plumped her own cushions behind her back and made herself comfortable on the other bed.

After a while, Richardson let out a breath. "Heard of Spencer Percival at all?"

"No. Can't say I have. Who is he?"

"He is the only British Prime Minister, ever, to have been assassinated whilst in office."

"God! Really? Can't believe we don't know more about him. We seem to know everything there is to know about JFK and Lincoln."

"Aha!" exclaimed Richardson. "You'll never guess who killed him?"

"I'll give you that one. No idea."

"John Bellingham of Liverpool."

"How the hell would I know…. Christ! The same name Wells used in Lincoln at the airfield?"

"Right. Obviously, a hero of his."

Walters slowly nodded.

"Come on. Let's go," said Richardson.

"Where to?"

"I reckon the first nine on the list were easy to get close to and could be taken out by handgun, knife or bare hands. Number ten, though, will prove more difficult and the sniper rifle is missing."

"Which means the accomplice has it and is probably on his way to take out number ten right now. Did you find out who it was?"

"No. I'll do it now." Richardson took out his phone and typed in First Lord of the Treasury. He waited for the page to load. "Bloody hell! Who on earth knows that?"

"Who is it?"

"It's the Prime Minister."

"To quote the Reverend Cruz, 'Blames everyone from the receptionist at the surgery to the Prime Minister.'"

"Come on," ordered Richardson. "I'll go get the car. You go and book the room for another two, no, three nights. Hang out a 'Do Not Disturb'. I'll bring out the hardware. No. Scrap the

'Do Not Disturb.' If someone takes a look in, it will look like we are still here."

Richardson retrieved the car and waited for Walters outside the front of the pub. When she was in, he instructed her to get hold of Cobbold and get him to obtain, by hook or by crook, a schedule for the Prime Minister for the forthcoming days. Then she was to let Edmundson know that they were headed back to London, without divulging why. Edmundson must not tell anyone. Then she was to get hold of Jones, Crawford, Newcomb and Thompson and tell them to meet them at HQ tonight. "And make bloody sure that Cobbold gets the Prime Minister to stay at home whatever his plans. Got that?"

"Yeah."

"Oh! And find out from Cobbold why Cooper has so much protection, and from whom. But tell him to be careful, just in case there is a government department trying to assassinate the PM."

"You what!"

"I doubt it but you never know. All sorts of people are pissed off with him following on from the fallout from the pandemic. Rule nothing out."

"Anything else or can I get started?"

"Yeah. Two more things. How far can a good sniper use that rifle effectively? And you had better tell Cobbold to let the currency person know we won't be here."

"Definitely over two-thousand metres and maybe, who knows, if they are really good up to two-thousand-five-hundred metres."

"Jesus!"

Richardson went quiet and Walters knew better than to interrupt him when his brain was in calculator mode. Area-equals-pi-times-radius-squared and circumference-equals-pi-times-diameter.

"That's an area of around twenty square kilometres and a circle of nearly sixteen kilometres. Bloody hell!"

"She's a numismatist, by the way."

"Who is?" asked Richardson, not really caring, trying to work out how to patrol such a big circle.

"Adelaide Wiggins the currency expert. It's the proper name for what she does."

Richardson shrugged his shoulders as if he were saying whatever but it stayed in his head.

EPILOGUE

Suffolk

The packed congregation stood as the sound of Adele's Set Fire to the Rain echoed off the medieval stone walls of the late-Norman church in the Suffolk village of Oakshott. The Home Security Team had now been in existence for just over twelve years and this was the first time they had needed to arrange the funeral of one of its members. The song had become the unofficial anthem of the group since they had brought down the Knights Tempest in 2011. Setting fire to the rain is impossible, which is why the tune was adopted as their song, because that's what they achieve: the impossible.

Some congregants looked around as the coffin processed through the ancient portal whilst others stared, resolutely, at the carpeted floor. Her Britannic Majesty's new Home Secretary, turned in the direction of footsteps betraying the arrival of one of the team member's last journey. Looking around, it was good to see that members of all faiths and none were represented at this traditional final goodbye. It was an image of unity that the British Government would like portrayed to the whole world. Britain always had been welcoming to all.

The pallbearers were all similar in height and dressed entirely in black suits, black ties, crisp white shirts and immaculately polished black shoes. They all wore the mourning uniform with a pride, like the soldiers two of them used to be, for they were saying goodbye to one of their own. They were paying their final respects to a former soldier, an incredibly brave soldier. The faces of the three men and three women carrying the wicker casket all looked like they had been hewn from granite. Neither a tear nor smile broke the rigid poses.

Behind the coffin, the chief mourners paraded through the nave. Some were tearful and some were equally stony-faced as the selected few carrying the deceased. Lady Isobel Walters, face shielded by a black veil, was flanked by two men. She was crying. To her right was her only grandchild, a grandson, Toby Walters, and to her left was Peter Jones, husband of Field Officer Michael Jones. Jones face was smeared with tears whilst Toby walked upright. Face grim but stoic, trying to reflect the soldier he wanted to be. Lady Isobel had buried her only son at this church before saying a last farewell to her husband, the late General Sir James Walters. The former had been sent off with rousing full military honours. The latter was justifiably an ignominious disgrace. The second rank was made up of the Bryant women, Amelia and her two daughters, Poppy and Daisy, tears streaked their faces.

The Reverend Darren Massey looked on sombrely as the coffin was placed on the collapsible catafalque. The pallbearers stepped back from the casket, stood in a line, saluted, before bowing in unison. With that, they turned and took their places reserved in the front pews. One of them, Curtly Richardson, felt a hand on his shoulder. He turned round and looked into the face of Duncan Cobbold. Until now he had held it together. When taking the slow march along the aisle, he had kept his eyes just below Jesus Christ's nailed feet, deliberately avoiding eye-contact with all gathered here. At the feel of the touch on the shoulder and the look in Cobbold's sorrowful eyes, it all gave way. His face was chilled from the cold, grey outdoors but the tears felt like rivulets of lava pouring down his cheeks.

His shoulders began to heave. He hated funerals but knew it was his duty to be here. He recalled the memorial service for his beloved Augusta in that little theatre in the Italian town of Sorrento. He remembered the tearful service, where he and his even more beloved wife, Gillian, had stood, arms around one another, in this same spot. That was to say a goodbye to their unborn son. Then, short months later, he had been back in this very same church to say goodbye to that same beloved wife after her tragic suicide. Now here he was again, the pain palpable as he had to say goodbye to another he cared for like it was his spouse or sibling.

The vicar opened with "We are gathered here today to say our final goodbye and pay our respects…"

Richardson kept his head high and found he was staring into the serene eyes of the Messiah. Even the pain from the bloodied crown of thorns could not take away the forgiveness from Jesus' face. A better man than me, thought Richardson. How can you forgive those who have performed the ultimate trespass against you. He had looked for, and found, revenge against the perpetrators of the previous sins against his loved ones. This time was no different. He let the all too familiar words wash over him as he cast his mind back to the day, nearly three weeks ago now, when he and his team had saved the Prime Minister's life. I note that cretin couldn't even be bothered to turn up! No wonder he was on Major John Wells' wish dead list. If they hadn't have interfered with Wells' campaign, it might be the PM being mourned today. Instead, though, it was one of the best friends he had ever known. We all do our duty for crown and country. What a load of bollocks that felt like at the moment! It felt like they had saved the life of someone who did not give a jot about those who served under him.

Yorkshire

On learning that the sniper rifle was missing, from the arsenal below the allotment shed, the entire HST, involved with the rescue of the migrants from Bartholomew's Woods, had convened at their headquarters in Central London.

They had, with some reluctance from the Specialist Protection Branch of the Metropolitan Police Service Protection Command, SO1, been given the upcoming schedule of the Prime Minister. They had spent hours pawing through the itinerary identifying two places of high concern and three of medium concern. Cobbold was finding it difficult to convince his counterpart at SO1 that there was a clear and present danger to the leader of the country and had to call in the back-up of Vanessa Forbes-Marriott to add substance to his claim. It was the same-old-same-old. SO1 had never heard of this new start-up, the Home Security Team. In the end, the plans were forthcoming provided all interested parties were briefed on any conclusions reached.

The commander of SO1 had almost sneered when Cobbold had come forward with the conclusions. "We have already come up with that," she had said.

Cobbold exploded. "Why the fuck didn't you tell us this before?"

"You never asked."

When Cobbold lost it, his face nearly went the same colour as a good claret. Richardson took him outside to calm him down. A way forward was agreed upon.

A handful of low, and one medium, concern events came and went without incident. Then, on the sixth day of tracking the Prime Minister's movements he was due to visit an old mining town in one of the so-called red wall seats. These were constituencies that had, hitherto, been Labour held areas as far back as people could remember. In the last general election, the blue tide of conservatism had flooded these landscapes and overturned the Labour boat, drowning all on board.

Thanks to Covid there were now rumblings that the new heroes of the socialist voters in the, mainly, northern and working-class districts were becoming agitated at being left behind. Many accused the conservative leopard of being incapable of changing its spots. This trip was to be the beginning of the charm offensive as Covid restrictions were beginning to ease.

Field Officers Sue-Beth Walters and Michael Jones were tasked with reconnoitring the destination. It was an old coal mining pit set in a vale in Yorkshire. The previous workings had been engineered to allow visitors to visit the coalface and experience exactly what it had been like to mine the black gold of England. In 2021, the journey was made in climate-controlled pods on rails, mechanically ventilated tunnels which were brilliantly lit by modern LED lights that had no chance of exploding the ever-present methane gas of yesteryear. There were no canaries in cages waiting to full off perches, if the gas levels became dangerous. The redundant buildings on the ground had been turned into workshops for artisans, retail outlets for local crafts and a museum depicting life in a period unimaginable to most alive today. The old slag heaps had been reduced in height and landscaped to reintroduce flora and fauna long since absent from these desolate acres. Trees had been planted in their thousands and boardwalks constructed so that visitors did not trample the wildlife back into danger. And, of course, no visitor centre attracting the investment of millions would be complete without the obligatory giftshop and restaurant.

Walters had driven the pair here in her Ford Mondeo. Jones had slept most of the way so she had been able to listen to her favourite Katherine Jenkins tracks without fear of interruption. The first port of call, after the washrooms, was the restaurant where they both ordered all-day breakfasts with coffee. There was a brisk wind bringing a chill from the north and they were both grateful for their HST issue coats.

There were two periods of danger. First was the arrival and the walk from the specially adapted Jaguar XJ Sentinel armoured car to the entrance through the giftshop. The other was the return walk back to the safety of the vehicle. Each stroll was about fifteen metres. SO1 had suggested, wisely in Walters' opinion, the construction of a retractable tunnel. Whilst it would not stop bullets, it would stop any shooter from seeing the target. The Conservative Party mandarins had rubbished the idea saying that it was imperative that the nation's leader should be seen by his people and not be hidden away. "His people, my arse!" she had allowed to no-one in particular, remembering her encounter with the man in Downing Street. He couldn't care less about his people, she thought, if it got in the way of his own self-importance!

Walters and Jones positioned themselves about halfway along the fifteen-metre walk. To their immediate front, directly opposite the entrance to the giftshop, were the old workshops that had been refurbished to house the artisans and craftspeople. Working on the theory that all areas would be scoured clean of occupants before and during the visit, these did not present any danger. Both ends of the yard were open to the high hills beyond. The lower slopes had been planted with saplings that offered no cover to a shooter. The higher slopes, which were outside the perimeter of the old mine, were more thickly wooded and would afford good protection to any assassin.

Walters drew a scope from her coat's inside pocket. On first glance, it appeared to resemble any gun sight. A closer observer would realise that it had no means of attaching to a barrel. She deduced that the woods to the left offered the best option to any gunman. At this time of day, which was exactly the scheduled time for the Prime Minister's arrival in three days from now, the sun, if out, would be directly behind the shooter. Walters peered through the scope.

"One-thousand-two hundred-and-sixty-seven metres," said Walters and waited while Jones noted the distance down.

She turned her attention to the right. "One-thousand-five-hundred-and-forty-two metres."

Jones noted the second dimension into his book and took the scope from her. He looked through it, up at the treelines to each end, and confirmed that the distance to the left was one metre less and the right was one metre more. That was explained by the eighty centimetres between them on the PM's walk.

"The difference is incredible," observed Walters. "They look roughly the same to me. It'll take a skilled sniper to hit the target from there, especially when you think he hasn't been anywhere near sniper school for thirty years or more.".

"It's like riding a bike to these guys, though," responded Jones. "Still a bloody long way, though."

"A top shooter cold kill a target from over two-thousand metres if he was in battle condition."

They climbed the hill to the left first. When they reached the treeline, they turned back and looked down at the spot where the car would pull up. They realised that they could settle back in the wood by a further ten metres and still have a commanding view of the fifteen-metre walk. Total cover was afforded by the season's remaining undergrowth and autumnal canopy. They agreed that this would be the best position. When they consulted the Ordnance Survey map, this confirmed that access from and, therefore, exfiltration, to a relatively substantial B-road was most convenient. The getaway would be easy.

The survey of the right hill did not throw up any advantages whatsoever. At least, not as far as the experienced ex-soldiers could identify.

They were just about to head back down the hill, render their report to Cobbold, when a voice with a strong Yorkshire accent interrupted their progress. "And what do you think you two are doing?"

The pair turned around and came face-to-face with a bull of a man. He held a broken shotgun over his shoulder. Jones and Walters, instinctively but surreptitiously, widened the gap between them. Any cartridge fired from the weapon would expand and, in theory, could take the pair of them in one shot. If the space between them was too great, the man would have to fire twice. Both fancied their chances of drawing and loosing off a retaliation before he fired a second shot.

"Just taking a look to see if I can get a good shot at the Prime Minister in a few days-time," Walters replied.

The man laughed and visibly relaxed. "Oh yeah. That. Hope you find a good spot."

"Not a fan?"

"Course not. Top wanker! My Dad used to work down there and then Thatcher shut it all down. Pity the IRA didn't get her at Brighton. Would've done us all a favour. One day, about five years after pit closed, he came up here with this gun and blew his brains out."

"I'm sorry."

"Don't be. He was a drunken bastard. He used to beat up mother. It was a community thing really. Now all me mates 'ave gone and voted enemy in again." They ain't real jobs they's creating down there. They's jobs for pansies."

"Okay. Point taken. Thank you for your input."

Exchange over, the two returned down the hill, filed their report and went off in search of a hotel they could use until the morning of the visit.

Suffolk

The congregation filed out as the coffin was taken to an excavated grave to the north of the church. The pallbearers carried the load to the graveside, placed it on some strops and lowered it into the final resting place. Four plots closer to the church were the graves of Colonel Nathan Walters, General Sir James Walters and Gillian Richardson, much missed headteacher of Oakshott Primary School. There was no grave for the unborn child as he had not actually taken a breath. The Richardsons, though, had kept his urn on their mantle. Richardson had taken it down and passed it over to the funeral director who had made sure Gill was at eternal rest with their son.

"Ashes to ashes, dust to dust...." The Reverend Massey started up again.

Yorkshire

Duncan Cobbold stood in line outside the giftshop at the renovated pithead and waited for the Prime Minister's visit. Adrenalin was pumping but was calmed by a niggling doubt. He, as usual, fully backed his field officers. His two best operatives, Richardson and Walters, had, in particular, never let him down. There was always a first time for everything. He was continually scratching his head just behind his right ear. It was nothing more than a nervous twitch. Pull yourself together, man, he chastised himself. There is absolutely nothing you can do about it now. He had assumed that the shooting of Major John Wells in Norfolk had been the end of the matter, so much so, that he and Mrs Cobbold had booked a two-week getaway on the remote little island of Lismore in the Inner Hebrides. He had seen pictures of the self-catering accommodation complete with its modern fitments, latest entertainment systems and jacuzzi on the deck that overlooked the waters of Loch Linnhe.

His mind was wandering as he fantasised of sitting on the edge of that deck with his rod dangling in the water whiling away the hours. Tanya would probably spend far too long in the whirlpool and end up with skin like a prune most days. What the hell and who knew, after the Covid months he had endured, he might even throw caution to the wind and sip on some well-deserved champagne. He knew he wasn't an alcoholic but had steered clear since that night in Birmingham.

The shooter had been in position since well before dawn. He wasn't a natural sniper but had handled weapons all his working life. He watched as members of staff reported earlier for this highlight of their lives. None of them had ever imagined meeting the Prime Minister. Today would be different. He observed as they went about their usual morning ritual, even if there was more purpose today. Brooms were being pushed around the paved yard, signage was being polished to an unnatural gleam and windows were being cleaned.

A man appeared from within the giftshop and stood about three metres away. Looking through the scope, he had a good view of him, he was probably in his fifties with a high forehead. He watched as he took a position ready to greet the very important person about to visit. Possibly the manager. He watched as the man repeatedly scratched behind his ear. He raised the gun's sight until it was a few inches higher and a few inches away from the centre of the man's head. The rifle's safety was disengaged for immediate action. His finger was inside the trigger guard waiting to squeeze.

The sound of the motorcade coming in through the museum's gate drew Cobbold away from the Scottish idyll. This returned his mind to the nagging thought that Richardson had over-egged the pudding and got it wrong. He knew the bitch of a woman head of SO1 would be waiting back in London to gloat in her belief that there was no real chance of an attempt on the PM's life. She had made it perfectly clear that this little upstart of a security group could not have uncovered plots that they, SO1, did not have on their own radar. Hence, he was now standing outside an old coalmine in Yorkshire rather than taking in the airs of the tranquil island. That would have to wait!

The shooter was watching the scratching man. He was clearly nervous about something. He calmed his breathing and tried to remember everything he had been told. Even the slightest of heart flutters could throw the missile away from its target at this range. His breathing controlled, the man's head a few inches away from his aim, he could now fire. He imagined the head bursting apart like an exploding watermelon. Then the sound of sirens from the Prime Minister's cavalcade.

Richardson was positioned in the trees to the west of the mine workings and was looking through his binoculars. Following Walters and Jones' report and recommendations, it was decided to split the three HST groups into two packs of three. The three former soldiers, Walters, Jones and Shane Thompson, had taken position on the eastern slope where they thought the attack would, more than likely, originate from. He along with the other two former police officers, Rowena Crawford and Amy Newcomb, were looking down from the western hill.

All six officers were fully armed and armoured. No chances would be taken. It was a given that the soldiers were more experienced at moving with stealth through the dense woodland of the eastern side. He could see Cobbold clearly and knew that he was having his doubts. Not only had he cancelled his leave, he was under pressure from more established security branches within the hierarchy of British protection. The only head who regularly came out on Cobbold's side was Vanessa Forbes-Marriott of the SIS. Richardson had no idea why and Cobbold would not divulge anything to him. Walters had told him that Ness, as Cobbold charmingly called her, had the hots for him. That was just so wrong on many levels, mainly that fifty-somethings did not get the hots for anybody! One of the real giveaway signs that Cobbold was nervous was the repeated scratching just behind his right ear. He had seen it before.

He scanned the far slope again before resting his eyes for a moment. Nothing. Then a blue light flashed in the periphery of his vision. The sound of police sirens hit his ears a few seconds later. He glanced to the right where the access road wound its way around to the museum entrance. Motorcycle outriders were the first into view, followed by the specially adapted Jaguar XJ Sentinel car, two Range Rovers and, finally, two more motorbikes. The car was more a fortress on wheels. It had a protected cell constructed from titanium and Kevlar, the windows were of triple-glazed polycarbonate bulletproof construction and the inside was impervious to chemical and biological attack, complete with its own oxygen supply. As soon as any threat, no matter how insignificant, was perceived, the man would be bundled back into the self-contained safe haven of the vehicle. The five-litre engine would then power him away from danger. The only worry was that the gun, if armed with the right ammunition, could pierce the windows of the car from the distance calculated by Walters and Jones. The inventory of the arsenal discovered on Wells computer had not alluded to any such armour piercing rounds.

Cobbold stood back and allowed the local uniformed police and the imported personal protection officers to form up. The motorbikes passed by the end of the protective lines, allowing the car to come to a rest with the back door perfectly lined up with the path formed by the protective ranks. Cobbold was stationed by the door leading to the shop with all of the mine's staff inside waiting to greet their leader.

This is the moment, thought the assassin. Protection officers were forming a rank on each side of the Prime Minister's walk from the car to the shop. He thought that this might happen and believed, if necessary, he could fire two shots in quick succession. The first would take out one of the officers whilst the second, following in the first's wake, would go right through the Prime Minister's head. The car pulled up at the end of the protected walkway.

As a flunky stepped forward to open the car door, Cobbold caught a flash from the corner of his vision. He processed the information immediately and knew, without any doubt, that it had been a muzzle flash up in the woods to the east. Confirmation followed about three-point-seven seconds later as the sound of an elongated gunshot started to echo around the valley. Cobbold was convinced that it was one of the HST's Heckler and Koch rifles firing with the auto-selector set to three. This was interspersed by two, maybe three, cracks. It was hard to tell with the echo.

"Police! Drop your weapon," a woman's voice demanded from behind the shooter.

The shooter turned in the direction of the voice. He saw three, what appeared to be soldiers, fanned out and dressed in black, all with weapons trained on him. It was over. He was a marine, though, and despite whatever odds are stacked against us, we get the job done. Maybe he might be able to take them by surprise. He had five rounds plus one in the chamber and he had to make each of them count.

"Drop the gun," the woman demanded again.

He stood slowly, carefully, holding his rifle out to the side. He sensed a relaxation in the hunters. He snapped his weapon back toward the firing position, his hip; No time to aim. Just let instinct take over. He got one round off. At the same time, one of the soldiers opened fire and he felt his gut explode as he was hit. Another shot left his gun but all that did was blow a few leaves from the branches above.

The Prime Minister, who had only managed to get one foot on the ground was unceremoniously bundled back into the Sentinel. The look of surprise on his face nearly caused Cobbold to laugh out loud but he managed to check the reaction. The air was blasted apart from the roar of the five-litre engine as the driver hit the gas and the wheeled fortress accelerated away. Even more amusing was the sight of the PM being thrown around in the back of the car. He lost his balance, lurched violently to one side and the last Cobbold saw was the Prime Ministerial arse filling the window as he grappled to right himself.

Richardson hadn't spotted the muzzle flash but he did sense

a panicked movement down at the car, short seconds before the reverberating sound reached his ears. He reckoned that there had been a violent but brief exchange of fire up on the distant hill. His helmet's built-in earpiece sprung to life.

"Target neutralised." It was Thompson's voice, the most junior of the pack. "We're one down. First aid being applied."

Richardson slumped back against a tree. It could only be Walters or Jones. It was probably only an injury as the armour protected nearly all vulnerable areas. Hold on, though, this was a sniper rifle with a range of two-and-a-half kilometres. What the hell would it be like from point-blank range? He closed his eyes and offered up a silent prayer to who knew who.

The pain was ripping the shooter apart. He knew his time was limited. He had no idea which organs had been hit but blood was now oozing between his fingers at such a rate it would not be long before he bled out. He could not staunch the life carrying substance from leaving his being. He knew, that with absolute certainty, he had hit one of the soldiers in the face. Yeah, for sure, it had been a lucky shot but it had done its job. He was pretty damned sure that it had been the woman who had ordered him to drop the weapon. He couldn't be sure, though, as it was hard to distinguish sex from the uniforms his attackers had been wearing. There had been at least one male voice as well.

Suffolk

Richardson found the tears welling again, as the vicar sprinkled some soil onto the coffin lid. The pallbearer to his immediate right embraced him hard. He hugged back and then tears streamed again. He took in the scent of Chanel Number Five, a classic perfume he had been told, that, in itself, provided a familiar comfort. One of the other's hands patted him and a woman's voice whispered. "He was a good man."

Richardson pulled back from the embrace of his long time HST partner. "I know," was all he could say.

She wiped away his tears, with a clean handkerchief packed with exactly that in mind, before adding, matter-of-factly as ever, said, "We all knew the risks."

"Yeah, I know," he said as he took her hand and they walked toward the group now huddled by the path leading to the gate. "It doesn't make it any easier. I should have said no when he rang and asked if I had anything he could do for us."

"It could've been any one of us. Me, you, Rowena, whoever."

"I thought it was you at first," he confessed. When Shane announced we were one down, I couldn't bring myself to ask. I treated no news as good news!"

Peter Jones was a wreck. Amelia Bryant was supporting him. Richardson couldn't say anything and headed for the gate. He had arrived in one of the official limousines but now, arm in arm, with Sue-Beth he walked the short distance to the pub where they would celebrate the life of Field Officer Michael Jones, ex of the Royal Anglians and the Special Air Service. This was not before Rowena Crawford had retrieved five H and Ks from the back of one of the limousines. They were only loaded with blanks. Five of the pallbearers stood to attention at the graveside of their fallen comrade. Walters, who was in the line with Richardson, Crawford, Shane Thompson and Amy Newcomb, barked out the orders and they fired a volley over the grave to mark the passing of this brave warrior. The only one of the team that had carried the coffin, Sean Bryant, who wasn't trained in firearms, did not take part. It was a spectacular send-off.

Glasses of champagne were poured and a toast offered up to absent friends, lest we forget.

Jones' widower was now doing the rounds and thanking everyone for coming. Richardson watched as he approached Rosina Ali, who had asked if she would be allowed to attend and pay her own respects. They shared a laugh. Neither of them had done much of that over the past few weeks.

All of the migrants that had crossed the channel with Sean Bryant had been given leave to stay and work, provided they did not have criminal records. The few men and older boys who had been sold onto labour gangers, without exception, had all been traced and reunited with the group. Even if they did have a criminal past, each case would be studied before any decision to deport would be enacted. Rosina Ali had been told that she might have to wait, six months or more, before residency was finally granted. In the meantime, she was employed as an interpreter within the Home Office, a dream job. On arriving in Oakshott, she had confided to Walters and Richardson that she had been blown away by how friendly everyone was to her. She immediately fell in love with the Suffolk village and vowed that, one day, she would make her home there. The prices of houses, though, were terrifying. She would need to find herself a very wealthy man.

A smile played on Richardson's face.

"And what are you smiling about, Field Officer Richardson?" asked a bemused Walters who had been looking at the exchange between Rosina and Peter Jones as well.

Richardson turned to face her and the smile broadened.

Walters returned the smile. "I knew that is what you were thinking! It's nice to see the scar above her eye has healed so well."

"Yeah. The physical has healed well but what about the mental scars? I can't see them clearing up any time soon."

"Maybe not. You never know what their future holds," she said still looking at the Afghan interpreter and the widowed businessman. "You know Peter likes girls too?"

"Really?"

"Yep. He's bi. So was Jonah for that matter. He told me when we were waiting to ambush the would-be assassin."

Richardson shook his head. "Incredible. I never knew. I'm surprised he told you. He often seemed to lose the power of speech in the company of women, especially pretty ones. I s'pose, then, that the signs were there."

Walters blew out through her closed lips at the back-handed compliment from her partner. "He told me because he reckoned he had a foreboding about the day ahead. He thought he was going to die. I told him to stop talking bollocks."

"Shame he couldn't patch things up with his Mum. He tried, you know. She wouldn't have it. According to her, her son died when she found out he was gay. No son of hers would be a poof. Why go to a funeral for someone who had already been dead for over ten years. Besides, there was Covid and there was no way she was going out of the house until it was all over. I've never had to inform a relative of a death before and, if I'm honest, I never want to do it again. That was weird. She even made me stand outside the front door about ten metres away, let alone two, and shout."

Manzoor Sajjadi proved most cooperative. It transpired that he had got himself in debt through an online-gambling addiction. He had then been approached by a colleague who had bought a franchise in an adult entertainment business. He had been reluctant at first, the thought had repulsed him, but he was in debt and was in imminent danger of having his house repossessed. He was one of over twenty franchisees who had invested additional money, borrowed from the franchisor, into this most lucrative of industries.

It was an absolute winner. All the victims were unknown to the authorities and if they disappeared or, even, died no one would miss them. All the bank accounts for the franchises were offshore and when he turned over one of his statements to the investigators, it showed a balance in excess of two-million pounds. All franchisees, except for six who had been tipped off and had fled, were arrested. Many of their lieutenants, not all, had also been arrested and charged. The Mr Big remained unknown, but authorities on every continent were forever following up leads and were convinced that the net was tightening.

Sajjadi, earlier in the week, that the HST had gathered for

the funeral, had been found hanging in his cell. It transpired that his father-in-law had visited him. They had had a bad-tempered exchange of words. Warders in the visitor centre of the prison had heard the father-in-law say "You have brought shame on my daughter and grandsons. Perverts like you make it ever harder for us to assimilate into British life. No wonder some racists out there are always picking on us. You must do the right thing."

Incredibly, not all the images of women were illegal and the users of that type of pornography would not be exposed for their obsessions. The more sadistic stuff along with the kiddie-porn was a different thing altogether. It appeared that Interpol had issued well over two-thousand warrants for arrest worldwide and there would be thousands more to follow. Matching credit card payments up with individuals was a laborious job but the task would be completed whatever the cost. No participant in this most sordid of affairs would escape punishment. The numbers were so overwhelming that consideration was being given to booking prison cells like hotel rooms, as in some countries abroad, as there were so many offenders.

Patrick Hunter was later confirmed to be the pimp, Joe Burns. Burns, it was discovered after a small amount of delving was the owner of Patrick Hunter Associates LLP and Patrick Hunter Services LLP. The other listed partner, Patrick Hunter himself, was totally fictitious.

The funeral of Major John Wells, Retired, also took place in the same week. The service for his wife, Kate, would have been packed out if Covid restrictions had allowed. That was in stark contrast to Wells' own send-off with only four persons in attendance. The Reverend Jordan Cruz officiated and the Sheringhams were present. Most of the village had decided not to attend as it would be seen to be publicly supporting a self-confessed serial killer. Privately, though, many were proud of his achievement in ridding the world of some undesirable people. The local surgery had learned lessons and the new receptionist was all smiles whenever anyone attended.

One other man turned up at the funeral. Villagers stared, agog, as the half-million pound red Ferrari glided into the church car park. Steve Carter cut a forlorn figure in the rearmost of the pews. He hadn't really turned up to say goodbye to a serial killer, who he happened to have liked, but was there to pay respects to the man's wife. Since the meeting with Wells, he often wondered what might have been. For Christ's sake, he would have met the costs of any medical intervention that both Kate and John had needed.

The French Gendarmerie confirmed that two of its officers had been dismissed for taking bribes and would be facing court in the new year. The British were, secretly most pleased with this revelation that French officials were corrupt. It was only the tip of the iceberg. They had uncovered a fund, provided by the French government, which was used to encourage people-traffickers to carry on their trade on their northern coast. It had materialised that the French, despite their protestations to the contrary, did not want the migrants in their country any more than the British. The British government placed that file in a locked drawer and it would only see the light of day again should pressure need to be brought to bear on the cousins across La Manche.

When he had been downed by enemy fire, Walters had

rushed to the prostrate figure of Michael Jones. Despite the gruesome injuries sustained by her colleague and friend, she still checked for a pulse. Nothing. Life must have ended like a light had been turned off by a flicked switch. She then made her way to the fallen assassin. He was clearly still alive. Eyelids were pulsing and he was trying to say something. She kicked his weapon away. She knelt beside him and using blood absorption pads from her own personal first aid pack tried to stem the bleeding. One was soon replaced by another. It was a forlorn effort. It wasn't long before Richardson was at her side.

Alan Cooper did not die on the hillside overlooking the old coalmine in Yorkshire. He was badly injured from a burst of fire from Field Officers Walters and Thompson but only after he had fired off a round at Michael Jones which had taken him in the mouth and killed him instantly. As he lay in the arms of the huge black man he had met once before, in the pub in John Wells home village, he asked, "How did you know?"

"It was nothing more than a hunch, although the clues were there."

"How do you mean?" Cooper asked as he grimaced from the pain in his abdomen. He had not bothered with body armour. Basically, he was in great pain and bleeding out.

"First of all, I could not understand your presence in the village," Richardson began. "Why did you visit both his home and the allotment. Then, curiosity got the better of me really, I looked on his computer beyond just his wish dead list...."

Cooper smiled but gasped at the same time. "He did actually write that list then? It wasn't just in his mind?"

"Yeah. Then I decided to take a look through his emails."

Cooper smiled again. "Oh shit! I told him to delete the bloody things."

"He sort of did. They had gone from the Drafts folder but he hadn't deleted them from the Deleted Items folder. From then on, it was easy. It was just one draft left in the folder, written by you, I assume, and not deleted that made me trawl through the rest."

"He was always bloody useless with IT. I should have thought to tell him but it never crossed my mind that he would be so stupid." Cooper laughed again. "Even so, how did you know it was me?"

"I didn't for sure. To be honest, I had no idea really. I guessed you might be involved. The draft emails gave no clue as to your identity but the final email pointed to you wanting the gun. Then, after scrolling back through older communications you had, sort of, applauded him in adding the First Lord of the Treasury to the list. We had to look it up. Neither Walters nor I had any idea that this was the same as the Prime Minister."

"Congratulations, indeed, Field Officer Richardson," gasped Cooper. "How did you know it would be here?"

"Obvious, really. It, in our opinion, could only have been here or one other place based on the PM's itinerary. This offered everything. Open ground, good cover, easy escape. Perfect."

Cooper grinned again. Richardson wasn't sure if it might be a grimace.

"Tell me. Nothing to lose now and you know it. Were you

and Wells, in any way, involved with the trafficking of women into the sex industry?"

Cooper's eyes widened at the suggestion. "No way. Why?"

"Not now. I need more answers, soldier, and you haven't got long left. I am going to ask but I don't expect an answer. Who are the people who wanted him dead?"

"Come clean time," said Cooper, barely above a whisper, grimacing once again at the pain in his gut. "Certain agencies and MPs were beginning to find him embarrassing and wanted to see the back of him. They had tried to get him to resign...."

Richardson listened in disbelief as the ex-marine divulged everything. Cooper had no family to embarrass so what was there to lose. Besides, the death of old soldiers had troubled him. He had no need to protect his paymasters any longer. What was more, he had taken a liking to the two HST operatives. By the time he had finished there were no unanswered questions. "One more thing?"

"What?"

"You're a decent man," he gasped. "My dog, Venus, a black labrador. Look after her. She's a good girl. Tell her -sorry."

Cooper's eyes closed. He never regained consciousness and died in hospital two days later.

"What are we going to do now?" asked Walters looking across at the new Home Secretary.

"Not sure. I understand we are on gardening leave. Never really sure what that was before. It's full pay so who cares."

Walters put a hand on Richardson's arm and said, "You know what? We could go take a break somewhere hot, just you and me, and, well, you never know how things might develop. Pina colada and the sands on the cape seem rather inviting right now."

"You what?"

"Just something I heard."

They exchanged coy smiles.

Teresa Burgess, the new de-facto head of the HST had stood the group down to allow thorough investigations to take place. She would not make a decision until all due process was complete. If that took a year or more, so what! They had meddled where they weren't wanted. If they had kept their noses out her friend, Javed, would now be the Prime Minister.

The Opposition was making hay following the arrest of the former incumbent of the Home Office. Not only was Javed Akhtar involved but a slew of high-ranking officials and one army general had been implicated in the conspiracy to assassinate the Prime Minister. There must have been other government Members of Parliament involved, even cabinet ministers, so they would keep digging.

Javed Akhtar had the full knowledge of Wells' plans from his constituent, Major Alan Cooper, Retired. As careless as Wells had been with the Drafts idea, Cooper had been equally casual. He had only been using the plan thanks to Akhtar. They had agreed to communicate that way when Cooper had reported back about Wells' plan.

Akhtar started to have reservations that things were going to cross over. It was clear, as an interested observer, that Sajjadi and Wells' bin Laden were one and the same. The surveillance photographs from Bartholomew's Woods had betrayed this and whilst the Home Security Team had been chasing clues, very efficiently in the absence of the knowledge that Akhtar held close to his chest, he and his co-conspirators had instructed Cooper to revert to Plan "A." It was obvious that any reliance on Plan "B" was going to die in an unknown woods in Norfolk.

Plan "B" was the ultimate "Get out of jail free" card. Or, rather, it was a "Don't go to jail in the first place" card. All the blame would have ended up at Wells' door and Javed Akhtar would have been Prime Minister.

Akhtar had simply held his head in his hands as he listened to a recording of Cooper's takedown and confession in Yorkshire. On Cobbold's return, Akhtar had summoned him to the Home Office and confessed all. There was no way that his team would overlook the clues and Akhtar knew his days were numbered. Cobbold called in partners in the NCA and the arrest was effected.

It was a forlorn sight as a tearful blind man was led away in handcuffs whilst his beloved guide dog looked on in dejected bewilderment. His master had never gone anywhere without him. Guide dogs are not allowed in the prison environment so this was the end of Blair's relationship with his owner. He would be taken back by the Guide Dogs' Association and, as he was still young enough, would be reassessed and provided to another owner. His sister, Venus, was put up for adoption; she was found a new home, in acres of countryside, within two hours of her picture appearing on the adoption site.

In early 2022, the Russian army under the direction of its dictatorial president, invaded the sovereign state of Ukraine. The world with only a few exceptions, universally condemned his actions. Civilised societies were given the time to employ economic, cultural and sporting sanctions against the Kremlin. Thanks to the interception of the twenty-pound notes and other currencies, the outbreak of the omicron variant of the Covid virus was nowhere near as bad as the Chinese had led their Russian allies to believe. Some of the virus escaped its polymer sacks and ravaged the population for a short time in late 2021 and early 2022. It proved to be highly infectious but did not pack a punch, so soon fizzled out to something more akin to seasonal flu.

As the Prime Minister had promised Cobbold and Walters, they received no formal thanks for their part in diluting omicron's effect. Instead, the brilliant NHS staff fighting on the frontline won endless plaudits for their sterling work in the face of adverse conditions. The rollout of the vaccination was also accorded enormous credit for laying the final threat of coronavirus to rest. The defeat of the pandemic allowed the western nations the time to turn and face the real threat from the east. A footnote to the saving of the Prime Minister's life irked Richardson. Walters was not surprised by the prick's failure to thank them for saving his life, either formally or informally. When asked by a journalist if he was going to thank the individuals for protecting him in Yorkshire, he responded by saying, "They were only doing their jobs. That's what they are paid for. Nobody ever thanks me for what I do so why should I be any different." So, was the acknowledgement of the NHS and the vaccination programme genuine?

The examination and testing of the thousands of twenty-pound notes discovered under the floor of Wells' garage proved negative. They did not contain the virus so, it was assumed that Wells did not have any links with the people traffickers. It was nothing but coincidence. After bickering between the authorities, the money was granted to the HST to be used for out-of-pocket expenses in future investigations, whenever they might resume. If they resumed at all.

The Chinese introduced coronavirus to the world to test the reaction. They were staggered to see that, with minor exceptions, it fought the threat on a united front. Trade with the rest of the world is the best way to bring their influence to bear. War, they now know, will only serve to make them pariahs. It will be a long time before Russia is ever trusted again.

The End.

Sign up to the **Travelling Blind eNewsletter**

Instagram: @blindtravelrobert